the red scream

▼

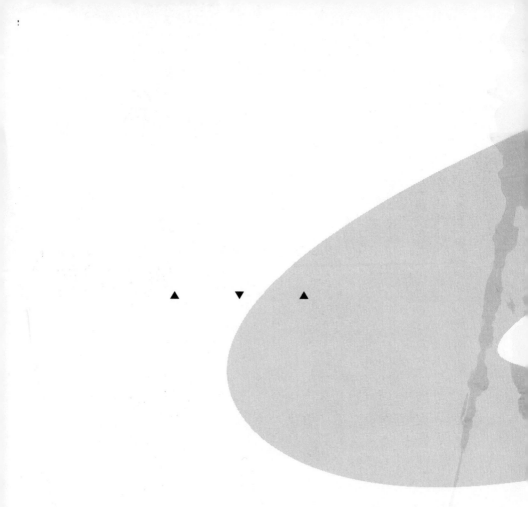

DOUBLEDAY

New York London Toronto Sydney Auckland

THE RED SCREAM

▲ ▼ ▲

Mary Willis Walker

PUBLISHED BY DOUBLEDAY
a division of Bantam Doubleday Dell Publishing Group, Inc.
1540 Broadway, New York, New York 10036

DOUBLEDAY and the portrayal of an anchor with a dolphin
are trademarks of Doubleday, a division of
Bantam Doubleday Dell Publishing Group, Inc.

Interior design by Susan Yuran

Library of Congress Cataloging-in-Publication Data

Walker, Mary Willis.
   The red scream / Mary Willis Walker.
     p. cm.
    1. Women journalists—Texas—Fiction. 2. Serial
murders—Texas—Fiction. I. Title.
PS3573.A425354R4 1994
813'.54—dc20   93-37418 CIP

ISBN 0-385-46858-X

Printed in the United States of America

August 1994

10 9 8 7 6 5 4 3 2 1

FIRST EDITION

To Amanda and Suzanna, always.

▼

acknowledgments

For abundant help and information my heartfelt thanks to Liz Cohen of the Texas Resource Center, Charles Brown of the Texas Department of Criminal Justice, Steve McCleery of the Travis County District Attorney's office, Linda Cooper of the Austin Police Department, Mike Cox of the Texas Department of Public Safety, and especially to "The Trashy Paperback Writers": Dinah Chenven, Susan Cooper, Susan Wade, and Jody Berls.

the red scream

▼

chapter 1

▲ ▼ ▲

Believe me
Nothing's free
My daddy told me.
He give me my life
And a hunting knife—
Nothing more.
He's out the door
We're left dirt poor.
Five bitches and me
Nothing's free.

LOUIE BRONK
Death Row, Ellis I Unit,
Huntsville, Texas

Definitely a view to die for, Molly Cates decided—180 degrees of
prime Texas hill country threaded by the sparkling blue ribbon of
the Colorado River. Far below, three turkey vultures floated, never
flapping a wing as they rode the late afternoon thermals along the
undulating ridge. This was the king-of-the-mountain location in all
of Austin, pick-of-the-litter real estate, the absolute high spot for
twenty miles around. It was refreshing to see that some Texans could
still live like this.

"Real pretty view, ain't it? You ought to see it sometime with a
norther blowing up." The voice behind her was low and raspy, with
an easy drawl, the kind of male voice Molly knew and liked best. If
she closed her eyes and let herself float back in time, it could have
been her daddy talking.

"Sure is. Real pretty," she said, turning from the window to look
at him and duplicating the languid vowels of his West Texas twang.
She did it with ease because it was her native tongue, too.

He reacted with a slow grin as he took the hand she offered in
both of his. "This is a pleasure, Miz Cates. I sure do appreciate you

coming here to visit with me." He pressed her hand warmly and looked her square in the eyes. His hands still retained the roughness of the manual laborer he had once been. A large man, Charlie McFarland was about six feet tall, his body still thickly muscled, though around the torso it was starting to go slack. He wore a red plaid shirt, baggy old jeans, and expensive hand-tooled boots.

"It's real gracious of you," he said, "since I know you must be remembering all the times I said no to you."

He was right; she *was* remembering. Back when she was covering the trial for the *Austin American-Patriot* ten years before and then later when she was writing the book, he had staunchly refused even to take her phone calls, much less give an interview. Of course, in her business you got used to people slamming phones down and she didn't take these refusals personally. But she sure did remember them.

Without returning his smile, she said, "When my boss asks me for a special favor, Mr. McFarland, I try to do it."

The grin faded slightly. "Yes, ma'am, I did have to lean on Richard a little to get him to ask you. I wanted to be sure you'd come. Hope you'll forgive me for that." He raised his heavy gray and ginger eyebrows to indicate he had asked a question.

She kept her face noncommittal; if he wanted forgiveness, let him work a little harder for it.

"Did he mention to you this was off the record?"

Molly nodded.

"Good. I wouldn't want to see any of this appearing in print." He gestured at his enormous showplace of a living room and said, "My wife just finished redecorating in here. As a wedding present I gave her a free hand. Only woman I know who can exceed an unlimited budget." He chuckled. "But it was featured in *Southern Living* this month so I guess it turned out all right."

Molly hadn't heard he'd remarried. She surveyed the room quickly. The oatmeal-colored Berber carpeting, the two walls of solid glass, the beige suede and chrome sofas, the white grand piano. No books or magazines, no litter, no family photos. Cold. No draperies for the windows; at night they would be huge black voids out into space.

She looked him in the eye and took a chance. "Handsome, but I sure wouldn't feel comfortable pulling off my boots and reading the sports pages here. Where's the room you *live* in?"

She was rewarded by a head-thrown-back laugh—a deep male whiskey-and-sex sound that reminded her of barrooms and hunting camps and visiting oil rigs with her daddy all those years ago. "Richard said you were a pistol."

"Richard's no slouch himself," she replied, getting more curious by the minute to find out what this man wanted from her. Whatever it was, she knew he would trot out all the big guns in his arsenal, including his relationship with her boss, to get it. This made her uneasy because Richard Dutton, the editor of *Lone Star Monthly,* was one of the few people in the world who had any power over her.

Charlie McFarland reached out and touched her elbow. "Let's go back to my office and talk, Miz Cates."

As he led the way, she was surprised to see how slowly and painfully he walked. His pace was a slow shuffle and he held his back ramrod stiff.

She followed him along a hallway that was a picture gallery with paintings hung only inches apart—all landscapes, Texas bluebonnet scenes mostly. Molly liked bluebonnets as well as the next person, but, God, she was sick of all those murky pictures of the damn things everywhere she went—one of the curses of being a Texan.

He stood aside at the open door at the end of the hall. When she entered, she couldn't help smiling with satisfaction. It was exactly the room she would have predicted for a West Texas good ol' boy who'd made it big—a large, dark-paneled study with a ten-point buck's head over the stone fireplace and a buck's rump over the door. A gun cabinet with a beveled glass door stood to the right of the fireplace. One wall was packed with built-in electronic equipment: stereo, large-screen TV, VCR, and other gadgets. On the desk sat an IBM computer with a twenty-one-inch color monitor that she coveted on sight; it was big enough so you could see two full pages of fourteen-point type side by side.

The window out to the view was covered with tightly closed miniblinds. How delightful, Molly thought, to be so rich that you could pay hundreds of thousands of dollars for the best view in Central Texas and then keep it covered.

He walked to a worn Naugahyde recliner, turned, and grabbed the arms so he could lower himself into it. With a movement of his head he directed her to an armchair slipcovered in a hunting print. Molly was glad to see that the new wife who'd decorated the living room had not been allowed to make a statement in here.

She sat down and was about to cross her legs when she paused, feeling a flush of heat radiate from her neck into her face. On an end table next to his chair lay a copy of her book, *Sweating Blood.* It was open at about the middle, the gaudy orange and red cover facing up. Somehow, she had never considered the possibility of this man reading it. And for just a moment, here in his house, the cover struck her as so tasteless, so sensational and tawdry, that she felt a hot blush prickling her cheeks—a reaction she could not remember ever having in her many years of being a crime writer who often violated the rules of good taste.

From the minute her publisher had first showed her the cover art, she had loved it because it was so attention-grabbing. The painting depicted a lonely stretch of highway with a woman's body lying in a ditch alongside; from the body blood flowed and surrounded the entire cover, front and back, with a shiny vivid red. She had recognized immediately that it would sell books. It was commercial, yes, sensational even. But that was the nature of true crime books and she wasn't going to apologize for it.

Certainly, when she was writing it, she had wrestled with the problem inherent in writing a book for entertainment which was based on other people's private disasters. And here was a man who'd been personally devastated by the violence she'd carefully researched and portrayed; from the place the book was open, she figured he must have already read that vividly detailed scene of his first wife's murder and the cold description of the act Louie Bronk had given in his confession to the police and again when she'd interviewed him in prison. Eleven years had passed since the murder, true, and McFarland had heard it all rehashed at the trial, but seeing it in print, dramatized, was a different matter; it had to be damned painful for him to read.

She forced her eyes away from the book and finally finished crossing her legs.

Charlie McFarland had been watching her. He steepled his thick callused fingers over his belly, closed his eyes, and took a deep breath. "Do you have daughters, Molly?"

She was glad he'd switched to first names. "Yes, Charlie. I have one daughter. She's twenty-four."

He nodded and opened his eyes as if that made it all right for him to go on. "Then you know that you'd do damn near anything for a daughter. Alison's twenty-two now. She's a real fan of yours, reads everything you write. Maybe you already know that since you've been in touch with her." He gave her a hard look as if he was expecting an answer.

Molly remained silent; she wanted to see where he was heading.

He reached out and placed a hand on the open book next to him. "The girl reads too much of this sort of thing if you ask me—always has. I can't believe it's good for her, especially when you consider her history." The thick, tanned skin of his brow furrowed. "Now I wasn't planning on even giving this a glance—no point to it—but she bought a copy the day it appeared in the bookstores and stayed up all night reading it. Then she gave it to me. Said reading it might help me lay it all to rest."

He kept his hand on the open book and drummed his fingers on it. "You're real good at what you do and I admire that. It's clear you do your homework; you're thorough, but"—he began to shake his head slowly from side to side as he spoke—"I just can't imagine why anyone would want to do this. All that time you spent with him—" He screwed up his mouth in distaste. "To get so close to him, to try to get inside—" He shook his head furiously now. "Even his poems. No, I can't see it, but maybe that's because I got hit so close to home. I wish I could just forget it, but it keeps coming back."

Molly thought about her own experience with violent death hitting close to home. She sighed and said, "I don't think forgetting is an option, Charlie. And I think Alison has a point. Sometimes looking at it closely and trying to understand can . . . well, this may just be rationalization for what I do, but I think that exposing it to the cold light of day can de-fang it some."

When she looked up, he was studying her face with increased interest. "In the book you describe me as a small but growing Austin builder. What do you know about me now?"

God, she thought, wasn't that typical of us all—out of a four-hundred-page book he picked out the one sentence that was about him. "You started McFarland Construction with two bulldozers and a wetback stone mason," she said, "and built it up to a hundred-million-dollar-a-year business. And you're one of the few builder-developers who's not only survived the real estate crash intact, but prospered during it. Recently you got the contract for a new office building downtown and you've got several environmentally controversial new developments under way."

He nodded. "That's all true, but your numbers are low." He grinned at her. "My company grossed almost two hundred million this year."

"Well, I was under-informed," Molly said. "Congratulations. I'm impressed that anyone in the construction business is still standing."

"Me too, me too. It hasn't been easy." He cleared his throat and looked away from her.

Now he was going to get down to it, Molly thought, whatever it was that had caused him to use his considerable influence to get Richard Dutton to ask the first favor he'd ever asked of her—"Molly," he'd said, "do something for me: when Charlie McFarland calls you, and he will call, just pretend to be nice if you can manage it. Listen to the man." Charlie had called the next day, and she had agreed to come see him at his house. Of course, even without Richard's intervention, she would have agreed; the book was finished, but her interest in the Bronk case sure wasn't. She still wanted to hear what this man had to say, even off the record.

McFarland was slumped down in his chair now, staring into the empty, blackened fireplace. Well, she had seen it before—people having trouble getting started. When you wrote about crime, you met people who had suffered grievous pain and they often had a hard time getting started.

She sat and waited for him, studying his face. Though she had watched him testify at the trial ten years before and had seen his picture in the business section of the newspaper often since then, she might not have recognized him on the street. She knew he was sixty-two, but he looked older. The powerful bone structure of his jaw and Roman nose was holding, but the flesh, being more transient, was sinking. Swollen pouches of skin under his eyes seemed to be dragging the lower lid down and pads of fat under his chin almost obscured his thick neck. Gravity was having its way with this man. Maybe grief had helped it along.

Finally he raised his head. "You must be sitting there thinking I'm some crazed old coot with a loose cinch. The thing is, this is a real delicate matter; I have a favor to ask, but I don't want to insult you."

Molly found herself suddenly even more interested in what he had to say, interested enough to help him along. "Would it help if I promise not to be insulted no matter how outrageous it is? Give you advance absolution?"

"Yes, ma'am, it sure would help. But that's not my only problem here; see, it's something I haven't talked about in so long it's like I've forgotten how to do it."

She hoped he wouldn't back down now; she was beginning to feel the erection of those sensitive little hairlike receptors in her brain that alerted her to the proximity of a good story.

He leaned forward in his chair and rested his hands on his broad knees. "Here's my problem."

Molly settled back to listen.

"Alison is having a difficult time of it right now. She's back at school now, at the University, after taking some time off. She's real smart, Molly. Valedictorian of her high school class at Austin High, National Honor Society, National Merit finalist—you name it. For the past two years she's been going to see this psychiatrist because she's been having nightmares and . . . oh . . . anxieties. She's come to the conclusion it all has to do with her mother's death. She was just eleven then. Of course, you know all about that—her being there when it happened and testifying at the trial and all. Now I know she's agreed to talk to you for the article you're writing; she told me. Here's where the favor comes in."

His eyes flicked up to meet hers and then lowered. "I want to ask you not to talk to her. As her father, I truly believe it would be harmful to her right now. Too much pressure. And I don't think any of this would help her brother either. He's doing a medical residency in emergency medicine. The last thing he needs is a revival of all this horror to distract him."

He put the heel of his right hand to his forehead and pressed as if he felt a headache coming on and could force it back. "There's more. I want to ask you not to write anything more about my wife's murder." He reached out his left hand and rested it on her book as if blessing it. "Doesn't this say it all? Let it be the final word." He picked the book up with one hand and snapped it shut. "Enough."

It wasn't the first time someone had asked her not to write a story, or even the first time that the welfare of a child had been invoked as the reason. But she sensed a difference here: Charlie McFarland wouldn't stop at just asking.

"Charlie, I've been following the Bronk case for eleven years and I am going to see it through to the end. The final word will be when Louie Bronk is executed."

He took in a long breath before speaking. "So this article you're planning to write is in honor of"—his mouth tightened into a mean slit—"Mr. Bronk's slated execution. My sources tell me this time it will go through since he's exhausted the appeal process."

"Yes," she said. "I think your sources are correct. The Texas Court of Criminal Appeals has turned him down. The Supreme Court has run out of tolerance and the governor's not about to intervene."

"They also tell me that he's asked for you to be one of his witnesses. At his execution."

"Yes. I'm planning to attend."

His black eyes flickered, alive with intelligence in his heavy, immobile face. "You ever seen an execution before, Molly?"

"No. Actually, I haven't."

"I thought that's something a journalist who writes about crime would do routinely."

"Well, it is, for some. But I—"

"I know," he said, his mouth turning down at the corners, "you and all those liberals over at the magazine are opposed to it. You think it's barbaric."

Molly sighed; she really didn't want to get into this discussion. "I am opposed to the state being in the killing business, yes."

"But you must admit," he said, "if we're going to do it, lethal injection is an easy way to go." He jabbed a finger at his thick forearm.

"Compared to, say, the electric chair, it is. More humane."

"Humane? I'm surprised you can even use that word in connection with Mr. Bronk." His voice rose for the first time to a challenging tone.

"It's not in connection with him, Charlie; it's in connection with us. The state does this in the name of its citizens. I don't want killing done in my name, but if they are going to do it, better it should be done quickly and with as little suffering as possible."

He shrugged. "Well, that sounds like nit-picking to me. I don't give a shit whether they boil him in oil, or hang him, or shoot him, or cut his sick head off. It seems like every time I pick up the god-damned newspaper, I read about a new murder committed by some Louie Bronk clone who's out on parole. We're letting these guys out to prey on our families. Now, Molly, do you think that's right?"

"No. I don't. I think they ought to keep habitual murderers like Louie Bronk in for life."

His voice boomed. "Life? According to the bozos on the parole board, life is about twelve goddamned years. Now that's just terrible."

Molly had to nod in agreement.

His chest was rising and falling as if he'd been running. He took several deep breaths. "Well, we aren't going to get anywhere on this subject. What I'm worried about is Alison. I don't believe she knows what's best for her right now. I'm her father and I know that bringing up the whole sorry mess will be harmful to her." He sought out her eyes with his. "Molly, I do wish you'd rethink it before you travel any further down that road."

"Charlie, every time I write an article, someone objects to it. What makes you think I'd let you talk me out of this one?"

He rested his head back on the chair and closed his eyes again. "Because you have a daughter, too." He paused to let it sink in. "Because there's no shortage of crimes out there to write about." He lifted his head and opened his eyes, meeting hers directly. "And because if you help me here, I can help you a great deal. A *great* deal."

She felt a catch of surprise in her throat. Never before had anyone attempted to bribe her and she couldn't imagine where this was heading if not to a bribe. "How could you help me?" she asked quietly.

"How much did you make last year, Molly?"

Molly smiled and shook her head. "Why should I tell you that?"

"Because I know anyway. You made forty-five thousand last year —thirty from the magazine and most of the rest from the advance on *Sweating Blood.* Your best year ever. Even so, you had to borrow at the end of the year to pay your taxes. You aren't a very smart money manager, Molly, but then you're an artist."

"You seem very well informed about my finances."

He raised a hand up in dismissal. "Hell, that's easy. You know that."

Yes, she did know that. She'd pried into other people's finances herself—often—but to have it done to her made her damn mad. Her hypocrisy, she thought, seemed to know no limits.

He went on: "Now I've always been a supporter of the arts—the ballet, the symphony—I give to them all. I know you need to do the magazine pieces for the money and that makes it hard to take the time you need for book writing."

He leaned forward and Molly saw by the grimace he made that it hurt him to do it. "Now what I have in mind is to endow an annual prize to be given to the Texan who . . . oh, contributes the most to crime writing—you know, to educate the public about the dangers and all that. And you'd be the first recipient. One hundred thousand dollars in cash, Molly—enough to support you while you write another book—on any subject in the world except my sorry family history."

Molly felt herself stiffening. The ignorant, redneck son of a bitch thought he could buy anything.

Charlie struggled up out of his chair. "I can see you're about to break your promise and get offended. Wait a minute before you do. Let me show you something." He shuffled to the bookcase behind his desk, which contained only a few books but scores of framed photographs. He picked up a silver frame and brought it to her. In it was a picture of a pale girl with limp, light brown hair, colorless eyes, and a startled expression. "That's Alison's graduation picture from Austin High four years ago. She was valedictorian of her class, out of three hundred kids—I guess I already told you that."

Surprised, Molly looked at the face in the photo again. She'd seen the girl only once, ten years ago when she was twelve, a key witness at the trial of Louie Bronk. The face stared back like a rabbit cornered by a pack of beagles.

Charlie McFarland jerked his head up as he heard the buzz of a security alarm and a door opening. He quickly took the photograph from her and put it back on the shelf. "That'll be Georgia, home from the fitness wars," he said. "I haven't told her what I was fixing to ask you, so please don't say anything about it. This whole subject just upsets her no end."

A door slammed shut and in a few seconds a slender blond

woman dressed in fuchsia tights, a flowered leotard, and sunglasses appeared in the office doorway. A very well-preserved fifty, Molly estimated.

The woman entered smiling. Before greeting Molly, she walked the length of the room to where Charlie stood at his desk. As she approached, Charlie straightened and made a visible effort to pull his stomach in. He's in love, Molly thought.

Charlie leaned over slowly to kiss the woman. She pushed her sunglasses up onto the top of her head and stretched her arms around his neck. It wasn't the perfunctory greeting kiss you usually saw in couples their age, but a warm, real kiss with sexual intent. Molly was impressed.

Keeping his arm wrapped around her waist, Charlie said, "Sweetheart, this is Molly Cates. I've been talking to her about doing some free-lance PR work for the company, but it seems Molly's incorruptible; can't be lured into the corporate jungle now that she's a famous writer of books."

Molly stood and held out her hand.

Georgia's smile faded a little as she heard the name and made the connection, but she took hold of Molly's hand and shook it. "It's a pleasure to meet you, Mrs. Cates. I'm Georgia McFarland."

Molly took a good look at the second Mrs. McFarland. Her short blond hair was artfully cut to show off a slender neck and her cheeks were slightly flushed as if exercising had been an aphrodisiac. She had a delicate upturned nose and luminous blue eyes. The only signs of aging were some faint lines around the eyes. Charlie certainly had a fine eye for women.

Molly wondered how Alison felt about her.

When Georgia caught sight of the book next to Charlie's chair, her smile died. She looked at Molly. "I haven't read your book and don't plan to. That's such an unhappy chapter in my life. I knew Tiny—we were friends in college—and I don't want any more reminders. None of us need any more of that horrible business. Thank God it's over." She looked immediately uneasy, as if she had just broken some rules of Southern womanhood and hospitality. To dispel the somber mood she had created, she gave a tinkling laugh and said, "Mrs. Cates, I bet Charlie hasn't offered you anything to drink —the oaf—has he?"

"Oh, no thanks," Molly said. "I've got to be going in just a minute."

Disengaging herself from Charlie's arm but holding on to his hand, Georgia asked, "Honey, are you feeling up to that dinner with the Merrimans at seven?"

"You bet," he said. "I've been having some back problems lately, Molly. May have to have surgery. It's hard for me to sit too long."

"You'll need to dress," Georgia told him. "Coat and tie. They're taking us to the Headliners."

He sighed.

"Good to meet you, Mrs. Cates," Georgia said and left the room.

When Molly turned back to Charlie, he looked flushed with pleasure. He waited until his wife's footsteps faded before he said, "Molly, I don't want you to give me an answer now. Why don't you take some time to think about this? Just go home and—"

Molly held up both palms to stop him. "Whoa, there, Charlie. Hold your horses. I'm sorry about Alison's difficulties—real sorry, and sorry for your pain in this matter, but that's not how I decide what to write about and I certainly wouldn't let money change my mind."

"Now hold on a minute, Molly. Just answer me this. When you chose to write about Mr. Bronk and his exploits, you saw it as a story with commercial appeal, didn't you?—a serial murderer on the loose for years, butchering women, and doing God knows what-all to them, Texas Rangers on the trail, five trials around the state— pretty sensational stuff. You made that decision with money in mind, didn't you?"

She paused, wanting to deny it, but from the first she had seen in Louie Bronk's five-year killing spree and subsequent confessions a story that would sell books. There was more to it than that, but money was a big factor. "Of course," she said.

The curt nod of his head said that settled it. "Well, I'm just asking you to make another commercial decision. There are lots of violent crimes out there. Choose one of the others and let me help you finance the project. Hell, you can return the favor by dedicating the book to me." He chuckled and held his hands out in a supplicating gesture. "What do you say, Molly?"

"I say that I don't take bribes."

"Bribes! Now goddammit, you promised not to get insulted and here you are sounding like a stuck pig."

She heard the echo of her voice in her ear and knew he was right. She relaxed back in her chair and smiled up at him. "It's just that no one's ever tried to bribe me before, Charlie. I guess it gets me feeling all officious and self-righteous, gives me the illusion that what I do matters a rat's ass in this world."

"You don't really think I was trying to bribe you, did you, Molly? No way. You should be flattered. I just want to be a patron of the arts like some of those rich old Eye-talians who paid Michelangelo to do their portraits. Only I'd be paying you *not* to do ours."

"I don't think Michelangelo would have been flattered by that." Molly looked at her watch and stood. "I've got to get going, Charlie."

As he started to limp toward the door, his face screwed up in pain. When he got to the doorway, he leaned against it and took several ragged breaths. "Well, I guess I haven't budged you at all," he said, facing Molly.

She shook her head. "I don't budge easy."

He looked down at her with his eyes narrowed. "Let me ask you something else. If you are determined to write this article, why not interview me instead of Alison or Stuart? On the record."

Molly lowered her eyes to give herself time to consider. Here was another bribe more tempting than the first—a bribe she might be able to accept. He was offering, after eleven years of never saying a public word, to give her an interview. And she still wanted to hear what he had to say. She felt the gears begin to turn in that cold journalist part of her mind, that icy lobe of the brain that was always weighing alternatives. On the one hand was the husband who keeps a stoic silence for eleven years and then finally speaks out on the occasion of the execution of his wife's murderer. And the husband is a rich and powerful man to boot. It could make a hell of a story.

On the other hand was the story she had been planning, the one about the eleven-year-old girl, who was in the house when her mother was murdered, who saw the murderer drive off in his car, and her older brother, fourteen at the time, who arrived home to see his mother's body lying in the garage. What were they like now? How had that event shaped their lives? And how did they feel about the approaching execution of their mother's murderer? Now *there* was a story.

She looked up at Charlie McFarland's big, mournful face and said, "You'd be willing to talk about the murder and your feelings about it all now?"

He stared back over her shoulder into his office. "Yes, if you'd agree not to interview my kids."

Molly felt a prickling of self-contempt in her chest, but she knew from experience it would pass quickly. For the past twenty years she had written about crime; it was her work and her obsession. She was a self-appointed messenger of the worst news society could generate; sometimes the message was ugly and painful to the living, but it *was* her job and to do it well she had to seek out the stories where they were.

"Let me think about it, Charlie. I'll talk to you tomorrow," she told him.

He stood aside to let her pass, then followed her down the blue-bonnet-lined hall to the front door. At the door he punched a code into the wall control box to deactivate the alarm. Then he pulled a key ring out of his pocket and leaned down to unlock the several dead bolts. Those precautions didn't seem at all excessive, Molly thought, in someone whose family had once encountered the likes of Louie Bronk.

"How long have you lived here, Charlie?" she asked to break the silence.

"Oh, I started this house right after the trial, about ten years ago. I couldn't stand the idea of staying on in the old house and I thought it might be safer here—closer to town, more neighbors. And I figured a change of location might help me and Alison forget." He straightened up and pushed the door open. "Didn't work a damn, of course. Neither of us forgot, and now she's moved out. But Georgia likes it."

Molly turned to say good-bye, but he stepped out into the court-yard ahead of her. "I'll walk you to your truck," he said.

They walked in silence, at Charlie's slow pace, across the brick-paved courtyard to her Chevy pickup parked near the wrought-iron gate. Molly unlocked the door of her truck and he held it open for her.

But when he saw the truck's customized interior with the reclining leather seats, wood-trim dash, phone, special CD player and stereo, he let out a whistle of surprise. "Looks like a regular old Chevy pickup from outside and a goddamned German luxury car inside."

"Yeah," Molly said, "I've always driven Chevy pickups, in honor of my father who thought they were the Second Coming. But now I'm older, I like a little more creature comfort than they come off the factory floor with."

He grinned and shut the door for her.

Molly looked out the open window. "Did Richard Dutton know what you were going to ask me?"

"No, ma'am. I just said it was a personal matter." He reached up through the window and took her hand in both of his. Squeezing it warmly, he said, "Thanks for coming and listening, Molly. Give it some thought. I'll be waiting to hear from you."

She looked into his big ravaged face. He was smiling and his eyes crinkled at the corner, but she was certain that no matter how genial he might appear, this man wouldn't stop pushing until he got his way. Well, if she had learned anything over the years, it was how to push back. "I'll be in touch, Charlie," she said.

As she started the engine and revved it, she felt her blood quicken. Before this visit she'd been lukewarm about writing anything more about Louie Bronk, but now she couldn't wait to get going on it. Nothing in the world gave her the motivation that opposition did. It was her own personal siren song. It reminded her of the time her Daddy told her never, not under any circumstances whatsoever, to go into the pasture where the old bull was grazing. That just made her spur her horse right on into that pasture. Of course, she'd gotten gored—she had the scar on her thigh to prove it—and her horse barely escaped alive. It was childish and contrary, but at forty-two she hadn't yet grown out of the impulse to go into the pasture.

As she drove out the gates she glimpsed off in the distance the buzzards still lazily working the ridge.

chapter 2

▲ ▼ ▲

When I was five
Oh, man alive,
I learnt to survive
All alone.
On my own.

When I was six
What a fix
Ma did tricks
With anyone.
Weren't no fun.

When I turned ten
She died then,
The big fat hen.
The sisters four
They settled the score.

I turned fourteen
They got so mean
Worst I seen.
It wasn't fair.
I wuz outta there.

LOUIE BRONK
Death Row, Ellis I Unit,
Huntsville, Texas

Turning out of the driveway, Molly glanced at the huge houses lined up close together on the ridge, each one edging out a little farther than the one next door, like rich matrons elbowing one another to get a better view, and she couldn't help thinking about money. What made Charlie McFarland think she could be bought off this story? And so cheap! If she were for sale, a measly hundred thou wouldn't do it.

As if she could stop now, before the end.

After all, she had chronicled Louie Bronk's sorry life and crimes from his miserable illegitimate birth in Laredo, through his twelve years in prison in Oklahoma for killing the oldest of his four sisters, and through his five murder convictions in Texas and his ten-year stay on death row. His lethal injection at Huntsville next week would mark the end of a case that had sucked her irresistibly into its vortex eleven years ago, on that miserably hot July day when Louie Bronk had been arrested in Fort Worth and extradited down to San Marcos where he was wanted for questioning in the death of Greta Huff. Lord, a lifetime ago.

Molly flipped on the fuzz-buster attached to her visor and hit the accelerator as she turned onto Mesa and headed back toward her town house, back to the unfinished story waiting for her there on her computer screen. As usual she was facing a deadline and even after twenty-two years in the business, deadlines still made her sweat.

Eleven years ago, back when she first got swept up in the Louie Bronk arrest, she hadn't known it would mushroom into a long and harrowing serial murder case that would absorb her attention as nothing else ever had. She'd been a police reporter for the *Austin American-Patriot* at the time, and when she dropped in at the Austin PD press room, it had looked like a slow news day, too hot even for crime, which usually thrived on heat.

Gus Drysdale, the head of the Austin homicide detail, had whispered the rumor in her ear. There was this drifter, Gus said, who was being arraigned down in Hays County for murdering an old woman he'd done some odd jobs for. "He's got one murder on his record, back in Oklahoma. Killed his older sister and shaved the hair off her head. Then raped her—in that order. Sound familiar?" he asked, his voice rising in excitement.

Molly had turned to face him and whispered, "The Texas Scalper?"

"Could be," Gus said. "But this guy wasn't driving a white Mustang. No car at all—he was on foot. Rumor has it that he's confessing to everyone who'll listen that he's killed more than thirty women, mostly in Texas, and mostly close to the Interstate. We're sending someone down to question him about the McFarland case." Gus grinned at her. "And if all that isn't bizarre enough for you, here's something that's sure to appeal to a literary type like you. Many *times* he makes up *rhymes* about his *crimes*. If he isn't our

Scalper, at least he should be good press. You get there quick, Molly, you might could scoop this.''

She'd given Gus a peck on the cheek, called to check with the city desk, and headed her truck toward San Marcos in the hope of interviewing the district attorney there and maybe catching the arraignment.

She entered the Hays County courthouse just in time to see three Texas Rangers and a U.S. marshal escorting a man who was handcuffed and chained at the waist down a long dark-paneled hallway. Because she'd come in from the bright sunlight outside into the dark hall, she couldn't see them well at first. She followed them to where they stopped and waited in front of a closed double door marked "Courtroom Four."

Her first impression of him, as he stood waiting, was of a small insignificant man who was slightly amused, as if none of this had anything to do with him. The chained prisoner was in his mid-thirties, she guessed, short and wiry, but with an unpleasant-looking hard paunch asserting itself above his belt. His stringy arms were covered in crude blue-green tattoos, the kind that were done in prison, and his skimpy dark hair was greased back on his scalp. Small dark eyes were set very close together. The gray T-shirt he wore was darkened with sweat stains under the arms and across the chest. She didn't know it then, but Louie was a prolific sweater. Even in cold weather, and even fresh from the shower, he smelled like a man who'd never had a bath.

One of the Rangers turned and said to him, "Want me to escort you to the gentlemen's before we go in, Louie?"

As he opened his mouth to speak, Molly recoiled slightly. The man's lower jaw was crowded with jumbled, crooked teeth. It looked as if he had twice as many as was intended for the narrow jaw. It was a shock, like going fishing and thinking you'd caught a perch, but when you opened the mouth to remove the hook you found you'd caught a piranha that was still very much alive.

On an impulse, sensing that this might be an important moment, she'd pulled her little Nikon out of her bag and snapped a picture. When the flash went off in the dark hall, the man whirled toward the light with a movement as quick and instinctual as the flicker of a snake's tongue testing the air for possible prey. He stared at her. Then he offered a twitch of the mouth which some might call the beginning of a smile, but Molly recognized it as something else entirely. She put the camera to her eye and snapped again.

That second photograph turned out to be the best she'd ever taken. It had been run nationwide by the Associated Press and was among the pictures that made the final cut in *Sweating Blood.* What made it such a good photograph, she'd always thought, was that it captured the smirk of amused knowledge that was Louie Bronk's characteristic way of looking at women. Looking past the camera directly at Molly, his expression that day suggested he was capable of knowing things about her that she herself could never know. Later on, when the details about Greta Huff, Rosa Morales, and the others emerged, she learned what those things were and that he was right—she could never know them about herself because when they were finally revealed she'd be dead, or dying.

During the two years it took her to write the book, she kept a copy of that photo pinned on the bulletin board over her desk, along with the autopsy photos of two of Louie's victims—Tiny McFarland and Rosa Morales. To remind her what the book was about.

Pulling up to the mailbox in front of her house, Molly maneuvered the truck as close as she could without knocking off the side mirrors. Leaning out the open window, she reached inside for her mail and fanned it out so she could see at a glance if the check she'd been waiting for was there—the one from *Texas Law Enforcement Quarterly* for the article she and Barbara Gruber from the ME's office had coauthored, on recent developments in blood splatter. It wasn't, of course. Damn, but this was a slow-paying business. You could starve while waiting for payment on work you'd done months before. She sighed, dropped the mail into her lap, and drove into her garage, punching the automatic door closer on her dashboard to shut it behind her. She turned off the engine and looked through the mail: several bills, a brochure for a self-empowerment seminar for women, a letter from her Aunt Harriett, one from her agent in New York, and a flimsy white envelope addressed to her in pencil with an Austin postmark and no return address.

She tore open the envelope from her agent, praying for a lucrative film or TV offer—a secret fantasy of hers. But it was just a note saying he was negotiating with a publisher in Tokyo for the Japanese rights to the book. Apparently the Japanese were big on serial killers right now. There could be some real money in it, he said.

Dropping the letter into her lap and picking up the penciled envelope, she ripped it open and pulled out a sheaf of folded papers.
They looked like printed pages that had been torn from a book. Just
as the timer switched off the overhead light and threw the garage
into total darkness, she recognized them as pages from *Sweating
Blood.*

Curious, she hurried into the house and tossed the rest of the mail
on the kitchen table. The pages—twelve of them—had indeed been
torn from *Sweating Blood.* They were the pages describing the murder of Tiny McFarland.

She sat down at the kitchen table and leafed through them. Attached to the last page was a yellow Post-it on which a poem was
penciled in small crabbed printing. It said:

> *Lady writer, you ought to know it:*
> *Louie is my favorite poet.*
>
> *Your depiction of his crimes*
> *Has inspired my poor rhymes.*
>
> *I give your book a rave review.*
> *Accolades from me to you.*
>
> *Now that Louie's doomed to die*
> *I may give his craft a try.*
>
> *Oh me, oh my.*
> *Who's next to cry?*
>
> *Sealed with a kiss.*
> *Remember this: I am the master poet here.*

Molly crossed her arms tight over her chest and raised her eyes
from the page. Then she leaned back and gazed out the kitchen
window where the cluster of gnarled live oaks had taken on a rosy
glow from the setting sun.

What she needed was to take a deep breath and fortify herself—
toughen up. Here it was: the first of the inevitable kook letters.
Richard had warned her when she told him she was going to write
the Bronk book that it would bring the nut cases streaming out of
the woodwork like cockroaches. Not that she needed warning,
really. Over the years, she'd had her share of crank letters and

threats. And, she reminded herself, not one of them had ever amounted to a goddamned thing.

She could toss this in the garbage and forget it; after all, she had work to do—a deadline in two days on an article for *Lone Star Monthly* about the Abilene Angel, a woman minister of a fundamentalist Christian sect who had just been convicted of persuading elderly parishioners to will their worldly goods to the church and then poisoning them. Molly had spent two mostly dreary weeks in Abilene researching it, interviewing sect members and families of the victims. An interesting story, she supposed, but it had never really captured her and she'd had a hard time stomaching all the holier-than-God religious extremists she had to talk to. She'd had to flog herself to get it written, but it was almost finished. All she needed now was a good ending.

She looked down at the poem again. One thing was sure: this was not from Louie Bronk. He couldn't possibly have written it. She'd seen more than enough of his work to be able to recognize his style. When she'd been making her weekly trips to Huntsville to interview him, he had given her page after page of the verse he turned out like pancakes from a griddle, all written in his childish round script on wide-lined paper. Could she get it published for him, he wanted to know, not in a magazine but in a real book. She'd promised to show it to someone and had actually persuaded her agent to send it out to a few editors with the suggestion of an anthology of poems by death-row inmates all over the country. Though Molly liked the idea, wanted to call it *Poetry from the Edge,* it had met with universal rejection.

Instead, with Louie's permission, she had used some of his poems in *Sweating Blood* as a device to give more insight into Louie and his background. She had paid him a flat fee of one thousand dollars, which went into his prison account for use in the commissary and kept him in cigarettes and Moon Pies for a year.

So Molly was all too familiar with Louie Bronk's poetry. The person who had written this was far more literate.

She rested her fingertips on the first of the torn-out pages and slowly caressed the heavy white bond. The print was so sharp it looked as if the letters should feel raised. Though she had been seeing her words in print for twenty-two years, this was the first book, and the pages seemed more durable, more authoritative somehow. But for some reason she didn't understand, Molly hadn't even glanced at the text of *Sweating Blood* since she'd completed the last of her editor's revisions more than a year ago. When she'd received her fifty author copies two weeks ago, she had just held one in her hands and stared at her name on the cover for a long time. She'd always intended to write a book and there it was, finally. Then she'd opened the cover to check out the photograph on the flap. But she hadn't yet opened it to read the text. Maybe because she was sure she'd find errors and it was too late to do anything about them.

Now she picked up the torn-out pages, beginning with 198, and read what she had written about the murder of Tiny McFarland.

It is difficult to imagine a more unlikely setting for the next murder, the one that happened on July 9, 1982.

In the rolling, cedar-covered hills of the Balcones Escarpment west of Austin, more than nine miles from the nearest exit off I-35, the McFarland family lived in a sprawling native stone ranch house set on forty undeveloped acres. The McFarlands loved the location because it was peaceful and private with a country ambiance for the children—a fine place for dogs, bicycle riding, and target practice—but only a twenty-minute drive from Charlie McFarland's office in downtown Austin.

It was a far cry from the drainage ditches and rest stops and squalid trailer parks along the Interstate highway that had served as Louie Bronk's usual killing grounds. And this time the victim was very different from the dark-haired young hitchhikers and waitresses who were his customary prey.

Andrea Wendell McFarland, nicknamed "Tiny" because she stood barely five feet tall and weighed less than one hundred pounds, was a thirty-seven-year-old mother of two with short honey-blond hair that was streaked lighter on top.

The indulged only child of Stuart Wendell, the owner of a Texas department store chain, she had attended public schools in Austin, but instead of going on to the University of Texas as did most of her friends, she went East to college—to Vassar, where she majored in art history and took her junior year abroad in Florence. After graduating from Vassar, she came back to Austin and worked for her father as a buyer in the business. A year later, she met and married Charlie McFarland, a builder who was fourteen years her senior.

Tiny McFarland had a keen interest in the arts, especially painting and music. She was active in the Austin Symphony, the Laguna Gloria Art Museum, and the Junior League, and she oversaw her own investments, which were considerable since her father had died five years earlier and left his entire estate to her.

A lifelong sportswoman and traveler, she had recently returned from a three-week hunting safari in Botswana. She was a fixture at charity balls and had been included several times on the list of the best-dressed women in Austin.

On this July day her husband, the chairman of a construction company he had founded himself, had risen at six-thirty and gone to work at his downtown office. At fifty-one, Charlie was a self-made businessman who had ridden the Texas real estate boom to modest success in the business of building homes and small office complexes. Business was brisk that year and he worked long hours, often leaving home at six and not returning until seven or eight in the evening.

Tiny McFarland, still feeling jet-lagged from her trip, had slept late that morning, according to her daughter, eleven-year-old Alison, who had gotten up to have breakfast with her father and then watched television by herself. Alison's older brother, fourteen-year-old Stuart, had ridden his bicycle to his cousin Mark Redinger's house about five miles away, where he was planning to spend the day and sleep overnight.

When Tiny got out of bed at ten o'clock, she dressed in a sleeveless white linen dress with a straight skirt and white Ferragamo shoes with three-inch heels. She wore her usual jewelry—a gold Rolex watch with a diamond bezel and large gold hoop earrings. She was planning on attending a Women's Symphony League board luncheon meeting and then seeing to some business at a bank downtown.

At about eleven o'clock, Alison, tired from having risen so early, had fallen asleep on the sofa in front of the television. Her mother had gone out to the garden behind the house to cut some flowers from her cutting garden, which she did almost every morning she was in town. Tiny loved having fresh flowers around the house.

David Serrano, the McFarlands' twenty-one-year-old live-in baby-sitter and handyman, was studying in his quarters above the detached garage, which was about ten yards from the house at the end of a long winding gravel driveway. A part-time student at Austin Community College, David was taking a summer school class in accounting and used all his spare time to do his schoolwork.

The final member of the household, the McFarlands' ninety-five-pound German shepherd named Mauser, was at the kennel having a flea dip. Charlie McFarland had dropped the dog off on the way to work that morning. Eight years after the murder, an old friend of the McFarland family said with tears in her eyes, "It would never have happened if Mauser had been there; he was the best watchdog, the most protective animal I've ever seen. He would have walked out to the garden with Tiny and he would have set up a racket you wouldn't believe when that old junker of a car drove in. I don't believe that man would have even dared get out of his car if Mauser had been there." It was just one in the series of random misfortunes that contributed to the tragedy that morning.

It had been only five days since Louie Bronk had murdered eighty-year-old Greta Huff in San Marcos, and he was cruising the highways again, driving up from Corpus Christi, where he'd fled right after the Huff murder. As he described it in a prison interview eight years later, "I was just cruising, you know how you do, and the Mustang was running real good, just purring along the Interstate, but in all that distance—Corpus to San Antone, San Antone to Austin—I didn't see but one opportunity—see I'm always looking for the opportunity—and that was some old bag with gray hair and glasses by the side of the road with a flat. She actually tried to flag me down. Isn't that something? But she was not up to my standards, definitely not. See, I never had to settle for no dogs.

"I'd been drinking pretty steady for two days and thinking those things which I try not to let take over, but them pictures, the real bad ones, you know, those things I told you about last week, had just got hold of my head and I was seeing those things real clear in my head, just like Technicolor movies over and over again, and by the time I get to Austin I'm in need, just looking for anything at all, not fussy at this point the way I am sometimes, wishing I'd settled back near San Antone for the old bitch. Would serve her right doing such a damn-fool thing like flagging down a stranger."

Bronk didn't intend to stop in Austin; he was heading to Fort Worth, but because he got in the wrong lane after he crossed over Town Lake, he was forced to exit off the highway and found himself in Austin, going west on FM 2222. He intended to turn around and get back on the Interstate, but then he decided to wait and see where fate took him. He was low on cash and thought he'd look for someplace easy to rob.

After about fifteen minutes he found himself out west of the city. "See, I always liked to stay close to the Interstate, but this time I thought to try something different. All the times I've drove through Austin, I never really seen it and this area was real pretty—these green hills and all. I saw this road, Something Park Road, off to the left and I don't know why, it just looked pretty, like where you'd take a Sunday drive or something, so I took it and drove about a mile to this driveway going up a hill. Made out of gravel. There was a mailbox with a number on it, I remember that. So I drove in just to see what's at the end of it and I come to this garage near a big stone house.

"I didn't see no one around, but it was clear rich people lived there. I knew there'd be stuff to steal. I went to the door and it was unlocked, just like it was waiting for me, so I walked in and took me a little Sony TV from the kitchen and a silver bowl and the prettiest carving knife with this white handle that looks like it's made of bone. I was carrying these out to the car when I saw a lady standing in the garage and the door was open. Yup. Mrs. McFarland—she was one of mine, sure was. See, I can have any woman I want. Any woman. She was all dressed in white, not a spot on her anywhere, had a bunch of flowers—these pretty red flowers. Yup. Just as easy to do the rich ones as them you pick up by the side of the road. Ain't no difference when you get down to the basics.

"Lucky I had this little .22 Saturday Night Special I got me down in San Marcos for twenty-five bucks. I'd it stuck into my pants under my shirt. I dropped the stuff I was carrying and I ran at her. She was real small, I can see why they called her 'Tiny,' but she was strong, fought like a wildcat. Pushed me away, and turned to run, so I had to shoot her. I would of preferred to use my knife, or something else, but she didn't give me no choice, fighting and running like that. She fell and I saw right away she was dead. That easy, it was."

Then he pulled his old straight razor out of his pocket, the same razor he'd used on Rosa Morales, Lizette Pachullo, and Greta Huff—the razor he'd bought when he got his first job as a barber in Oklahoma after he was released from the state prison, where he was trained as a barber.

"I opened my razor and started on her hair. This Texas Scalper thing—well, I didn't always do that, just sometimes. When I was done I thought about . . . well, you know, having sex with her. I took her dress off and looked at her. But this time I know it's not going to work. I don't know if it's all the beer I drunk or it's so damned hot or a strange place or maybe that she was a blonde and they've never appealed to me. They don't seem . . . finished somehow. So I took her watch and earrings off of her, 'cause they looked like they'd bring in some cash, and I got in the car and drove off. And that was it, like it was just a detour from the road I was taking. I don't think the whole thing took more than three, four minutes."

In one of his confessions Bronk told Sheriff Dwayne Gaskill in Hays County that he sold the pistol and all the stolen items at different flea markets and pawnshops that same day between Austin and Fort Worth. He has also told other versions of what he did with the items. In court, he said he got scared and threw them in a river outside Austin, but he couldn't remember where. None of the items have ever been recovered.

He said in his confession that he took the dress the victim had been wearing and threw it into the back seat of the Mustang. When he pushed the car off a cliff into Eagle Mountain Lake near Fort Worth, it was still inside. Although the lake has been dragged twice, the Mustang was never recovered.

As for the hair he shaved from Tiny McFarland's head and from his other victims, Louie Bronk has never been willing to talk about what he did with it.

After he got back onto the Interstate that day, he drove on to Fort Worth where he'd planned to go all along, before he got in the wrong lane that made him take the exit, that led him to FM 2222, that enticed him to the hills, that took him to City Park Road, that lured him to the gravel driveway, that ended at the McFarlands' garage on that hot July morning.

Molly looked up from the page, remembering that interview with Louie when he'd taken her through the steps of the McFarland murder. As usual, she'd kept her face neutral, her manner encouraging. Of course she already knew the story. She'd read his confession and then heard it all again at the trial where he had unsuccessfully claimed insanity. But hearing it from his own mouth, as they sat inches apart in the visitors' room in Huntsville, separated only by a few layers of wire mesh, was something else—his cool recital of it, his occasional smiles and head shakes at the ironies of fate. At the time she'd just listened and recorded. But now, reading the words, she wondered how she was able to endure listening to it.

She looked back down at the page:

David Serrano was lying on his bed in his apartment above the garage studying an accounting textbook. He wore only a pair of boxer shorts because his quarters were not air-conditioned like the main house was, and the heat was intense, already ninety-one degrees at quarter past eleven in the morning.

He heard a noise that he recognized immediately as a gunshot, but that didn't concern him. All four members of the McFarland family often practiced shooting in the field out behind the house where they kept some targets and cans to shoot at. During the summer the kids would often wander out there and do some shooting. Tiny also liked to shoot, was the best shot in the family, better even than Charlie and the kids who had all won trophies over the years in shooting competitions at the Travis County Rifle Club. It could be any of them out practicing.

David went back to his book.

But a few minutes later he put down his book. It occurred to him that there had been just one shot, and he began to worry. He couldn't remember anyone ever going out to shoot and shooting only once. And as he thought about it, that shot had sounded closer than usual. He decided to check, and anyway, he knew Mrs. McFarland was planning to leave at about eleven-thirty when he would take over supervising Alison.

He pulled on a pair of jeans and a shirt and stepped into his tennis shoes with no socks and without bothering to tie them. As he was walking down the staircase that led into the garage, he heard a car engine start up, and when he came to the bottom of the stairs he saw through the open garage door a white car, old and beat-up, driving out the driveway. He didn't recognize the make of the car because he says he's never been interested in cars, can't tell a Ford from a Buick. Though he saw only the back of the driver's head, he thought it was a man with dark hair, though he wasn't absolutely sure. He was sure about one thing, though: the car was white with one brown door, the one on the driver's side.

He watched the car drive off, wondering who the McFarlands knew who would drive an old clunker like that. Most of their friends drove late-model cars, new and shiny.

By then he was inside the garage and saw that a woman, naked except for a pair of white panties, lay in the empty space, the space where Charlie's Cadillac was parked when he was home. David says he knew two things immediately—that it was Mrs. McFarland and that she was past help. Even though she was lying facedown and her hair was gone, he recognized her because her head was turned to the side and he could see her profile. "Also," he said, "it was the size of her. No one else I knew, no grown woman, I mean, was so small. It had to be her."

He walked slowly toward her and when he squatted down and saw her glazed, open eyes, he knew instantly that she was dead, even before he saw the blood oozing from under the body, beading up on the grease spot from where the Cadillac had leaked oil.

David Serrano was familiar with the look of death, he says, because his family, including his father, grandfather, and three uncles, was in the funeral business in Brownsville, Texas, where he grew up. For five summers he worked assisting in the embalming and preparing of bodies for burial. He didn't need to feel for a pulse. He knew death when he saw it.

Only then, he says, did he think to look around the garage. It was a three-car garage, but the McFarlands parked only two of their three vehicles in it because the third space at the north end was taken up with storage of bicycles and lawn mowers and boxes. The big electric door was open and the small side door was shut, he says, though it was never locked. Mrs. McFarland's white Mercedes occupied the center space and Charlie's Cadillac, the space on the south end where his wife now lay. Scattered around her body lay a bunch of scarlet gladioli and a pair of garden snippers.

David backed out of the garage and ran to the house to telephone for the police, suddenly afraid that whoever had killed her might come back. He was shocked to find Alison standing in the doorway looking up the driveway where the car had just been. He took her in the house with him, locked the door, and called the Austin Police.

APD records their response time that day as thirteen minutes. David Serrano says it felt like forever, as he sat with Alison in front of the television worrying about Mrs. McFarland, feeling she shouldn't be left alone outside. But he felt his first loyalty was to his young charge, so he remained with her. He didn't call Charlie McFarland at that time. He says he didn't know what to say and thought he'd let the police handle it.

During that time, Stuart McFarland, who had decided to come home early from his cousin's house, arrived on his bicycle, went to put it away in the garage, and saw his mother lying there. He knelt down and tried to revive her, thought about doing CPR which he'd just learned, until he saw the blood pooling under her and understood that his mother had been shot.

Molly stopped reading there, though the account went on to detail the arrival of the police and the early stages of the investigation before Louie Bronk confessed eight days later.

Molly stood up, then suddenly dropped the pages to the table. Oh, God. Fingerprints. Here she was a former police reporter, a former wife of a cop, and a present crime writer, and she hadn't given a thought to fingerprints on the pages. If there had been any, she had certainly messed them up.

Not that it mattered; this was just some kook. There was no reason to worry about prints.

But that poem was damned unsettling.

She walked to the back hall closet and rummaged on the shelf for a pair of old cloth gardening gloves she rarely wore. This time touching only the edges with her gloved hands, she reread the poem. The line, "I may give his craft a try" bothered her. Was there a threat of violence there?

And, of all the 421 pages of her book that could have been torn out, why these? And why right now, just after her meeting with Charlie McFarland?

Glancing up, she saw that the kitchen window had darkened. She rose and pulled the blinds, then walked into the living room and closed the shutters on the big windows so she wouldn't be tempted to look into those black voids. She poured herself a Scotch and water, a rare indulgence for her, and sipped at it while she changed into her exercise clothes. Maybe some strenuous sweating would help her get rid of this clutch of dread in the pit of her stomach.

It was a feeling she'd almost forgotten. She hadn't experienced it for two years—not since the last time she went to visit Louie Bronk.

chapter 3

Always their hair
Their long black hair
Combing and brushing,
Washing and fussing.
Black hair everywhere
You could drown in hair,
Hair in the sink,
Hair in the drains
Long black hair instead of brains.

LOUIE BRONK
Death Row, Ellis I Unit,
Huntsville, Texas

▲ ▼ ▲

"**B**ut what if it isn't just some nut case?" Molly Cates grunted as she did the seventh push-up in the set of twenty-five; she was damned if she'd let herself collapse at this point the way she usually did, even though the muscles in her back were screaming. "I mean, what if it isn't a *harmless* nut case?"

She glanced up at her daughter who, as she rose and sank on thin, shaking arms, wore her usual serene expression in spite of the big drops of sweat dripping off her face. Jo Beth Traynor, who now wanted to be called Elizabeth, had the kind of determination that just didn't recognize pain, Molly thought.

"Mother, calm down. You've had this sort of thing before." Jo Beth just managed to make herself heard over the thrumming beat of the hard-rock booming from the overhead speakers. "Remember that guy who kept threatening to load his dump truck with explosives and crash it into the *Lone Star Monthly* offices if you didn't stop writing about developers ruining the Barton Creek watershed. I hope you aren't getting paranoid in midlife."

"No," Molly gasped. There was no way she was going to last through fifteen more push-ups. "I've always been paranoid." She closed her eyes against the stinging sweat that was dripping into them. "God, this is torture." She stopped for a minute to grab her towel and wipe her face. Then she hoisted herself up immediately and joined back in, determined to make this the first time she did all the push-ups. "Wait until you read this poem before calling me paranoid," she panted. "It has a crazy feel to it. Of course I suppose it goes with the territory of—" She couldn't finish; she'd done thirteen —thirteen!—more than she'd ever managed before, and her back and shoulders were burning. She collapsed on her stomach and watched Jo Beth persevere through all twenty-five.

Push-ups finished, the class of twenty sweating bodies looked to the front of the room for instructions. On a platform in front of the mirrored wall, the instructor, a forty-five-year-old freak of nature with tight beige skin, a twenty-two-inch waist, and a concave abdomen, flipped onto her back. "Now let's work those abs," Michelle bellowed out over the deafening music. "Backs flat, glutes squeezed tight, suck in, let's *go.*" Hands behind her head she began to demonstrate sit-ups. Molly and Jo Beth turned onto their backs and followed her lead.

"But this poem—" Molly said, "it could be read as a threat."

"Maybe you should show it to Dad then. You know, get his opinion."

Molly shook her head as she raised and lowered her torso. "No. Austin homicide won't want to bother with this. Too subtle. I'll take it to the DA's office—tomorrow. Stan Heffernan can take it to APD if he wants. God, these sit-ups always make me feel like I'm going to throw up."

Now Michelle was pulling her knees into her elbows on each sit-up. It was difficult to do that and talk, but Molly managed to say, "This thing with Charlie McFarland bothers me, too."

"You sure he tried to bribe you?" Jo Beth said, pulling her knees in to touch her elbows.

Molly grunted. "Yes. I can't figure any other way to take it."

"Tell me the truth. Weren't you tempted? Just for a minute?"

Before Molly could answer, Michelle bellowed out from the platform, "Okay, as a special treat, let's end on some more push-ups— another set of twenty-five."

"No-o-o," Molly wailed. "Just when I thought we were safe." She wiped her brow and turned over again to her stomach, hoisting herself up on shaky arms. "Yeah, I was tempted. Maybe that's why I feel so angry about it." Molly stopped in mid push-up. "You know something?"

"What?" Jo Beth asked, not even short of breath.

"I'll really be relieved when this Bronk thing is over."

Jo Beth stopped, her arms extended, and looked up, wide-eyed. "Mother! What's this? Do I detect some blood lust here?"

Michelle was counting to help them get through the push-ups: "Fourteen . . . fifteen . . ." Molly was groaning now from the strain and her arms were trembling, but in the five months she'd been doing this class she'd never gotten so far before. "Sixteen." Only nine more; she didn't want to give up. "Seventeen . . ." Her back felt like it was ripping. With a moan, she collapsed onto her stomach. So close, so close.

"Well, Mother," Jo Beth finished off the last eight and added one extra for good measure, "what about it? Don't tell me that an old liberal like you is looking forward to poor Louie getting the needle?"

Molly was silent for a moment, resting her chin on the floor. Then she said, her lips barely moving, "If I weren't in a weakened state right now, I probably wouldn't say this—and if you repeat it I'll deny I ever said it—but," she closed her eyes and said it very low so Jo Beth might not hear it over the music, "the world will be a better place with Louie Bronk out of it. I can't wait to see that sneering, smug, murdering, evil son of a bitch dead."

Jo Beth looked at Molly with her eyes open wide and said nothing.

They both did the cool-down stretching in silence. It was Molly's favorite part of the class because it didn't hurt and it meant they were almost finished.

When it was over, Molly stood up and wrapped the towel around her neck. "I'm going to get a little dinner at Katz's. Want to come?"

"If you're paying, sure," Jo Beth said. As she followed her mother down the stairs to the women's locker room, she said, "For a woman your age who can barely do a push-up, you've got a pretty firm butt."

Molly looked back at her. "I'm bowled over by the praise."

▼

The menu at Katz's Bar and Deli included several items that Molly had never identified—things like latkes and knishes, which she wouldn't know how to pronounce even if she did order them. An unadventurous eater who stuck to the tried and true, Molly ordered her usual turkey on white bread and a Coors Light. Jo Beth ordered pastrami on Jewish rye and a Coors Light. Beer was one of the few things mother and daughter agreed on.

As the waiter left, Jo Beth said, "It may be your lucky night. Don't look now, but there's a man standing in the doorway of the bar who's been staring at you."

Molly glanced over that way. A dark-haired man in a well-tailored blue suit was indeed staring at her. He nodded his head when he saw her look over.

"You know him?" Jo Beth asked.

"No," Molly said, turning back to the table.

"Gorgeous," Jo Beth said.

"He is good-looking," Molly agreed.

"I knew you'd think so. He's just slightly sleazy and since that's the way your taste in men runs—"

"Sleazy? You think your daddy's sleazy?"

Jo Beth smiled the gentle, loving, maddening smile she always got on her face when she talked about Grady Traynor. "No. Not Dad. The other two. And some of the boyfriends. My God! Sleaze personified."

Molly decided not to rise to the old bait. Instead, she shifted the topic slightly: "Speaking of your father, that marriage can't still be holding together?"

Jo Beth opened her mouth to speak, then seemed to think better of it and shook her head. "You know my rule about that, Mother."

It was damned maddening. Jo Beth, always mature beyond her years, had from the beginning refused to talk to one parent about the other, throughout the divorce, Molly's subsequent two marriages, and Grady's one.

Molly sighed. From her bag on the seat she pulled copies she'd made of the twelve torn-out pages and the poem and laid them in front of her daughter.

Jo Beth read the poem over twice and scanned the pages. Then she looked at the poem again as if she were memorizing it. When she looked up, the smooth skin of her forehead was creased. "I see what you mean about the poem. If you take it literally, this part about Louie inspiring his rhymes and giving his craft a try could mean this person actually likes Louie Bronk's poetry and wants to write like that." She shook her head. "Unlikely."

"Yeah. And poetry being metaphorical, I'm afraid the writer is using the poetry as a symbol for something Louie does do well."

"Killing," said Jo Beth.

Molly nodded.

"I agree you should show this to the DA. And I don't like to nag, but I really think you should show it to Dad, too. Tonight if possible. I'm going to call him now. Maybe he could—"

Molly grabbed her daughter's arm and pulled her back down. "No. I'll take it to Stan Heffernan first thing tomorrow."

Jo Beth sighed and sat back down in the booth.

The waiter arrived with their beers and both women took long drinks, putting their glasses down at exactly the same moment and looking at each other across the table.

"Could this be Louie Bronk's last gasp?" Jo Beth asked. "He could have gotten someone here to mail it for him."

"That's the first thing I thought about, but the language is far too literate for him. Louie has trouble spelling cat; his vocabulary doesn't include words like 'depiction' and 'accolades.' The poetry of his that I quote in my book has been cleaned up—my editor corrected the spelling and added some punctuation." Molly took another long sip of her beer. "You know, after fifty hours of interviews I feel I know Louie better than anyone in the world. He didn't write this. But I've wondered whether he's read the book; it would take him a while with his fifth-grade reading level."

"Where he is, he's got plenty of time."

"Until it runs out altogether, sometime between midnight and sunrise on Tuesday," Molly said, shaking her head. "Tell me something that makes sense, like tax law."

Jo Beth grinned. "Well, yesterday I started working on the Overton case, directly for Benson Williams."

"One of the partners. Honey, that's great."

"Uh-huh. Ben's a super teacher; it's heaven working with him. He's letting me do most of the prehearing preparation, and I'll probably go to Houston with him if it goes to trial."

While she listened Molly marveled at what an accomplished and beautiful daughter she had produced in spite of all her own manifest deficiencies as a mother.

"So if we can prove that Paul Overton didn't know about the—" Jo Beth stopped midsentence and looked up. So did Molly. The man in the dark suit was standing at their table, looking down at them. Molly felt her shoulders tense; now that he was closer, the bulge she thought she'd seen under his left arm was unmistakable.

"Mrs. Cates?" His soft voice carried the slight singsong intonation that characterized Texans of Mexican descent. "I don't think you recognize me."

Molly studied the smooth-contoured olive face with its straight nose and lustrous, slightly slanted black eyes and felt just a prickle of memory stir. "Sorry, I—"

"Well, it's been a long time. Ten years. I'm David Serrano. We met during the Bronk trial." His expression remained grave.

Molly stifled a gasp. David Serrano. The McFarlands' baby-sitter-handyman. How could she have forgotten? "Yes, of course. David. Mr. Serrano," Molly blurted out. "Sorry I didn't recognize you; you've—" She stopped, afraid of offending. This well-dressed, soft-spoken man had been a scruffy young student at the time, handsome but threadbare and unsophisticated. He had changed tremendously over the years.

He shrugged. "People change. It's been a long time."

"David, this is my daughter, Jo—uh, Elizabeth. Elizabeth, David Serrano."

He reached out to take Jo Beth's proffered hand and shook it gravely. Jo Beth's eyes were bright with interest as she scanned the bulge under his arm. The daughter of a policeman, she had no trouble spotting a man who was carrying.

"I hate to interrupt you," he said in a low voice, "but I wonder if I could have a word with you in private, Mrs. Cates. I was going to call you tomorrow, but since you're here . . ." He gestured toward the bar. "I have a table there. I won't keep you long."

Molly looked over at Jo Beth, who nodded at her. "I'll be right back, honey," she said, sliding out of the booth, noting the intensity of interest in her daughter's eyes. She has inherited something from me after all, Molly thought as she followed David into the bar; she is afflicted with that same damned sordid curiosity; she can't wait to hear what this is all about. And neither can I.

The bar at Katz's, with its low, black-tiled ceiling and dim lighting, was notorious as the hangout for many of Austin's heavy drinkers. The sign outside said *"Katz's Never Kloses,"* and several of the good ol' boys drinking and laughing at the bar looked like they hadn't been home in years.

David Serrano with his courtly manners, serious face, and business suit looked decidedly out of place there. And so did the gun under his arm.

He led her to a small round table against the brick wall and pulled a chair out for her. He waited until she sat before he did. "Can I order you a drink, Mrs. Cates?"

"Call me Molly."

"All right. A drink?"

"First call me Molly," she said with a smile.

He let out a puff of air which might have been a laugh if he'd allowed it to take shape, but his lips looked as if they'd been trained to solemnity. "Molly," he conceded. "How about that drink?"

"No thanks."

He motioned the waiter over and ordered a double Scotch on the rocks.

Molly sat back in her chair and took a good look at this man she had not seen for ten years. Last time she had seen him, he'd been testifying at Louie Bronk's trial, wearing a shiny ill-fitting suit he'd obviously borrowed for the occasion. And he had wept throughout his testimony.

Now his long delicate fingers were tightly interlaced on the table in front of him; on his left hand he wore a wide, hand-hammered gold band and a heavy gold watch. His thick black hair, combed straight back from his face, was graying at the sides—prematurely, since he was only thirty-two, Molly calculated—and he was as svelte as he had been at twenty-two. She should have recognized him.

She found herself brimming with questions, but decided to wait and hear what was on his mind first.

When he started to speak his voice was shaky, like a nervous public speaker. "I've only been back in Austin a few days and I was going to call you." He shifted his weight on the chair as if he was having trouble getting comfortable. "I've been living in Brownsville for the past ten years, you know."

"No. I didn't know," she said.

The waiter set his drink down on the table. David picked it up and drank as if it had arrived in the nick of time.

Then he took a deep breath and said, "The reason I wanted to talk to you—I wonder if I could ask you something. About Louie Bronk?"

"Sure. Ask."

His tongue flicked over his lips. "Do you think the execution will go through this time?"

It was the second time today she'd been asked that. Molly studied him before answering. His body was so full of tension that his shoulders were hunched up close to his ears. "Yes," she said. "I think so. Why do you ask?"

He shrugged, but his shoulders stayed tense. "Well, the last two times, his attorneys have managed to get him a stay. I thought you might have some inside information. You know, what last-minute maneuvering was going on."

She shook her head. "I really don't have any inside information, David. When I talked with his attorney last week, she said the state court had rejected Bronk's appeal."

"What about the governor? Do you think she might pardon him, or reprieve him?"

"Not a chance. She's tough on law and order. And she really believes in the death penalty." She leaned forward across the table. "What brings you back to Austin, David?"

He hesitated. "Well, it seemed time. I haven't been back since I left ten years ago."

"Why not?"

"Bad memories, I guess. But really I came here on my way to Huntsville. I'm going to witness the execution on Tuesday—if it happens."

"You are?" Molly tried to conceal her surprise.

"Yes. Weird isn't it? He requested me as one of his witnesses."

"And you accepted."

"Yes. My first reaction was to say no, but then I decided I should. It might be good for me."

"Good how?"

He didn't answer right away. He took a sip of his drink. Then he said, "So maybe I could stop thinking about it. This thing almost ruined my life. It changed everything for me. I suppose I was hoping that seeing him die might erase it all, so I could—not go back—I wouldn't want to do that, but put it behind me. Eleven years ago when Mrs. McFarland was murdered, I was just a kid really, only twenty-one. Innocent. I had no idea how things were." His face tightened up and the skin around his nostrils went white. "But I learned fast."

Molly suspected he harbored anger that he hadn't even begun to fathom. She wanted to pull out her tape recorder but was afraid that asking might spook him.

"I was so dumb back then," he said, "I didn't even know how vulnerable I was, how I couldn't do noth—anything to protect myself."

He paused and looked at Molly miserably; she nodded to encourage him.

"The cops assumed I'd killed her. That I was the Scalper. They tried to pin every murder they could think of on me. They treated me like I was some sort of mad dog. Even when Alison and me told about seeing the car drive away and Mr. McFarland went to bat for me. Even though I'd never done nothing, never been in trouble with the law. Even with those things, they still knocked me around and tried to pin it on me." As he talked on, he lost his controlled grip on grammar. "If it hadn't been for Louie Bronk confessing right then, they probably would have indicted me. It was like a miracle, him confessing. If that hadn't happened it'd be me on death row now." He took a drink. "I decided right then I was going to do everything I could to get some power in this world so that couldn't happen to me again."

"And have you?"

He looked up at her, puzzled.

"Gotten power?" she said.

He emitted the gust of air that might have been a laugh if it hadn't contained so much bitterness. "Well, I made some money. A lot of money actually." He finished off his drink in a quick move and held the glass in the air to get the waiter's attention.

Once she started asking questions, Molly believed in asking the rude ones—the questions everyone else was too tactful to ask; lack of tact, she believed, was one of the main things she had going for her as an investigative journalist. "How did you make money?" she asked.

For a minute she thought he might not answer, but he did. "Funeral parlors," he said. "My grandfather had one old one in Laredo and when I went back we acquired some more and now we've got a string of fifteen along the border. It's a good business. Death is a growth industry there."

Molly studied his face to see if his last sentence had been a joke, but there was no sign of it. Maybe funeral directors didn't make jokes.

"Did it work? Did money bring you the power you'd hoped for?"

He narrowed his eyes as if he didn't understand the question. "Not really. Maybe I feel a little safer than before."

"Is that the reason for the gun? To be safe?" Molly nodded toward the bulge under his arm.

His face stayed blank, his black eyes steady; it was hard to believe this was the same emotional young man who had wept as he testified a decade earlier. "I suppose," he said. "I got a permit for it."

"But does it make you feel safer?"

"Not really. But in this world some people are safer than others. I want for me and my family—I'm married now and we have three kids—to be in the safer category. Whatever it takes."

He fell silent. When the waiter put a drink in front of him, he just stared at it.

Molly wished she knew what the hell was really going on here. Serrano seemed to have a great deal more on his mind than he was saying. She decided to try fishing around a little.

"David, do you stay in touch with the McFarlands?"

He took a long draw on his drink. "Sure. I saw Alison last night, and Mark, you know, her cousin Mark Redinger. We've kept in touch over the years. I really loved those kids, and they were real fond of me, especially Alison, 'cuz their mother was gone a lot of the time. Most of the time, really. I saw much more of them the two and a half years I worked there than their parents did."

"What about Stuart? Have you seen him?"

"Not yet. He's been busy at the hospital. But I'm planning to."

"And Charlie?"

He shrugged.

"The kids have had a hard time of it, I imagine," Molly said.

"Yeah, as hard as people like that can have."

"What do you mean—people like that?"

He looked away. "Oh, people who have it all so easy—Anglos with a fancy education and a rich daddy. When they run out of money, they just whine for more. For those people there's always a safety net."

"How is Alison?" Molly asked. "Her father says he's worried about her mental health."

He sighed. "She had a sort of breakdown when she first started college, had to drop out for a year, but I think she's in pretty good shape now."

"David, I suppose you know the book I wrote about Louie Bronk just came out."

He lowered his eyes and stared into his drink.

"Two years ago I wrote you several letters asking for another interview, but I never heard back from you."

He didn't lift his eyes.

"Have you read it?"

He hesitated a betraying fraction of a second. "Yes. I read it last week."

"What did you think of it? I'd welcome some feedback on the part that involved you."

His eyes darted toward the door. For all the world, Molly thought, like a trapped animal. "You mean was it accurate?"

She nodded.

"Well, you must have used my testimony at the trial for your information."

"That, and the interview you gave me at the time," she said.

"You stuck close to it, so it was accurate in that respect. I guess that's what you got to do, but—" He took a long swig of his drink.

Molly shifted her weight on the hard chair; the man's tension was contagious. "But what?"

He didn't answer and he didn't look up.

This was so unexpected a development that Molly found herself floundering around for the right question. Finally she said, "David, are you having some second thoughts about your testimony in the McFarland matter?"

When he looked up, there were several tiny droplets of liquid just above his upper lip; Molly wasn't sure whether it was sweat or Scotch. "I just wondered," he said softly. "There wasn't anything in your book about the nicks."

"Nicks?"

"Yeah. The nicks on her scalp."

Molly felt short of breath and her fingertips prickled. "What are you talking about, David?"

He lifted a hand and used the back of it to wipe the moisture off his upper lip. "Well, those little cuts Mrs. McFarland had on her head—you didn't mention them in the part about the autopsy. I read it a couple of times to be sure."

"There weren't any little cuts," Molly said.

"Yes there were. Like I've seen sometimes when our clients—you know, the departed—have been shaved by someone in the family who had a shaky hand instead of having it done by our professional mortuary barber."

When she had caught her breath, Molly said, "David, the Travis County ME who's been doing the postmortems for thirty years didn't mention any nicks. And I had one of the autopsy photographs on my bulletin board for a year, looked at it every day, and I never saw any nicks."

"They weren't very big," he said, "and when they're done after death, there isn't any bleeding."

"Why didn't you mention this before?"

"No one asked. I thought it was obvious and would come out in the autopsy. I didn't know it hadn't until I read your book." His black eyes watched her so intently Molly got the feeling that he was giving her a test of some sort.

"I'll check on it tomorrow," she said, looking at the tight set of his handsome red mouth and wondering what else he was holding back. "Is this what's been bothering you?"

"I guess."

"Is there anything else I can check on for you?"

He lifted his glass, drained the contents, and set it down carefully on the table. "Molly," he said, using her name voluntarily for the first time, "you're against the death penalty, aren't you?"

"Yes," she said.

"Are you Catholic?" he asked.

"No. I'm not any religion. I'm just against the state killing people. What about you?"

He lifted his right hand to his chest and put the index and middle fingers inside his shirt between the buttons. Molly was certain he was touching a small gold cross that hung there. "I'm against it, too," he said. "Thou shalt not kill."

Molly thought she understood now what his problem was. "It sounds like you're having some last-minute discomfort about your role in putting Louie Bronk away. That's not unusual for witnesses, David. Among the many things wrong with the death penalty is that it can be devastating for witnesses."

He let out a stream of air through his lips; all the way across the table she felt it on her face and smelled the Scotch.

"David, I'm doing an article about the execution, sort of an update on Louie Bronk, for *Lone Star Monthly.* I wonder if you'd talk to me about this, on the record? About your religious scruples as a witness. I'd like to record what we say, if it's all right with you."

He ran his tongue over his lips and looked around the room. "Now?"

She smiled at him. "Why not? No time like the present." She leaned over and pulled her little recorder and her notebook from her bag.

He leaned back in his chair and looked down into his drink. "Not tonight. I'm tired. Let me think about it."

Push, her instinct told her. "We could take twenty minutes now and get it done. It could be helpful in changing people's minds about capital punishment, David. Showing the difficulty a religious man has after he does his duty and testifies in court."

He shook his head slowly and held up his empty glass as explanation. "I can't even think straight now. I don't usually drink like this. I'll call you tomorrow. Maybe we could talk after you check the autopsy stuff."

Molly sighed, took a card out of her purse, and handed it to him. "What time will you call?"

He slid the card into his breast pocket and folded his hands again on the table, as though they might escape if he didn't hold on to them. "In the afternoon," he murmured.

"Where are you staying if I should need to get in touch with you? There's always the chance I might get some information about the execution."

"I'm staying with my cousin, Reuben Serrano, on South Fifth. 1802 South Fifth."

Molly jotted it down. "What's the phone number there?"

David put a ten-dollar bill on the table. "He's got no phone."

She decided to try once more to get him to talk, but just as she was about to speak, he stood and slid his chair into the table. "I've got to go," he said, reaching out to shake her hand. "Got a date." When she put her hand in his, he shook it with a firm, professional grasp and then made a slight bow from the waist.

"Talk to you tomorrow," Molly said.

She watched him walk away in his dark suit and his dignified posture. A funeral director—he had certainly mastered the body language.

Molly could see from all the way across the room that Jo Beth's eyes were sparkling with anticipation. As she slid into the booth and picked up her sandwich, Jo Beth said, "He was the guy who worked for the McFarlands, wasn't he?"

Molly nodded and took a bite of the sandwich.

"Don't get coy on me, Mother. What did he want that was so private?"

"Not coy," Molly said with her mouth full, "just eating." After she swallowed, she said, "I'll tell you after I eat." She started to take another bite, then stopped. "Something's going on. First Charlie McFarland trying to talk me out of the story, then this stuff from the master poet, and now David Serrano. It's like out in the oil fields when the rigs start drilling and all the snakes for miles around are set into motion. I just want to go on the record here as predicting that things are on the move."

Jo Beth shook her head. "If you want to get credit for being a prophet, Mother, I think you need to be a little more specific than that."

chapter 4

Here on death row
All set to go.
Ain't scared,
All prepared.
Got no fear, they say,
Ready anyday.
All set to die,
Easy as pie—
What a fucking lie!

▲ ▼ ▲

LOUIE BRONK
Death Row, Ellis I Unit,
Huntsville, Texas

Molly Cates looked down at the familiar photos spread out on the desk—eleven-year-old photos of a dead woman whose body was probably reduced to dust by now. The oval face, with its small even features, was appealing even in death and even without hair to soften it. The body stretched out on the stainless-steel autopsy table could have been that of a ten-year-old girl, except for the swelling of small breasts and the wispy hair growth in the groin. Tiny McFarland had been one of those women who pass from child to adult with only a minimum of external physical change.

Barbara Gruber, assistant to Travis County Medical Examiner Robert Perez, looked over Molly's shoulder and demanded, "What on earth are you looking for, Moll, that you didn't see the first hundred times?"

"I'd rather not say, so you can be impartial here," Molly told her. "Let's have a closer look at this head shot, Barb."

A sturdy, middle-aged blonde in horn-rimmed glasses, Barbara Gruber was an old friend. Over the years the two women had pored over a great many autopsy pictures together. They had recently collaborated on an article for the *Law Enforcement Bulletin*. Barbara had contributed her expertise on body fluids, which was her old specialty, and blood splatter, which was a new passion. Molly had organized it and translated it into words regular people could comprehend.

Barbara picked up the photo and carried it to the long table next to the wall where she switched on a high-intensity goose-necked lamp, and positioned the photo under a large magnifier. Then she stood aside to let Molly look.

As she bent and looked through the lens, Molly felt a fluttering in her chest, like hundreds of furry moth wings. It was incipient panic —her usual reaction to having made a mistake. She moved the photo down slightly so the top of the head was right in the center of the lens and studied it. Yes, there they were, goddammit—some faint lines just a little darker than the mauve-toned skin of the scalp. She closed her eyes for a moment and looked again to see if they were really there. Then she stood back and said, "Look at her scalp, Barb, and tell me what you see, if anything."

Barbara bent over and put her practiced eyes to the magnifier. She looked in silence for what seemed to Molly a long time, moving the photo around continuously. Then she stood back from the table. "Hard as hell to see them, but looks like some tiny hairline cuts, probably made postmortem, maybe when he shaved her head."

"Sure does," Molly said, crossing her arms across her chest. "You don't have pics for any of the other Bronk victims, do you?"

"No. But if it's important to you, we could call and have the other counties check. Let's see, they did the post on Greta Huff in San Antone, and Rosa Morales—that was Corpus, right?"

Molly nodded. "And Candice Hargrave in McLennan County. And Lizette Pachullo in Denton. Could you call them, Barb?"

"You bet."

"Could I talk to the good doc for a minute?" Molly asked.

"No way. He's out of town for the week. First vacation in fifteen years. Hope it improves his temper some. Even if he was here, he probably wouldn't talk to you after what you said about him in your book. Calling him dour and irascible in print is not going to improve your relationship with him."

Molly nodded. Robert Perez had been the overworked and underpaid Travis County ME for thirty years and Molly had often endured his vile temper and hostility toward the press, first when she was a police reporter, then as staffer for *Lone Star Monthly,* and finally when she was researching the book. "When he calls in, will you tell him I need to talk to him—urgently."

Barbara shook her head. "You kidding? There's no way I'd tell him that. He'd bust a blood vessel. Uh-uh. When he gets back I'll tell him. Maybe. If I find a good moment."

Molly didn't really care; she knew what she had come to find out. She had a powerful hunch that when she reported this back to David Serrano, he would have some more to say.

"Barb, I hate to ask this, but would you do something else for me —as a reality check? Would you read through the McFarland file today and see if your boss made any mention of those cuts? I sure didn't see any. I just want to make sure I'm not losing it."

Barbara squeezed her eyebrows together and pretended to be thinking it over. Then she draped an arm across Molly's shoulders and hugged her. "For you, Molly Cates, anything. I've been meaning to call you. I read the book and especially enjoyed the acknowledgments." She closed her eyes and recited: " 'And special thanks to Barbara Gruber who knows more about body fluids than anyone in the state of Texas. Her eagerness to share her knowledge makes her one of the best teachers I have ever run across, and her cheer and efficiency make her the heart and soul of the Travis County Medical Examiner's office.' " She opened her eyes. "You didn't have to say that, but I'm glad you did; my mom thinks I'm famous now."

Before she left, Molly borrowed Barbara's phone and called the DA's office to make an appointment with Stan Heffernan. His secretary, someone new whom Molly didn't know, said Heffernan was in court all morning and booked in meetings all afternoon so he couldn't possibly see her today.

"Who is this I'm talking to?" Molly asked.

After a pause, the voice said, "Ella Sue Jenkins, ma'am."

"Well, Ms. Jenkins, I'm Molly Cates and I got a real urgent problem that only your boss can help me with. Now I know you can get him on his pager, so please tell Stan that I've received an anonymous letter concerning the Bronk case and that it sounds threatening. I need his help in deciding what to do and I need it today. I can come in anytime he's got five minutes."

"Okay, I'll try, Mrs. Cates, but—"

"Honey, if he doesn't get that message, he'll be all horns and rattles when he hears he missed it."

"Well, I—"

"I know what," Molly said, talking fast. "Stan usually comes back to the office at twelve-thirty to read and eat his lunch in peace. Why don't I come over and catch him then? Yes, that's a good idea. You go ahead and tell him that when you buzz him. Thanks, Miz Jenkins." She hung up quickly so the secretary couldn't get another word in.

She looked at her watch and decided to spend the three hours until her appointment over at her *Lone Star Monthly* office. These days she usually worked in her home office and sent things in over a modem, but it was good to appear in person occasionally, remind them she was still around. Maybe a change in working environment would help her discover an ending for the Abilene Angel story. At least it would give her a chance to fill Richard Dutton in on what was going on.

Richard Dutton looked up after less than thirty seconds. His fine long nose with the dent in the tip wrinkled in distaste. "Forget it, Molly. This is just the usual nonsense." He dropped the copy of the poem and the twelve pages on his desk.

Molly reclaimed them. "You're probably right, but I'm going to show Stan Heffernan—just in case."

Richard shrugged under his loose fawn-colored jacket. "Didn't I tell you the Bronk book would bring out the squirrels? I'm surprised this is all you've gotten. Of course it's only been out for a month."

"But, Richard, doesn't this poem read like a threat to you?"

He sat back on the edge of his desk and crossed his arms over his narrow chest. "If you want to call that dreck a poem. I think 'verse' or 'doggerel' is more appropriate for something so dreary."

"Compared to Louie Bronk's stuff, it sounds like Shakespeare. Anyway, things are heating up as the execution approaches. I'm going to—"

"Give it a rest, Molly. Enough's enough." He uncrossed his arms and slapped his hands down on his thighs. "How's the Abilene piece going? We need it tomorrow, first thing, so the fact-checkers can get going on it."

"Richard, have you ever known me to miss a deadline?"

He tilted his long bony head to the side. "Not once. That's one reason I like to hire old reporters—you work like coolies and you always meet your deadlines. Listen, tomorrow after you sign off on that, I want you to plan on going to Houston right away to cover the defenestration of that banker—what's his name?"

"Griswold. Banker Griswold," Molly muttered.

Richard chuckled low in his throat. "How could I have forgotten? Absolutely Dickensian, isn't it?" In spite of having grown up in Fort Worth, the son of an oil executive, Richard Dutton spoke with a slightly British accent—an affectation Molly had always considered amusing and eccentric. But now, for the first time in the eight years she had worked for him, she found it irritating.

"Listen, Richard. That's going to have to wait. The Bronk execution's next Monday, well Tuesday really, just after midnight. I need all the time I can get to cover it right—interviews with families of victims and some of the original investigators like the old sheriff down in Hays County and the Rangers who were involved early on. You know—where's the old gang and how do they feel now that the execution is finally about to take place."

She got increasingly excited as she talked about it; it would be the best of the series she'd done on Louie Bronk, the final word. "I want to cover the actual execution in detail, Richard. His last day, what goes on in the death chamber—I think people are fascinated by that —last visitors, last meals, last words—all that. Then I'll go outside and talk with the protesters—the Amnesty International faithfuls, the candlelight chanters, and all the usual prison groupies. And here's something else I've been thinking about—how an execution affects the other inmates on death row. I want to talk to them, find out what they thought of him, whether they stay awake for it. You could call the warden to arrange that, couldn't you?"

She stopped to gauge his reaction, but his face was blank. He just shrugged in answer to her question. She was surprised. Usually she could rev him up when she tried to sell an idea.

She just needed to do a harder sell, she decided. "And this is the perfect chance for me to do an update on capital punishment now that Texas is gearing up for an unprecedented surge in executions. After all, we lead the nation; we've executed fourteen already this year, two of them last week. We can do a sidebar on the executions this year to date and compare it with Florida and some other states that are executing aggressively. And, now, with the Supreme Court decisions limiting habeas corpus, there's no telling what sort of records our great state might set this year."

He looked bored. "Hell, Richard," Molly said, "Banker Griswold's just a stain on that Westheimer sidewalk; he ain't going nowhere. I can do him next month."

Richard looked down the length of his legs to his shiny tasseled loafers. "Molly, with the indictment of Griswold and his partner and the other Resolution Trust Corp bribery cases, Griswold is hot stuff. And we haven't done zip on it. And anyway"—he looked up and grinned, revealing some of the charm for which he was notorious— "it's worth doing the piece just so you can revive the use of the word 'defenestration.' Trust me, this is much better than trotting out your moldy old Bronk thing. You've had a good run with it. Now lay it to rest."

"But, Richard, I'll come up with new angles; you know how just rooting around in an old case like this can stir up something new. David Serrano, the McFarlands' old live-in baby-sitter, is back in town, and he's going to attend the execution as one of Bronk's witnesses. Now that's an interesting wrinkle—asking for someone who testified against you to come watch you die. And David's a devout Catholic fretting over his role in sending Bronk to the death chamber. There's juice there. And Charley McFarland is willing to talk for the first time. And surely," she said, holding her hands out, palms up, "you haven't forgotten the two Bronk issues outsold everything we've ever done."

Richard crossed his arms over his chest again in a way that made her heart sink. "Molly, the Bronk case is all over but the needle prick. I'm sick of that animal cracker. If you feel you have to do something, make it a brief piece on the execution itself, his last words, how long it took for the injection to work, blah-blah—you know, three pages at most. We'll put a blurb at the end plugging your book, sell a few copies maybe."

Molly felt like wailing in frustration, but she forced her voice to stay low and spoke slowly. "Richard, we talked about this last month when the court set his execution date. We agreed a story would be a good idea. I've already made plans, set up some interviews."

"Cancel them."

Because she felt like squealing, she lowered her voice even more. "Why have you changed your mind?"

"I don't remember ever thinking it was a good idea. Anyway, I don't think so now and we've got better stories waiting for your attention. At the last staff meeting, which you missed, Molly, there was general agreement that we should do something on the S & L indictments." His mouth was set in a hard, thin line she didn't like the looks of.

Molly took a deep breath to push the anger down. Usually they saw eye to eye on what made a good story. When they disagreed, it was over the best approach or angle to take. And on those rare occasions, he usually turned out to be right, so she trusted his instincts. She was willing to acknowledge that she sometimes got carried away with something. Yes, sometimes she did go too far. But now she knew he was wrong, knew it for certain.

"Richard, *Lone Star Monthly* has covered the Bronk case intensively. We need to finish it with a flourish; our readers expect it." She tried to stop her voice from rising, but it defied her control. "Just give me one good reason, Richard."

"I already have. It's a vein we've mined out. Ancient history. Everyone's tired of it. Except you."

She looked at the smug set of his mouth and felt her anger surge; she couldn't contain it another second. "I just can't believe this, Richard! There's more to this than you're saying. It has something to do with Charlie McFarland, I bet. Yeah, that's it. He says the two of you are *real* good friends. McFarland's gotten to you, hasn't he?"

Richard rolled his eyes upward. "What is this, Molly?" he asked the ceiling. "You know these good ol' bubba types who talk like they just dropped off the back of a turnip truck. Sound dumb as dog shit. But everything Charlie says is calculated. He knows I'm your boss, so he tells you we're great friends to impress you."

Molly was quiet for a moment, thinking. Then she slapped the palm of her hand against her forehead. "Oh, God. I'm so slow. I know what it is. He's head of the Builder's Association and they buy all that advertising from us. You've been *bought!*" She all but barked the words out.

He snapped his head upright. His eyes were blazing amber pits.

"Come off it, Molly. You know I have nothing to do with that part of the magazine."

Her fists clenched themselves into balls and she gave voice to the suspicions which had just flooded through her bloodstream. "But the publisher sure does. If you haven't been bought, then he has, and he's leaning on you. That's it, isn't it?" She was on a roll now. "McFarland's a man with some powerful connections. Don't deny it, Richard."

"Why would I want to? McFarland's an old crony of the governor, one of her major campaign contributors, friend of all the fallen wheeler-dealers, one of the few who was canny enough to pull in his horns just before the crash. Now he's back bigger than ever. Sure, he's rich and powerful, but that has nothing to do with my editorial decision that Louie Bronk is stale news."

"McFarland tried to bribe me, Richard."

Richard looked back at her with raised eyebrows and bright, amused eyes. *"Bribe* you? How?"

"He said he wanted to endow an award for worthy crime writers and make me the first recipient—one hundred thousand dollars not to write anything more about his wife's murder."

Richard threw his head back and laughed. "Worthy crime writers!" he said when he caught his breath. "That's marvelous. I hope you snapped it up, Molly, since you aren't going to do the story anyway. God knows you could use the money."

"But, Richard, I *am* going to do the story."

He stood up. "Not for *Lone Star Monthly* you're not."

She felt it like a kick in the ribs. "Richard!"

"I'd hate to lose you, Molly, but I am the boss here. I've never pulled rank on you before, but I say we're going to do the piece on Banker Griswold, not Louie-fucking-Bronk."

She wasn't about to let him intimidate her with that macho posturing. Through gritted teeth she said, "Richard, if I didn't know what an opinionated, snobbish, aesthete you are, I'd really suspect that McFarland got to you on this."

She could see by the barely perceptible flinch of a muscle in his cheek that she'd gone too far. His brown-orange eyes narrowed. "Well," he said in his clipped, mock-British intonation, "if I didn't know what a death-obsessed, morbid ambulance-chaser you are, I'd suspect you just want to rake up something new to boost the sales of your book."

She felt breathless, as if she'd been flattened by a steamroller. Finally she managed to croak out, "Oh, Richard, I never even thought about book sales."

He was breathing heavily. "Molly, I think we need a time-out here. We both need to go back to our corners. Why don't you hold off on a decision for today." He walked to the window. "And I need to get a grip on my temper. I really think—" A buzzer on his desk went off. "Damn. Just a minute."

Keeping his back to her, he picked up the phone. "What is it?" He listened a minute, turning so Molly could see his smile spreading. "Hold on, Becky," he said in a light voice, "I'll see if she'll take it."

Pushing the hold button, he held the receiver out. "For you. Your benefactor. Charlie McFarland calling. From his private plane. Says it's urgent."

Molly took a deep breath and stepped forward to take the phone. As she was raising it to her ear, Richard leaned over and whispered into the other ear, "Be smart, Molly. Tell him you'll take his offer." He chuckled and clapped his hands together softly. "Worthy crime writer of the year, indeed. That's delicious! If you play it right maybe next Charlie'll set up a retirement home where old crime writers can go in their sunset years." He went into peals of laughter so loud Molly had to cover her other ear so she could hear McFarland.

chapter 5

▲ ▼ ▲

In comes this shrink
A four-eyed fink
Asks how I think
Rinka Dink
Says he'll help me
I should talk free.
Was I damaged at birth?
Born under a curse?
Or something worse?
Maybe I'm just scared to die.
He's got a tic in his eye.

LOUIE BRONK
Death Row, Ellis I Unit,
Huntsville, Texas

In spite of the heat, Molly Cates was glad she'd decided to walk instead of driving the six blocks to the Travis County district attorney's office. Parking at the Stokes Building was impossible, and anyway, she needed to work off some steam. What a horse's ass Richard could be! She'd never seen him act like that before. Of course she hadn't exactly covered herself in roses either—losing it like that and calling him names.

Sweat began to drip down her hairline, but she walked faster, passing the white-pillared Greek Revival governor's mansion without even glancing up at it.

Why had he changed his mind in midstream? Months ago at the staff meeting everyone had agreed that it was a good idea to use Louie Bronk's execution, when it came, as an opportunity to recap the case and to look at the capital punishment situation in Texas. Then when Bronk's date was set last month, they'd discussed it again.

It made her jaw clench to think about Richard Dutton calling her morbid and death-obsessed. Then, to top it off, while she talked on the phone with Charlie McFarland, he had leaned against his desk with that just-swallowed-the-canary look, insinuating she had capitulated just by taking the phone call. When she hung up, they'd looked at one another in hostile silence.

Finally Richard had said why didn't she take a day to think it over before saying anything else she might regret. She'd been on the verge of saying it wouldn't matter if she took a day or a month; she *was* going to write the article on Louie Bronk and if he didn't want to print it, well, hell, she'd find another publication that would. But she stopped the words before they escaped. She had a sudden vision of herself unemployed, out pounding the pavements for a new job, maybe having to go back to the grind of a police beat on some daily rag—a hard job at her age. As jobs went, hers was a great one; she couldn't afford to lose it.

As she approached the Stokes Building at the corner of Guadalupe and Eleventh, her sweat was flowing. In other parts of the country September might be fall, but in Austin it was often the hottest month. Today it felt like living inside a blast furnace.

The two flags—U.S. and Texas—that flanked the entrance of the Stokes Building hung limp in the still air. Across Guadalupe the white limestone of the county courthouse shimmered in the heat and gasoline fumes.

Molly took the elevator to the second floor. When she gave her name at the reception desk, the woman there checked her list and said, "Mr. Heffernan said he'd be in by twelve-thirty and he could see you then if you don't mind him eating his lunch while you talk. He said for you to wait on him in his office."

The receptionist buzzed the glass door open and Molly wended her way through the warren of cubicles toward the DA's office. Inside, she shut the door and settled down on his big red leather sofa. She let her head drop to the back of the sofa and closed her eyes.

Charlie McFarland had said he needed to talk to her—privately, not over the phone—today. Could she meet him at his house again, at five-thirty when he got back to town? It would be worth her while, he said. She agreed. Her curiosity was piqued, and anyway, it was on her way home.

Yes, things certainly were on the move, but try as she might, she couldn't figure out where they were going.

Head still resting on the sofa back, she opened her eyes and let them roam around Stan Heffernan's office. Except for this sofa, it was pretty Spartan—an institutional metal desk and two imitation wood bookcases, old maps of Civil War battle sites on the wall. Not really the sort of office a boy growing up poor in South Texas would fantasize about having when he made it big.

When she had researched Stan's background for *Sweating Blood,* she had been intrigued to find his early life not all that different from Louie Bronk's: both came from extreme poverty in small South Texas towns, both had alcoholic, absent fathers and domineering, often abusive mothers. But the similarities ended there. Stan Heffernan's rotten childhood had propelled him out into the world determined to work hard and succeed. Louie Bronk's rotten childhood sent him forth determined to kill and rape. One of the questions she had tried to answer in the book was why.

Stan Heffernan had grown up in George West, one of those dusty, dying towns where the local Dairy Queen was the only place to eat and the high school football game on Friday night the only entertainment. An all-state tackle and a solid student, he had gotten a football scholarship to the University of Texas. A serious knee injury his senior year left him free to pursue what he really wanted: law school.

Right out of school, he joined District Attorney Warren Stappleton's staff as an assistant and immediately acquired the reputation for taking on and winning tough cases. Ten years ago, when he was still an assistant DA, he had prosecuted Louie Bronk for capital murder in the robbery-slaying of Tiny McFarland and gotten a death sentence. The following year, when his boss retired, he ran for DA and won. He was one of the most tenacious and steady people Molly had ever met.

When she heard his heavy tread approaching down the hall, she felt a twinge of apprehension: she hadn't seen him since the book came out and she wondered how he felt about it. He was an important source for the section on the prosecution of Louie Bronk in the McFarland murder and he appeared as a major character. As a courtesy, she had sent him one of the first copies she got from her publisher, but she hadn't heard from him. Did he find it accurate? Was he offended at her frank portrayal of him as slow and steady—the plodding tortoise who always won the race? Had he even read it yet? Of course he'd read it; not even Stan-the-Man-Heffernan could resist reading about himself.

As he entered, he was pulling on his tie to loosen it from his thick bull neck, which was every bit as wide as his head. He closed the door behind him. "Molly, Molly, what's this I hear about someone threatening you? We can't have that." His hoarse, whispery voice was almost inaudible. When he spoke to a jury, he had to wear a microphone. It always came as a surprise to her that such a big man had almost no voice—sort of like seeing a Saint Bernard opening its mouth and letting out a tiny mew. People tended to get very quiet and lean forward when Stan was around.

She said, "I don't know if it's me being threatened, or just some general threat, or nothing but a crank letter, but I'd feel better if you'd take a look." From her briefcase she pulled a plastic bag containing the envelope, the torn-out pages, and the poem. She set it down on the coffee table. "I didn't think about prints when I was opening the mail, so I may have messed them up."

His tie hanging loose now, he took off his suit jacket and tossed it on his desk. Then he sat down in the chair across the coffee table from her and pulled a handkerchief out of his pants pocket. He used it to take the pages out of the plastic bag. Looking at the envelope through the plastic, he said, "Came by mail yesterday?"

Molly nodded.

In his usual unhurried, methodical way, which often drove his legal opponents to fury, he read the pages, moving his lips slightly as he did. When he got to the poem stuck to the last page, the deep line that ran vertically between his heavy brow ridges deepened. Finally, still silent, he put the pages back in the bag, stood, and walked to a cabinet under the bookshelves. When he opened the door, it revealed a small refrigerator inside. "Like something to drink, Molly? A soda water?"

"No thanks," she said.

He pulled out a brown bag and can of Diet Dr Pepper which he carried back to his chair. As he lowered himself, he pulled over a magazine—*Texas Lawyer*—to put the can on, and with the little finger of his left hand he popped the top. Then he pulled from the bag a sandwich wrapped in plastic. He peeled it back just enough to allow him to take one big bite, which he chewed slowly, meditatively, for a long time. After he swallowed, he said, "It's not from our old friend Bronk."

"Oh, no," Molly said.

"Has this shaken you?"

"A little. I hate to be a sissy, but the line 'Now that Louie's doomed to die/I might give his craft a try' is troublesome. The idea of a more literate version of Louie Bronk out there does worry me." As usual when she talked to him, she found herself almost whispering so she wouldn't sound loud and shrill in contrast. This phenomenon always made a conversation with him feel very intimate.

Stan picked it up and read it again, then dropped it on the table. "Nah," he said. "This is the kind of nutty stuff we get all the time. We just stick them in the file marked 'mail from outer space' and forget about them. But if it'll make you feel better, I'll send it over to the DPS lab, see if they can pick up some latents and run them through the computer. Since you've touched it you'll need to drop by there and leave your prints. Okay?"

Molly nodded. "Stan, there's something else. I ran into David Serrano last night at Katz's and he seemed upset about Louie's execution coming up—the usual willies people get when they're involved in capital cases maybe, but he did say there was something that bothered him about my book. He said there was no mention of the nicks on Tiny's scalp."

He tilted his head to one side. "Nicks?"

"Uh-huh. I was over at the ME's office this morning looking at the autopsy photos. If you look closely under a magnifier, there *were* some nicks on her scalp, just like David says—the first I ever heard of it. Did you know that?"

"Not that I recall. But it was ten years ago and one hell of a complicated case. As much as I hate to say it, there are always some details that get away from us. You're much more current with the case than I am. Even if we did overlook this, what difference does it make?"

"Well, probably none. But Barb Gruber called the MEs in McLennan, Bexar, and Denton counties and had them check the autopsy photos of the Bronk victims there. Absolutely no nicks. Not one. Perfectly shaven."

"So the day he did Tiny McFarland he had more caffeine than usual, or he just felt jittery in the lavish surroundings; he's probably more at ease mutilating people in drainage ditches." He grinned at her.

Molly nodded, but she couldn't work up a smile. "Yeah. Maybe. It's just that Louie was trained as a barber when he was doing time for murdering his sister in Oklahoma and he's got a steady hand. I've never seen him shake."

Stan's eyes were pinpoints of light under the heavy protruding ridges of his brow. "Molly, something's got hold of you." He took another bite and chewed, waiting for her to speak. "Maybe it's the execution coming up. When you write a book where you get as close as you did to the subject, there's bound to be some . . . identification with him, some empathy."

"No," she said, too loud. She lowered her voice. "No, not in this case. Usually I do find some area of empathy with people I write about, but not with Louie. No," she repeated, shaking her head, "that's not it."

Stan pulled a carrot stick from the bag. "Attending the execution might be a bad idea for you, Molly. Given your feelings about the death penalty. Why subject yourself to it if it's going to be a problem?" He bit down on the carrot and chewed it.

"No, I need to be there, to see it through. Stan—" She suddenly felt ridiculous, like a lifetime religious believer who loses faith for no reason at the last minute. "Stan, let me ask you something. You've prosecuted more than ten capital cases and got the death penalty in eight of them. Right?"

"Right."

"Would you answer something, not as DA, but just as a reasonable citizen, an old friend? No ass-covering, no macho posturing, okay?"

He laughed—a low, pleasing, raspy sound. "I can try."

"Do you ever wake up at night worrying about how easy it is to make a mistake and how you might—just might—send an innocent person to the death chamber?"

"Louie Bronk is not an innocent person."

"No. I know. He's not. But if we overlooked something like these nicks on the scalp, we could make other mistakes, too. Don't you ever worry about it?"

He pointed the carrot stick at her. "Did you say this was off the record?"

"Would it affect your answer?"

"Damn right, it would; I'm a politician."

"Okay. Off the record."

"First of all, I never wake up at night, Molly; I sleep like a baby. And second, that's something I don't worry about because we don't prosecute innocent people."

"Goddammit," she wailed, "that's an on-the-record answer."

He took a bite of the carrot stick. "I can't help it. It's the truth."

They sat silently for a while as he chewed. Finally Molly said, "So you never have doubts?"

He didn't answer right away. He took a long swig from his can and nodded to show her he was thinking about it. "Well, I wouldn't say that; there's always some doubt. Let's take Louie Bronk as an example here. If I'd been there and seen Bronk shoot Tiny McFarland with my own eyes, I'd be ninety-nine point eight percent certain. As it is, I'm ninety-eight point five percent certain."

He leaned forward and used what was left of the carrot stick to emphasize his words. "When the little girl and the baby-sitter gave the description of the car, that white Mustang with the one brown door, I was up to twenty percent. When Louie confessed, that only raised it to twenty-five, because he's a born confessor. But when he picked out a photo of Tiny and told us what had been stolen from her body and the house, I shot up to seventy-five. And when he described how to get to the house and where the body lay, and where the gunshot wound was and the caliber of the bullet, it went up to ninety-eight. The other half a percent happened from watching him during the trial."

"His other convictions must have been worth a percentage point or two."

Stan's eyes closed. "Rosa Morales," he whispered. "Greta Huff. Lizette Pachullo. Candice Hargrave. I like to say their names every so often. It keeps me focused. And helps me sleep like a baby."

Molly let out a long sigh. He was right, of course.

"Sounds like you're having a bad case of the eleventh-hour willies here. That's not unusual for people involved in capital cases as the moment of truth approaches, you know. Jury members have been known to seek psychiatric help and send us the bills."

"I know. I hate to be such a pain in the ass. I'm just having a rotten day and it's not Louie's execution really. I can actually see that it's best to put him to death."

"Damn right. If we don't, twelve years from now those moronic incompetents we've got on the parole board will read the file upside down and let him walk. And do you have any doubt that he'd kill as soon as he got out?"

"It might take him a day or two to get organized. He's a living, breathing argument for the death penalty. So it's not that. And I have no feelings for him personally at all. Isn't that strange? After all the time I've spent with him?"

"So what's the problem?"

"This is going to sound dumb," she said. "It's just all this power —the attorney general and his staff, you and your certainty, the governor in her white-pillared mansion, public opinion favoring capital punishment, Charlie McFarland and his money—the entire criminal justice system like an inexorable steamroller out to flatten one miserable wretch. It's like going after a rat with a Sherman tank."

"Remember when he was out killing on the highway, Molly? It seemed like he had all the power then."

"I know. But I can't help flinching at the idea of a mighty state taking blood revenge on a man who hasn't known a day of kindness in his life. We'll watch them strap him to the gurney and put a needle in his arm. Then we'll watch him sputter a few times and die, and we'll walk away feeling like crime fighters, like we've done our duty."

Stan Heffernan looked her in the eye. "Goddamn right we will. My job is to use all my energy and skill to keep people like Louie Bronk from preying on citizens." His eyes were burning. "And when we put him to death, I will damn well feel I've done my duty. If your sensibilities have gotten too delicate for this, Molly, make a job change. Write about the environment or ladies' fashions."

Molly felt her cheeks heat up with the rebuke; maybe he was right.

He reached across the table and patted her hand. "It is harsh and barbaric," he whispered, "but so is he. We're fighting fire with fire."

She nodded. "Anything new on his appeals?"

"I don't know. It's out of state court now so I haven't kept up. You might say that the baton has passed to the attorney general. I suppose you're doing an article on the execution."

She hesitated just a moment before answering. "Yes, I am. What can I quote you on?"

He smiled broadly; his teeth were as wide and solid as the rest of him. "Anything but my calling the parole board a gang of moronic incompetents. Even though they are."

"You *will* be there, won't you?"

He picked up his sandwich. "Wouldn't miss it. Did you know Bronk actually put me on his witness list? I got a note from him asking me to come, sort of like a party invitation."

"No." Interesting; Louie was on record as saying he thought Stan Heffernan was the sorriest son of a bitch he ever saw.

"And just guess who else is on his list." He looked at her with a big smile of anticipation.

"You, me, David Serrano," she said. "Who else?"

"It's the goddamnedest thing," Stan said. "You know he's allowed five. You and me I can understand him asking for. Serrano is a weird choice. But he also asked for the two McFarland kids— Alison and Stuart. And he made sure they were on his visitor list at Ellis, so it would be legal. First time I ever heard of a condemned killer asking for a victim's family members as witnesses."

Molly kept making the mistake of thinking life had no more major surprises for her and then she got hit with something like this. After she caught her breath, she said, "Do you know if they're going?"

"They both said yes. I know that because their daddy called me yesterday with a burr up his butt. How could I allow this? I should have called him first, got his permission. I tried to tell him this had nothing to do with me, but he didn't listen. He demanded I not let his offspring attend such a barbaric ritual, said it would be real bad for his little girl's mental health." He shrugged his massive shoulders. "Hell, she's an adult and when I've talked to her in the past she sounded tough as nails. This might be just what she needs."

Molly was still digesting the news. What was Louie up to? This certainly had the makings of a dramatic story; she couldn't have planned it better.

"Now," Stan said, using his handkerchief to lift the pages from his lap to the table, "about this. We get this sort of bullshit all the time, you know. It's probably just some casual craziness; ninety-nine times out of a hundred you don't hear anything more about it. But I will send it to DPS and notify APD, too, just to be safe. Okay?" He stood.

Molly nodded and rose, too. He didn't see this as serious. Neither did she, not really.

He shook her hand, walked with her to the door, and opened it for her. As she walked out, he said, "Oh, Molly, about your book—"

She turned.

So quietly that she had to lean her head toward him to hear, he said, "It reminded me that we did real good to nail that mother-fucker. Thanks for sending it to me and thanks for the kind words in your acknowledgments. Give me a holler, if anything else comes up."

Molly felt much better as she walked back to the *Lone Star Monthly* office. Her first impression about the letter had been right: it was just some crank. And if she worked like a maniac this after-noon, she might be able to finish the piece on the Abilene Angel before her meeting with Charlie McFarland at five-thirty.

Then she'd have time tonight to get cracking on the final install-ment—the very last word, finally—of the Louie Bronk saga.

chapter 6

Blood needs to get out,
It's dying to spout.
It presses the veins
And squeezes the brains.

The first drop of blood
Turns into a flood,
A blanket of red
To comfort the dead.

LOUIE BRONK
Death Row, Ellis I Unit,
Huntsville, Texas

When she pulled through the open gates, Molly Cates noticed something she hadn't on her first visit—the gate's ornate, flowery design formed the initials "CMcF" in wrought iron. She parked in the courtyard, which was enclosed by the two curved wings of the house meeting a high stucco wall. When the gates were closed, it formed a circle, a fortified space at the top of the world. Nice for security, if they'd just keep the gates shut.

She got down from her truck and walked to the front door which had a center panel of heavy frosted glass with a swirling pattern of clear glass. She pushed the bell and heard it chime, then echo through the big house. When no one came, she rang again and checked her watch. Five minutes early; he must not be back from the airport.

She got back in her truck to wait and turned on the ignition so she could sit in air-conditioned comfort. Even though it was almost five-thirty, the heat was stifling, still over ninety degrees in the sun, and she was feeling every degree of it. She picked up the sheaf of papers resting on the seat. Might as well finish editing the Abilene Angel while she waited. Rummaging in her bag for a pen, she glimpsed

three huge shadows flitting across the brick-paved courtyard.
Quickly she glanced up through the windshield, scrunching her neck
so she could see the sky. There against the clear blue, a bunch of
turkey vultures circled overhead. As she watched, they circled lower
and lower. When they were just above the roof of the house, they
seemed to hang motionless in the air, so close that Molly could see
the crepey red skin of their small heads and the silver flight feathers
that formed the fringed tips of their wings. That familiar clutch of
dread in her stomach, she told herself, was just a hangover from
growing up on a West Texas ranch. There, the sight of buzzards
circling low like that always meant death.

Lowering her eyes to the page, she tried to concentrate, but a
prickle of misgiving had started in her fingertips and spread up her
arms to her chest. Buzzards, after all, were buzzards, and likely to
behave the same in this fancy Austin suburb as they did out in
Lubbock.

She got down from the truck, keeping an eye on the birds. They
seemed to be zeroing in on an area just behind the house. She
walked up to the front door and rang the bell again, really leaning on
it this time and trying to peer through the swirls in the glass panel.
When she got her eye right up to one of the thin clear ribbons, she
could see straight through the house out to the hills behind. There
was no movement inside.

Molly glanced at her watch again. Five twenty-seven. Still a few
minutes early.

She walked back to the truck and opened the door, intending to
climb in, but instead she tossed her purse onto the seat and slammed
the door so hard it echoed off the courtyard walls. The noise didn't
spook the buzzards a bit; they were too intent on something.

Molly walked out the gate and turned left, following the stucco
wall around the garage at the side, toward the back of the big house.
Just killing time, she told herself.

She stopped where the mown grass ended and the slope de-
scended sharply. The hill was a tangle of scrub oak, cedar, tiny
yellow wildflowers, weeds, and prickly pear—wild and snaky-look-
ing. But about fifty yards down, she could make out a flat clearing
and a white trellislike gazebo.

The birds were circling right near the gazebo. They'd probably
found a nice ripe rabbit or an armadillo. She needed to get a grip on

herself and get back to the air-conditioning. It was a furnace out here.

Just as she was about to do the sensible thing, she caught sight of four or five more buzzards soaring in to join the original group.

Word was out.

She peered hard through the brush. Just below the circling birds something white was visible through the underbrush. And then she glimpsed movement—several large dark shapes. Some of the buzzards had landed. She took a few steps to the left where she could get a better view of the clearing. There. She could see what looked like a leg—a bare human leg. She shook her head. No, it couldn't be. But she held her breath and took three little steps down the hill to get a closer look. God. It was a leg. There was someone down there, lying on the ground, right where the buzzards had landed.

Flustered and confused, she looked back toward the road and the driveway. If a car had driven in while she was standing here she would have heard it. She could run back to her truck and use the phone to call for help. That would be sensible. But someone was down there, only yards away, and they might need help right now.

She turned and looked down the hill again; there must be a path somewhere down to the gazebo, but she sure couldn't see one. A trickle of sweat ran down her rib cage to her waist. Wishing she'd worn her usual jeans and tennis shoes instead of this damn dress and high heels, she started down the hill. Thorns and thistles snagged her stockings and grabbed at the hem of her skirt. Her thin heels sank into the soft ground. *Shit.* In a perfect world she'd never wear panty hose.

With difficulty she made her way to a limestone ledge, then hesitated before stepping on it. This was just the kind of place rattlers liked to sun themselves on a hot day—the kind of place she firmly believed in staying away from. She wiped away the sweat that was running along her eyebrows.

When she saw another buzzard thump to earth in the clearing, she stepped down onto the rock. Lord, the ugly brutes were aggressive, and with her so close. Another one bumped to earth as she half slid down toward the clearing.

Now she could see better—she could make out a human form, stretched out on the ground, facedown, surrounded by tugging, hissing buzzards. Now sweat was running freely down her back and between her breasts. She wanted to turn back, but it was too late.

"You go out looking for trouble, darlin'," her daddy used to say, "and you usually find it in spades." How right he was.

"Hey!" she shrieked down at the birds as she made her way through the brush. "Get away, goddammit. Scram!" They only increased their jerky motions, darting in, pecking and tearing.

In her forty-two years, Molly Cates had seen her share of death, both natural and unnatural; on the ranch in West Texas and as a police reporter, she'd seen calm, dignified deaths and messy, clawing, screaming deaths. And she had certainly seen buzzards doing what they were born to do, eating what nature decreed they should eat.

But this was more than she could stand.

She bent over, picked up a rock, drew it back over her head, and took aim at the bird closest to her. Using her wrist to give it some snap, just the way her daddy had taught her, she flung the rock at the closest bird. It landed at the buzzard's scaly, red feet, kicking up a puff of dirt.

The buzzard hopped backward, stretched out its wings, flapped a few times, and took off. The flapping sound made the others stop and look around; then they went right back to their grisly work. Molly felt like a child who'd stumbled through the forest onto a coven of witches, their long black wings drooping at their sides like cloaks, their wrinkled, blood-smeared hags' heads jerking up and down.

She shook off the vision and hurried toward them. Skidding, she made her way to the small clearing, waving her arms like a madwoman and screaming, "Shoo now! Get away, dammit. Get away from here, you hags!" One by one, the other seven buzzards hopped away from her. With a few strong wing beats, they rose almost straight up until they caught an air current to ride.

That left only Molly, alone in total silence with what had once been a human being. A rivulet of sweat trickled down her hairline, from her temple toward her ear. She made no move to brush it away.

The smooth naked body—a woman's body with a narrow back, tapering at the waist and flaring at the hips—lay facedown in the clearing, a few feet from the gazebo. One hand, stretched out above the head, was still caught inside the sleeve of a white terry-cloth robe that lay in a heap on the ground. A sudden stab of fear made Molly glance around the clearing and down the deserted hill, then back up to the house. But there was no one around. Whoever had done this was long gone. She knew it from the smell—that sweet, sickly smell that was all too familiar from other homicide scenes. She needed no medical examiner to tell her this was a body that had been dead in the heat for many hours.

Reluctantly she turned her eyes back to the body. The face of the corpse was turned down to the ground, but Molly could see just enough of the profile—the turned-up nose and full mouth—to recognize that this was Georgia McFarland. Yes, it was Georgia, even though the artfully frosted blond hair was all gone.

Her head had been shaved.

Just like Louie Bronk's victims years ago.

Just like the first Mrs. McFarland.

Molly held her breath and leaned forward to look closer at the scalp. It had been carefully, cleanly shaved. Someone with a steady hand had done this. She began to tremble. How could any human being keep such a steady hand right after committing a murder?

Two bloody holes marred the smooth narrow back. She had seen enough autopsies to recognize the entrance wounds made by large caliber bullets. But those ragged torn edges were not typical. She glanced up at the buzzards in disgust. They had managed to get their licks in.

All that earthly beauty, all that effort to stay young—in the end just food for buzzards that didn't care whether the flesh was firm and well exercised or old and wrinkled.

As she looked, she saw a thin red line snaking along the naked rib cage. Ants. She shuddered. When we die we descend the food chain pretty goddamned fast.

She glanced around the clearing. In the rays from the low western sun, something shiny glinted next to the single wood step up to the gazebo. She walked closer. It was a metal cylinder. She reached out for it, but checked herself in time. This was a murder scene.

She squatted down to get a better look. It was one of those sleek, stainless-steel Thermoses from Germany that you saw in expensive kitchenware shops.

Molly rose and took a step backward. She needed to call this in immediately. She could do it from the phone in her pickup. But the minute she left, the buzzards would be back in force. And she couldn't allow that to happen. No way.

She turned around and looked up the hill. Along the ridge two other houses might be in earshot. She called out, "Help. Is there anyone up there?" She raised her voice to a scream. "Help! I need some help down here! Help me, dammit!"

But no sound came back. No one would be out on this blistering hot afternoon. All the windows would be closed, air conditioners on full-blast.

She looked up into the cloudless Texas sky. The birds were still there, circling patiently, wings held in a vee, tilting from side to side. Waiting for her to go.

It was intolerable.

She picked up another rock and took aim, but let it drop back to the ground when she saw how hopeless it was. Instead, she cupped her hands around her mouth and shouted at them, "Ha! Get away, you hags." Then she waved her hands in the air.

She jumped when a man's voice called out from above. "What's going on down there? This is private property."

Molly looked around frantically for the source of the voice.

"What the hell are you doing down there?" the voice called.

She looked up the hill to the back of the McFarland house, shading her eyes with her hand. He must be standing at the top of the hill, but it was so steep she couldn't see the top. "It's me, Molly Cates," she called. "Something very bad has happened here. Who are you?"

"Franklin Purcell. Security director for McFarland Construction. Come up here, please."

"I can't. Call the police. Now. Then come down and help me. Hurry."

"What should I tell the police they're coming for?"

It seemed all wrong to yell it out, but she didn't see an alternative. "There's a body down here, with two bullet holes in it. A woman." Molly was having trouble catching her breath in the hot, still air.

"Okay. You just hold on a minute, ma'am." The voice was calm and competent. "I want to make sure Mr. McFarland's settled inside, then I'll call APD and be down. Do you know who it is?"

Molly hesitated. "You better come see."

"Okay. Just hold on."

Just hold on. In the silence, Molly turned back to the body. Lying there in the weeds, it looked so naked, so white, so vulnerable, so in need of protection that she kept her eyes on it. Charlie McFarland's second wife. Dead at home. Shot in the back. Naked. Head shaved. Hot day. It was all too familiar. She knew this scene, had written it once before. Unbidden, the lines came to her mind:

> *Lady writer, you ought to know it:*
> *Louie is my favorite poet.*
>
> *Your depiction of his crimes*
> *Has inspired my poor rhymes*
>
> *I give your book a rave review.*
> *Accolades from me to you.*
>
> *Now that Louie's doomed to die*
> *I may give his craft a try.*

She hadn't realized that she'd memorized the words. She certainly hadn't intended to. Once you memorize something, it becomes part of you forever. And she didn't want that.

She raised her right sleeve to blot the sweat that was dripping off her chin and neck. Lord, was it possible that her account of Tiny McFarland's murder had inspired someone to imitate it?

No. She turned her back to the corpse and stood watching up the hill instead. No. It was absurd. She was just an observer, a recorder of events. Not a participant. This had nothing at all to do with her; she just had the bad luck to get here first this afternoon.

But what if some maniac read her account of Tiny McFarland's murder and decided to do the same thing? To the same family? It hadn't occurred to her that the poem might be directed at the Mc-Farland family, even though it had come stuck to the pages about Tiny's murder. She felt a flush of hot confusion, like waking pan-icked from a nightmare not knowing what was real and what wasn't. Sweat was streaming down her back now and she didn't know how much longer she could last, standing here in the heat.

A spray of scattering pebbles made her look up. A man was bar-reling down the same route by which she had come.

Franklin Purcell was a real can-do sort of fellow. He had done what he said he would and scrambled down the hill in less than four minutes. Running and sliding, with heedless abandon for his neck or for his impeccably tailored charcoal-gray suit and shiny black shoes, he arrived on the scene in a shower of stones and clods of earth.

His right hand rested on the semiautomatic pistol tucked into his belt. His eyes surveyed the scene with the practiced efficiency of a man whose business it was to spot danger before it spotted him. Only after he had looked the area over thoroughly did he focus in on Molly, buttoning his suit jacket over the gun, as if he were suddenly aware of exposing something unseemly in the presence of a lady. "You all right, Miz Cates?"

"Yes," Molly said, looking closer at his face—the thin lips and flat nose, the cheeks that were purplish with broken blood vessels. She'd seen him somewhere before; she was sure of it. But she couldn't remember where.

He nodded and then turned his attention to the body. He hunkered down to get a better look at the two bloody holes, wincing slightly as Molly had done. Then he studied the face, as if he wanted to be absolutely certain he knew who it was. When he finally turned to Molly, sweat was pouring down his forehead. "Jesus Christ, Miz Cates, this looks like history repeating its bloody self."

He pulled a white handkerchief from his pocket. "One of us is going to have to go up there and tell Charlie it's his wife down here." Blotting his face and neck, he looked up at the buzzards, still relentless overhead; his fists clenched. "And one of us needs to stay and keep those fucking bastards away until the police arrive."

"I'll go," Molly said.

Franklin Purcell rose to his feet and looked Molly over carefully from her muddy shoes to her snarled, sweat-dampened hair. Then he nodded at the path that curved up to the opposite end of the house, a much easier route than the one they'd both taken down. "I think we should leave the path alone. There might be prints. Can you manage to get up the way I came down, ma'am?"

Molly hated condescension from men; she was accustomed to it, but she hated it. She gave Purcell back the same scrutinizing look, noting the breadth of shoulder and the suggestion of muscle definition under his suit. Where the devil had she seen him before? "Well, I got down here, didn't I?" she said.

His eyes opened wider. "Didn't mean to offend you, Miz Cates."

Molly turned and started up the hill. Behind her, Purcell called, "Miz Cates, don't let Charlie come down here. It would kill his back and it would . . . just kill him. Keep him up there."

Molly turned and nodded and then made her way back up the hill much faster than she'd come down. She dug her heels in and grabbed at branches to pull herself upward. As she climbed, she thought about the flush of pleasure on Charlie McFarland's face when his wife had arrived home the day before.

Instead of approaching the house from the rear and taking the chance of startling him, Molly walked around to the front and rang the bell. After a second, a door opened at the far end of the house near the garage. Charlie stuck his head out. "Molly. Come in this way. Frank didn't want me going to the glass door until he figured out what happened down there. What the hell is going on?"

As Molly approached him, she noted his hands clenched in front of him and his face blotched red with agitation. "Who's down there?" he asked.

"Let's talk inside, Charlie."

He preceded her into a back hall which led to a huge, white-tiled kitchen with restaurant-size stainless-steel appliances. Then he faced her, bracing a hand on the round butcher-block table. "What's happened?" he asked in a tight voice.

"Let's sit down, Charlie," she said, "and I'll tell you."

He sat heavily and looked at her with the world-weary expression of a man who, in spite of all his financial good fortune, has heard a great deal of bad news along the way and knows he's about to get hit with some more.

"I'm afraid it's bad news—very bad," Molly said. "The worst. I walked down the hill a ways because I got here early and saw the buzzards circling. It's Georgia down there. Looks like she was shot, Charlie."

His jaw fell as if he'd suddenly lost all control of it. "Dead?" he said, his voice little more than a croak. "Georgia's dead?"

"Yes. I'm afraid so."

His big head slowly drooped forward until she could see only the bald spot on the crown. A few lonely strands of wispy gray hair stood up from the freckled skin. She looked away.

His head still hanging, he said, "She shouldn't be alone. I need to be down there with her." He started to push himself up. "I should help Frank. I need to go down there and—"

Molly reached out and took hold of his arm. "Oh, Charlie, you don't want to do that. Your man has it under control, and the police will be here in a shake. They're professionals. Let them do it."

As if to validate her advice, the sound of sirens in the distance rose and fell and rose again.

As though rooted, they sat listening as the sirens got louder, shriller, closer. It seemed only seconds before the squeal of tires and the sound of slamming doors and radios filled the courtyard. It was a combination of sounds Molly Cates used to find exciting, but somehow along the way she'd lost the taste for it. "I'll go," she told Charlie.

When she pulled open the side door, Molly gasped. There in front of her stood her first ex-husband, his black hair and mustache gone mostly white, his skin more tanned and seamed than she remembered. "Grady," she said, her hand fluttering to her breast and her voice higher than she liked.

A man rarely taken by surprise, Grady Traynor merely lifted his eyebrows. They were still black and they still met in the middle.

Suddenly Molly was aware of the sticker burrs in her shoes, the runs in her panty hose, and the tickle of tattered fabric at the hem of her dress. She resisted the impulse to reach up and smooth her hair. Lord, but this female vanity habit was hard to fight down; after forty-two years she wasn't even gaining on it. At the rate she was going, on her deathbed she'd be wishing she'd remembered to shave her legs.

Two uniformed officers jogged up behind Grady and an EMS van squealed in through the gates.

"Well," Grady prompted, "what's going down here, Molly?"

"The body is back of the house, down the hill," she said. She lowered her voice. "It's Mrs. Georgia McFarland. Her husband's in the kitchen, Charlie McFarland. Frank Purcell is down there waiting for you; he's the head of security at McFarland Construction. Just walk around that wall there and head west until you find a path down the hill. And, Grady, I don't know if it rings a bell with you, but his first wife was one of Louie Bronk's victims."

Grady nodded. One of the things she'd always liked about him was the quick way he entered into new situations; he was the only man she'd ever been close to who she felt might possibly be smarter than she was.

"I'll take a quick look-see. Tell Mr. McFarland we'll be in to talk in a few minutes," he said, turning to lead the way for the two officers and two EMS techs. He looked back over his shoulder. "You stay inside with him, Molly. I'll leave one of my men out front to send the next wave down."

Molly paused to watch him go, so he wouldn't think she was following his orders. After all these years, the macho son of a bitch still thought he could boss her around. Some people just never learned.

When he had disappeared around the corner of the house, she turned and strode back to the kitchen. Charlie McFarland was still sitting at the table, but now he was talking into a cordless phone. "That's all I know, honey." His voice quavered. "I don't understand it either. She was fine this morning when I left for Dallas. Yes, she had just gotten up and was taking a shower. Yeah, Frank's here. I don't think you ought to, honey. I'll call you when we—" He paused to listen. "Yes, do tell him, but I don't think he—" Again he seemed to be interrupted. "Well, all right, if you feel that way, but be careful. Drive real careful." Tears oozed from the corners of his eyes. "I couldn't stand it if something happened to *you.*" He reached across the table for a red and white checked linen napkin which he used to blot his face.

He lowered the phone slowly to the table as if it had gotten too heavy for his hand. "Alison," he said, glancing up at Molly. "She's coming over as soon as she gets in touch with Stuart. Christ, this can't be happening. . . ."

He rose painfully to his feet and, with his hands pressed into the small of his back, shuffled over to a cabinet near the sink. He took out two glasses and a bottle of Cutty Sark. Molly quickly took them from him. "Here. Sit down. Let me." She put the glasses and the bottle on the table, unscrewed the top, and poured several ounces into one of the glasses.

Shuffling back to the table so slowly it looked like he was moving underwater, Charlie said, "There couldn't be anyone in the world who'd want to kill Georgia. She was my wife. For it to happen twice, it must have something to do with me. This must be my fault. I made some horrible mistake somewhere. I am to blame."

He took a long swallow from the glass, closing his eyes as the Scotch slid down his throat.

Molly reached out and rested a hand on his arm. "Charlie, have you looked around the house? Is anything disturbed?"

He shook his head. "I don't think so. I walked through after Frank heard you shouting down the hill. I'd have to look more closely to be sure but . . ." His voice trailed off.

They both flinched at the sound of heavy knocking on the side door. "Police, Mr. McFarland," a voice called through the door.

Molly jumped to her feet.

Charlie looked up at her and said in a pleading voice that seemed strange coming from a man who was accustomed to giving orders, "Molly, I know this sounds crazy, but could he have escaped?"

"Louie Bronk? No. People don't escape from death row. And even if he had, I think we'd have heard."

The knocking intensified. It sounded now like a violent assault on the door.

"Molly? Help me out here. You know some of the brass at Huntsville. Just to humor an old man, will you call them and check?"

Molly looked down into his brown eyes that were set deep into the heavy flesh and thought she saw there the real thing—genuine despair. Still, she wished she could be certain. "Of course. Sure, I'll check."

chapter 7

Shrink asks about my childhood.
Only one thing ever felt good:
Ma let me brush her long
black hair,
And let me touch her anywhere.
But when I turned ten
She stopped me then.
She didn't care.
She lost her hair
And left me there.
Life sure ain't fair.

LOUIE BRONK
Death Row, Ellis I Unit,
Huntsville, Texas

▲   ▼   ▲

Molly sat in Charlie McFarland's big leather desk chair and stared at the telephone. It was comforting to pretend that all the random violence in the world was concentrated in one evil man, a criminal locked up in a nine-by-twelve-foot cell in East Texas. If he had escaped and come back to prey on this family again, then he could be recaptured and contained again and the world would be restored to sanity. No wonder that was the first idea Charlie had grabbed at.

She felt stupid making the call, but she'd promised, so she decided to get it over with quick while Charlie was still talking in the kitchen with Grady Traynor and another detective. It took four tries but she finally reached Steve Demaris, the warden of the Texas Prison System's Ellis Unit in Huntsville. She got him on his car phone as he was driving home from work.

"Louie Bronk?" he said in his distinctive East Texas drawl. "You don't have to worry none about that sucker, Miz Cates. We just did our body count and he's right where he ought to be—locked up tight

on death row, in ad seg. We're keeping him healthy and safe for his
date Tuesday; he ain't going nowhere nohow. Why you asking?"

When Molly explained what had happened, he was silent. For a
moment Molly thought she had lost the connection. "Well, hell," he
said finally, "I'm real sorry for your troubles there in Austin. The
wives of Mr. McFarland seem to attract bad luck. But you tell old
Stan Heff to catch this one and send him on to us. We know what to
do with his kind."

"I'll tell him," Molly said. "And I'll see you in Huntsville Monday
night, Mr. Demaris. I'm coming for the execution."

"God willing," he said, "the creeks don't rise and the federal
courts mind their own damned business."

Molly cradled the phone and tilted back in the chair. She gave a
start when she saw that Frank Purcell was standing in the office
door; she hadn't heard him approach. His jacket was slung over his
shoulder and his white shirt showed half-moons of sweat under his
arms.

"Mr. Purcell. I didn't know you were there."

"Didn't want to interrupt your call. They finished with me in the
kitchen. Now they're talking to Charlie alone. Could I fetch you a
glass of ice water, ma'am? I don't know if you lost as much fluid as I
did down there on the hill, but I am parched."

"Yes. Thank you," Molly said. "I sure could use one."

He walked to a panel in the wall and gave it a tap. The panel
swung open, revealing a full wet bar with crystal glasses on a glass
shelf and an ice maker below. He filled a tall glass with ice cubes and
poured over them some bottled Utopia water. He carried it to her
where she sat at Charlie's huge mahogany desk. "I guess Louie
Bronk's right where he oughtta be," he said.

As she took the glass from him, Molly looked up into his face and
said, "Mr. Purcell, I keep thinking I've met you before, but I can't
remember where."

He put a big hand to the back of his neck and rubbed. "Everybody around here calls me Frank, ma'am."

"If you'll call me Molly."

He nodded.

"Can you think where it might have been?" she asked.

"Well, ma'am, I don't believe we met as such, but I recollect
seeing you once or twice when you came down to Hays County. You

were reporting on Louie Bronk when we had him in custody down there back in '82." His hand still cupped the back of his neck. "Just like he was some sort of celebrity," he said in a low voice, "rather than the vicious animal he is."

Molly looked at him more closely. Of course. She would have known him right away if he'd been wearing a gray Stetson pulled down low on his forehead like he used to. "You used to be a Ranger down there," she said.

"Yes, ma'am. I sure was. For seventeen years."

"When did you go to work for Charlie?"

"Oh, about six, seven years ago. There's better money in corporate security and the wife likes it 'cause I'm home more."

"And how long have you known Charlie?"

"Charlie? Oh, I knowed him for a long time; he had some projects down our way, years back. There was some vandalism—pilfering and such—on the construction sites. I got to know him then. Did a little security work for him on my off hours. Always was the most decent fellow." He shook his head slowly, as if it had been Charlie killed down the hill.

"Yes. I was wondering—" She stopped speaking when they heard the noise of several more vehicles squealing into the courtyard.

He began to back away. "If you'll excuse me, ma'am, I need to check on that."

Molly watched him hurry down the hall to the front door. She felt the vague uneasiness that always afflicted her when someone knew more about her than she knew about him. Would this man have mentioned that he'd been a Ranger involved with the Bronk case if she hadn't asked?

She checked her watch. It was after seven and it might be a long time before she could leave. Grady and Detective Caleb Shawcross had listened to her account of finding the body, and her story of the anonymous poem and pages from her book. They said they'd send someone to pick them up from the DA's office and told her to stick around while they talked to Charlie. She suspected it might be a long time before they got back to her.

She walked to the front of the house to see what was going on. Frank Purcell stood at the open door impassively watching the black coroner's van back up in the driveway. When it stopped, two men in white jackets climbed out and walked around to the back where they opened the double doors and pulled out a litter. A uniformed police-man approached them and gestured to the path down the hill.

Just then, a beat-up red Toyota labored up the driveway and chugged to a stop in the courtyard. The driver, a young man with black hair, drove with one arm around a young woman whom Molly recognized from the photograph Charlie had showed her: Alison McFarland.

The young couple got out of the car and gazed around, looking stunned at all the police vehicles filling the courtyard. They talked for a minute with the uniformed cop standing in the middle of it all. He gestured first down the hill, then to the door where Molly stood behind Frank Purcell.

A week ago Molly had spoken to the girl on the phone about an interview, but this was the first time she had seen Alison in person since she testified at the trial ten years ago. Amazingly, she hadn't really changed much. Very small-boned and pale-skinned, she wore old jeans with holes in both knees, a dingy-looking T-shirt, and hightop sneakers that were laced only partway up. Looking at her narrow hips and shoulders, Molly couldn't help thinking about the photos of her mother stretched out on the autopsy table. Mother and daughter had the same childlike build, as unlike Charlie McFarland as it was possible to get, as if they were different species as well as different sexes.

Frank stepped out to meet the girl and put an awkward hand on her thin shoulder. "Alison, I'm so sorry about this."

"How's Daddy?"

"I don't know, honey. He's in the kitchen talking to two police detectives. They've been in there for about a half hour."

"Mrs. Cates. I recognized you from the picture on your book jacket. I'm Alison."

Molly extended her hand. Alison's fingers felt small and sticky.

The dark-haired young man appeared at Alison's side, towering over her. He draped a protective arm around her shoulders. "This is Mark Redinger," Alison said, her arm automatically reaching out and snaking around his waist.

This was Mark Redinger, the cousin. Molly had never met him, but she knew the name. He was a first cousin of the McFarland children, several years older than Stuart. Stuart had been at his house the day Tiny was killed. What confused her was that just now she would have sworn the interplay between Alison and him was of a sexual nature.

He smiled down at Molly, his deep-set navy-blue eyes glowing under thick dark lashes. His face was tanned, and close-up, she could see that he was older than she had first thought, near thirty probably. Like Alison, he wore old jeans and a white T-shirt, but his jeans were soft and faded and his shirt was snowy white. Definitely a hunk.

Mark Redinger and Frank Purcell stood aside for the two women to enter the house, then stayed at the doorway, talking in hushed voices.

Inside, Alison wrinkled her nose in what looked to Molly like distaste. "Poor Georgia. This should have been such a happy time for her. She and Daddy were really in love, but she married into an unlucky family."

Unlucky, Molly thought. That was certainly one way to explain getting hit twice by lightning. Maybe the McFarlands were unlucky, but she had always suspected that when lightning strikes twice, it must have had a real good reason for striking in the first place—maybe because you lived on the highest hill around or next to a huge oak tree. Or maybe it struck the second time because the first had created some sort of electromagnetic field that attracted a second strike—some sort of unfinished business.

Alison wandered around the big living room as if she were looking for a place to sit but couldn't find any surface that suited her. Finally she perched on the arm of one of the immaculate suede sofas. "Can you tell me about finding her, Mrs. Cates? Daddy said on the phone you got here first."

"The police asked me not to discuss it until they've had a chance to talk to everyone."

Alison's gray eyes widened. "Does that mean me? Will they want to talk to me?" She pressed both hands against her breastbone.

"I imagine so." The girl was very pale. Her skin in places was transparent; at her temples and along her jaw you could see the delicate lavender veins under the skin. The startled look which Molly had noticed in the photograph came from round lashless eyes and an upper lip which naturally lifted to show her prominent front teeth.

Alison lowered her head, raised a thumb to her mouth, and began to chew furiously on the side of the nail. Then she pulled her hand away from her mouth and gripped both hands together in her lap. "It's hard to think of Georgia as dead. She was always so . . . lively. And so pretty. But dead? God." She looked down at her bony knees, visible through the holes in her jeans. "Poor Daddy."

She lifted her head and the intensity of her gaze almost made Molly take a step back. "Isn't this weird? Daddy said she was shot. Just like my mother. And right now, when Mom's killer is about to get executed." Her voice grew higher as she began enumerating how very strange it was. "And you're here. You've written a book about my mother's killer and you happen to be here and find Georgia's body." She held her hands out, palms up, as if she were waiting to receive something. "I mean don't you think that's all really strange?"

"Yes," Molly said with conviction, "I do. Very strange."

Alison's eyes opened wide, showing white all the way around the light irises. "He hasn't escaped or anything, has he?" she asked.

"No. I just talked with the warden in Huntsville. Louie Bronk's locked up in his cell on death row."

The girl let out a sigh. She looked toward the kitchen. "I wish they'd finish, so I could see him. He must be devastated."

"Yes. I believe he is devastated," Molly said.

"It's just so unfair he should have to go through something like this again. I mean you don't see that many happy marriages, and even though they were so old, Georgia and Daddy, they really . . ."

"Yes. They seemed to have a good thing going," Molly said softly.

Alison's eyes teared up. She lowered her head.

Molly said, "Alison, I hear you're planning to attend the execution next week."

"Yeah, I am. Another weird thing, isn't it? He asked for me and my brother to witness it. Can you believe that? And David, too."

Molly looked at the girl's thin arms and birdlike wrists and felt the aura of vulnerability surrounding her. It wasn't difficult to see why her father would want to protect her. "How does your father feel about that?"

Alison whipped her head up and fixed Molly with a fierce look. "What difference does that make? I'm twenty-two years old. I make my own decisions, Mrs. Cates. Daddy doesn't want me to do an interview with you, either. He doesn't want me to live with Mark; he doesn't want me to study journalism—he thinks it will be upsetting. My God, of course it's upsetting. Life's upsetting."

She gripped her knees with her hands. It was the same gesture Charlie had made. "Daddy thinks I should avoid anything difficult or unpleasant. As if that were even possible. When I decided to attend the execution, it was because I thought it might be, oh, like a ritual or ceremony where I could finally say good-bye to the whole thing. But now, this—with Georgia, I don't know. I just never expected that anything—"

The sound of voices in the courtyard made Alison jump up and hurry to the door where the two men were still standing. Molly walked up behind her.

The two coroner's men were loading a litter with a long green body bag on it into the back of the black van. Sweat stains broke through their shirts. From the stunned look on Alison's face Molly could see that the reality of Georgia's death was just now registering on the girl. Hearing about death over the phone was a different matter from seeing it up-close.

Alison glanced toward the closed kitchen door and said, "I'm glad Daddy's not seeing this. He hates death."

Well, Molly thought, he can join the club.

A silver Lexus pulled into the courtyard and Alison let out a long breath. "Oh, good. It's Stuart." She glanced at Molly. "He must have found someone to cover for him in the emergency room." She ran out into the courtyard. As soon as her brother got out of the car, she threw her arms around his neck and held on to him for dear life. Stuart returned the hug with one arm, then disengaged himself.

Molly remembered Stuart McFarland well from the trial; he'd been an excellent witness for one so young—articulate and forthright. At the time he'd been a skinny, forlorn-looking fourteen-year-old with wire-rimmed glasses and dry tan hair. His hair had darkened and he wasn't skinny anymore. He was shorter than his father by six inches, she guessed, and husky, his upper body muscled like a weight lifter. He no longer wore glasses, but he still had that forlorn look of someone who'd just lost something important but couldn't remember what. A bit like his sister's look. Molly had a sudden flash of an idea. Maybe it had to do with losing a parent early in life. And maybe she, Molly, had that look, too—as if she were roaming the world, room to room, and place to place, looking for someone who was never there.

In the courtyard, the officer on duty was asking them some questions. Then he talked into his radio, probably informing Grady Traynor in the kitchen of the arrivals.

Brother and sister came into the house side by side. Stuart shook hands with Frank Purcell and raised a lackadaisical hand in greeting to Mark Redinger who was leaning against the door frame, looking like a male model in a J. Crew catalogue.

Alison pointed toward Molly and said, "Stu, this is Molly Cates. You know, the lady who wrote the book I gave you."

He took her hand and looked at her with interest. "Yes. Mrs. Cates, we've talked on the phone," he said. Up-close you could see the shadows under his eyes and the gray tone of his skin. Molly had heard how difficult medical residencies were and it certainly showed on this young man. Both McFarland children looked as if they led stressful lives and didn't get enough sleep.

"What the hell happened here, Frank?" Stuart demanded.

"I don't know, Stu. I went with your dad to Dallas this morning. Picked him up at ten to seven and Georgia was just getting up."

"Did you see her?"

"Uh, no, but—"

He broke off when the uniformed policeman entered. He was holding his radio to his ear and said into it, "Yessir. Ten-four." He said to Alison, "Miss McFarland, the detectives would like to talk to you in a few minutes. Could you please wait for them in the office?"

Alison looked at Mark before replying. "Just me? Alone? Sure. Right now?"

"Yes, please," the cop said. "And Mr. McFarland—"

"Doctor," Stuart said, under his breath, so low Molly was certain she was the only one who'd heard it.

"They'll see you right after your sister, sir. Lieutenant Traynor asked if you would wait for them in the master bedroom."

Stuart shrugged and walked off.

Frank was still standing in the door and Mark had sat down on one of the suede sofas and draped a long leg over the arm. His shoe wasn't quite on the upholstery, but close. He was surveying the room.

Molly walked over and sat next to him. "Dramatic room, isn't it?" she said.

"Yeah." He looked up at the cathedral ceiling. "I bet it costs more to air-condition this barn than I pay in rent. All that glass, in this climate." He crossed his arms across his chest and looked directly at Molly. His scrutiny started at her waist, studied her breasts, and moved up to her face. Then he smiled as if they shared some secret. It took her breath away, it was so insinuating and suggestive, so totally offensive.

"You're the one that wrote the book about that guy Bronk, right?"

Molly nodded.

"I didn't read it. Alison's obsessed with that sort of stuff—cops and robbers stuff. Not me. Too creepy."

"Mr. Redinger," Molly said, "am I remembering right that you're kin to Alison and Stuart?"

He leaned back and let his hands fall into his crotch. "My mother was Charlie's sister."

"Was?"

"Yeah. She died when I was eighteen. She was his poor relation and now I am." Again he gave her the smile and narrowed his eyes in an Elvis Presley way, to suggest all sorts of possibilities. Molly wondered if it actually worked with anyone.

"Well," she said, "compared to Charlie, most people would be poor relations."

"And does he ever love to rub it in," Mark said sourly.

"He does?"

"Boy, howdy. You should have seen the way he treated my mom."

"How was that?" Molly asked.

"Like trash. Just because Charlie got lucky and made big bucks he's always pretended the rest of his family just doesn't exist."

"That surprises me. I wouldn't have pegged Charlie McFarland as the sort of man to repudiate his family."

"Well, he is," Mark said. "Until the day of her death, he never had anything to do with my mother, his own sister. He didn't approve of her and he's never approved of me."

"Why not?"

"Because I don't have any money, of course. I teach tennis and wait tables and he doesn't think that's sufficiently classy."

"Am I remembering right that Stuart was at your house the day his mother was killed?"

"Yup. He stayed with us lots, liked to get away from home. My mom was a lot more . . . motherly than his." He raised both eyebrows to insinuate something.

"What do you mean?" she asked.

"Oh, I don't want to tell tales out of school, but my Aunt Tiny was something else." He lifted his right hand in the air and shook it as though he'd just burned himself.

Molly was choosing the right words to pursue this when Grady Traynor stuck his head through the swinging door in the dining room and called out to her to come in for a minute. Molly made a mental note of wanting to get back to Mr. Redinger. She was trying to remember if sexual congress between first cousins was considered incest in Texas.

It was nine-thirty, a dark and muggy evening, before the police had finished with the crime scene. With Charlie's help, they had looked through Georgia's things and found nothing amiss or missing. They had talked with everyone, several times.

The last of the officers to leave was Grady Traynor. He looked reluctant to go as he stood in the cavernous living room with Charlie McFarland, Alison McFarland, Mark Redinger, Frank Purcell, and Molly Cates. Stuart McFarland had left an hour earlier, after talking with the detectives. The hospital was shorthanded and they'd had an emergency.

"Mr. McFarland," Grady said to Charlie, "if you'd come to police headquarters tomorrow around ten to sign your official statement, we'd sure appreciate it. And you, too, Mr. Purcell, and Miz Cates. We've cordoned off the immediate area down the hill, just in case we need to come back tomorrow, so please stay away from there, just until tomorrow afternoon."

He handed a card to each of them. "Here's my number. Call if anything comes up or you think of anything more you'd like to tell me." He handed Molly her card last and as he did it, he angled his back to the others and flashed her a quick smile, raising his eyebrows as if he were asking something. To her amazement, it made her pulse quicken.

As soon as Grady Traynor was out the door, Alison turned to her father, whose shoulders were bent and whose face looked as if the flesh were dripping off. She put her arms around him and rested her head on his chest. "Daddy, you must be exhausted," she said, not seeing Charlie's face screw up in pain. "Go on to bed. I'm going to stay here tonight and take care of you."

When she tipped her head back to look up at her father's face, she exclaimed, "Oh, your back. Sorry."

"It's okay. You don't have to stay, honey. Frank will stay with me." Charlie glanced at Frank. Purcell gave him a thumbs-up sign.

"No," Alison insisted, "I want to stay. I'll drive you to the police station in the morning."

"Well, thanks, honey." Charlie kissed his daughter's cheek, then without once looking at Mark Redinger, or saying a word to him, he turned away and put a hand on Molly's arm. "Could you stay for a minute, Molly? I need to have a word with you."

Charlie led the way down the hall, limping and bent forward at the waist. Molly looked back and saw Frank Purcell let Mark out the door and then start doing up the multiple locks.

Once they were in his office, he closed the door and leaned against it. "Molly, it must've been awful for you, finding her like that. I'm just sorry me asking you to come here let you in for that experience."

Molly nodded and waited. One thing you had to say for Charlie, the man had grace even under the most intense pressure.

"They're treating me like a suspect in this thing even though I was gone all day, out of the city. It feels real bad to have people think I might do something like that. I suppose I'll have to get a lawyer now, pay the bastard an arm and a leg to see me through this. On top of everything else."

"I think that's a good idea, Charlie," Molly said. "It sure can't hurt to have a good attorney in your corner when you're dealing with the cops."

He made his way over to his recliner. Slumping down into it with a low groan, he said, "You called the warden over in Huntsville?"

"Yeah. Louie Bronk's in his cell."

Charlie nodded as if he'd known it all along. "There's someone else out there, then." His voice was dispirited. "A copycat. Traynor showed me that stuff you got in the mail—poem and the pages about the murder. He asked if I knew anything about it. As if I'd know anything about that craziness." His whole body seemed to slump even farther down in the chair. "So sick."

Molly said, "Alison's right; you need some sleep."

"I reckon so. Molly, you haven't asked me what it was I wanted to talk to you about."

"I knew you'd get around to it when you felt up to it. You don't have to tell me right now."

He didn't seem to hear her. "Well, I got to thinking about our talk yesterday and I felt bad about it. Sometimes I get a little crazy on trying to control things. I wanted to tell you if you still wanted that interview, I was willing to talk about it—on the record. I think I have some things to say I'd like printed, might do some good. As for my children, they'll do what they want no matter what I do so I might as well give up. Of course now isn't a good time, but I'll carry through on this if you want—when I feel better."

Molly knew that the humane thing was to say it wouldn't be necessary; it might be too much of a strain for him. But that cold part of her mind that was always hunting for the good story just couldn't allow that. Now more than ever she wanted to hear what he had to say. "Thank you, Charlie," she said. "When you've gotten some sleep."

About to leave, she thought of something that had been bothering her. "Charlie, about Frank Purcell—was he directly involved in the Bronk investigation when he was a Ranger in Hays County?"

He looked up as if he were slow in registering the question. "Frank? Directly involved? Oh, I think there was so much to do early on with all Bronk's confessions that all of them down there got involved some. Why?"

"Just wondered. I recognized him from when I was going down there as a reporter. He's been working for you eight years?"

"For my company, yes. A damn good man, best we've had. The Rangers train 'em good." He struggled to his feet. "Well, I guess I will try some sleep. This has been one hell of a day and tomorrow's not gonna be much better. The condolences again. God. I've had enough condolences for a lifetime."

Molly wanted to take his elbow and help him, but she restrained herself. "It'll get worse before it gets better. But you already know that."

His left eye twitched involuntarily. "Yes, ma'am," he said. "Unfortunately, I do know. And this is going to be worse than last time, if that's possible." He squeezed his eyes shut. "If that's possible," he repeated.

chapter 8

Oh man, sweating feels so sweet,
I do my best work in the heat.
A hundred degrees,
Not a breath of breeze.
I find someone,
Have my fun,
Do what I do
And when I'm through
I feel that gush, a red-hot flood
And I am fucking sweating blood.

LOUIE BRONK
Death Row, Ellis I Unit,
Huntsville, Texas

▲   ▼   ▲

It was nearly ten when Molly Cates drove out of the McFarland driveway. She recognized the white Ford Tempo parked in the bushes across the street as an unmarked police car, but she drove right by.

In her rearview mirror she watched the car pull behind her, tailgating her in the aggressive way cops do when they want you to sweat it out. She turned onto Greystone, staying right at the speed limit, and smiled when she saw the concealed lights under the grille begin to flash, throwing red and blue beams into her truck.

Molly rolled down the window and kept driving. She felt transported, as if she were seventeen again, riding in an open convertible with her hair streaming in the wind and a beer can in her hand. She threw her head back and laughed. When she'd gotten almost to Mesa, she pulled over to the side and waited, staring straight ahead through the windshield.

The white car pulled up behind her, its light still whirling.

His shoes crunched the gravel shoulder as he approached. His flashlight flickered into the back seat, then around the front. He let out a low whistle. "Some fancy custom interior you got here." Finally he looked at her. "Howdy, ma'am. See your driving license please."

"Didn't bring it with me, Officer," Molly said, still staring forward.

"How about some other identification then. A library card or your voter registration."

"I forgot my purse, Officer. I don't have any identification. What was I doing wrong?"

"Doing wrong? Why, not a thing that I know of. This here is just a routine traffic check. Could you get out of the vehicle, please, ma'am?"

Slowly Molly turned her head and looked at Grady Traynor. His head and shoulders filled the window. In the flashing light, the deep seams that ran the length of both cheeks looked like saber scars and his eyes, which were just a shade paler than Oriental Avenue on the Monopoly board, seemed transparent.

"I believe this sounds like the beginning of an illegal search, Sergeant."

"Lieutenant," he corrected.

"Oh, yes. Lieutenant!" she said. "Well, Lieutenant. I refuse to get out of my car. I've heard about all this po-lice brutality and I'm just a poor widow-woman trying to make a living as best I can—"

He snorted. "Widow-woman!"

"Well, yes. My third husband *did* die."

"Yeah, four years after you divorced him."

"So," she said with a smile of satisfaction, "you've been keeping track."

He sighed and switched off the flashlight. "I suppose I have. How about following me over to the Cadillac Bar?" He leaned in the open window, so close she could smell that he still used English Leather after-shave. "Maybe we could have us a drink there and talk this situation over real peacefullike."

Molly broke the mood; she couldn't help herself. "What would what's-her-name, Jane, say about that?"

"Janine. It's not a problem."

"Oh?"

"I'll tell you all about it, if you come."

Molly hesitated, but the outcome was never in doubt. Just like the outcome was never in doubt when she was a seventeen-year-old orphan, a high school dropout being seduced by a twenty-four-year-old rookie patrolman. Now, as then, her curiosity was fueled as much by hormones as by interest in the way things turn out in the end.

Molly had never been to the Cadillac Bar. It was a fairly new place on Red River, only a few blocks north of police headquarters. As they entered, several men at the bar, whom she recognized as off-duty policemen, turned their heads and watched as she and Grady walked to a booth in the back. Grady stood aside for Molly to slide into the semicircular booth, then he slid in next to her and took his jacket off, quickly transferring his pistol from his belt to the jacket pocket.

"Molly," he said in his official voice, "I want to warn you about something: if you have in mind writing anything about this murder —even so much as a word—forget about it."

Molly crossed her arms over her chest. "Don't try to bully me, Grady; you know I hate that. You promised some personal revelations, a nice chat. If you've brought me here under false pretenses, I'm leaving."

"Let's get this out of the way first," he said. "I'm not sure yet how we're going to handle this with the media, but you know we'll withhold some details, details you were in a position to observe. So I want you to assure me you will not write anything about what you've seen or heard at the scene today, or any other inside stuff you've gotten, including that crazy stuff you got in the mail. This case is off-limits for you until I tell you different."

"Grady, do you know you're the third man in the last thirty hours to tell me what I shouldn't write? You may remember how I feel about men trying to boss me around."

He rolled his eyes upward. "How could I forget!" Then he looked at her with interest. "Who else tried to boss you around?"

"Yesterday Charlie McFarland tried to bribe me not to write anything more about his first wife's murder and not to interview his kids for the article I'm planning on Louie Bronk's execution."

"Bribe you with what?"

"One hundred thousand bucks, in the guise of a writing award."

He let out a low wolf whistle. "Well, I find that highly interesting. Who else?"

"My boss at *Lone Star Monthly,* Richard Dutton, vetoed the article this morning. Said he'd fire me if I went ahead and did it the way I want to."

"Well, good luck to them—trying to persuade you of anything. But this is different, Molly. I'm not trying to persuade you, or bribe you. I'm *ordering* you. If you write about this without checking it out with me, I'll make sure no one in the Department ever tells you the time of day again. You may remember how I regard press interference in police business."

"Oh, I surely do," she said.

He nodded to indicate an end to the subject, leaned back against the booth, and said, "McFarland says he asked you to come to his house today to tell you he'd changed his mind and he would cooperate with you after all."

"That's what he told me, too."

"When did he tell you that?"

"Just now, before I left the house."

"I wonder why he didn't tell you that when he called earlier." He raised his eyebrows. "From his private plane."

"He's a man who likes to wield power and one way he does that is to get people to come to him."

"And you were willing to let him do that?" He narrowed his eyes.

"Sure. I was curious."

He grinned. "Yeah," he said slowly, "I remember that about you."

She looked down at the table to avoid his eyes. "I wanted the interview; it's how I make my living. And as I told you, we had an ongoing discussion about the article I'm planning on Louie Bronk."

"Oh, yes. Louie Bronk. I suppose I'm going to have to ferret out the old case files on him. I was in IA back then, but I sure remember Louie Bronk. And of course I know he's one of your obsessions."

Molly decided not to take the bait. She had a good excuse since the waitress was approaching their table. She wore a Mexican peasant blouse dipping off one shoulder and an expression of utter world-weariness. Molly ordered a Coors Light and Grady ordered a frozen strawberry daiquiri.

When the waitress left, Molly laughed. "You've got to be the only homicide detective in Texas who drinks strawberry daiquiris."

He didn't smile. "Molly, I can't let this go until I get a commitment from you. I have a feeling about this case. I'm going to give you some good advice; write about the Bronk burning if you feel you must, but leave Charlie McFarland out of it for now. Don't see him. Don't talk to him. Don't write about him."

"Thank you for the advice, Grady. That must mean you actually think he did it."

He planted his elbows on the table and glared at her. "You know the percentages. Odds are ten-to-one when a wife is dead, her old man did it. Here we have an older husband, beautiful younger wife. She probably had a lover—you know how it goes with women, don't you, Molly?" His glance was sharp. "He finds out, he's jealous, he shoots her. The old story."

"Yeah. I've heard it. Is it your theory he did it himself or had someone else do it?"

He paused, then said, "I see two itsy-bitsy problems with his having done it himself, but nothing I can't deal with. I can talk about this to you because you already know most of it and also because you know if you breathe a syllable of it, I'll slam you in jail for obstructing justice, right?"

Molly nodded to keep him going.

"Purcell says when he got there this morning at exactly ten minutes to seven to take his boss to the airport, he went into the bedroom to carry his briefcase for him—seems McFarland has a back problem—and he heard McFarland shouting to Georgia who was in the shower, or so McFarland says, and Purcell could hear that the shower was on. But he didn't actually hear Georgia's voice or see her. That's number one. Number two is that Purcell saw a stainless-steel Thermos leaning against the back door. He identified it as identical to the one found next to the body."

"What was in the Thermos?"

He laughed. "What I love about you, Molly, is that there's no predicting your questions. Coffee. And it was still hot, since that's probably your next question. She was cold and the coffee was hot. A great Thermos."

Molly said nothing.

"McFarland and Purcell left the house together at a few minutes before seven and Purcell saw the Thermos at the door as they left."

"What about the shower? Was it still running?"

"Purcell couldn't hear because by then they were in the kitchen, too far away to hear."

"And you've checked that Charlie was with people all day after that, right?"

"On the plane, meetings in Dallas all day, then on the plane again, and Purcell drove him home. No way he could have come back before you found the body."

"Purcell's a good witness?"

"According to our preliminary check, Molly. He was with the Rangers seventeen years, excellent record, quit to make more money in corporate security. And, anyway, if he was lying, he would of said he'd actually *seen* the lady as they left. No. This sounds like truth."

"So if Charlie killed her," Molly said flatly, "he would have had to kill her before he left with Purcell at seven. A lot is going to depend on the ME's time of death."

Grady let out a long sigh. "You know those things are about as reliable as the fucking rhythm method."

"Yeah. So if he did it himself, how would you explain those two things?"

"Easy for a smart guy like that. The shower thing—he just turned it on and talked to it so Purcell would hear, turned it off before he left. And the Thermos—well, he just had a duplicate he'd left with the body down the hill before Purcell got there."

"And how did he get rid of the Thermos he'd left in the house?" she asked.

"While Purcell was down the hill with you and the corpse, he hid it."

"But you didn't find it when you searched the house."

"Nope. But that doesn't mean much."

Molly digested this in silence for a minute. "You know," she said, "his back is so bad he can barely walk."

"So he says. But it doesn't matter. Rich guy like that—he could hire the whole thing done."

"Why would he, Grady?"

"Damned if I know—yet." He grinned at her. "They'd been married almost two years. According to McFarland she had no money of her own. No enemies. Even his kids liked her, he swears. Imagine that—being liked by your stepchildren.''

"Where were they?"

"The kids? Well, young Alison was asleep in bed in South Austin with her live-in boyfriend, who happens to be her first cousin, until six-thirty when the cousin got up to run and then went on to work without coming back. She studied at home without seeing or talking to anyone all morning."

"What about Stuart?"

"Stuart McFarland started his shift at the hospital at five this morning, but nothing much was going on so he slept in one of the rooms until nine when business got going. He doesn't think anyone can vouch for that."

"What about business enemies of Charlie?"

Grady toyed with his drooping mustache and watched the waitress approaching with their drinks. "He says he's got some. We'll check them out, of course, but that will come up dry. The wife didn't have anything to do with his business."

The waitress set their drinks in front of them and left.

"Molly," Grady said, still toying with his mustache, "save me some time here. You're more familiar than anybody with the murder of Charlie McFarland's first wife. I'll read the case files tonight, but tell me something about it."

"It's all in my book. Read it."

He grinned. "Nah. I'm waiting till they make it into a movie, and then I'll probably wait until it comes out in video. Just give it to me now in a nutshell."

"How many words are there in a nutshell, Grady?"

"About five hundred."

"Okay. It was eleven years ago, in July. Tiny and Charlie lived out west of the city on fifteen acres off City Park Road. Charlie was an up-and-coming builder-developer, self-made. She was a little bit of a thing, ninety pounds, blond, sort of a society matron, an heiress; her daddy owned a chain of department stores. The children were young —Stuart was fourteen and Alison was eleven. Tiny was gone a lot, most of the time, actually—tennis, charity work, parties, travel— that sort of thing—so they had a live-in baby-sitter, David Serrano, age twenty-one, a part-time student at ACC. He lived in an apartment over the garage."

Molly took a sip of her beer. Grady still hadn't touched his daiquiri.

"About eleven o'clock on the morning of July ninth," Molly continued, "Serrano hears a shot, goes down to check, and finds Mrs. McFarland in the garage, dead, naked except for a pair of white panties, her head shaved. He sees a car driving out of the driveway —an old white car with a brown door on the driver's side. Just then the daughter, Alison, emerges from the house, in time to see the car drive off. He hustles her back inside and calls the police. Meanwhile, young Stuart arrives home on his bicycle to find his mother lying dead. The cops arrive in fifteen minutes. She'd been shot once in the back with a .22 caliber bullet. She hadn't been raped. David Serrano was their chief suspect at first—young, Hispanic, helpless—you know what cops are like. They tried to pin all the Scalper murders on him."

"Where was McFarland?" Grady had been listening intently and still hadn't touched his drink. Molly remembered that she had always loved the way he listened—with total concentration.

"At work. But he left the office at around ten-thirty to go to his health club for a swim; he got there, but no one knows exactly when. So he had an alibi but it wasn't perfect."

He ran an index finger along one side of his mustache. "This was right before Bronk was arrested, right? And dead women with their heads shaved had been turning up all over Texas?"

"Yes. Tiny McFarland was murdered eight days before Louie Bronk was arrested in Fort Worth. They had been trying to link David Serrano with the other crimes when Louie confessed. What made the Tiny McFarland case particularly interesting, beside the fact that she was rich and beautiful, was that it was the only chance to nail Louie on a capital charge."

"Why was that?" Grady asked.

"Because he was in the process of robbing the house when he killed her," Molly answered. "He also took her jewelry. That made it murder in the course of committing another felony, hence, a capital crime."

"Oh, yes. I remember. He raped some of his other victims but the sequence was wrong for a capital charge. And this was before they added serial killing as a capital crime."

"Yeah." Molly could hear how hard her voice sounded. "He killed them first, then screwed them. So the most they could get him for was murder and the desecration of a corpse. Louie enjoyed submissiveness in his women."

Grady let out a long, deep sigh. "So there's no doubt Bronk did her, huh?"

"None. He was able to tell the detectives details that weren't in the news—that she was wearing only panties under her dress, that red flowers she'd cut from her garden were strewn around her, that the garage door was open, that she was lying on an oil spot, that the driveway was gravel. And he listed all the stuff that was stolen. Two eyewitnesses saw the car drive away—a very distinctive car that he did own. And he confessed to it."

"So his confession saved young David in the nick of time?"

"Yes. After the trial David moved back to the valley and went into the funeral parlor business." She tried, but she just couldn't keep the excitement out of her voice. "I just saw him last night, Grady. He's back in town."

His eyes brightened. "That's interesting—exceptionally interesting. Why?"

"Just a sentimental stop on the way to Huntsville, he claims. For Bronk's execution."

He raised his eyebrows. "We'll have to talk with him, I think. I won't tell him it was you who told me he was back."

That was another thing she'd always liked about this man: he could be very sensitive. And if he said he wouldn't mention something, you could count on him not to.

"Grady, did you look at that poem and the pages from my book?"

"Yes. I did."

"I've been worrying that it's a copycat and that I wrote the manual for him."

"I can see why you would be, but breathe easy. It won't turn out to be any copycat, just someone clever covering his tracks, Molly. Trying to make it *look* like some copycat crazy is at large. Bet you a steak dinner it turns out to be the usual thing—a dude killing his old lady. Only difference here from the ones we get all the time in East Austin is in this case they're filthy rich."

"Why are you so sure?"

"There are some things I can't tell you. It'll turn out to be McFarland," he said and smiled at her in a teasing way that made her want to slap him. Now she remembered what she couldn't stand about him—his cocksureness.

"You're wrong, Grady."

He smiled sweetly and shook his head. "So you think Charlie McFarland just couldn't be guilty?"

"Well, he's certainly guilty of something; we all are. But not of killing his wife."

Grady kept his eyes fixed on her. "Why are you so certain?"

"Yesterday when I was at the house, Georgia got home from her exercise class. When she came in the room, Charlie stood up and sucked his stomach in, even though I could see it hurt his back to do it. It was the noble gesture of a man in love. There's no way he killed her twelve hours later. That dog just will not hunt, Grady."

Grady began chuckling low in his chest. "Oh, I'd forgotten how you can do that, Molly. It's wonderful. How could I have forgotten that about you?"

"What?"

"That trick you have of summing up a person's character by their choice of neckties or how they eat an ice cream cone."

She studied his face to see if he was making fun of her or if he was really impressed. She decided it was a bit of both. "Anyway, he was really and truly surprised when I told him she was dead, Grady, and devastated."

"You've made it to middle age, Molly, still believing you can tell whether people are lying just by watching them? Well, we'll see." For the first time, he lifted his bright red daiquiri and held it up to Molly, inviting a toast. Some drips of icy red sludge spilled over the lip of his glass. Molly raised her beer glass and clinked it against his. A trickle of red ice transferred itself to her glass. She scooped it up with her finger and licked it off.

"To our daughter," Grady said.

"To Jo Beth," Molly said, taking a sip of beer.

"To old times," Grady said, still holding his glass up.

"Okay," Molly said with a shrug, "to old times." She raised her glass again.

"And to new ones," he said, finally taking a sip and watching her over the rim of the glass.

Molly paused with the glass almost at her lips. "New ones?"

He nodded.

"Tell me about Jane," she said.

"Janine. She left."

Molly was silent as she absorbed the news. "Why?"

He shrugged. "It's hard to know for sure with women, but she said it had gotten to the point after six years that the only surefire way she could think of to attract my attention was to get murdered during my shift."

Molly grinned.

He smiled back at her, the wrinkles at the corners of his eyes radiating upward. "She also said *some* people were not cut out to be married."

"I think Jane has a point there."

Grady nodded his agreement, then leaned back in the booth, stretching his arm behind her along the back of the booth. "Do you remember what was best about our marriage, Molly?"

To her everlasting astonishment, she felt a flood of hot blood pumping into her cheeks. She lowered her head in the hope that he wouldn't notice. It was ridiculous. A woman of the world, three times married, with more lovers in between than she had ever counted, and here she was reacting like a virgin librarian.

"I see you do," he said. "Good. So do I." He sat watching her in silence for a minute while he sipped his drink. "I have a proposition for you."

Molly took a long drink of her beer. "Shoot."

"I was just thinking that now we are real adults, both of us single, we could enjoy what was best without having to suffer with the rest of it." He drained his glass and held up a finger for the waitress. "I've missed you all these years, Molly. Not just the sex, though I have thought a lot about that, but you're the only woman I've known who isn't a silly romantic." He leaned his head in very close to hers. "And I've always loved talking with you."

Looking down into her beer, Molly Cates thought that if you just wait long enough in this life everything comes full circle.

She considered the proposition. The thought of taking Grady Traynor home right now and trying to relive the sexual fireworks of their early years made a pulse in her neck begin to throb. There sure hadn't been much passion in her life lately and she'd missed it.

She glanced up at him—his longish hair and drooping mustache almost white against his beach-boy tan, the three scars across the bridge of his nose, the single black line his eyebrows made. It was a face that had moved her twenty-five years ago and it still did. She would like to run her fingers over the scars in the dark, see if the old playfulness and inventiveness were still there. Yes, it might be fun.

"For a long time," he said, "I was bitter about what you did, but it's ancient history now. I've forgiven you completely. I just want you to know I'll never throw it up to you."

The hell he wouldn't! He just did throw it up to her, the son of a bitch! Molly had to struggle to get her breathing under control. And what made him think he had the *right* to forgive her? No! The last thing in the world she wanted to discuss—or even think about—was what she did when she was twenty. She was goddamned if she'd let him do that to her.

She looked at him long and hard. There was something in his expression she remembered—the smug set of the mouth, the possessive way his arm draped above her—that reminded her of the tong warfare they had waged against one another during four long years of marriage.

She met his eyes and smiled.

He released a puff of air through his nose and sat up a little straighter.

"It's a nice offer," she said. "Very flattering, Grady, but I think I'll pass." She finished her beer in a last smooth swig and stood. "Thanks for the beer. I've got an early morning tomorrow, so I need to get going."

"Molly—"

"I'll be in at ten to give my statement. Count on it," she said over her shoulder as she walked out.

Molly gripped the steering wheel to steady her hands. It had been one hell of an upsetting day.

She started the engine. It was almost midnight. She should go home, like a normal person, and go to bed, but she wasn't even the least bit tired. What she really wanted was to talk to her father. She wanted to tell him about the Louie Bronk situation, and about her book. And she wanted to tell him about Grady Traynor reappearing in her life and how confused and agitated she was.

Since she wouldn't be able to sleep anyway, she drove south toward Town Lake. To find David Serrano. He'd want to hear about Georgia's death. And they needed to finish the conversation they'd started the night before; she should never have let him get away so easily. They were just getting to the interesting part. She took the Lamar Street Bridge and drove into South Austin, to Oltorf and then to South Fifth. It was a neighborhood which a realtor might describe as "in transition." But right now, in the dark, it seemed pretty tough, with groups of men drinking on sagging, shadowy porches. It was the sort of neighborhood David had left behind him, she thought.

She fished her little notebook from her bag and paged through, resting it on the steering wheel, until she found where she'd written down the address. 1802 was a small house made of tan siding and, hallelujah, some lights were still on.

She parked the truck in front of the house and looked up and down the sidewalk before unlocking the door and getting out. She walked up the dark dirt and grass driveway to the front step. Behind the house a dog started to bark. A battered baby carriage was chained to an iron rail next to the door. Molly pushed the bell. When she didn't hear anything, she knocked, at first softly, then louder.

The porch light came on. A woman's voice, sounding angry, called, "Yeah, who is it?"

"Molly Cates. Sorry to bother you this late, but I saw your light was on. I'm looking for David Serrano."

There was the rattle of a chain and the thunk of locks and the door opened a crack which was enough for Molly to see almost the entire woman she was so thin. Dark-haired and pale-skinned, she wore a dirty halter top and shiny blue running shorts. She looked Molly over and said, "He ain't here."

"He gave me this address. Do you know where I could find him?"

"No idea. He ain't been back here since yesterday morning, got us all worried."

"Do you think he might have gone back to Brownsville?" Molly asked.

"Without his clothes and his briefcase?" the woman said. "No way."

Molly felt a tremor along her spine. "Could I leave him a message?" she asked.

The thin shoulders lifted in a bored shrug. "Suppose so."

Molly pulled out her notebook, wrote her name and phone number and *"Please call me right away—at any hour."* She handed it through the narrow opening in the door and decided it wouldn't hurt to press a little. "Has anyone else been looking for him?"

"Why you want to know that?" The harsh voice had sharpened.

"Well, just wondering because something's happened he'd want to know about and I thought other people might be looking for him, too."

"I couldn't say."

"All right. Thanks for giving him the message."

"Good night." The door closed.

Molly had had lots of doors closed in her face and phones slammed down, but she had a rule: always give people a second chance to talk. About seventy-five percent of the time it worked—if you gave them some time to think about it. She counted to sixty, then knocked again.

This time the voice sounded even angrier than the first time. "What?"

"Mrs. Serrano, it's Molly Cates again. I think there's something you ought to know."

"What?"

"It's hard to talk with the door closed. Could you open it, please?"

There was a lengthy silence. Then the woman said, "Not now," and turned off the porch light. Molly could hear her walking away. Well, sometimes it worked and sometimes it didn't. She headed to the truck in the dark.

When she got home, she didn't turn on the light, she didn't look at the mail or get her messages from the phone machine the way she usually did. And she didn't go to her office.

Instead, in total darkness, she walked through the house to the living room and sat down in the wing chair facing the big window. The shutters were open so the window loomed in front of her—that familiar black void to another world.

She curled her feet up under her and leaned back. Until she did that, she hadn't known the night was to be a vigil. She never knew when the need for one would arise. It seemed to come about once a month. Maybe it was connected to some sort of lunar phase or hormonal cycle. She didn't know.

She only knew that it would last until dawn and that she had been doing it for twenty-six years—in remembrance of the dead.

chapter 9

▲　▼　▲

Time to make bones?
Go without groans,
No whining, no crying—
I seen that kind of dying.
Life's just a bad dream,
Not worth the red scream.

LOUIE BRONK
Death Row, Ellis I Unit,
Huntsville, Texas

Making it through to sunrise filled her with a sense of mellow well-being, as usual. Everything looked so different in the morning light —rosier, more hopeful. Molly got up out of the wing chair and stretched.

After putting some coffee on to brew, she walked out the front door into the humid morning air to see if the paper had come. It hadn't. She'd have to wait another hour to read what Grady Traynor and his cohorts had chosen to tell the press and public about Georgia McFarland's murder.

The flag on her mailbox was up. In all the excitement yesterday she'd forgotten to get her mail—certainly the first time that had happened in years, since it seemed she was always waiting for one check or another to arrive.

She opened the box and pulled out a larger than usual stack. As she flipped through it, her eye was caught by a flimsy white envelope with pencil printing. She stared down at it. Her heart pumping hard, she lifted her head and glanced around. Three cars and one van were parked on the street. All looked empty.

She turned back to the mailbox and put the stack down inside. This time she wasn't going to make the same mistake about prints. Looking around again to make sure no one was watching, she lifted her skirt up above her waist and used it to take the letters out and carry them to the house.

Strange. It hadn't occurred to her that there would be more anonymous messages, but the instant she saw the envelope she'd known it was the master poet again.

She dropped the stack onto the kitchen table and lifted the envelopes off one by one until she got to it. Yes, the address was penciled in the same crabbed printing as the first one. And again there was an Austin postmark and no return address. She lowered her head to read the postmark which was a little blurry. September 23, yesterday.

She picked up her cotton gloves which were still lying on the table. After putting them on, she took her sharpest knife from the drawer and carefully slit the envelope. Then she held it open and peered inside. Again, there were torn-out pages. Carefully she drew them out—five pages from *Sweating Blood*. This time it was the account of the murder of Greta Huff in San Marcos. She turned quickly to the back page where another Post-it was stuck, with another penciled poem.

> *Lady writer, your book's my guide*
> *For sending folks to the other side.*
>
> *You may think I'm mighty screwy,*
> *But I am just as good as Louie.*
>
> *I can kill or I can rhyme.*
> *I'm inventive all the time.*
>
> *At first you thought I was a crank.*
> *Now you know it's no one's prank.*
>
> *Monday we'll cheer poor Louie's demise,*
> *But from his ashes I will rise*
>
> *To show you death's no fate to fear;*
> *Yours is whispering in my ear,*
> *Predetermined, drawing near.*
>
> *Get one thing absolutely clear:*
> *I am the master poet here.*

She set the pages down. With a trembling hand, she poured herself a cup of coffee. Then she rummaged in her purse for the card

Grady Traynor had given her and dialed the number on it. As the phone rang she checked her watch: five fifty-five. When he answered the phone himself on the second ring, she wondered if he'd been up all night, too.

"Grady," she said, surprised by the rawness in her voice, "Molly here." She cleared her throat. "I just looked at my mail from yesterday. There's another master poet communication—same cheap white envelope, same handwriting, five more pages from my book, the part about the Greta Huff murder. And a poem."

"Another poem? I'm starting to hate these fucking poems. Read it to me."

"Okay. I think it'll mean more to you, Grady, when I tell you that it's postmarked yesterday."

Without touching it again, she read it to him.

"Well, shi-it," he said. "God, Molly, do not touch it."

She felt a flash of annoyance. "I'm not. Anyway, I'm wearing gloves."

"Read it once more," he demanded.

"Master poet, my ass," he said when she finished. "I don't know much about poetry, but I know what I hate. I'm going to send someone to pick it up right now and take it to the lab. You okay?"

"I'm fine. Will you let Stan Heffernan know about this or should I?"

"Let me take care of it, Molly. Now there's no question you've got to stay out of this. What I want you to do is hunker down and stay uninvolved."

"Uninvolved? How the hell can I be uninvolved, Grady, when I get letters like this? Christ, he's saying he's using my book as a guide to killing people. And that my death is whispering in his ear." The hand which held her coffee cup was shaking so much the coffee was sloshing over the edge.

"That's a good reason for you to keep out of it. What time does your mail come?"

"Usually around two."

"Tell you what—I'm going to send a man in an unmarked car over about one. Let him get the mail when it comes today. You just stay in the house."

"I won't be home. I work for a living, you know." She softened her voice. "Do you know anything about David Serrano, Grady? I tried to find him last night, but the relatives he's staying with over on South Fifth don't know where he is."

"Yeah, I know. Listen, I got another call, Molly. But it's real important that you don't mention this master poet stuff to anyone. No one. Right now I'm sending a uniform over. Expect him in ten minutes."

She didn't want to let him hang up. "Wait a minute, Grady. It's our murderer, isn't it? He mailed this before anyone else knew that Georgia McFarland was dead. When he writes, 'Now you know it's no one's prank,' he's talking about that murder, isn't he?"

"It's possible, Molly. Sit tight."

"Wait," she said. "Maybe you should call Greta Huff's family—there's a niece. And a brother in a nursing home, I think."

"Don't fret, Molly. We'll take care of it." The phone clicked and he was gone.

Molly sat staring into her coffee, then lifted the cup with both hands to keep it steady and took a long sip. She thought about reading the pages from her book, but decided she couldn't face it. Instead she went into her office, got a notebook and pencil from her desk, and brought them back to the kitchen. Very carefully she copied the poem into her notebook, trying to duplicate the handwriting as closely as she could. As she was finishing, the doorbell rang, startling her even though she had been expecting it. Lord, this was making her jumpy.

A very young policeman stood at the door with his hat in one hand and an evidence kit in the other. When she led him into the kitchen, he pulled on a pair of rubber gloves and carefully pushed each page into a separate plastic bag and the envelope into another.

After he left, Molly stripped off the clothes she'd worn for twenty-four hours straight, took a thirty-second shower, and dressed in her most comfortable old khaki skirt and white T-shirt.

The last thing in the world she felt like doing now was working on the Abilene Angel piece, but it was due in two hours. She forced herself to sit down at her desk and read it from the computer monitor. When she came to the end, she felt like weeping; she hated every word of it, especially the ending. But she didn't know why.

It was the kind of high-interest, off-beat, Texas-flavored crime the magazine favored.

It was meticulously researched. Yes.

It was written with careful craft and even had a few nice phrases. Yes.

It had some colorful characters speaking from the page. Yes.

But the fact remained—she loathed it.

She spent the next hour rewriting the ending. Then, without even rereading it, she hit the save key and swiveled around in her chair to switch on the printer. It was finished, not because it felt right or satisfied her, but because she had a deadline in an hour and because she always met her deadlines.

She sent it over the modem to the office and gave the command to print it out so she'd have a hard copy for her files; she still didn't trust computers completely.

While it was printing out, she looked at her Day-Timer. Last week she had scheduled an appointment with Stuart McFarland for today at noon. She wondered if he'd keep the date after what happened to his stepmother yesterday, but she wasn't about to call and give him the excuse to break it. He had a tight schedule at the hospital and it had been difficult for them to arrange a time to meet. This interview would give her a jump start on the Louie Bronk article—the beginning of the end of Louie Bronk.

Molly arrived at the *Lone Star Monthly* offices at eight-thirty to find the usual uproar that accompanied putting the magazine to bed. She talked for a few minutes with Hazel Williams, the fact-checker for the article, and for a few minutes with Jerry Kovac, the attorney who vetted the piece for libel. She fended off a host of inquiries from other staffers, who had all read the morning paper and, under the guise of commiseration, wanted to hear the gruesome details about finding Georgia McFarland's body.

The summons from Richard came, as she knew it would, before she'd been there ten minutes. When she entered his big office with the wraparound windows looking out over Town Lake and the Congress Avenue Bridge, he was leaning way back in his desk chair staring up at the ceiling. Slowly he tilted the chair upright, keeping his hands clasped behind his head. "Molly," he said, "what a thoroughly rotten day you had yesterday—first fighting with a good friend who really has your best interests at heart, then finding a corpse and getting caught up in all that messy police red tape. It must have been so vexsome.''

She crossed her arms over her chest and said, "But when a person's morbid and death-obsessed, there's no telling what she'll do to boost book sales.''

Just a twitching of a smile quirked the corners of his mouth. "Okay. So I lost my temper. You did, too. But let's forget that. What happened yesterday changes the entire complexion of the McFarland case, of course. It'll be months now before any of it comes clear enough to write about. And since you are actually involved, being first on the scene and all, surely the gendarmes won't let you write anything about it now.'' His smile broadened.

He sat up straight, rested his right ankle on his left knee, and jiggled his foot up and down. "Listen. Don't start in right away on the Griswold thing, Molly. Take a day or two off in Houston first, stay at the Galleria, go shopping, sleep late—God knows it looks like you could use a little sleep, and''—he looked at the familiar khaki skirt—"why don't you buy some new clothes?''

She sat down. "Richard, this has been the best job I've ever had.''

"I know,'' he said, his voice steely. "So don't muck it up.''

"I'm trying not to, but asking me to stop covering the Bronk story now is like asking a fisherman to stop just as he's about to pull a seventeen-pound bass into the boat. I need to see this through.''

"No problem, sweetheart. Go ahead and cover the execution. I saved you three pages.''

"You know that's not nearly enough. Especially now, with this new murder. My God, Richard, the man has had two wives murdered in eleven years and he says he'll talk to me about it. The children are going to the execution and they've agreed to talk to me. I'll need at least twelve pages.''

"Molly, let's not go through this again. You've got a blind spot here. Trust me. It's best to drop this for now. A monthly can't compete with the newspapers on live cases—you know that. We wait and cover them in depth later if they're sufficiently interesting.''

She paused and took in a deep breath. "Listen, Richard. I have a proposition for you: let me do an outline and a few opening paragraphs for the story I have in mind. I can have it ready tomorrow. You read it with an open mind and then decide. Okay? Just give me two days and an open mind.''

His face darkened. The smile was gone. "Molly, I know you can write the hell out of this. But it would be a waste of time. We've got just so much space in the next issue and it's all spoken for. I can't give more than two or three pages to Louie Bronk. Just his execution. Period. Finis. You can do capital punishment next year."

Molly couldn't afford to lose this job. But she couldn't knuckle under here either. "You said for me to take two days off in Houston. Just do this—let me take them off to write this outline." This was a gamble. "Then if you read it and still don't want me to do it, I'll let it go and never mention it again."

His long face brightened. "Promise?"

She nodded.

"I want to hear you say it."

Molly remembered how easy it was when she was a child; just cross your fingers behind your back when you promise something you might not be able to deliver on. Adult morality was trickier. "I promise," she said.

Molly looked around the noisy, steamy cafeteria in the basement of Brackenridge hospital. When she'd phoned him last week, Stuart McFarland had agreed to talk to her about Louie Bronk if she could come meet him at the hospital. Since he usually managed a break around noon, they decided to combine the interview with lunch.

At quarter past twelve she leaned back against the wall and began to doubt he was coming; she should have called to confirm. At twenty past, a group of men in white coats came walking down the corridor talking and laughing. As they approached, she saw that one of them was Stuart McFarland. He was right in the middle of the group, but he was the only one not laughing.

When he saw Molly, he walked over to her and took her hand. His grip was firm and the fingers felt dry and cool and competent. "I'm late because we had an emergency. Of course." His eyes were bloodshot and he needed a shave.

"You look like you need to sit down," Molly said.

"Yeah. Let's get some chow first. It's not great, but it's right here and it's cheap."

Molly followed him through the line, amazed by the amount of food he crowded onto his orange tray: chicken-fried steak, mashed potatoes, carrots and peas, three rolls, a bowl of beans with sour cream, a dish of fruit and a piece of cherry pie. She got a salad and an apple and followed him to a table against the far wall.

"Is that all you're having?" he asked as he unloaded his dishes from the tray.

"Afraid so," she said, sitting down. "The real tragedy of middle age is a slowed metabolism."

He smiled and began to eat immediately.

"I don't know if I got a chance to tell you yesterday, but I'm sorry about your stepmother."

"Me too," he said after swallowing a mouthful of mashed potatoes. "Georgia was a really nice woman and she was making my father happy. She didn't deserve to end up like that." He sliced a big piece off his steak. "God knows my father could use a little happiness. He's had so much misery."

"You mean in addition to your mother's death?"

"Her death, her life, her memory. I don't know which was more miserable for him."

"Her life?" Molly said. "Her life was miserable for him?"

"I suppose most marriages are pretty miserable when you look at them up-close. Theirs certainly was. But that's an old story and I really don't want to get into it."

"Okay." Molly leaned down and pulled her little tape recorder out of her bag. "Stuart, it helps my accuracy if I record. Is that all right with you?"

He shrugged. "Sure."

"I'd like to know a little more about you, Stuart. Where did you go to medical school?"

"Baylor. Finished last year. Before I went, I spent a year working in Dad's business, but it didn't work out."

"Why not?"

"I was lousy at it. And I hated it. I thought I wanted to go into medicine, but he talked me into trying the construction business first. Big mistake."

"Maybe it helped affirm your decision to go into medicine."

"I guess. Yeah, it did work that way for me but not for him. Dad doesn't much like any decision he hasn't made himself." He managed a small smile between bites.

He cut off another big chunk of steak. "I never did hear yesterday what you were meeting him for when you found Georgia."

"It had to do with this article I'm writing."

Stuart glanced up at her without lifting his head, just flicking his eyes upward. The eyes were full of color: the whites were threaded with thin red lines and the large hazel irises had flecks of gray and yellow mixed with the green. On top of it all floated a contact lens that from Molly's angle looked like a thin layer of slime. "What about it?" he asked.

Molly hesitated.

Stuart opened his eyes wider and said, "Oh, I know. I bet he was trying to buy you off. Right?" He smiled and for the first time Molly could see in his prominent incisors a resemblance to his sister Alison.

"Yes," she said.

He tapped his fork twice against the plate. "What a piece of work the guy is." He shook his head. "But you're here interviewing me for the article so it didn't work. Good."

"Stuart, why do you think he'd want to buy me off the story?"

"Oh, I suppose because he thinks poor little Alison can't take it."

"Is he right?"

He thought about it for a minute. "Well, that's a hard question. Al is something of a mess emotionally. I guess I agree with my father on this—not with his trying to bribe you, but I agree that this won't help her any. A few years ago she had what used to be called a nervous breakdown, but she seems to be functioning now. I'd hate to see you upset her equilibrium, such as it is."

"She lives with Mark Redinger?" Molly asked, though she knew the answer; she hoped he'd elaborate.

"Yeah, for almost two years. She moved out of the house when Dad and Georgia got married, but she didn't much like living alone. Al's never been much for being alone. She wanted to come live with me, but I declined. She only lasted a few weeks on her own before she moved in with Mark. There's no accounting for taste."

"You aren't fond of your cousin?"

"No. He's a jerk."

"Your father seems to feel the same," Molly said.

"Yeah. It gives Dad fits."

"Because Mark's her cousin?"

"Among other things," Stuart said. "Lots of other things."

"For example?"

"Oh, Dad always thought Mark was a bad example for us when we were kids. And I suppose he was, but Alison and I both had crushes on him, especially Alison, didn't know any better. Mark's three years older than me and he knew about all the neat stuff—sex, poaching rabbits, evading parents, smoking pot. . . ."

He lathered some butter on his roll and took a bite of it. "He's kind of a sex maniac. It's all he thinks about, or talks about. Let's not talk about him anymore."

It was time to get down to the real business of the interview. "I hear you're coming to the execution, Stuart."

He shrugged. "Yeah. How about that? I had to get my schedule here changed so I could go watch my mother's murderer be put to death. My supervisor said that was the first time in thirty years he'd ever heard that particular excuse."

"I bet. But as a physician, Stuart, you are committed to saving lives. I was wondering if that makes it more difficult to contemplate the death penalty."

He pushed back slightly from the table and gently massaged his closed eyelids with his index fingers. When he opened his eyes they looked even redder and he had the confused look of someone who wasn't quite sure how he had come to be where he was.

"I know this is going to sound pretty bloodthirsty and unhealer-like," he said, "but I agree with the Bubba majority on this. I think we need the death penalty. Not for deterrence; it doesn't deter shit. But for retribution. I think certain terrible crimes demand that we respond with a terrible anger. It preserves the moral order." He looked at her with a half smile. "Come on. You see some pretty heinous crimes in your work. Don't you think that some people are so evil and dangerous that we need to get rid of them, just cut them right out of the society?"

"People like Louie Bronk?"

He nodded, picked up his fork again, and went after the little bit of remaining mashed potatoes on his plate.

"What do you think it's going to be like Monday watching him being executed?" she asked.

"Well, probably easier for me than you. I witness death pretty frequently, you know. I doubt this will be much different."

"But the deaths you witness are not inflicted coldly and deliberately by the state."

"True. But I think death by sodium thiopental is one of the easiest ways to go. Some of the deaths we see here are messy and painful."

"Do you think it would be better if Louie's were like that? Messy and painful?"

He looked down at his empty plate for a long time before saying, "Do you?"

"Sometimes," she admitted. "When I think of the pain and fear he's caused. But, then, I'm afraid I have a vengeful nature. What about you?"

"Sometimes I feel very angry when I think about my mother. It really affected Al more than me. So I get angry on her behalf."

"I was wondering, Stuart, if your mother's murder had anything to do with your choice of medicine—and emergency medicine in particular."

The question seemed to surprise him. "No. Why would it?"

"Oh, I was just thinking about your coming home and finding her there, and how it might make you want to do something where you wouldn't be so helpless in emergencies. I've often thought medicine would be comforting in that way. You'd always know something to do."

He laughed bitterly. "Now that's a romantic view of medicine, Mrs. Cates. Lots of the time there's nothing to be done. Like in my mother's case. By the time I got to her the best surgeon in the world couldn't have done anything for her."

"Stuart, if it's all right I'd like to ask you a few things about that day."

He wiped his mouth with the paper napkin and pushed back from the table. "Sure."

"When you found your mother in the garage, did you notice any little cuts on her scalp?"

He looked up, eyebrows raised. "Cuts? On the scalp? I don't think so. Why do you ask?"

"Oh, just something an assistant ME called to my attention. There were a number of tiny nicks done post-mortem."

"First I've heard of it," he said. "But you know it was kind of dark in that garage. Even with the door open. Since I didn't even notice the bullet hole at first, or the blood, I could easily have missed something else."

"And in moments like that, it's hard to observe," Molly said, remembering when the sheriff's deputy came to tell her a body that fit her father's description had been found floating in the lake. She'd been sixteen then, just two years older than Stuart had been when Tiny was murdered. It was something they had in common. She wondered if it had affected him as profoundly as it had affected her.

"It really is. When I rode my bike into the garage and saw her, it was like I was underwater or in another dimension."

"When did you know she was dead?"

"I was so dumb. Doesn't say much about my aptitude for medicine, I'm afraid. I saw her there and I thought immediately I'd try CPR which I'd just taken a class in. Then I noticed the bullet wound and the blood."

"I've wondered, Stuart, why you came home early that day. Weren't you planning to stay at Mark's all day and spend the night?"

"That was the plan." He reached out and picked up a tiny piece of roll, the only morsel left on his plate, and popped it into his mouth. "But I changed my mind."

"Why?"

He sighed. "I already told you Mark's a world-class jerk. And I've always been a loner, basically. I just wanted to go home." He pushed farther away from the table, stretched out his legs, and yawned. He didn't cover his mouth.

"Do you ever dream about it?" Molly asked, thinking of her own underwater dreams.

"Never have. Knock on wood." He rapped on the Formica table.

"What about the long delay between conviction and execution, Stuart? It's been more than eleven years since the murder."

"God. Eleven years—long enough for me to finish high school, college, and medical school. Almost half my life. And they're just now getting around to carrying out the sentence." His head moved slowly from side to side.

"So what are you thinking?" Molly asked.

"It sure is a long time, but on the other hand, I think it's important for someone to have every chance to appeal, make sure the trial was fair and all. That's the vital part of this—that we get the right person."

"Do you think Louie got a fair trial? You were pretty young, but you were there."

"I wasn't so young—fourteen. I remember it all perfectly, kept a journal, watched most of it. I think it was fair. After all, the guy said he did it. And there was plenty of evidence." He pushed his plate away. "You've been asking me a lot of questions. Now may I ask you one?"

"Sure."

"I told you over the phone that I just finished your book, the only nonmedical thing I've read in five years, by the way. My sister gave it to me." For the first time he looked at her with interest in his eyes. "I wondered about your motivation for writing it."

"My motivation?"

"Yes. Why this case? So unpleasant. It was a gargantuan chore. Lots of tedious research. Why did you do it? Was it worth it?"

"I have a living to make," she said, watching his face to see if that explanation would satisfy him. "And whether it was worth it I won't know until I get some royalty statements."

He shook his head. "Uh-uh. No. There have to be easier ways than that to make a living."

"In the beginning, I covered the case for the *American-Patriot* and I just got hooked on it. I don't know if I can explain it, Stuart."

He planted his elbows on the table and rested his chin in his hands. "Maybe you feel that if you can really understand one murderer, then violence will lose its mystery."

Molly was about to answer when Stuart frowned and raised a hand to someone across the room. "Oh-oh. There's Alison."

Molly turned and watched the girl approach. She wore the same torn jeans and white T-shirt from yesterday. Her narrow shoulders sagged and her hair hung in her face, limp and greasy. She looks like she did a vigil last night, too, Molly thought.

Alison leaned down and kissed her brother on the cheek. "Hey, Stu," she said, resting her hand on his shoulder.

He got up and pulled a chair over for her from a nearby table. "Sit down, Al. God, you look awful. Don't you ever wash your hair?"

"I know. I was going to have lunch with David, but he stood me up, so I decided to come see you before my shrink appointment." She turned to Molly. "Hi, Mrs. Cates."

Molly was feeling a cold chill at the news about David Serrano. "Did you try going over there?" she asked.

"No. I might have gotten the time or place wrong, though." She put a hand to her forehead and closed her eyes. "Lately I seem to be getting lots of things wrong." Eyes still closed, she said, "Mrs. Cates, I don't want to be rude, but I need to talk to my brother in private. Are you almost done?"

Stuart answered before Molly could get a word out. "Yes. We are. And I have to be back in a few minutes anyway."

Molly didn't feel anywhere near finished, but Alison looked so desperately in need of some comfort from her brother that Molly decided to withdraw quickly. She stood and said, "Thanks, Stuart. Could we talk again?"

"Maybe in Huntsville," he said. "I know the execution's not until after midnight, but I'm going to drive over early Monday—take the day off. Maybe I'll see you there."

"Okay." Molly was about to walk off when the thought of David Serrano stopped her. She turned back to the table. "I'm worried about David. I've been trying to get him since yesterday. When did you-all last see him?"

"I haven't had a chance to see him at all yet," Stuart said.

"He was over Monday night," Alison said. "Mark was going to go running with him Tuesday, but he didn't. I can't remember what happened. David finked out, I think."

"Well, if you hear from him," Molly said, "please tell him to give me a call right away." She looked down at Alison. "And we're on, Alison, for tomorrow at eight-thirty?"

Alison pushed her hair back from her forehead. "Oh, yeah. You're coming to my house so we can talk for your article. I already gave you directions, right?"

"Right. Take care," Molly said, thinking it would take a great deal of care indeed to fix whatever was wrong with Alison McFarland.

chapter 10

▲   ▼   ▲

Roses are red
Violets are blue
We all end up dead
Whatever we do.

LOUIE BRONK
Death Row, Ellis I Unit,
Huntsville, Texas

Molly's town house in Northwest Hills was her refuge from the world. It was perfect—sunny, compact, tranquil, and, best of all, she didn't have to share it with anyone. No child, no roommate, no dog, no husband. Only recently had she admitted to herself how much she loved having a space that was all her own, where she could arrange things as she liked and have them stay that way, where she could live according to her own time schedule. Her single women friends all said they would sell their souls for the presence of a good man in their lives and Molly could see their point for sure. She'd enjoy a good man in her life, but not in her house. One of her goals in life was never again to share a bathroom with a man.

The phone rang just as she walked in the door; uncanny, as if someone were watching her.

"Molly Cates, Grady here. You're home finally. Listen, how about dinner tonight?"

"Grady, was there anything in my mail?"

"Well, now, it's real interesting you should ask. That's one of the things we can talk about over dinner. How about the County Line? I'm in the mood for some serious grease."

"I can't, Grady. Jo Beth and I exercise tonight."

"Exercise? Molly! You? Since when?"

"Grady, you don't know me anymore. I've been exercising regularly for years now," she lied.

"Hmmm. I'd have to *see* that."

"So, what about my mail?"

"Can't discuss it over the phone, Molly, you know that."

He was playing with her. She wouldn't let it get to her.

"But I could come in and deliver it to you," he said.

"Where are you?"

"Outside your front door."

Molly set the receiver down on the table and walked to the door, smoothing her hair. She opened the door and looked out. The white Ford Tempo parked across the street had a long straight antenna on the back.

She closed the door and walked back to the phone. "You don't give much notice when you drop in, do you?"

"I called first, didn't I?"

He was waiting at the door when she opened it, looking freshly shaved and showered, his shirt creamy white, his suit surprisingly unrumpled. Jane, or whatever her name had been, had certainly up-graded his wardrobe and his grooming.

He looked around and whistled in appreciation. Then he pulled some envelopes out of his pocket. "Oh. Here's your mail. Two bills, one that's overdue, your car registration renewal, a note from your agent about possible British rights at a nice figure, and a letter from one Charles Logan, attorney-at-law, who says he still thinks about those nights in Abilene." He looked down at her with a sour expression. "Still at it, huh?"

Molly reached out and grabbed the envelopes from his hand.

He took a step back and said, "But nothing from your poet pen pal today."

She leafed through the envelopes. They were all sealed, looking as though they had never been disturbed. "Why did you open them?"

"Just to be on the safe side. Now that he's threatened you di-rectly." He glanced at his watch. "Five fifty-nine," he said. "I'll be off-duty in one minute."

He wandered around the living room, looking it over, then settled himself in her most comfortable armchair and checked his watch again. "Six on the nose," he said, leaning back. "Officially off-duty."

She ignored the hint for a drink. "Do sit down, Grady. Make yourself at home."

He smiled up at her, his tanned skin breaking into a sunburst of lines radiating out from the corners of his eyes.

"Now," Molly said, still looking through her mail, "you can tell me what you've found out about David Serrano."

He crossed his legs. "Same thing you found out when you went by his cousin's house last night. He's vanished, leaving behind his clothes, his briefcase, and his high blood pressure medication. We know he's not back home in Brownsville. There's a BOLO out for him and his vehicle—a black Lincoln Town car."

Molly put the mail on the hall table and walked toward him. "This is bad news, isn't it?"

"He's either on the run or he's belly up somewhere. You know him. What do you think?"

Molly recalled Serrano's nervous gestures, the sweat on his upper lip. "I think he was afraid of something. I told you he was armed, but he looked too nervous to shoot straight. I think he may be dead."

Grady nodded again. "Molly, why don't you stand Jo Beth up and come to dinner with me?"

"Because I want to go to exercise class with her and I don't want to go out to dinner with you."

He leaned his head back on the wing chair and ran an index finger along his mustache, just above his long upper lip. "Oh, Molly, that's one of the things I've missed about you."

Molly found herself watching his finger and thinking about how it would feel to run her own finger along his lips. Damn. She promised herself not to do this. "Grady," she said in a hard voice, "are you courting me, or did you just come to spy on my correspondence?"

He frowned. "Are those my only two choices?"

She sat down in the other chair, across from him. "Tell me about the postmortem and I'll tell you something juicy sometime."

He sighed. "All right. The postmortem. Forty-eight-year-old Caucasian female. Dr. William Mixter, Travis County Assistant Medical Examiner, began with a Y incision, the standard cut from each shoulder to the pit of the stomach, and then a straight line down to the pubic bone."

"Come on, Grady, you don't think you can gross me out, do you? I've probably seen as many posts as you have."

"Oh, you just want the results? Why didn't you say so? Death resulted from a forty-five-caliber hollow point bullet—what we police like to call 'controlled expansion'—that entered her back at the left shoulder and nicked the heart. A second bullet entered the middle of the spine and lodged in the left lung. We've got the bullets, but those dumdums tend to self-destruct so they aren't in good shape for a ballistics comparison even if we had a weapon, which we don't. We've checked all the McFarland guns and there isn't a .45 among them. The shots were fired from more than two and a half feet away. The head was neatly shaved, with a safety razor, probably after death. She does not appear to have been sexually assaulted. Is that what you wanted to know?"

"Time of death?"

"Well, I wish this were a more exact science like on TV where the ME says the deed happened between 7:42 and 7:44, but Mixter tells us it happened between 6 and 9 A.M. Maybe. The month he can pinpoint exactly."

"So it's not going to help eliminate any of the family members as suspects, is it?"

"No."

She leaned forward. "Grady, something's been worrying me and I want you to be honest with me."

"I will," he said.

She took a deep breath. "When I got the first master poet letter, you know the I-may-give-his-craft-a-try one, it seemed like it could possibly be a threat, some sort of general threat. You may find this incomprehensibly stupid, but it never occurred to me it might be a threat to the McFarlands, in spite of the fact that the pages he sent with the poem were about Tiny McFarland's murder. I got it at about five o'clock and later, when I showed it to Jo Beth, she said we should call you right then and let you look at it. I wouldn't let her do that. I took it to Stan Heffernan the next day at noon and he didn't think it was anything to get excited about. Of course, Georgia was already dead by then, lying out there in the sun with ants and buzzards at her."

Molly took another deep breath. "What I want to know is, if I had shown it to you Tuesday night, would you have seen in it a threat to the McFarlands and would you have warned them?"

He studied her face. "This has really been worrying you."

"Yes. Of course it has. It's bad enough having this master poet creep saying he's going to use my book as a blueprint for killing, without thinking I've contributed to it with my negligence, too."

"I can see that," he said.

"Well? Would you have warned them?" she demanded.

"No."

She let out a breath she didn't know she'd been holding.

He smiled. "Actually Jo Beth did call me after she got home. She'd memorized the poem—clever girl. I told her it sounded like business as usual. So if there's blame here, Molly, we can split it."

She felt an urge to get up and kiss him on the cheek, or maybe on the mouth.

He leaned closer to her. "It's no fun being brought into this as a participant, is it?" he asked.

"No. While I wrote the book, I kept telling myself that writing about a real-life crime with the purpose of entertaining readers was possibly a bit voyeuristic and sleazy. But I couldn't see any way it could do any harm. And on my best days, I thought it might even be educational in some way."

"I think it's very unlikely that it's done any harm, Molly."

"Don't you think those poems are from the killer?" she asked.

"They could be. But even if they are, I think it will turn out to be someone trying to focus attention away from the likely suspects on to some crazy Louie Bronk copycat. I believe Georgia was killed by someone she knew well."

"Why?"

"Several reasons. Here's one. You remember the Thermos?"

She nodded.

"Guess what was in the pocket of her robe?"

"What?"

He stood abruptly. "Let's continue this conversation over dinner. And a drink, especially a drink."

She reached up and took hold of his arm. "Tell me what was in her pocket and I'll get you a drink here," she said.

"Deal." He sat back down and crossed his legs.

"So—" she said, "what was in her pocket?"

"Two foam cups and a packet of Sweet'n Low. Now how about that drink?"

Molly headed to the kitchen. "She was expecting to meet someone for coffee at the gazebo," she said back over her shoulder.

Grady got up and followed her. "Looks that way doesn't it? If your master poet is the killer, it's also someone she'd have coffee with in her robe."

The thought made Molly queasy. "What do you want?" she asked, opening the fridge.

"I don't suppose you've learned how to make a strawberry daiquiri."

"How about a beer?"

"Okay. A beer."

She got two Coors Lights out of the refrigerator and opened them. Then she took two tall glasses down from the cabinet. When she turned he was watching her, his head tilted to one side.

"A glass?" she said.

"Of course. What do you think I am? Some crude cop who drinks out of the can?"

"Did she use Sweet'n Low in her coffee?" Molly asked as she poured a beer into one of the glasses.

"No."

She poured the other beer into a glass and handed it to him. "Who in the family does?"

"Sweet tooth seems to run in the family. All of them use it, including Mark Redinger, who turns out to have a juvenile record."

"For what?"

"Those records are sealed, you know."

"But you looked at them anyway," Molly said.

Grady held his glass up waiting for her to touch hers to it.

As she reached her glass up to his, he moved in a step so he was looking directly down into her eyes as their glasses clinked. "To you, Molly," he said. "Redinger had three arrests. Two were for peeping in windows, when he was sixteen. The third was assault. He got into a fight with the husband of a woman he'd been seeing. He was fifteen, the woman was thirty-five."

Molly moved back a step and leaned against the counter. "What else makes you think Georgia was killed by someone she knew?"

"Oh, I suppose I've been at this too long. But you know the odds. If it turns out Charlie didn't do it, then one of the kids or Mark Redinger did it. Did you know that Charlie had written Georgia into his will in a big way?"

"No. How big?"

"Half his estate—about ten million probably. The other half is to be divided between the two children, in trust, with Georgia as trustee until each is thirty. Don't you think that must have pissed them?"

"Yes. I do. Especially since a large chunk of that came from their mother."

Grady nodded. "Experience tells me when you have children, a second wife, and lots of money around, that's a real combustible combination."

Molly had to nod in agreement. "What else have you learned about Georgia?" she asked.

"A nice woman by all accounts. A widow. He'd known her forever. Her husband died of a heart attack seven years ago. Charlie courted her for four years before they got married two years ago. Everyone agrees he loved her madly and she got along well with the children, better than Charlie did, actually. She had very little money of her own coming into the marriage and he wanted to give her something. Hence, the will. But we're still working on it. Even nice women sometimes have affairs, I'm told."

Molly walked into the living room. "Have you read the Louie Bronk file yet?"

"Stayed up all last night reading it." He took a long sip of his beer. "Interesting. But like I told you before, ancient history."

"So you're going after Charlie," she said.

He followed her into the living room. "I'm sure as hell interested in Charlie. Molly, I've told you more than I should have here. Now—I know you need to earn a living. And God knows it looks like you make a better one than me, but we are agreed, aren't we, that you won't write anything about this until we've made an arrest?"

She sat down. "Charlie was really surprised yesterday, Grady. And horrified. I *know* it."

He leaned forward and patted her knee. "Well, Molly, I'm not sure you're an unbiased judge here. I think you like the man—I recognize the signs. He's that type you have a soft spot for. Reminds you of your daddy, I expect."

She moved her knee away from his hand. "Time for you to mosey, Lieutenant. I've got to change clothes."

"That's okay. We can continue our conversation in the other room while you change."

She walked to the front door and opened it wide. "Thanks for stopping by."

He walked slowly toward the door, paused just before walking through it, and turned to face her. "Let's make a wager on this, Molly. I'll bet you a steak dinner with a bottle of red wine at Steak and Ale that Charlie McFarland is responsible for his wife's death."

Molly looked into the pale eyes and smiled with all the confidence she could muster. "It's a deal," she said firmly.

He tapped the dead bolt above the doorknob. "Pretty good lock you got there. So's the one on the back door. If you remember to lock them. But I sure wish you had an alarm system."

"How do you know about the one on the back door?"

"Oh, I checked it out while I was waiting for you to come home." He raised his palms to her as if expecting an attack. "Just doing my job, ma'am. You're a woman who lives alone and you've gotten a death threat from someone who has most likely killed one woman already."

Molly felt a thump of alarm in her chest. "Then you do think the master poet killed Georgia."

"I said 'likely.' "

"But wait a minute. If you really think this was a family matter and the master poet notes are just a cover, why should I worry?"

He looked down at his feet. "Oh, Molly, it's just that I'm wrong so often and I don't want you to take any chances."

Her surprise was so total, she felt her jaw drop. This was a man she couldn't ever remember admitting an error in the past. "Grady," she said, her voice full of amazement.

"What I really wish is that you'd go away for a month, and not tell anyone where you're going. Just wait this one out until we make an arrest." He looked directly into her eyes. "I don't suppose you'd—"

She grinned up at him.

"No, I didn't think so," he said. "And I suppose you still refuse to have a gun around."

"That's right. I still hate the damn things."

"Well, then, I have a present for you." He pulled out a key chain with a small cylinder-shaped canister the size of a fat lipstick attached and handed it to Molly.

She read from the canister: " 'Super CSX Tear Gas.' " She

dropped it into her big bag which was open on the hall table. "Just what I always wanted. Very kind of you, Grady."

He shrugged. "They gave me a box of free samples when I spoke to a Citizens Against Violent Crime meeting last week. It's better than nothing. Will you put it on your key chain right now?"

"Sure. Now I'm going to give you a gift, too. Wait a minute." She went into her office and grabbed a copy of *Sweating Blood* from the box of fifty complimentary copies her publisher had sent. She got a pen from her desk and walked back to the front door.

Grady was attaching the tear gas to her ring of keys. "God, you've got a lot of keys. Must weigh a ton."

Molly put the book on the table, opened the cover, and signed it on the title page. Then she handed it to Grady. "In case you don't have enough crime in your life," she told him.

He opened the cover to look at the inscription. " 'To Grady,' " he read aloud. " 'All the Best, Molly Cates.' So intimate. I'm touched."

He reached out, took her hand, and pressed it against his chest, hard. "Stay out of trouble now, Molly. You hear?"

chapter 11

▲ ▼ ▲

Made of dust
Die we must.
Made of mud
and clotted blood.
Skulls and scalps,
Skins and sins.
The worm wins.

LOUIE BRONK
Death Row, Ellis I Unit,
Huntsville, Texas

"**O**kay. Let's work the gluteus medias," Michelle said from the platform. She had to shout so the class could hear her over the blast of the music. Down on all fours, leaning forward on her elbows and forearms, she lifted one bent leg up behind her and twitched it out to the side.

Molly could feel the thrum of the music in her hands and knees as she followed suit. She watched herself in the floor-to-ceiling, wall-to-wall mirror and shook her head. "I feel like a male dog peeing," she told Jo Beth. "I can't believe I'm spending my middle years doing this."

"Not to worry, Mother. You aren't spending very much of your middle years at it."

"Just a small movement," Michelle shouted. "Make the glutes do all the work. That's right. Four, three, two, one. Now cross it over the other one like this."

After suffering in silence for a minute, Molly said, "I'm so sick of telling everyone about finding a dead body. Let's talk about something else. How's the preparation for your case going?"

"Well, I ran into some snags yesterday," Jo Beth said, head down, leg moving up and down behind her, "but Ben always seems to have time to help and he has the gift of getting right to the heart of the issue. We worked late last night and he helped me get back on course. So it looks like I'll meet my deadline next week."

"Ben?" Molly said, raising her head. "Benson Williams?" Molly had met Jo Beth's boss, one of the senior partners in the Rutgers, Diamond and Williams law firm, several years before, in connection with a story she had been writing about a bank fraud case. She remembered him as a big, charismatic, middle-aged man with a twinkle in his eyes. Williams had been a U.S. congressman for several years and it was rumored he was planning to run for governor.

"Yeah," Jo Beth said. "You've met him. What did you think of him, Mom?"

"I only met him briefly, honey, but I thought he was very competent. And attractive."

"Yeah," Jo Beth said in a small voice, "he is."

Molly felt a mild tingle of misgiving. "Refresh my memory here, Jo Beth. How old a man is he?"

"Oh, hard to tell. Ben's one of those ageless men. Like Dad. Early forties probably."

"Married?" Molly asked, aware she was edging into dangerous territory.

Jo Beth kept her head down and kept lifting her leg. "Yeah, but—"

"But what?"

"Oh, I don't know. She was at this office party we had last week, for John Seton's retirement, and she seems so . . . I don't know, dour and old, and he's so vital and open to new things. They don't really seem to match up."

The tingle of misgiving turned into a buzz. Molly wanted to question and probe, to issue advice and warnings. Instead she pressed her tongue hard against the roof of her mouth and kept on lifting her leg. She looked at the back of her daughter's head and admired the shining straight brown hair hanging forward onto her hands, the slender leg in black tights moving diligently up and down.

She felt her chest tighten with affection. Jo Beth, now Elizabeth to everybody but Molly, had mapped out a life plan when she was just thirteen: she would go to college in the East, to Bryn Mawr, she'd decided, though neither of her parents had ever heard of it, nor could they imagine why anyone would want to go anyplace other than Texas; her plan was then to come back to Texas for law school and to practice law in Austin. She would make a lot of money, have two black Labs and an apartment of her own, and never get married.

So far the plan was right on track. When she'd been accepted at Bryn Mawr, Grady and Molly between them could come up with only half the tuition. So Jo Beth had gotten some student aid for the other half. She had worked summers as a lifeguard and saved enough money for law school. Now she had a job in one of the best law firms in Austin, an apartment in Westlake Hills, and two Labrador puppies. As for getting married, she divided her time between a middle-aged veterinarian and a young attorney from her office, both of whom she said were only good friends. And, knowing her, Molly believed it.

Molly was in awe of her daughter's discipline and steady resolve, but she also worried that the illusion of control could come crashing down when the unexpected came to call. Which it always did, eventually.

Just when Molly felt like her leg was about to break off at the hip, Michelle stopped and called out, "Good news. Push-up time. We're going to do thirty. Molly Cates, I'm watching you."

Molly moaned and stretched out on her stomach, then hoisted herself up on her hands with her knees on the floor. The thing she hated most about her inability to master the push-ups in this class was that they weren't even real push-ups; they were wimpy from the knee push-ups, and still she couldn't do more than twelve without collapsing.

Michelle began counting. Molly was flagging at eight and ready to drop by twelve.

"Mrs. Cates," a voice from above said. Molly glanced up, pathetically grateful for the interruption. One of the young men who worked at the desk stood over her, his face wide-eyed and flushed. "Telephone. He says he's a police officer and that it's an emergency."

Molly rose and followed him, weaving through the sweating bodies, then out the glass doors to the extension phone near the drinking fountain. She poked the lighted button and lifted the receiver. "Hello."

"That you, Molly? Grady here. Sorry to interrupt your chin-ups, but I promised I'd call when I heard something on David Serrano."

Molly leaned her shoulder against the wall.

"Officer in Edward sector just responded to a bad odor call over at Burnet Road U-Store-It. Turned out to be a ripe one for us—it can really heat up in those storage units. Male Hispanic, middle thirties, slender, dark blue suit, empty shoulder holster, GSW to left side of head, looks like. No papers on him, but the description sounds a lot like your Mr. Serrano. I don't have a recent picture and can't get in touch with the cousin. One of my detectives is working the scene now and I'm going to stop by. Why don't you come along with me, take a look? Maybe you could make the ID for us."

Molly glanced through the door to where Jo Beth and the rest of the class were still doing push-ups. "Okay, but I don't have a car here. Jo Beth drove."

"I'll pick you up in one of the patrol cars. As I remember, you always enjoyed that. You can work the siren like in the old days. Should be about twelve minutes, Molly. Bring your hankie."

Molly walked slowly back into the room where sixteen women and two men were now doing one-armed push-ups, which were the worst.

Molly hadn't told Jo Beth anything about her recent encounters with Grady Traynor, except that they had met at the McFarland murder scene. Usually she could discuss anything with her daughter, but each time she had thought about mentioning Grady, she found herself unable to broach the subject. Maybe it was because the subject had gone undiscussed between them for so many years that it had become taboo. Or maybe she was afraid Jo Beth would see right through to her true feelings.

She squatted next to her daughter and said, "That was your father. He's picking me up in a few minutes. There's a body over at Burnet Road U-Store-It that could be David Serrano."

Jo Beth raised her head but kept up the rhythm of the push-ups. "The man from Katz's the other night!"

"Yes."

"This is connected to the McFarland thing?"

"If it's him, yes, I think so. It must be. I'm going to get dressed now, honey, but don't let this change your plans."

Jo Beth studied Molly's face, then tilted her head to the side and squinted her eyes as if some new idea had just occurred to her. She opened her mouth to speak, but then pressed her lips together and shook her head, as if the idea was so outlandish that she couldn't bring herself to give voice to it.

Grady hadn't been kidding; Molly *had* always loved riding in police cars, especially at night and especially when Grady Traynor was driving. It was embarrassing to admit it; she'd expected at her age that the fascination would have passed, like a child outgrowing a passion for dinosaurs or cowboys and Indians. But as they sped across town on Koenig Lane toward Burnet she felt it more intensely than ever. The pulsing light captured quick frames of the world speeding past her open window and intensified them. It transformed the familiar, benign landscape she saw every day into a quick succession of alien images, peeling away the top layer and exposing all the secret nighttime things underneath.

And the power of the siren! Traffic scattered in front of them like ants. As Grady sped through the openings, she felt as if the Red Sea were parting before them.

And the way he handled the car hadn't changed since his patrol days when she used to keep him company on the night shift. He still drove fast, very fast, aggressively, purposefully, as if he had no doubts about anything in the world.

Life in a police car was simpler, she decided as Grady executed the left turn onto Burnet and accelerated north—simpler and more intense. That was why she loved it.

The storage place stood on a stretch of Burnet Road which also had a Church's Fried Chicken, a Pizza Hut, a tiny donut shop, a junior high school, and an Academy Surplus—one of those franchised, hard-edged, familiar pieces of American road that could be anywhere in the country.

Molly had passed the U-Store-It entrance a hundred times, but she had never driven in. Never accumulated enough possessions to need a place to store them, she thought.

Two patrol cars flanked the gate in the high chain-link fence next to the huge sign that said "U-Store-It, U-Lock It, U-Keep-the-Key." Grady flashed his badge in the window and got a salute as they drove through.

At the back of the huge complex, the night was illuminated with strobes of red and blue. They drove toward the lights, down row after row of long, low, flat-roofed buildings that looked like cheaply constructed barracks with no windows. "Place gives me the fucking creeps," Grady muttered.

When they got to the last building, where patrol cars blocked both ends of the narrow road running between two buildings, they pulled in and parked. The drone of police radios on different frequencies competed with the screech of crickets for control of the night air. Several groups of uniforms were gathered behind the morgue wagon, which was a Chevy van with blacked-out windows.

If this was all for David Serrano, Molly thought, he had certainly never gotten this sort of attention while he was alive. Or maybe he had—just once—during those eight days back in 1982 when he was a murder suspect, before Louie Bronk had confessed to the crime.

They both got out of the car. Grady raised a hand in greeting to each group as they passed. Outside the open door of unit 2870, in the glare of headlights and spotlights turned to illuminate the place, Detective Caleb Shawcross and two uniformed cops stood talking and laughing. A corpse lay at their feet, half inside and half out of a closet-sized unit. The legs rested outside on the asphalt, while the rest of the body lay across the threshold on the cement floor.

As she and Grady approached, the men stopped talking. Molly felt like an intruder into some sort of male ritual that was spoiled by the presence of a woman. When they reached the body, Grady took hold of her elbow and drew her around to his side. Molly breathed shallowly through her mouth, trying to avoid the full impact of the smell—that sweet, spoiled smell of raw chicken forgotten in the refrigerator weeks past the expiration date on its package.

Molly started with the polished black lace-up shoes and moved her eyes up the slender, relaxed-looking body in the well-tailored blue suit. The jacket had fallen open to reveal an empty leather holster under the left arm. On his handsome cheeks a dark stubble caught the cold light beams and glittered. The eyes, which just forty-eight hours ago had been dark and shining, were now dull and dried, half open as if he were just awakening to some unexpected noise. His mouth had relaxed into a soft smile. Death didn't look as bad on David Serrano as it had on Georgia McFarland.

Two days, two bodies—things were indeed on the move.

Just above and behind the left ear was a black, messy-looking wound.

"Is it Serrano?" Grady asked.

"Definitely," Molly said.

Grady nodded to Caleb Shawcross. Molly had met him at the McFarland scene the day before, but until now she hadn't really looked at him. He was a big man in a shiny gray suit. The sides of his head were shaved, although the slicked-back hair on top grew long and black. It looked as if he'd started to get a military haircut and changed his mind halfway through, or as if he were expressing two warring sides of his personality with one haircut.

"Howdy, Caleb," Grady said. He gestured toward Molly. "You met Miz Molly Cates at the McFarland scene the other night. Molly, you remember Detective Caleb Shawcross from homicide, the primary on this one."

Caleb reached a powerful-looking hand across the corpse and shook Molly's. "Howdy, ma'am," he drawled.

Grady flicked his eyes down toward the corpse. "And, Caleb, this here is Mr. David Serrano, an undertaker from down at the border. Brownsville. Former handyman-baby-sitter for the McFarland family some eleven years ago. We got ourselves a real murder mystery here."

Caleb squatted and stared into the corpse's half-open eyes. "Howdy," he said to the dead man.

"What we got so far?" Grady asked, squatting down so he was on the same level with his detective.

Caleb pointed at one of the uniformed cops, a slight man with a dark mustache. "Senior Patrolman Cavallos was the first officer. Cavallos, the lieutenant here will appreciate hearing about how this stiff jumped out of the closet at you."

Cavallos laughed uneasily and glanced at the uniformed man next to him. "Well, sir, when we finally sawed the lock off and opened the door, the body was like folded up against the door and the feet fell out, just like you see 'em here, sir. It really did look for a second like he was jumping out at us." He forced another laugh. "You shoulda seen Jackson jump, sir. I think he set some kinda world record for the standing broad jump."

The other cop took a step away and looked hard at Cavallos. "Yeah, but it wasn't me who pulled his gun and screamed, 'Freeze right there, motherfucker.' "

The men laughed, louder and longer than Molly felt the story deserved. But it was no news to her that people who witnessed a great deal of sudden death felt a desperate need to joke about it. The funniest jokes she'd ever heard were all told at murder scenes.

Caleb Shawcross straightened up. "Looks like he was done somewhere else and dumped here, Lieutenant. And I think I know where —we just found his black Lincoln Town car over in the corner of the grounds near the fence. Blood all over it. Lady in the office says this unit was empty, so the killer must've put his own lock on it when he left. Barrow already took that in for prints. Along with the gun— Smith & Wesson .38 caliber Combat Special."

"Can we give him a ride now?" a voice behind them asked. Molly turned to look. The young man wore white shorts and a gray sleeveless T-shirt with dark patches of sweat across the chest. Molly recognized him as Bill Mixter, the Travis County assistant medical examiner. He must be filling in while Robert Perez was on vacation.

Grady said, "Hey, Bill. You know Molly Cates? She just ID'd this guy as one David Serrano of Brownsville, Texas." He tilted his head toward the corpse.

Bill and Molly nodded at one another; she'd met him on one of her many visits to the county morgue.

"How long?" Grady asked him.

"Now, Lieutenant," the young ME said, "you know how hard this is to figure in the heat and all." He shrugged. "Decomposition is well under way."

Grady wrinkled his nose. "For that information I don't need an eighty-thousand-dollar-a-year assistant ME."

The ME held up his middle finger. "Eyes are dried. He seems to have come out of second-stage rigor. My wild guess is maybe fifty hours."

Grady nodded. "Well, this should help you. Molly here saw Mr. Serrano alive and drinking at Katz's Tuesday night at"—he glanced at Molly—"what time?"

"Around nine-thirty," she said. "And, Bill, I'm sure he was clean-shaven at the time." She glanced back at the corpse. "There's definitely been some growth since I saw him then."

The ME pulled a notebook out of his pocket. "That's real interesting, Molly. Are you aware that contrary to the widely held belief, hair does not grow after death?"

She nodded. "I am aware of that."

"It's understandable that people think that"—he jotted something down in his notebook—"because often both hair and nails appear to have grown, but it's just that the skin around them desiccates and recedes. Bearing that in mind, could you take a close look and try to estimate how much growth?"

Molly took a few steps toward the body. "May I touch his cheek?" she asked, looking back at Bill Mixter.

"Be my guest," he said.

Holding her breath, Molly knelt next to the body. She brushed her fingertips against his cheek. Under the prickly stubble, the skin was clammy, like she imagined a marine mammal would feel. She let her fingers rest on his cheek as she conjured up his face across the little table at Katz's—it was olive-skinned and as smooth as if he'd shaved only an hour before.

She withdrew her hand slowly and stood. "When I saw him, there was no stubble at all, not even a five o'clock shadow. So allowing for some receding of the skin—" She thought for a minute. "I'd guess that's quite a few hours of growth since I saw him, maybe five or six, or more even."

Grady stuck his hands in his pockets. "Believe me, Bill, this is a lady who should know her beards."

Molly refused to look at him or take the bait.

The ME looked a little confused and said, "That's real helpful, Molly. Thanks." He turned to Grady. "That means he's probably been dead less than forty hours. We'll see what we can do with stomach contents."

Grady knelt down next to the body again. "That puts his death close to the time Georgia McFarland hit the ground. It sure would be helpful, Doc, if we knew whether he died before or after that lady. If you can tell me that you've earned half your eighty thousand. And if you can tell me whether they were done by the same weapon, that would be worth the other half."

Bill Mixter thought a few seconds. "One thing I can tell you just from eyeballing—the gun was in contact with the skin when the shot was fired and he didn't commit suicide, unless he figured out how to padlock himself inside here. We're ready to take him to the chop shop now, if it's okay with you, Lieutenant."

Grady shrugged. "It's Caleb's scene. I'm just stopping by with my lady friend." He grinned. "What do you say, Caleb? Don't let anyone rush you on this. It's a big one because of its tie-in to the McFarland murder, so take all the time you need."

Caleb silently surveyed the scene. Then he punched a thumb up in the air. "Yeah, Doc. Go ahead, take him. We're finished here."

The assistant ME gestured. Two attendants pulled a litter from the back of the van and set it down next to what remained of David Serrano. They bantered cheerfully as they wrapped a sheet around the slender body and lifted it onto the litter. They reminded Molly of carpet layers going about their business in a good-natured and workmanlike way, showing about the same amount of respect for the mortal remains of David Serrano as they would for a roll of mid-priced broadloom. She understood. In her business, too, it was often necessary to detach herself from the misery and misfortune of the people she wrote about; self-preservation demanded it. But the way the system treated a body as nothing more than any other piece of evidence—tonight it offended her, made her head throb. Their voices were too loud and the laughter too forced.

Molly took a few steps back and closed her eyes. Damn. Those whirling lights were enough to give anyone a headache. You'd think they could turn them off now. But cops seemed to find them energizing.

She glanced over to see if Grady was ready to leave. He and Caleb Shawcross were talking in front of one of the squad cars. His back to her, Grady had one foot propped up on the car's bumper. The fabric of his pants was stretched tight across his narrow hips. She began to think about what it used to be like. So damned ridiculous. This was the wrong time and the wrong man. And it just made her headache worse. The morgue wagon pulled away. She looked around and thought about human perversity—*her* human perversity—wherein death becomes the ultimate aphrodisiac. Something about the nearness of death makes you want to go out and do something to prove how alive you still are.

"Okay, Detective, don't spare the horses on this one. And give me a holler after the autopsy." Grady thumped Caleb on the back, then took Molly's arm as they walked back to his car. He opened the car door for her with a flourish, something Molly hated.

As they drove out the gates, Grady adjusted the rearview mirror and said, "You okay, Molly? You look a little green around the gills. It wasn't the body, was it?"

"No. Of course not. I'm fine. Just a little headache. Didn't get much sleep last night."

He glanced over at her. "Neither did I."

They drove in silence out of the storage complex.

"Molly," he said as he turned right onto Burnet Road, "tell me again about your conversation with Serrano Tuesday night."

Molly closed her eyes, leaned her head back on the seat, and described the encounter—David's nervousness, his repressed anger, his queries about the execution, his feelings about the McFarlands and the past, his story about the nicks on Tiny's scalp. "Oh, Grady," she said, "I wish I hadn't let him get away so quickly. If I'd stuck with it a little longer, pushed him harder, asked a few more questions, he might have told me more. Haven't I learned a damned thing all these years?"

Grady reached his arm out around the shotgun that stuck up like a barrier between them and rested his hand companionably on her shoulder.

She didn't move away.

"Do you think he was just bragging or had he really struck it rich?" he asked.

"I think he really had. But you'll check it, won't you?"

"Oh, yes indeed. Molly, let's just brainstorm a little here, see if we can concoct a possible story for these two murders. Let me try one out on you." He glanced at her, then back at the road.

"Go ahead."

"For whatever reason, Charlie McFarland needs to get rid of Georgia. It's been known to happen, you know. He sets up that elaborate alibi for himself with the shower and the business trip. And he plans for you to find the body."

"No. How could he do that, Grady? It was just chance I went to check out the buzzards."

"Now hold your horses, Molly. This is just a fragile idea aborning. We're brainstorming here and the rules are not to jump on anything too quick. Just listen. Charlie's a big executive who's used to delegating life's unpleasant tasks. He may have decided to hire someone else to do his dirty work, maybe an old employee. Maybe David Serrano was an undertaker, but of a different sort. Maybe he created business for undertakers, opened new markets. After all, from your own mouth, Molly, Serrano came to town armed. He was an angry sort. He had prospered. None of that is inconsistent with his having gone into the killing business. And those border towns are known to breed violence. Right?"

Molly didn't answer. She slipped her shoes off and stretched her feet out to the dashboard.

Grady continued, "After the deed was done and Georgia was dead, Charlie didn't trust Serrano to keep the secret, so he paid him off with a bullet in the head and stuffed him in a storage closet."

Molly nodded. She didn't buy it, but it was possible. "Of course, that scenario would only work if David was killed after Georgia."

"Yeah," he said, deep in thought.

"You know," she said, "David might have been killed just a few hours after talking to me in Katz's—that really bothers me. Do you think his talking to me could have had anything to do with his death? Maybe someone was worried about him telling me something."

Grady turned right on Koenig and headed toward Northwest Austin where Molly lived. He was driving the speed limit for a change.

Molly said, "Look at the timing here. A month ago Louie Bronk gets his execution date. Three weeks ago my book is released. On Tuesday Charlie McFarland tries to get me to stop writing about Louie Bronk and his first wife's murder. The same day I get an anonymous letter saying the writer is going to emulate Louie. That night David Serrano, the old baby-sitter who was the original suspect in the first murder, wants to talk, and later that night—probably—we aren't sure when—he's murdered. Wednesday morning Charlie's second wife is murdered, also shot to death. Oh, I don't know. This just makes my head hurt more."

"Well, one thing's sure," Grady said, "this one's not going to be a slam-dunk."

"Mmmmm," Molly said. "And all of it five days before the convicted killer of the first wife is scheduled to be executed."

Grady said, "Things look worse and worse for McFarland, don't they?"

Molly didn't answer.

In silence, he turned onto Steck, then left into Molly's complex, pulling up in front of her town house. Jo Beth's white Volvo was parked in the driveway.

Grady shut off the engine and headlights and turned to face her. "Head still hurt?" he asked in a low voice.

Molly had a sudden flash of remembrance from years past: Grady Traynor used to have the best technique in the world for banishing headaches. She wondered if he still had the touch. "Yes," she said, "it still hurts."

"May I try my hand?" he asked, sliding out from under the wheel. With surprising agility, he managed to get over the protruding shotgun and the apparatus that locked it in place so he was on her side of the seat.

She knew it was madness to go any farther with this. But her head was now thrumming with pain.

He reached out his long-fingered hands, put one on each side of her head, and pressed gently against her temples with the heels of his palms.

It felt so good she was instantly lost in the sensation. He rotated her head so she had to turn her back to him, and then he moved closer so he was right behind her. "Lean against me," he whispered in her ear. "Relax, so it has a chance to work."

Knowing it was a mistake, that she was passing the point of no return, she let herself sink against him, feeling the heat from his body and the solidity of his chest against her back. With the tips of his middle three fingers, he pressed against her temples, making tiny circles. Gradually he increased the pressure until it felt as if his steady pressure was pushing the pain back.

At the same time he pressed little circles with his thumbs behind her ears. It was heaven. The tingling sensations radiated from her head down her neck into her body, producing little flutters low in her abdomen, and a feeling of bonelessness, a liquefaction right down to her toes.

Slowly he moved his hands down to her neck and shoulders, and began to massage. "Is that a good place?" he asked, pressing his fingers into the tight place between her shoulder blades.

"Mmmm," she said. He certainly hadn't lost his touch. She remembered it all, now that she was allowing herself to. This was a man who loved foreplay—endlessly creative, tireless foreplay—not her first lover, or her last, but her best.

"Better?" he whispered, his breath warm in her ear. Then she felt his breath lower, on the back of her neck, then the brush of his lips there. He moved his hands slowly along her shoulders, down her arms toward her breasts.

A car squealed up to the house next door, catching them in its headlights. Startled, Molly sat up and pulled away.

Grady tried to draw her back, but she shook her head.

Molly's young neighbors got out of their car and stood laughing and talking in the street, glancing over at the parked police car.

Grady looked at the Volvo in Molly's driveway and sighed deeply. "I guess Jo Beth is here," he said.

"I guess so," Molly said, running a hand through her hair.

He reached out for her hand and squeezed it. "Maybe we could talk some more tomorrow. Take up where we left off."

She started to open her door, but he held on to her hand. "Thanks for the help tonight, Molly. Be careful; we've got a killer out there. And it looks like the dam has broken."

She nodded at him, disengaged her hand, and got out of the car, feeling dazed.

Inside the house with the door locked behind her, she switched off the outside light and peered through the narrow window at the side of the door. He was still sitting there in the dark, hadn't started the engine yet.

When she heard a footstep behind her, Molly jumped and spun around.

"Well," Jo Beth said, "was it him?"

"Huh?"

"David Serrano—was it him?"

"Oh. Yes, it was."

"Is that *Dad* out there in the patrol car?"

Molly looked out again as if she wasn't sure who it was. "Oh, yes," she said, "it is."

chapter 12

Lying makes your nose grow long—
Lying is wrong, wrong, wrong.
Lying keeps them guessing.
Lying is a blessing.
Everybody lies,
Cries,
Dies.

▲   ▼   ▲

LOUIE BRONK
Death Row, Ellis I Unit,
Huntsville, Texas

Molly Cates woke with a gasp, her head jangling. It was the god-damned telephone ringing—surely the worst sound in the world to wake up to. She reached up and fumbled it down from the shelf in the headboard. "Hello."

"Mom, have you seen the morning paper yet?" Jo Beth's voice sounded breathless.

"Jo Beth. No, I just woke up. Why? What's it—"

"Just go get it and read the article on the front page of the City-State section in the *Patriot*. Listen, I'm late for a meeting. I'll call you when I get out."

Molly put the phone down, exhaled a long breath, and sank back to the pillow for a minute to regulate her breathing. The David Serrano murder probably wouldn't have made it into this edition of the paper. Whatever this was, she knew she wasn't going to like it.

She got up and threw on her old terry-cloth robe. Then she put some coffee on to perk, so she could fortify herself while she read whatever it was.

She hurried out and scooped up both papers—the *New York Times* in its blue plastic bag and the *Austin American-Patriot* in the clear one—and stripped the bags off on her way inside.

Back in the kitchen, she poured a mug of coffee and pulled out the City-State section. The headline stopped her dead. With the cup poised at her lip, she read it one word at a time to see if she'd gotten it right at first glance. "BRONK RECANTS CONFESSION IN 1982 MURDER." She felt a slow churning in the pit of her stomach. She sat down and proceeded to read the article:

Huntsville, Sept. 24 (AP) Convicted serial killer Louie Bronk claimed today from his death-row cell that he lied eleven years ago when he confessed to the 1982 slaying in Austin of Andrea "Tiny" McFarland. Bronk is scheduled to die here Tuesday by lethal injection for the robbery-slaying of the thirty-seven-year-old woman, who was shot to death outside her Northwest Austin home.

Bronk, 48, was convicted by a Travis County jury of capital murder in 1983 and sentenced to death. He is believed to be the notorious Texas Scalper who during a five-year period from 1977 to 1982 murdered as many as fifteen women along the Interstate 35 corridor. Beside his conviction in the McFarland murder, he has been convicted of four other murders in Texas—Greta Huff in San Marcos, Rosa Morales in Corpus Christi, Candice Hargrave in Waco, and Lizette Pachullo in Denton. In each case he received a sentence of life imprisonment.

Bronk has also confessed to at least fifty other murders in twelve states, but many of those confessions have been shown to be invalid.

Bronk made his statement Thursday through Texas Prison Ministries founder Adeline Dodgin, whom Bronk calls his spiritual adviser and best friend.

Bronk's attorney, Tanya Klein of the Texas Assistance Center, who has been handling Bronk's appeals, was out of town and unavailable for comment.

In his handwritten statement, Bronk said he was confused and under severe pressure when he made the confession. He claimed that officials who questioned him supplied him with enough information about the crime that he was able to confess to it convincingly.

Bronk said that the reason he has waited until now to recant the confession is that he has recently become a Christian and wants to set the record straight before he dies. "I know now that the only way to make up for the bad things I done is to tell the whole truth and nothing but the truth. God as my witness, I didn't never even set eyes on Mrs. McFarland. I been reborn in Christ and I want to live whatever is left of life to me as a real Christian. That's why I got to tell the truth about it now.

"The book that was wrote about the murder is totally false," Bronk also said in his statement, referring to the recently published Catton Press book about the crime, *Sweating Blood*, by *Lone Star Monthly* writer Molly Cates. "At that time I wasn't a Christian and I did like to spin a story, so I gave that lady who wrote the book a long tall tale. She just believed everything I told her and put it in that book but none of it is true. She encouraged me to tell that pack of lies. I can't believe in this country you can get lies printed like that."

Molly clenched her teeth and read on:

Travis County District Attorney Stan Heffernan, an assistant DA at the time, prosecuted the case. Asked about Bronk's recanting of his confession, Heffernan said, "This is just the sort of thing I would expect from Mr. Bronk, who enjoys manipulating the media. Here at the eleventh hour, with his appeals running out, Mr. Bronk is merely making a desperate gesture."

When questioned about the murder Wednesday of Georgia McFarland, 48, the second wife of Charles Clegg McFarland, whose first wife Bronk was convicted of murdering, Heffernan said Austin Police were actively following up several leads.

Molly let the paper fall to the table. That perverse, lying son of a bitch! After all his talk about going down with dignity and not giving in to the red scream. The macho code on death row dictated that when your time came, you went stoically. The worst thing was to give in to the red scream—to give voice to the terror of the execution chamber. Now here he was whimpering and getting ready to scream the red scream.

But why on earth should she be surprised? Like her daddy used to say, "Lie down with dogs, darlin', and you get up with fleas."

When she had decided to do the follow-up interviews with Louie and include some of the material in her book, everyone had advised against it. Her editor, her agent, Richard, Jo Beth—they had all warned that he was too crazy, too unreliable a source. And she hadn't really needed it; there was plenty of information available in the trial transcripts, case reports, and interviews.

But she had been determined to hear about it in his own words and write part of the story from his point of view.

She picked up her coffee cup and brought it to her lips. Her stomach gave a little heave of protest before she could drink. She dumped the coffee out into the sink and watched it run down the stainless-steel drain.

Why was she feeling so queasy over this? Louie was a liar making a last-ditch effort as the reality of his approaching death hit him. No one was likely to take anything he said seriously. If she was going to get upset over a little heat like this she ought to write about charity balls or the golden-cheeked warbler.

She glanced at the clock on the oven. It was seven-thirty and she had an appointment at eight-thirty with Alison McFarland. This development was all the more reason to get going on the story: a killer making a last-minute repudiation of the confession that got him convicted—this was good stuff. It would make a much better story. She needed to keep that in mind.

Molly took a long hot shower and put on what amounted to her working uniform: tan slacks, a white T-shirt, and an orange linen blazer she liked because it was supposed to look wrinkled and did. After she was dressed, she felt slightly better, but her stomach was still roiling.

She looked in her Day-Timer for the instructions to Alison McFarland's house in South Austin. Then she picked up her notebook and little Panasonic tape recorder, checking to be sure there was a tape in it.

Molly drove through the seedy old South Austin neighborhood to the tiny frame bungalow at 1202 Monroe where Alison McFarland lived with Mark Redinger. The roof was patched in places. Tarpaper sheets hung raggedly over the edges, and the sidewalk in front of the house had undergone an upheaval where the roots of an old oak had cracked and lifted it. This sure was a long way from her daddy's modern mansion on the hill.

As she parked in front of the house, Molly was glad to see the red Toyota in the driveway. Yesterday Alison had looked so distraught Molly had wondered if she was going to keep the appointment. And by now she'd probably heard about David Serrano; she could well be a basket case.

Molly walked up and rang the bell. She frowned when she saw that the door was standing open and tried to peer in through the warped aluminum screen door. God, if the murders of two people who were close to you couldn't get you to lock your doors, what could?

Alison McFarland's bare feet made absolutely no noise; suddenly she just materialized on the other side of the screen. She wore cut-off jeans that looked like they'd been chewed off rather than cut, leaving a stringy fringe of denim threads hanging down her thin pale thighs. She opened the screen door and held it for Molly. "Mrs. Cates, did you hear about David?" There was a shrill edge to her voice.

"Yes, I did. And I'm so sorry. How did you hear?" In the morning light that streamed in through the open door the girl's face was milky pale. Under her eyes the circles looked like week-old bruises.

"My father just called. The police called him real early this morning. They want to talk to all of us about David. I just called down to the police station to tell them about the lunch date he missed with me yesterday. Remember when I saw you at the hospital?"

"Yes, I do."

"And Mark was going to stop by the police station after running to tell them about when we saw him last."

"When was that, Alison?"

"Monday night. He came over and the three of us went out for pizza."

"The three of you? You, David, and Mark?"

"Uh-huh."

"Did you say Mark had seen David after that?"

"No. They were going to go running and out for a drink Tuesday night, but David called and canceled it." She crossed her arms tight over her thin chest. "And here I was feeling annoyed yesterday that he didn't show up." Her eyes squeezed shut. "He was probably already dead. God. This is like some nightmare that doesn't ever end."

Keeping her eyes shut, she said, "And I saw the article in this morning's paper—the one about Louie Bronk saying he didn't do it. I feel like the whole world's collapsing."

Molly rested a hand on her shoulder and felt a tremor under her hand.

Alison turned and led the way into a stuffy dark living room furnished with a few mismatched chairs and a card table with a goose-necked lamp. She sat at the table, which was covered with open books and loose papers, and started to chew on a thumbnail. When she looked up and saw Molly watching, she stopped. "Sit down. Please."

Molly chose the chair closest to Alison.

"I just don't know what to think now." Alison's voice sounded close to tears. "It's too much."

"I can see how you'd feel overwhelmed right now, Alison. And I see you're trying to study."

"Have to—paper due," the girl said, glancing down at the books on the table. "Here I was looking forward to this whole awful thing about my mother finally being over. And it all starts up again. Georgia gets killed. And then David. And now with him—you know, Louie Bronk—saying he didn't do it . . ." Her voice trailed off.

"But he did. No matter what Louie Bronk says now, Alison, I believe he killed your mother. Most death-row inmates protest their innocence to the end. What's unusual about Louie is that he's waited so long to start doing it."

Alison began chewing the side of her thumb. She nodded. "Yeah, he's just trying to save his ass. But it won't work."

"No, it won't," Molly said. "Alison, I don't want to add to your worries now, but I do think you should keep your door locked. When I arrived, it was open."

Alison gave a nod. "Yeah. I forget. My father wants me to move back home while this is going on; he's going to hire an extra security person for the house, in addition to Frank Purcell, who follows him everywhere, like a shadow. They're both putting a lot of pressure on me to do it but . . ."

Thinking of the open door, Molly said, "That doesn't sound like a bad idea. For a while. Can't hurt."

Alison shrugged. "Yeah, you're probably right. I guess I will. He needs me now." When she pulled her thumb away from her mouth, Molly could see that it looked red and raw.

Molly held up her little tape recorder. "Is it all right with you if I record this conversation? I like to do it because my note-taking breaks down when people get to talking fast."

"I don't mind," Alison said in a voice that suggested there wasn't much she did mind. "But like I told you on the phone I don't have anything earth-shaking to tell you."

Molly put it in her lap and switched it on, watching to make sure the tape was spinning. "I'm not looking for earth-shaking," she said, "just your reaction now to what's going on, how you feel about the coming execution. Your father's concerned that this is going to be too difficult for you, set you back somehow. I sure don't want to do anything like that."

A shadow of a smile crossed Alison's wan face. "My father doesn't know anything about me anymore."

"How come?"

"Well, ever since he got married and I moved in with Mark, I don't see him much."

"I gather your father doesn't approve of your living arrangements."

A small smile threatened again. "He doesn't like it. As a matter of fact, he hates it, but he can't do anything about it."

"Oh?"

"Yeah. He threatened to cut off my allowance. You know, if I'm old enough to make a decision like this I'm old enough to support myself. I think he thought it would bring me running home."

"But it didn't," Molly said.

"Nope. And he didn't do it anyway. I knew he wouldn't. But I got a part-time job anyway, just in case."

"With school that must be difficult," Molly said.

"It's only twelve hours a week, so it's not too bad. Mark's been a good influence on me there."

"How's that?"

"Well he's been on his own totally since his mother died when he was eighteen. He's had to drop out of school a couple of times because of money, but he's about to finish up now. Of course my father would never even think of helping him."

"Mark's mother was your father's sister?"

"Yes. But Daddy didn't have anything to do with her."

"Why was that?"

"Oh, he thought she was trashy and lazy. Anyone who doesn't work twenty-four hours a day is lazy, according to Daddy. We're trying to figure out how Mark can afford to go to graduate school. He wants to get an MBA. And we've thought about getting married, too, so . . ." She shrugged, but her pale lips were tight with what looked to Molly like resentment.

"What are you studying, Alison?"

Alison picked up a pencil off the table and rolled it between her palms. "Journalism. I'm thinking of being a crime writer—like you."

Molly looked at her in surprise. Very few people set out to be crime writers; they usually fell into it like she did and found they had a knack for it.

"I was wondering if you'd tell me how you got started, Mrs. Cates?"

Molly hesitated. This was a question she got asked all the time, but something about the girl made her reluctant to give the stock answer to it. When she opened her mouth to speak, she surprised herself with a truth she hadn't spoken in years: "A long time ago when I was sixteen, my father was murdered, out at Lake Travis. The sheriff didn't do much about it, so I started looking into it myself. In the process I got to know some reporters at the paper and later when I had to earn a living, I went and applied for a job. The reporter on the crime beat had just left and no one else wanted to do it so they let me try. I just sort of learned on the job."

"You didn't study it in college?"

Molly sighed. It was one of her major regrets in life. "Never went to college. But this was more than twenty years ago, Alison, when the business wasn't so competitive. I sure don't recommend anyone trying to do it that way today."

Alison leaned forward. "Did you find out who killed him? Your father, I mean."

Molly felt the old anger rising hot and thick in her throat. "No. I never did. I narrowed it down some, but I never have known for sure." She heard the whiny quaver in her voice, and as always, she despised her inability to control it.

Alison let the pencil fall to the table. "God, that's awful, not to know. That must've been so hard for you."

Once you let even a little piece of truth slip out, Molly thought, it opens the spigot. "I adored my father," she said, "and, more than anything, I wanted to do that last thing for him." She closed her lips, determined not to let this start a flood of truth-telling.

Alison looked down at her bony bare feet and said very quietly, "Maybe that's why you're still writing about crime. Because that didn't get solved."

"Maybe," Molly said impassively. "What about you, Alison? Why do you want to be a crime reporter?"

"Maybe part of it is like with you—something to do with my mother's death. But even before that happened, I was fascinated with murders and things. When I was eight I started reading mysteries. I exhausted Nancy Drew and the usual stuff and went on to adult things pretty quick."

"What things?"

"Oh, like detective magazines and true crime books. I've read just about everything. Joe McGinness, Anne Rule. But my all-time favorites are *In Cold Blood* and *Blood and Money*."

"Those are two of my favorites, too," Molly said.

"I told you over the phone how much I liked your book," Alison said. "It must've made you real mad this morning to read what Louie Bronk said about it."

"It sure did." Molly realized for the first time how angry she really was.

"Does it . . ." The girl hesitated, looking for the right words. "You know. Does it make you have any doubts?"

The girl probably had a future as a crime reporter; she certainly knew how to ask the right questions. "None. Bronk's a pathological liar. It's hard to know whether you can believe anything he says. But I do believe he killed your mother and I believe the version he told me which I related in my book is essentially accurate."

"Have you talked to him today?" Alison said. "Asked him why all of a sudden he's changed his story?"

"No."

"Aren't you going to?" Alison asked. "I think that's a lot more interesting than talking to me."

Molly stopped breathing for a minute as she considered it. She hadn't acknowledged it yet, but of course that's what she was going to do. As soon as this interview was over. And if this was going to be an interview where she interviewed Alison rather than the reverse, she'd better take charge of it now.

"Yes," Molly said, "I'm going to drive to Huntsville this afternoon. Alison, why did you agree to be a witness at the execution?"

"Oh. If I'm going to be a crime reporter, I guess I should get used to this sort of thing." As if she couldn't last too long without doing it, her thumb went up to her mouth and she ripped at what little bit remained of the nail.

"What else?" Molly prompted.

The girl put the hand in her lap and held on to it with the other hand. "Since I can remember I've been this poor little girl without a mother who everyone felt sorry for. I'm tired of that; it's so passive and pathetic. Witnessing the execution sounded like a way to have a part in avenging my mother." She shook her head. "I don't know. I guess I'm trying to stop being a victim."

Molly nodded. "Being a victim is the pits. I agree."

"And this may sound snobbish, but to have your life devastated by someone like Louie Bronk, this filthy, subhuman, stupid drifter who barely lives in the same world. I mean, it's humiliating in a way." She looked directly into Molly's eyes. "Isn't it?"

Molly felt like cringing from the sentiment, but she couldn't help sharing it. "Yes, it is," she admitted. "What about the death penalty, Alison. How do you feel about that?"

"Oh," the girl said fiercely, "anything less wouldn't be enough. It has to be death. I know you're opposed to it because I've read your things in *Lone Star Monthly,* but I think that's a philosophical thing. I get the impression from reading your book that you won't shed any tears when he dies."

Molly looked at the girl in wonder and said, "I think you're very perceptive. Alison, tell me if this is something you'd rather not talk about, but I'd like to hear what you remember about the day your mother was killed."

Alison said slowly, "I was only eleven and it was so long ago so . . ." Automatically her hand went up to her mouth and she chewed on the side of her index finger, pulling at the skin. "I remember waking up from a nap, but you know how you tend to be all hazy for a while. It's mostly a blur. Well, I heard this noise outside— probably it was a gunshot—and I looked around the house for some-one—my mother or David. David was usually there in the afternoon. My mother wasn't home much. But no one was in the house and I remember feeling scared. I guess that's my main memory—the empty house and feeling scared and alone. I never liked being alone."

"When you were looking around, did you notice that some things had been stolen?"

Alison shook her head. "But I wasn't really looking. I was hot and sweaty and I wandered to the door and saw David. He was coming out of the garage and then he came running at me and made me go back in the house and I could see how upset he was. He could barely speak he was so upset. But he didn't tell me my mother was dead. I didn't find out until later."

"When?"

"That night, I think. My father told me. And it's hard to separate what I really remember from the day and what I heard at the trial."

"What about the car?"

"Oh, when I was standing in the doorway, I saw it pulling away—that white car." Alison stood up abruptly. "It's so warm in here. Would you like some iced tea, Mrs. Cates? I'm really thirsty, after talking your ear off, and it's cooler in the kitchen anyway."

Molly followed her through a narrow hall to the kitchen, which was a pleasant sunny room. A breeze wafted in through an open window, rustling the newspapers that lay open on the linoleum table.

Alison took a pitcher of tea from the refrigerator and an ice tray from the tiny freezer. She poured two tall glasses and plopped a few ice cubes in afterward.

As she handed the glass to Molly she said, "When you said in there how much you loved your father, it reminded me of me. This is not part of the interview—just between us. I adore my father, too. He can be pretty overprotective, but I love him lots, maybe too much." She let out a big sigh. "When he and Georgia got married it seemed like a good time for me to leave."

Alison sat down across the table from Molly, wrapping her hands around the cold glass. Her nails were all chewed down to nubs. The skin around some of them was bloody.

"Of course, I can see why he's the way he is," she said. "All he's been through. Now that he's alone again, I suppose I'll spend more time with him. It's really tragic about Georgia because I think he'd finally found the right mate. They were so happy together they really didn't need anyone else."

"Your mother wasn't the right mate for him?" Molly remembered Stuart saying yesterday that both Tiny's life and her death made Charlie miserable.

"Oh, God, no. That wasn't his fault, though. She shouldn't have been anybody's mate."

"Why not?"

"Oh, even as a young child I knew it. I mean not exactly but—" She stopped and looked down into her tea.

"What did you know?"

"That she wasn't cut out to be married. It just wasn't in her. She didn't even try to hide it."

Molly felt the familiar tingling in her fingers. "Why wasn't she cut out for marriage?"

"Oh, she liked men too much. You know."

"You mean she had affairs?"

"Screwed around is more like it," Alison said, her mouth grim.

Only long practice in not showing surprise kept Molly's voice level. "Alison, when I was researching the book, I talked at length with several people who knew your mother well. To get some background on her. None of them ever mentioned that."

"Well, why would they?" Alison took a sip of her tea. "She was dead. They wouldn't want you to write stuff like that about her. And Daddy would be furious, and I mean *furious,* at anybody who told you that." She wrapped her arms around herself.

Molly thought of the childlike, pure-looking body in the autopsy pictures and reminded herself for the millionth time that you couldn't tell anything about people from appearances. It looked like she'd stopped asking questions about Tiny McFarland too soon—the cardinal sin for a reporter.

"Who did she have affairs with?" Molly asked.

"I don't know. Friends of my father, anyone. She was hardly ever home. That's why we needed a live-in baby-sitter."

Alison stopped to listen to the sound of a motorcycle outside. The roar stopped and in a few seconds the side door opened. There in the doorway stood Mark Redinger wearing neon pink running shorts and a white T-shirt. He had a knapsack slung over one broad shoulder.

"Hello, Mrs. Cates," he said, leaning over to shake Molly's hand. He dumped his knapsack on the table and gave Alison a kiss on the cheek. Then he went to the refrigerator and took out the iced tea pitcher. He refilled Alison's glass and Molly's before pouring himself one. He sat down next to Alison.

"You heard about David Serrano?" he asked, leveling his eyes at Molly.

"Yes, I did," Molly said.

"I've just been to the police station. I knew they'd want to hear about us seeing him Monday night and him breaking the date for Tuesday."

Molly nodded. "Did you know him well, Mark?" she asked, admiring the way his short thick black lashes made fringed shadows of deep blue on his irises.

"Not well. Not like Alison knew him. But I remember him from back when he lived at the McFarlands'. And then of course we got reacquainted Monday." He glanced at Alison, as if for confirmation.

"How did he seem to you?"

"Nervous," Mark said.

Alison said, "David was upset about the execution. He was a Catholic. The idea of even somebody as awful as Louie Bronk being put to death was hard for him to accept."

Mark nodded. "Yeah. He was real upset that he played a role in it. I got the idea he was hoping the courts might call it off again."

"How did he cancel for Tuesday night?" Molly asked.

"He called and left a message on the machine. The police wanted to know that, too. I wish we hadn't recorded over it because they wanted to hear it. But it just said something important had come up and he'd call to reschedule." Mark shrugged. "Of course, he never did."

Molly lifted the recorder to show him. "Mark, I was just getting some of Alison's memories about the day her mother was killed and I wondered if you'd tell me what yours are."

"Mine?" His voice was squeaky with surprise, as though he had just reverted to adolescence. "I was at my house all day, so I don't know anything you'd be really interested in." He wrapped his hands tight around his glass.

"I always wondered," Molly said, "the day Alison's mother was killed, when Stuart was over at your house, he was planning to stay all day, wasn't he? He'd even brought things to spend the night."

"Yeah. We were going to shoot skeet at the range and then go to a movie. I'd just acquired my first vehicle, an old pickup." He clasped his hands behind his head. "God, I loved that truck! We were going to do the town in it."

"In court Stuart said he changed his mind and decided to go home," Molly said. "I was wondering why?"

"Oh"—Mark shrugged—"just what he said. He decided he wanted to go home."

"Why?"

"Oh, you know Stu." He glanced over at Alison and shot her a grin. "He's always getting ticked off at something silly. You might say he's kind of prickly."

"You had an argument?" Molly said.

"You could say that, but really it was just Stu being touchy."

"What about?"

"Are you kidding? It was eleven years ago."

"Yes," Molly said, "but on a very significant day, which you have surely gone over in your head many times."

"Sure, but that was an issue that never came up," Mark said, decisively forcing his voice back to its adult baritone.

Molly nodded. "Well, it was just one of those little things I was wondering about, trying to reconstruct that day." She sipped her tea and then said, as if it were an afterthought, "Oh, why didn't you drive him home? It was four or five miles between your houses, wasn't it?"

"He had his bike," Mark said.

Molly took another sip of tea. "But you could have put it in the back of the pickup. As I recall, a teenager with a new vehicle takes every opportunity to drive it."

"We could have," Mark answered. "But we didn't. I told you he was pissed. It was good for him to make the ride. Old Stu does better when he gets his exercise. Works off his frustrations."

"What frustrations?" Molly inquired.

"Oh, you name it. Frustration's his middle name. A girlfriend would do him wonders, but he says he's too busy. Of course, that's what he's been saying for years." He smiled at Alison, but she was gazing out the window and didn't see it. "But," he said, "there is one thing I regret about my behavior that morning."

"What's that?"

"I regret that we didn't let Alison come with us. Then she would have been out of it. It was such a bummer for her being there and having to testify, her being so young."

"Yes," Molly agreed. "Why didn't she go with you?"

Mark laughed and reached across the table to mess up Alison's hair, but she just continued looking out the window with no change of expression. "Oh, you know. She was just this dippy kid sister. We didn't want her along 'cause she'd crimp our style." He lowered his head and tried to catch her eye, get her to look at him. "But now we do," he said in an ingratiating voice.

Alison finally looked at him. Her smile was distant and cool.

Molly switched off her recorder and dropped it into her pocket. "Thanks for the tea and your time," she said, standing up.

Alison and Mark both walked her to the front door. Alison said, "I guess I'll see you Monday night in Huntsville, Mrs. Cates. They told me to come around eleven-thirty."

Mark looked down at Molly and said, "Oh, I meant to ask you. I'm planning to drive her to Huntsville and I hate to have her do this alone. Is there some way I could get on the list for the execution? The guest list?" He gave a little laugh.

Molly looked into his dark blue eyes and wondered what was really inside there. "I think you'd need to talk to the attorney general's office about that, Mark. He's in charge of execution protocol."

"I'll do that. Thanks," he said.

Molly took a card out of her purse and handed it to Alison. "Give me a call if you think of anything else you want to say." She took hold of the girl's hand and squeezed it. "And please remember to lock that door."

"Mrs. Cates?"

She turned around.

"It's a good thing I didn't drive Stu home that day, isn't it?" Mark said. "We would have gotten there sooner and we might have met up with the killer. We could have been killed ourselves."

"Yes. You could have," Molly said, looking at Alison who was furiously chewing on her left thumb.

As she got in her truck she watched through the screen door as Mark wrapped his arms around the girl, who, with her thin awkward limbs and translucent skin, reminded Molly of a young bird fallen from the nest too soon, unfeathered and not quite fully formed.

chapter 13

Years on death row
Nowhere to go
Nine by twelve cell
Hotter'n hell.
Nothing to do
But one more tattoo.
To work off a debt.
Am I paid up yet?

LOUIE BRONK
Death Row, Ellis I Unit,
Huntsville, Texas

▲　▼　▲

It was ten o'clock when Molly Cates drove away from Alison Mc-Farland's house and it was fast heating up to one of those end-of-September scorchers.

Of course she'd go see Louie—for the final interview. Of course. She was already feeling the old pre-Louie jitters of bats flitting around her chest cavity. She knew from experience it would subside during the drive to Huntsville. By the time she got to the prison she would have achieved an icy hardness that would allow her to talk to Louie about the things that, with Louie Bronk, were inevitable.

She headed up South Congress toward the Lake and downtown Austin. First she would stop in at the Texas Assistance Center. Maybe she could surprise Tanya Klein, catch her in her office. Nothing else had worked. She hadn't been able to reach her by phone, and for the past week, Tanya had not returned her calls although Molly had left many messages. Among other things, she wanted to know why Tanya was avoiding her.

Molly parked in front of the old gray stucco house on San Antonio Street and put a quarter in the meter. A tiny sign to the left of the door said "Texas Assistance Center." A fine generic name, Molly thought, sure to confuse anyone who didn't know that the Center was an organization of lawyers formed in 1988 to provide legal representation to Texas inmates facing the death penalty. In a neighborhood of old houses now converted into offices for lawyers and architects and real estate agents, the house was not far from the county courthouse and the main branch of the public library.

At the desk just inside the front door sat a very young woman reading a *Mad* magazine.

"Good morning," Molly said, breezing right past, walking fast and businesslike. "I'm here to see Tanya Klein. I know my way up," she tossed over her shoulder.

"Wait . . . I'm supposed to buzz first. . . ."

But Molly was halfway up the stairs. She ran up the rest of the flight and then another to the third floor. The door to the office was open. She stuck her head around the corner and caught Tanya sitting at the desk with her feet up and the phone to her ear. "It's all right, Beth," Tanya was saying. "It's not your fault."

Molly knocked on the door frame—her one concession to courtesy.

Tanya put the phone down and lowered her feet. She swiveled her chair around and faced Molly with a tight mouth and narrowed eyes. Molly could not imagine what she'd done to deserve that hostility.

Louie's lawyer, Tanya Klein, wore black bicycle pants with magenta stripes down the outside of each skinny leg, a shiny magenta jog bra that matched the stripes, and black high-top aerobic shoes. Her black frizzy hair obscured a great deal of her deeply tanned narrow face. "Mrs. Cates." She clipped the words off in her curt New Jersey accent. "I just do not have a spare minute today. You can see we are swamped." She spread her arms out.

Molly stepped in and looked around at the boxes of files and the piles of paper all over the floor. "I can see you're real busy here and I sure hate to interrupt. But five minutes would satisfy me, stop me from bugging you all the time so you don't have to worry over all those unreturned phone calls." Molly moved a few steps farther into the room. "Mainly I just want an update on Louie Bronk's appeals and I wondered what you know about this new development."

"You mean the statement in today's paper?"

"Yes."

"Well. All I know is I had a call yesterday morning from this person—Sister Adeline Dodgin, if you can believe it—from some religious group that visits inmates. She's been visiting Louie and he gave her this statement yesterday and asked if she could get it in the paper."

"I wonder how she managed that," Molly said.

"She told me on the phone that she was going to give it to some friend of hers in the Associated Press Dallas Bureau. She wanted me to know in case the publicity might affect his appeals."

"Will it?" Molly asked.

"Not a chance."

"The Associated Press?" Molly said. "I wonder if—"

"Yeah," Tanya said. "It was picked up by the *New York Times, Miami Herald, Chicago Tribune,* and a bunch of other papers around the country. Pretty amazing."

Molly's heart sank. She sat down in the one chair in the room not covered with stacks of paper. "Yeah, pretty amazing. But I must admit I don't much like being called credulous and a liar in the national press."

Tanya smiled for the first time since Molly had known her. "Yeah. The pot calling the kettle black."

"Well, I'm not sure I like that metaphor. Louie is certainly a pathological liar. I may be a member of the press, but I don't like to think of myself as a kettle to his pot."

Tanya looked a little lost at that. "Well, anyway. It's amazing this Dodgin person could arrange that kind of coverage. A death-row inmate saying he's innocent is not exactly hot news."

"How do you figure it?" Molly asked. "His recanting."

"Pretty simple. Louie sees that our great state has executed fourteen men already this year, two of them last week. For the first time he believes they're actually going to do it to him, too."

Molly nodded. "He's trying to save his sorry ass. Where are you with his appeals?"

"We've filed his federal habeas petition in U.S. District Court, Western Division. We claim his constitutional rights got violated during the trial, the confession was illegally obtained—the usual stuff. Now we're waiting for the attorney general to make his response."

"When will you hear?"

"Tomorrow probably." Tanya's expression didn't change. "But Louie's got no issues. Like I told you when his date was set, this is a loser of a case. But this publicity might be good for us in the long run.''

"How do you see that?" Molly asked, getting out her little tape recorder. She held it up to Tanya and raised her eyebrows.

In response, Tanya shrugged. "Well, you know how it works. With public opinion being what it is, the capital punishment issue is going to be a long fight and we're going to lose lots of the battles. Lose. Lose. Lose." On each word, Tanya's voice got more dour. "You get an article like this where Louie says he's innocent and no one really believes it. But then he gets executed. And maybe some people, just a few, are left with a tiny doubt. Maybe he was innocent. Maybe an innocent man can get put to death and they begin to think, well, maybe we shouldn't do something that's so final."

She pushed her hair away from her face, but it sprang back immediately to its original position. As determined as a Brillo pad, Molly thought.

"Actually," Tanya continued, "I'm so busy right now with fifteen active cases—four with dates set already. And this new case—Edward Silvas—has some real merit, so I don't have much time for Louie Bronk."

"A matter of triage?" Molly asked.

Tanya winced. "We're doing everything we can for Louie. But we are overwhelmed with 368 men on death row right now and the speeding up of executions. We are down to 13 lawyers and our original idea of getting volunteers to do it pro bono just does not work. We can barely keep out heads above water. And funds are shorter than ever."

Molly knew it was all true. It might make a good article sometime, but it wasn't what she'd come for. "Have you seen Louie recently?" she asked.

"Monday. When I was in Huntsville to see Edward."

"How is he?"

Tanya shrugged. "How long since you've seen him?"

"Two years."

"Well, he's really changed. In the year and a half I've been handling his appeals, he's aged twenty years. He's still harping on those god-awful poems of his, of course, trying to get me to take them to someone who would make them into a book. Who would be that crazy? And he's been converted or brainwashed or something by this Sister Addie who works the prisons. He talks about her constantly and spouts all this Christian sentiment—more God's wills and Sweet Jesuses than you ever heard. It's enough to make you spit up."

Molly had to chuckle. "Yeah, I feel the same way about it."

"It amazes me how all these self-professed good Christians down here are panting to put their fellow man to death, while we heathens are reluctant to allow the state to take life."

"I've got a theory about that, Tanya. It has to do with a belief in an afterlife. They feel, well, if we make a mistake it's not such a big deal; there's still the hereafter."

Tanya actually laughed aloud. "I think you may really have it there, Molly. I may steal that line."

Seizing on that sign of humor, the first she'd ever observed in Tanya, Molly decided to ask the hard question: "Tanya, I know you're real busy here, but I wondered if there was any other reason you didn't want to talk with me. I can be pretty dense sometimes. I wondered if I'd said something to offend you."

Under her suntan the lawyer's face went red. "Oh. Not really. I—"

"Or maybe someone suggested it wasn't a good idea to talk to me."

"No!" She nearly shouted it, then lowered her voice. "I just . . . I knew you wanted to talk about Louie and there really wasn't anything to tell you. No. I'm sorry about the phone calls."

"Just wondering," Molly said casually. "I ask because it seems like everywhere I go lately people are trying to get me to stop writing about Louie Bronk. Tanya, tell me. Am I still on Louie's visitor list? Do you think he'd see me if I drove over there today?"

Tanya hit her head with her open palm. "Oh, I forgot to tell you. When I saw him on Monday he said he was sure you'd call and I should give you a message from him." She paused dramatically with her dark eyes open wide. "The message is, he's waiting for you."

In spite of everything, the three-hour drive from Austin to Huntsville affected her the way it always had. As soon as she got past Elgin on Highway 290 West she began to feel it—the soaring sensation, that old open highway siren call of freedom.

It carried her back to her childhood in Lubbock when she and her daddy went on vacations. They'd take off in his pickup, leaving all the problems of the ranch behind, and just drive. Without any plans or time schedules. Thinking only of the stretch of road they were on at that very minute, he'd drive them wherever the spirit moved him —to San Antone, or Corpus, or Austin. They took whatever back roads looked interesting and stopped to eat at tiny cafes in dusty town squares.

Two and a half years ago, while she was writing *Sweating Blood,* she had made this same drive once a week for four months to interview Louie Bronk about his life and crimes. Every Monday she'd leave her town house in Northwest Austin early in the morning with a cup of coffee to sip along the way and by ten o'clock she'd be in the visitors' room at the Ellis I maximum security unit outside Huntsville.

While making that drive she'd have the same breezy feeling even though she knew what was waiting for her at her destination: Louie Bronk's highway stories, which were a far cry from hers.

A love for the open road was one thing she and Louie shared. Louie, too, loved to get in the car and drive. Even more than she did. That's how he had spent the only five years of his adult life when he hadn't been in prison—cruising the highways. Often he'd drive thousands of miles in a few days, trolling the Interstate, just him in an old beat-up used car he'd bought for three hundred bucks, a six-pack or two on the floor, his hunting knife on the seat beside him, and sometimes a gun he'd picked up at some pawnshop. His face when he talked about those days took on a dreamy, beatific glow.

As he described it to Molly, he would often drive many hundreds of miles in the grip of a growing fantasy before finding exactly what he was looking for. But eventually he'd find her—a woman in distress by the side of the road, her engine overheated or her tire flat, a woman who could have no inkling the kind of trouble she was in when Louie Bronk pulled up behind her and grinned.

After each interview, Molly would sit in her car and breathe deeply as if in a decompression chamber. Then she'd open the windows and drive back to Austin. At about the halfway mark she'd stop to eat. She'd get home at five, sit down at her word processor, and write long into the night, absorbed in re-creating Louie Bronk's road stories, his vision of the Texas highways as the very lowest reaches of hell.

Some of the chapters she wrote from his point of view—showing how the movies in his head (as he called them) made him get in the car to look for the dark-haired woman waiting for him by the side of the road, enticing him; how long and hard he'd drive looking for just the right one; how exciting the moment of recognition was, the terror and helplessness in her eyes when she knew what was about to happen; how he craved that feeling of control, of total mastery of another person; how it thrilled him as nothing else could; how he did it once and found it easy to get away with. So he did it again. And again. And again.

In each session he told a fresh installment of his road trips. After forty-eight hours of listening to the world according to Louie Bronk, Molly had had enough. She had the material she needed and his stories were breaking through the barrier of cool objectivity she'd erected for the interviews. She thanked him, said good-bye, and hadn't been back to death row once in the two years.

Until today.

After turning onto Texas 21, she stopped in dusty Caldwell to pick up a Dr Pepper to sip as she drove. When she got to College Station, she caught Route 30 toward Huntsville. Here the landscape changed abruptly from flat prairie into the piney woods of East Texas. Tall pine trees shaded the road and the air felt cooler, so she turned off the air-conditioning and rolled down the window.

She skirted the pretty old East Texas town of Huntsville, following a series of little-traveled back roads to the prison twelve miles north of town.

When Molly turned in at the gate and drove toward the huge prison complex, she was awed, as always, by the red brick, more red brick—hard-edged, cold, and sterile—all in one place than she'd ever seen. From the flat clearing, hundreds of tons of red brick rose, surrounded by double Cyclone fences, twelve feet high and topped with swirls of shining razor wire.

God knows we need prisons, she thought, but she was never able to reconcile her feelings about this place. Here in the midst of these beautiful East Texas woods and flower-studded fields, in this remote place, away from human eyes, we build brick fortresses to hold our most violent citizens. We lock them up and don't think about them again—until they are paroled or executed, when they force themselves into our consciousness.

As she drove by the first tall guardhouse at the corner of the complex, she could feel the eyes looking down on her. It had always been with her when she visited—the constant feeling of being watched by eyes seen and unseen. But at least it would please Grady; she'd gotten out of town as he'd suggested, and there probably wasn't a safer place to be than right here.

She pulled into the parking lot and sat in her truck for a minute watching a dozen trustees in their white prison coveralls working outside the fence, digging in the neat beds of lantana and petunias at the front gate. The first time she had come here many years ago she had been astonished by the meticulous maintenance and manicured landscaping of the place. The secret, she now knew, was that they had lots of free labor and a horticultural school for the inmates. Somehow all that effort only added to the sterility of the place.

In her jacket pocket she put her driver's license, her credentials from *Lone Star Monthly,* her car keys, a ballpoint pen, and her Steno book. Louie had never liked tape recorders, so she didn't use one. After tucking her purse under the seat, Molly got out of the truck and locked it.

As she walked toward the gate, she looked around for the horseman she knew must be somewhere near. Finally she located him in the shade of an oak tree, a gun on his hip and a shotgun in a sheath on the saddle. The horse's head pointed directly at her, and as she walked, the horse took little steps so that it continued to face her.

She entered the small brick gate-house just across the walk from the prison gate and picked up the phone there. When a man's voice answered, she gave her name and said she was here to visit Louie Bronk on death row. After a wait of a few minutes, the voice told her to leave any purses or weapons at the picket and come on in.

She stopped at the tall guard tower next to the front gate and looked up to the little room on top where the guard stood. She held up her key chain that had a Swiss Army knife and Grady's tear gas attached to it. Weapons by anybody's definition. The guard stuck his head out the door and lowered a plastic bucket at the end of a rope. She dropped her keys in and took a step back so he could pull it up. Then he motioned her to go on through.

She opened the first heavy gate and let it clink shut and lock behind her before pushing the next gate. She walked across the narrow grassy strip, through the front door, and turned left into a small antechamber to the visitors' room. A sign said "Death Row visitations weekdays 8–4." The first few times she'd come here, she'd been surprised that "Death Row" was the official name they used in all the signs. It was such a raw and direct description, rare for a system accustomed to euphemisms.

The visitors' room was a long brick-walled room divided lengthwise by a partition that separated inmates from visitors. From the floor up to a height of three feet the partition was made of brick, and from there to the ceiling it was made of several thicknesses of tight wire mesh reinforced with glass. A wooden ledge at table height stuck out from it on both sides where the brick and mesh met. Old oak chairs were lined up along both sides of the divider.

Though the room was entirely empty, as it often was on weekdays, which were reserved for death-row visitors, the guard motioned her down to the far end.

"Set yourself in front of the interview cage, please, ma'am," he said in a deep East Texas drawl. "The prisoner's in ad seg."

Ad seg was administrative segregation, a type of isolation in which a prisoner was locked in his cell twenty-four hours a day, and on the rare occasions when he was brought out for a shower or a visit, he was cuffed and shackled.

"Why?" she asked.

The young guard looked at her as though she were a slow child. " 'Cause his date's been set, ma'am," he said.

"Is that the rule?" she asked, surprised. "Sometimes they get their date more than a month ahead of time."

"Yes'm." He sounded bored. "Go on and set down."

Molly sat opposite a steel-mesh cage on the other side of the divider. It was about the size of a phone booth and contained only a chair. She put her notebook and pen down on the ledge and waited, trying to relax herself into what she thought of as her Louie mode— that state of mind in which all usual judgments and morality were suspended. She thought of it as letting herself fall down into a rabbit hole where, at the bottom, there was a different reality—Louie Bronk's world, which she was about to enter again.

chapter 14

Pretty gal all alone
On the highway, car broke down.
You pull behind her quick.
She gets to looking sick,
Mouth all dry
Starts to cry
Like a flood,
Sweating blood.
Please, please don't.
Honey I won't
Won't hurt none.
There it's done.
Weren't that fun?

▲ ▼ ▲

LOUIE BRONK
Death Row, Ellis I Unit,
Huntsville, Texas

After a few minutes a door opened on the prisoner's side of the room. Louie Bronk shuffled in, dwarfed by the two guards, one on either side of him. His hands were cuffed and chained to his waist. His feet were shackled and he clanked with each step.

One guard left while the other led Louie to the cage, unlocked it, and, holding tight to his upper arm, sat him down on the chair. As he locked the cage door, the guard said to Molly, "I'll be right here, ma'am, if you need me." He walked back to the door and stood at attention.

During this procedure, Louie had kept his eyes glued to the guard. He kept his head turned away from Molly and continued to stare at the guard.

Molly looked through the several layers of mesh at the man in the cage—a small figure dressed in a coarsely woven white prison shirt and pants. On his feet he wore the cheap soft slippers that were issued to all death-row inmates.

From the first, Louie's appearance had struck Molly as one of insufficiency in every feature. It was as if his unwanted birth and stunted childhood had supplied barely enough love and nutrients to create a full human being. He was short and, except for the hard lump of a paunch that protruded above his belt, scrawny. His hair was sparse and limp, his lips mere gray lines, his eyes squinty and narrow, close-set, with no lashes or eyebrows. And his skin was papery-looking, insufficient to cover his body decently; his sharp, beaky nose and flat cheeks and long chin looked like naked bone.

He had aged in the past two years, just as Tanya Klein had said. His hair was even thinner now and totally gray, so you could see his scalp through it, and his arms, which used to have at least a stringy, tensile strength, had gone slack; the skin on the underside had loosened from the bone, making the crude blue images tattooed there wrinkle into an unrecognizable mess. If she hadn't known what the tattoos were—a hawk, a serpent, and a naked woman—she wouldn't be able to make them out now.

Still turned, staring at the guard, he said in a reedy, singsong voice,

"Time to die?
Go bye-bye?
Don't you cry.
Gonna cook my goose?
Make me the caboose?
Set me loose.
Time for the red scream?
Or just a bad dream?
Man, let off some steam."

The guard didn't bat an eyelash.

"Still rhyming, Louie," Molly said in a low voice.

He turned quickly and looked directly at her. Molly stifled a gasp. His mouth was collapsing. The flesh around his slit of a mouth had wrinkled and sunk inward like a rotted Halloween jack-o'-lantern. He was drying up, caving in. If the state didn't kill him soon, there wouldn't be much left to kill.

"Two years, Molly. You ain't been here once in all that time."

"Yes, I know."

"As soon as you got what you wanted out of me, you stopped coming."

She felt herself pulling up from somewhere in her chest the voice she had always affected with him in the past. It was a low, calm voice that never expressed judgment or anger, a voice that entered the most appalling of discussions without rising or cracking. "Louie," she said in that old familiar voice, "you knew the deal was for the series of interviews. Did I ever say I would keep coming after that?"

"No." He sat with his chained hands in his lap and tilted his head to the side coyly. "But it don't seem right, not polite."

Accustomed to his bursts of rhyme, Molly had always treated them as regular conversation. "It don't seem polite to call me a liar either."

He let his head drop back so that his long chin pointed at her and his stringy neck with its huge Adam's apple was exposed. "I knew that would bring you."

"If you wanted to talk you could have written me, Louie."

He shook his head and said nothing, waiting for her.

They sat in silence. Then he said, "You wrote a book. Does it cook? I'd like to look."

The hairs on the back of Molly's neck prickled at the thought of his reading the book. "Are you saying you'd like to look at my book?"

"I ain't a big reader, as you know, but I would like to see my poetry printed in a real book." He grinned without opening his mouth. "I thought you might bring me one."

"So you haven't seen the book at all?" Molly asked.

"Nope."

"But you recently made a statement saying it was a pack of lies," she said.

"You wrote down the things about Mrs. McFarland just like I told 'em, didn't you?" His voice was thin and aggrieved.

She nodded.

"Then you wrote lies. God as my witness." He moved his hands up in the start of a gesture which was cut short by the chain attached to his cuffs. Quietly, he said, "Sister Addie says we are forgiven, but we need to set right the things we can."

"All right," Molly said. "Here's something you can set right. I have some questions for you."

He was silent and she could see from the way his eyeballs shifted down and to the right that he was conjuring up a rhyme. Finally he said, "Sure thing. Give it wing. Let it sing. Ring a ding."

"Okay. An article in the *American-Patriot* this morning said you made a statement yesterday and gave it to Addie Dodgin. I want to know if the newspaper quoted you right."

He made a little puckering motion with his lips that she recognized as an indication to go on.

"First of all, the article said you made a statement claiming you did not kill Tiny McFarland, that your confession was not true." She tried to catch his eyes but he was staring down at the tabletop. "Did you say that, Louie?" she asked.

"What else did it say?"

"That you said the authorities in Hays County fed you information about the killing so you could make a convincing confession. Did you say that?"

"What else?" he asked.

She tried to keep her voice neutral, as if she were just listing another item. "That you said everything you told me about the McFarland case for my book was a lie and that I led you on and encouraged you to tell those lies. Did you say that?"

He looked directly at her and smiled so she could see what had happened inside his mouth: many of his teeth were gone, leaving big empty gaps. Prison dentistry, no doubt.

"Well, did you?" she asked again.

He closed his mouth. "That's the one that really gets ya, ain't it?" He moved his head forward, closer to the mesh cage. "Ain't it? Got you where you live."

Molly had forgotten how infuriating he could be. "The article also said you have become a born-again Christian and that you want to do the right thing." Molly put her hands together in a mocking prayer gesture. "Did you say *that*, Louie?"

"Well, I answer to God now. Don't have to answer none of your questions, do I?"

She waited, trying to keep a grip on her temper.

"I mean what good's it to me to answer? What did I ever get out of answering all them questions took up so much of my time two years ago?"

She said nothing.

"Yoo-hoo," he said in a high voice, "I'll tell you. I got zip. I got dip. Goose egg. Mumbly peg. Molly Cates. Special rates."

"What are you saying, Louie?"

"Maybe you should share some of the wealth with me since I cooperated so good. Maybe I deserve some of them big profits you're raking in."

Molly had to struggle to keep her voice low. "Louie, we talked about that and you signed a waiver, if you recall. I paid you for the use of some of your poems and you agreed."

"You're cheating me, just like people always done. You used some of my poems in your book, but you never did nothing to get the rest of them printed down in a book of their own like I asked. And the money I got's all gone." He lapsed into the high whine she remembered from his monologues about how unfair the world had been to him. Of course, it *had* been unfair to him, savagely unfair, but she hated the whining anyway.

"Louie, I told you at the start I would never pay a penny for interviews or give you any kind of approval over what I wrote. But you chose to talk to me anyway."

"Worked out real good for you, didn't it? You got a book. Gonna get rich. Television movie—miniseries maybe. About me. Why shouldn't I get some money from it, huh?"

She felt anger building in her like a steam kettle. "First of all I'm not getting rich. And second, I don't think it would be ethical for you to benefit from your crimes."

"But it's just dandy for you to benefit, ain't it?"

He had her on the defensive, squirming and explaining, and she hated the feeling. It was so ludicrous she should laugh, but it made her furious. "What good would money be to you anyway, Louie?"

"What do you mean?" he asked with his eyes narrowed almost shut.

"You're going to be dead in three days." The minute the words were out, she wished she could recall them. It was inexcusable—to bully a helpless, chained, condemned man like that.

He looked up quick, with a grim set to his thread-thin lips. "No, I ain't. I ain't gonna be dead in three days."

Christ, he was thick. Her anger flared again. She'd already proven herself a bully; why not go all the way? She planted her elbows on the tabletop. "Louie, believe me. No matter what you say or do, you're going to die in three days. Your goose *is* cooked. It *is* time for the red scream."

He shook his head and bent his lips into the smile she hated. "No, ma'am," he said. "It won't happen 'cause you won't let it."

Breathless with surprise, she rose partway out of her chair. "Me? Louie, I have nothing to do with this. Nothing. I have no power to change it, even if I wanted to."

The guard, seeing her sudden movement and hearing the rise in her voice, came to life and took a step toward the cage door. Molly sat back down and waved him away with a sheepish smile.

Louie was scowling at her, his tiny close-set eyes narrowed. "What do you mean, 'if you wanted to'? You always said you was against the death penalty."

Molly took a deep breath. "I am against it."

"So what did you mean?"

"I meant that you're caught up in the mill of the criminal justice system and no one can stop it from grinding you up."

"Ain't you even going to hear what I got to say?" Louie demanded. "Before, you always listened to me. That's why I talked all them hours—because you listened so good. But that was when you wanted something from me, I guess, before I was a cooked goose." The whine had returned.

"Louie, you were a cooked goose then. You were cooked ten years ago when that Travis County jury convicted you of capital murder. But sure I'll listen. What you got to say?"

He raised his head and spoke in a loud, firm voice. "This is true. Through and through. I tell it to you." He stopped and glared at her.

"So tell me," she said, through tight lips.

He raised his cuffed hands as high as the chain permitted and placed his spatulate fingertips against his chest. "God above as my witness, I really didn't do that Mrs. McFarland." He shook his head. "She wasn't one of mine and I shouldn't ought to of said she was. Sweet Jesus and Sister Addie forgive me."

She felt her anger rising sour in her throat. His syrupy tone of voice and the sight of him with his hands over his heart enraged her. "Cut out that phony 'Sweet Jesus' crap, Louie. Don't try that old jail house con on me. You sat right over there"—she pointed to the spot where they had sat for the interviews—"and hour after hour you told me about the movie in your head that built up from the time you were eight years old, the fantasy of killing women and having sex with them. You told me about all those black-haired women on the highway."

"That's true," he whined. Then he repeated it in a whisper: "That's true. God will forgive me."

Molly found herself gripping the ledge in front of her. "Then you told me about driving into Austin that hot, hot day, with the fantasy bursting out of your head. You hadn't been able to find a woman, you told me, so you took the 2222 exit in Austin and drove west and found this little windy road and the gravel driveway. You told me about driving partway in and parking your old white Mustang with the one brown door." She felt her speech speeding up and couldn't stop it. "You went into the house, you said, the door was open, and you stole a Sony television and a silver bowl and a knife. When you were walking back to your car you saw a small blond woman in a white dress standing in the garage. You shot her and stripped off her clothes and shaved her head so you could have sex with her, but you couldn't do it because she was a blonde and—"

"Wait, wait, wait," he protested. "I know what-all I told you. I shouldn't of." His chains rattled as he tried to lift his hands. When they held him back he shoved his hands down into his lap. "I shouldn't of said it. But it wasn't my fault. You asked me to tell you about it. You kept asking me. I was already convicted and you came here to hear about it, the big one—Tiny McFarland—the one that really interested you. You wouldn't of kept coming if I didn't tell you. It was what you wanted to hear. So I told you. You're to blame, too. 'Cause it was like we told the story together."

He leaned his head forward until it was a bare inch from the wire mesh, so close Molly could smell his sweat and rotting breath. "But it ain't true. I never even saw the bitch. She weren't one of mine. Back then, down in the jail in Hays County, I just said I did it because it was the easiest thing to do. They come in—the sheriff and all them Rangers—and said my car had been seen at this one and sure I done it. She was rich so they paid more attention to that one and there was like this movement that caught me up. It was kind of exciting, like being famous."

He was an effective liar, she conceded to herself. No wonder he could often talk stranded women into his car. "Louie, I don't believe you. What about the jewelry you described, the television, the silver bowl? That wasn't in the paper."

"One of them Rangers, a big one, told me about that. He described the house and all, told me what happened there. I don't recollect his name, but the one with the nose all pushed in like it had got broke more than once."

Molly felt that her body temperature had just gone up several degrees. She wanted to take off her jacket, but she had never wanted to do that in front of Louie.

"But even if he hadn't told me those things," Louie said, "I still could of made a good confession."

"How?" Her voice cracked on the word.

"It's easy. They ask you questions. You know. Like 'Louie, what did you do after you parked your car on the gravel driveway?' And then I know where I'm supposed to have parked. They ask, 'Louie, did you get to the west part of town on 2222 or did you come on such and such?' See, I can figure out almost everything. And I got a real good memory. And when I made a mistake they'd just say, 'Oh, he's done so many women he can't keep all them bitches straight.' "

That's exactly what they did say. Molly sat back on the hard chair and took a breath to try to get rid of the buzz of fear in her brain. This couldn't be true; it was just Louie doing his thing again. "Louie, you disappoint me. I thought you were going to be different from the others. I thought you'd go down owning up to what you did. Remember what you told me—how on death row the men make a big deal about going down tough, not letting the red scream break out? You said you'd never cry and you'd never give in to the red scream. What baloney! Here you are at the last minute suddenly whining you're an innocent man."

His face tightened as though the skin had just shrunk another size and the area around his nose yellowed. "I'm not saying I'm innocent. I'm saying I didn't kill that Tiny McFarland. Not her. And now I'm a real Christian I don't lie no more. You just ask Sister Addie."

She snorted and said, "What kind of fool would believe that?"

He tried to lift his hands again, but remembered about the chain this time before it jerked him back. He let his hands fall back into his lap. "I want to tell the truth and, Molly, I been thinking. There might be a way to prove it."

She felt like putting her hands over her ears; she didn't want to hear any more of this.

He leaned forward so far his bony nose almost pressed against the mesh of his cage. "I think you can prove I didn't do it. Molly, listen. It's about the car. That white Mustang I had, the one with the brown door on the driver side? The one I told 'em I dumped in Lake Worth and got rid of?"

They had dragged the lake for several days but never found the car. It was one of the ragged ends left in this case.

"Those witnesses at the trial—the little girl and the baby-sitter—they said they saw that car at the McFarland house. I never did understand that—little girl like that lying. See, they were lying through their goddamned teeth. They had to be. They had to be. That's why I put them on my witness list. So they could see what they done. Not for revenge. God don't like that. But for them to see and repent." His face was screwed up with an intensity she had never seen in him before.

"Are you listening?" he asked. "This is important. After the Greta Huff thing in Hays County I heard on the TV that they'd connected me and my car to it. So there I was in Forth Worth having a bad moment, I got to admit. Greta, old Greta, she was one of mine —Jesus forgive me—and I did have that car. So what I did, I went and had it painted—see, ordinarily I would have just dumped it somewhere but I was real fond of that car, best car ever, so I had it painted—a real pretty bright blue. Cost me $150 cash money, my last cent in the world. And the next day the damned thing broke down. Radiator burnt out, after all that money I spent on it. Had to junk it."

Louie Bronk lifted his eyes and looked right into Molly's. "Now here's the thing," he said. "That was over the Fourth of July 'cause I remember I took it to the body shop up there in Fort Worth to get painted and they said it'd take four days 'cause it was over the holiday. So I got it back on the sixth and it broke down on the seventh."

Molly was listening hard in spite of herself, caught up in his account. He must have noticed some change in her because he said, "Yes, ma'am, now you got it. Miz McFarland, she was done on July the ninth. There ain't no way in hell those people in Austin seen that car because by then it was blue and it was broke down."

Molly held her hands up to stop him. She felt like he'd been digging a hole in front of her and if she wasn't very careful she would fall right into it. "Louie, stop right there. If you have something like this, you should give it to Tanya Klein, your very able attorney, and let her look into it. That's what she's there for."

"No. Molly, I tried to. When she was here Monday. I tried, but she don't listen. She's not . . . like you say, able. Or maybe she's just not trying. You're the only one who—"

"Louie, you've had eleven years for this. Why do this now, with only three days left?"

His eyes opened in surprise. "Why? I heard on the TV about Charlie McFarland's second wife. Then this morning that baby-sitter. Can't you see? Someone got away with it eleven years ago. And if you get away with doing it once, you're going to do it again— sometime. Like me. Someone's copycatting me, just like they done eleven years ago." He sat up straighter. "Now that just ain't right. Sister Addie, she says you got to do what you can to set things right. She believes me, Molly. She got my statement in the newspaper."

Molly sat up straight in her chair. She was getting damned sick of hearing about Sister Addie. "Louie, I want to be perfectly clear about this so you don't have any false hopes. There is nothing I can do. For you to tell me any more would be pointless." She looked down at her watch. "I'm going to have to leave now, but—"

"You got to do it for me." His whole body tensed.

She shook her head. "No."

"You got to."

In exasperation, she held her palms up in front of her. "What makes you think I got to?"

"Because I know you."

She pressed both clenched hands against her chest. "You *don't* know me!"

"In all them hours we talked and you was asking questions, you don't think it was just you getting to know me, do you?"

Molly looked at him in horror. Suddenly she remembered a quote she'd read somewhere—Nietzsche she thought—something about having to be careful when you deal with monsters because when you look into an abyss, the abyss also looks into you.

She said slowly, emphasizing each word. "Your case is over. If you think I'll do this, then you don't know me." She gathered up her notebook and pen from the table.

Louie leaned so far forward his forehead bumped against the mesh of the cage. Like a shot, the guard started toward the cage. "No," Louie said to him, "it's okay. I just leant too far. Really. I didn't mean nothing."

His eyebrows raised, the guard looked at Molly.

"It's okay," she said.

When the guard took his place back at the door, he kept his eyes fixed on Louie. Louie glanced over at him a few times, then took a deep breath. "Remember when you was coming here all those weeks and I told you about the cross they found in my box, that little gold cross with real diamonds in it?"

"Yes, but, Louie, I don't know what this—"

"Listen. They said I stole it from some woman I killed and I always said no, I didn't, that I bought it to give to my sister Carmen-Marie for taking me on after my parole in Oklahoma, you know, for doing my sister Angela. I wanted to give her something nice. I told you I bought it with cash money from a jewelry store in Corpus. After I told you that, you went down there to Corpus and you went from store to store asking about those little crosses. When you found some stores that sold crosses like that you got them to look back in their records—and at that time it was back nine years—until you found the store that had a record with my name on it. When you came back the next week, you told me about it. Remember? And I asked you how long it had took and you said all week. All week! You spent a whole week doing that," he said with awe in his voice.

"So what, Louie? That's my job. I do lots of boring research like that."

"No. No. It's your . . . the . . . I don't know how to say it. You're like this pit bull bitch I saw fight once down in Laredo.

"Little bit of a thing," he said, rushing on, "but she had these big jaws and she just never let go of nothing once she got her teeth sunk in." He clenched his teeth to illustrate. "She was all ripped up and bloody, guts hanging out, but she still didn't let go. After she was dead, they had to break her jaw with a wrench to get her off the other dog." A smile of pure pleasure had spread over his face as he told the story.

Molly sat back in her chair disgusted by the image he'd drawn in her mind. She'd had enough of this for a lifetime. She was leaving. She started to stand.

"Wait." It was a command, a tone of voice she'd never heard out of him before.

"I ain't finished with the story," he said. "You done all that work for this little bitty thing that don't make no difference to no one. But you done it because it showed something good about me and you wanted to be fair. And I bet you put it in your book, didn't you? See, that's what I learned about you: you're fair and you never let go of nothing you've started on." He nodded his head up and down. "Yes. That's why you'll do this for me. God will provide."

Molly stood, this time making it all the way up. She shook her head decisively. "No. Louie, I hate to disappoint you. God won't provide. I know it's a devil of a hard time for you, but I'm not going to do anything but drive home and get back to work."

She felt like running, but she looked toward the guard and said in the calmest voice she could muster, "I'm ready to leave now."

The guard nodded at her and walked toward the cage.

Molly took a step away, then looked at Louie one last time. His head was drooping on his scrawny neck. "I'm sorry, Louie," she said.

She turned and walked to the door.

Behind her he said, "It's because of the book, isn't it? You're mad about what I said. And you're afraid what I'm saying here is true."

She stopped and turned her head. "No. It's because I *don't* believe you."

As she stepped through the door, she heard him say, "Because it's already wrote down in the book and you can't take the chance of finding out it's wrong. You want to be perfect. Don't want anyone to know you made a mistake. But you did. And like Sister Addie says, you got to face up to your mistakes. You got to admit them and give them over to God. Sister Addie says."

Fuck Sister Addie. Molly set her mouth and walked as fast as she could through the anteroom and out the front door. Her blood was boiling and when she stepped out into the beating sun she felt the heat was equal on the inside and the outside of her skin.

She took a deep breath, struggling to regain some equilibrium. One thing was sure. She'd liked Louie better before he found God.

chapter 15

It's never to late to pick up
the pieces
And find your way to Jesus.
Sister Addie teaches
Preaches
Nothing's too bad for God
to forgive
No matter how wicked you might
live.
She says just lay down your load.
Course she never seen what I left
on the road.

▲ ▼ ▲

LOUIE BRONK
Death Row, Ellis I Unit,
Huntsville, Texas

The manipulative son of a bitch wasn't going to suck her in like
that. No bloody way. God, you could chain him up, lock him in a
cage, and that didn't stop him from trying to control people. Well,
she was not about to get conned into some wild goose chase through
the junkyards of Fort Worth, for God's sake, just to make drama out
of his last days on earth.

Let him rot in hell. Not that she believed in hell. But if there was
anybody in the world who was likely to rot there, it was Louie
Bronk.

Molly approached the first gate and looked up to the top of the
picket for the guard to buzz the gate open. Instead, he came out on
the walkway and leaned over the railing. "Miz Cates," he called
down, "the warden just phoned. Asked if you'd stop by his office
please before you leave."

Puzzled, Molly waved at him and turned around.

This time, she turned right when she entered the prison and

walked down the corridor where the administrative offices were located. She stopped at the third door, the one marked "Warden Steven Demaris." It was open.

The warden sat at his desk talking to a fat woman in a pastel print house dress. She was knitting and the two of them were leaning toward one another, so deeply engrossed in conversation they didn't see Molly at first. When the warden saw her, he got to his feet and came forward to shake Molly's hand. "Thanks for stopping by, Miz Cates. This here"—he gestured to the fat woman—"is Sister Adeline Dodgin."

Molly looked down into the woman's large, placid white face. Of course. Louie's Sister Addie.

Adeline Dodgin smiled up at Molly without dropping a stitch from her knitting, which was something large in brown and pink—a shade of pink so garish it was almost neon.

"Could you sit and visit with us for a minute?" Warden Demaris asked.

Molly glanced at her watch. "I can stay for a minute," she said, feeling bushwhacked.

Sister Addie Dodgin looked up at Molly with the kind of sweet Christian charity smile that always set Molly's teeth on edge. She wore an enormous wooden cross tied around her neck on a braided lanyard. Molly had hated this brand of Christianity ever since she was nine years old and the Baptist women of Lubbock had gone on a campaign to save her soul after her mother died. They dropped in at the ranch regularly to bring tuna casseroles and tell Molly and her daddy they were destined for hellfire sure as Judgment Day if they didn't start coming to church. It wasn't until one of them, who looked a whole lot like this woman here, had suggested that Molly's mother had got cancer and died because none of them ever set foot in church that her daddy threw the woman out and told her never to darken his door again. When they moved to Austin one of the things both father and daughter had relished was the scarcity of Baptists.

It was a bias that had remained with her. She looked down at the woman without returning her smile.

Steve Demaris patted the back of the chair right next to Sister Addie's. "Have a seat," he said.

Molly sat down and watched the warden walk back around the desk. She hadn't seen Demaris in several years, since he'd been promoted from assistant warden to the top job. He used to be a lanky, dashing cowboy, but no more; his body had thickened everywhere, especially around the neck and waist. It seemed that men in law enforcement were compelled to honor a tradition of taking on bulk with increased responsibility.

Demaris sat in his chair and tilted it back until it bumped the wall. "Miz Cates, I've been wondering since your call on Wednesday what's going on over there in Austin. Do they have a suspect in this new McFarland killing?"

"Not that I know of," she said.

He clucked his lips. "Well, too bad. What a sad business—Mr. McFarland having something like that happen twice." He studied Molly for a few seconds, then said with the attempt of a smile, "Are you here on business today, Miz Cates? Maybe fixing to write some bad things about us in that liberal magazine of yours?"

Molly smiled at him. "You know better than that, Warden. For you, and the work you do here, I have nothing but the deepest respect. You do a difficult job in a very professional way, and I admire that." She meant it and watched his face to see if he accepted it.

His ruddy face deepened in color. "But that's not going to stop you from writing about how we're guilty of killing all these poor misunderstood boys like your Mr. Bronk, is it?"

"Mr. Demaris, you've got the job of carrying out the policies of the state. It's not you I have a quarrel with."

"But I support the state policy. You liberals, you're always saying we need to do away with capital punishment and have life without parole instead. That's because you've never put yourself on the line working in a prison." He brought his chair back to the floor. "A guy like Bronk—you get him in here on a life term, he's got nothing to lose. He rapes other inmates, attacks my officers. The only safe way is to keep him locked down twenty-four hours a day, and the courts don't allow us to do that." He slapped his palms down on the desk. "No. If you got someone so dangerous he needs to be locked up for the next fifty years it's better to kill him." He shifted his gaze to Sister Addie. "Sorry, Addie. You may see me as guilty of butchery, but that's the hard truth of it."

Molly was sorry she didn't have her tape recorder along. The warden would be a good interview for her Bronk article. She said, "You're no more guilty than Miz Dodgin and I are as citizens."

The woman turned to face Molly. "Please call me Sister Addie," she said. "Everybody around here does."

In a pig's eye I will, Molly thought, barely able to meet the woman's gaze.

"How was your visitation?" Steve Demaris asked.

"Oh, it was vintage Louie Bronk. He's denying the McFarland murder now. Trying to work his con on anyone who'll believe it."

"So I heard," he said. "Now, I'm inclined to your way of thinking, but Sister Addie here, she sees this one different. She wondered if she could have a word in private with you?"

So that was it! Well, she was trapped now, but since she was, the situation had certain interview possibilities. She looked directly into the large woman's faded blue eyes. "Certainly, Miz Dodgin. I'm doing a story on Louie for my magazine and I'd like to ask you some questions, too. I hear you've been a big influence in his life lately."

The warden got to his feet. "You ladies can talk right here; I've got some duties to attend to. Can I get Ginger to bring you a cup of coffee or a soda?"

"Oh, you know me, Steven," Addie Dodgin said, still knitting steadily. "I surely would enjoy a Co-cola."

"Miz Cates?"

"No. No thanks," Molly said.

As he left, Molly could hear him asking his secretary to fetch a Coke for Sister Addie.

Molly rested her notebook on her lap, pulled her pen from her jacket pocket, and watched Addie Dodgin take a handkerchief from her pocket and wipe her damp face with it. Molly had once thought of doing a story on the women who took an unusual interest in prisoners—sort of criminal groupies. Some of them just became pen pals with inmates or visited them regularly. Others went so far as to marry them, even men on death row. Yes, it might make an interesting story. And this might be just the one to start with; how on earth did this woman with her graying tight-permed hair and her doughy face ever get hooked up with Louie Bronk?

"It was Thanksgiving two years ago when I was making my rounds," the woman said, resuming her knitting.

"What?"

"The way I got involved with Brother Louie," Addie Dodgin said, looking Molly square in the eye.

"Oh."

"Yes. I was delivering Bibles from my Sunday school in Waco like I always do before holidays—holidays are such a lonely time for these men—and he was huddled in the corner of his cell looking like a miserable sack of meal. I said, 'Brother, have you heard the word of God that echoes through these halls like trumpets?' " She smiled and seemed to be recollecting the moment with pleasure. "In that thin voice of his he says, 'All I hear is punks jerking off and taking craps.' " Adeline Dodgin grinned, showing tiny, pearl-white, baby-like teeth. "And I said, 'Then you *have* heard the voice of God, brother.' "

Almost against her will, Molly found herself returning the smile.

"I asked him if he'd like a Bible. He said he wasn't much of a reader and I said it would be my pleasure to come read it to him. That's how it started. It was a month or so after you finished your talks with him and he missed the attention, I think."

Molly didn't know what was happening to her. The backs of her eyes got hot as if she were going to cry. Ridiculous. This emotional seesaw must be a delayed reaction to the scene with Louie.

The door opened and a young woman entered with a can of Coke on a plastic tray.

"Thanks, Ginger, honey," Addie said, reaching up to take the tray. As she turned her head, Molly could see snaking down the left side of her neck, from the earlobe down the side of the neck and disappearing into her dress, a long scar, raised and red. It was the kind of scar Molly had seen before—on gang members who had been in knife fights.

Ginger stopped and rumpled the fat woman's hair on her way out.

"Nothing like a cold can of Co-cola in this heat," Addie murmured, turning back to Molly and taking a long drink. "Louie's talked a lot about you, Miz Cates."

"Oh?" The idea of Louie discussing her had never occurred to her. Now that it did, the thought made her very uneasy.

"My, yes. He says some nice things about you—that you're a real handsome-looking woman, and you listen good. Louie says you've treated him fair and that you have the stick-to-it-iveness of a pit bull." She set the can down on the desk and smiled at Molly. "He also says you hide your feelings real good."

"What did he mean by that?"

"He didn't say, but I suppose he means that the disgust you feel for him is almost imperceptible."

Molly was stunned; she didn't know if it was because of the woman's use of the word "imperceptible" or her insight into Molly's feelings. The disgust was certainly there. But who could hear those things without disgust? Who could look at Louie without feeling it? It was impossible.

"It's hard, I know," Addie Dodgin said, "to separate the man and his immortal soul from his hateful acts."

"Can you?" Molly asked in a more challenging and aggressive tone than she'd intended.

The only sound in the room was the click of knitting needles. "Sometimes," Addie said finally. "I think I'm getting better at remembering that we are—all of us—forgiven."

"Well," Molly said, "that's something I'll leave to you. But I've spent twenty years interviewing criminal offenders, Miz Dodgin, and I've always before been able to see our common humanity. Louie is the first one I haven't been able to . . ." Unable to finish the sentence, she let it trail off.

Addie chuckled. "Louie is a challenge."

Molly leaned forward. "But how can you stand it?" she said. "You've seen the phoniness just like I have—how when their parole hearing gets near, or a court appearance, they all miraculously find God. It's such hypocrisy. Like Louie now. Surely you aren't taken in by his so-called conversion."

Addie Dodgin smiled and Molly suddenly realized that it wasn't one of those Christian charity smiles at all; it was a smile that contained a lot more knowing irony than sweetness. "Of course, they do it for reasons of their own. They pretend at first, but it doesn't matter."

"Doesn't matter!"

"No. Not at all. The reason they begin talking with God is not important; at least they are going through the motions, learning the words. And when the time comes that they need the words, they have them. Then it becomes real. Very real."

Molly thought about Louie on Monday getting ready for the executioner, being strapped down on the gurney.

"The nearness of death can work wonders," Sister Addie said. "On the last day, when they're taken from here to the holding cell over at the Walls—that awful, melancholy place next to the death chamber—and when the jailers ask them if they've made provision for their possessions and for the disposal of their body, then the words become real right quick, even if they haven't been before. And they usually die well—real well."

Molly was silent for a minute before remembering that she was trying to interview this woman. "You stay with them at the end?" she asked.

"When they're particular friends of mine, like Louie, the chaplain usually asks me to keep them company and pray with them that last hard day."

"Is it true that they usually admit to the crime then?"

"Oh, yes. They talk freely then. When the appeals are done and there's nothing left to lose, when they know for sure they're going to die."

"But Louie seems to be an exception to the rule. He's waited to the end to start proclaiming his innocence."

"That's one of the reasons I believe him."

Molly shook her head; she didn't want to hear the other reasons. "How on earth did you manage to get his statement picked up by the Associated Press?" she asked.

Sister Addie put her head back and laughed a rumbling, deep laugh. "That's another story. I won't bore you with it. But Jim Ledbetter, the AP writer in the Dallas bureau, is a dear ol' boy who was on the board of Amnesty International when I was. He believed I once did him a good turn and that he owed me one." She laughed again. "Now I owe him a couple. The eternal favor bank, huh, Miz Cates? I'm afraid it'll be like that even in heaven, should we be lucky enough to get there."

Addie's expression turned serious. "Did you agree to do what Louie wanted you to do?" she asked.

Molly sat back and her pen rolled off her lap onto the floor. She looked down at it where it came to rest near her left foot. This woman had a hell of a nerve. She didn't have to answer a question like that. She leaned over and picked up the pen.

After she straightened up, she said, "No."

Addie Dodgin nodded sympathetically. "It's hard with Louie because every time you do something for him, you know he thinks it's because he finagled you into doing it, rather than you doing it of your own God-given free will." She shook her head. "Makes you want to close up and give nothing. I think he's been inspiring that in people all his life." She took another long sip from the can. "All his life."

"I think he's lying," Molly said.

Addie chuckled. "It's the only thing he's good at."

"That and killing," Molly said. "He used to be good at killing."

Addie nodded. "Quick with a knife, our Louie. I agree with you on the death penalty. I'm dead set against it, too."

Molly remembered that she should be taking notes and opened her notebook. "Why?"

"Oh." Addie heaved a sigh that made the cross resting on her huge bosom rise and fall dramatically. "Each one of us has a life to work out in some special, individual way. To interfere with that cuts off the process. Like Louie. I don't know if you could see it today, but he is in his own way working on his issues and it ripples out to you and me. It's like letting the snail darter, or those blind slugs, go extinct—we don't know how exactly, but its absence will have an effect on us."

Molly let her head rest back on the chair and closed her eyes for a second. She had a sudden urge to tell this woman about the master poet, about her fears, and her vigils. When she looked up, Addie was studying her. "Miz Cates—"

"What?"

The big woman let out a long sigh. "You ever know something that defies all reason and proof, but you know it anyway? Something if you say it out loud will make you sound all preachy and melodramatic?"

Molly remembered the night her father died. She had been certain there was bad trouble waiting for him and had begged him to stay home. "Yes."

"Well, I know something like that and I'm afraid if I tell it to you, you'll call me a Bible-thumping busybody, which I am of course, and walk off; but if I don't tell it to you, I'm not going to have a moment's peace."

Unable to resist any longer, Molly smiled at her. "Then you better tell me, Sister Addie."

Addie sighed, put her knitting down, and pulled her handkerchief out of her pocket. With a grin, she said, "Well, Sister Molly, I don't even know the details of what Louie wants you to do for him." Slowly she wiped her face and neck and tucked the handkerchief back into the pocket. "But I know this: if you don't do it, you will lose your soul."

Molly was breathless with the shock. It sounded so . . . medieval. "Lose my soul? What is this? Some sort of curse if you refuse a dying man's request?"

"We're all of us dying, sister; Louie just knows his date."

"But what do you mean 'lose my soul'?" Molly asked. "That's not something I even believe in. I—you see I—" She found herself sputtering.

Sister Addie Dodgin sat with her hands clasped in her lap. "Sorry. That was a negative way to put it and I fall into a sort of shorthand religion talk sometimes. What I mean is that agreeing to do it, saying 'yes' to him, will give you more abundant life. I feel this about you— that you're at a big decision-making time."

Molly tried to laugh, but the sound emerged more as a wail. "Sister Addie, this is ridiculous. What Louie wants me to do is go look for a car that he says was junked in Fort Worth eleven years ago. Even if it's still there, which is so unlikely I can't count high enough to tell you the odds against it, it's not going to matter. It isn't going to save him from dying."

"No," Addie said slowly, "it probably won't save him from dying."

"It would be a waste of time," Molly continued. "A wild goose chase."

Addie shrugged. "Maybe."

"Well, then. Why should I do it?" Molly asked.

Addie shrugged again. "I told you there was nothing logical about this. I think you should do it because Louie expects you to, and in all his forty-eight years he hasn't had many expectations that got met." She picked up the can of Coke and drained it. "It is mighty hot in here," she said, pulling out her handkerchief again. "Mighty hot. I do believe the temperature in this place is adequate to keep me from a life of crime."

Addie pushed up out of her chair and said, "No rest for the wicked. I've got my rounds to do. Thanks for hearing me, sister."

Molly stood and said, "Thanks for telling me what was on your mind, Sister Addie. I'll think on it."

Addie Dodgin folded the long piece of brown and pink knitting and tucked it into her huge plastic handbag. From the bag she pulled out a card which she held out to Molly. "In case you'd like to chat again sometime," she said.

Molly took the card.

Addie hefted her bag up and slipped the strap over her shoulder. "They let me have a handbag because that's how I carry my Bibles."

As Addie trudged out the door, Molly glanced down at the card. It read: *"Sister Adeline Dodgin, Texas Prison Ministries, 121 Pecos Street, Waco, Texas, 817-555-9080.* WE ARE FORGIVEN."

Molly sighed, sat back down, and closed her eyes.

When the warden returned ten minutes later she was still sitting there with her eyes closed. She opened them and looked at Steven Demaris, who was staring down at her. "I'd like to talk to Louie Bronk again," she said.

Molly sat in the same chair in the visitors' room for about twenty minutes before the same two guards brought Louie back in and locked him in the cage. This time without a word, the same guard stationed himself at the door and stood watching.

When Molly saw Louie's thin lips twist up slightly into that knowing smirk, she felt like walking right out and being done with it, whether she lost her soul or not. But instead she picked up her pen. "Okay, Louie, tell me about the car."

"Good golly, Miss Molly. You came back. Right on track."

"I'm a jerk. Let's get to work," she said. The rhyme was unintentional.

For the first time since she'd known him, Louie laughed. It was a creaky, thin sound, but a genuine laugh nonetheless and Molly felt terrifically pleased with herself. She'd made Louie Bronk laugh. And without shedding blood. Or maybe this was Sister Addie's work— maybe the woman was converting him into a real human being.

"It's a Ford Mustang. You already know that. 'Seventy-two model, two-door, of course, hardtop, notchback."

"What does notchback mean?" she asked as she wrote in her notebook.

He looked at her with his skinny eyes as wide open as they would go. "You don't know nothing about cars?"

"I can drive. That's about it."

"Well, notchback means it's got a trunk, not a hatchback like lots of Mustangs."

She wrote it down.

"Before I had it painted blue, it was white," he said. "With grabber blue stripes down the hood."

"Grabber blue?"

"Yeah. This bright blue Ford came out with in the trim packages for the Mustang. My favorite color. The color I had it painted all over was like that—real bright blue—electric blue, you might call it."

"And before you had it painted, when the car was still white, one of the doors was brown?" she asked.

His smile faded. "Yeah. The driver's side. It was a repair that was did before I bought it. You'd of thought they would of painted it, but some people don't care."

"Louie, didn't you worry about driving a car that would be so easy to spot—a white car with a brown door?"

His face narrowed in displeasure. "No. I told you lots of times—I never thought about doing them things until they happened. They wasn't planned out."

She nodded. He'd always said that but she'd never believed it. She still didn't. "But when you found out the police were looking for a car like that, then you worried about it?"

"Sure. That's different."

"Okay. What else might help me recognize it?"

"I don't remember the vehicle identification number. Wish I did, but it had a 351 Cleveland engine, vee-eight, air-conditioning that worked, automatic floor shift."

Molly wrote it down. "Louie, if that car's still in the wrecking yard, the engine and some other parts of it are probably gone. What do you remember about it that would make it different, distinctive?"

"You mean other than being blue painted over white? You ain't gonna find many others like that. . . . It had a decal on the rear bumper that was there when I bought it—said some radio station,

KBJM or some such. Oh. And the passenger door was rigged not to open from the inside."

Molly's breath caught with a little clicking noise as she wrote it down. He'd never mentioned that before. It would have been a good detail for the book.

"I guess I forgot to tell you that before," he said.

"Mmmm," she said. "What else?"

"On the back seat there'd be some spots. Blood, you know."

Molly nodded impassively. "A lot of it?"

"Right much. The vinyl part of the seat I could wipe off, but most of it was this fabric that just wouldn't clean up. It had got kind of smelly and drew flies for a while, I recollect."

Molly nodded again as if he were telling her about spilling coffee on the rug. Talking with Louie had always seemed to her like being down a rabbit hole in some X-rated wonderland where doors rigged not to open and bloodstains that spoiled the upholstery were matter-of-fact, everyday subjects.

When she looked up, Louie was saying "—off of this lot in El Paso for three hundred. It was in 1981, so I had it for about a year. Best car I ever had. Never no trouble; all it required was just the littlest attention. I put more'n sixty thousand miles on it. When I junked it, it had almost a hundred and fifty thousand."

Molly looked over her notes. "All right, Louie. Now tell me how I can find the wrecking yard in Fort Worth where you sold it."

He let out a breath. "Okay. Now I'm not exactly sure of the name —something-something-auto parts, but it was on Rosedale near 820 and there was a sign that said 'Bring your own tools'—I remember that—and it was run by a big nigger with only one hand. He weren't the owner, just ran the place. He's the one who towed my car in and gave me seventy-five cash for it."

"How far from 820?" she asked, writing fast.

"No more than a mile. Toward Fort Worth, that's west."

"Which side of the street?"

"Uh—" His hands moved slightly and finally the right one pulled out to the limit of the chain. "Right side when you're going toward Dallas. It's a large place, more'n twenty acres, I think. Coupla real mean dogs there, too. Thievery's a problem in them wrecking yards you know. Dogs is the only protection at night. And that's a real bad area, Molly. You watch it."

Rabbit hole time again, she thought: Louie Bronk worrying about the criminal element.

"Okay, now, Louie. Let's think about this. Suppose I get lucky and find the car. There's not much chance of it after all this time—that yard is probably a shopping mall by now—but if I do, it won't do us any good unless we can establish the exact date you had it painted and junked. Now I don't think these places keep good records. What do you think?"

"Not the wrecking yard. But the place I had the car painted, this auto body place on Mansfield Highway, it was a high-class operation. They might still have records going back to then. The Fourth was on a Saturday and I took it in two days before that hoping I could have it back by the Fourth to take some friends to the fireworks, but it was real humid and they said it would take a few days to dry so I couldn't get it back until Monday. That was the sixth. So I picked it up then and it was blue. Wouldn't that show my car wasn't at Austin July ninth? Wouldn't it?"

"It might. Tell me everything you can remember about the painting place."

"Well, now. I don't rightly remember the name—but it was right on Mansfield Highway in the south part of the city—a mostly nigger area. There was a man's name, you know, like Jim's Auto Body or Mike's, something like that, and it was right near the city limits, where Mansfield and Loop 20 come together."

Molly was writing it down. "What did it look like and which side of the road was it on?"

"Going south it was on the left." His chains rattled because he had to use his hands to give directions. "I don't remember much about what it looked like, but it was real close to the road and you could park off to one side. It had a big sign and the sign said the name and that they had the best prices on body painting. And they did, too, because I got estimates different places. It was run by a man, the man whose name was in the sign—Bob or whatever."

Molly finished writing and looked up. "Okay. Anything else?"

"Oh, yeah. The name I used was 'L. Bronson.' " He paused, seeming out of breath after all the talking. Then he said, "Molly, are you going to do this like you did them crosses?"

"What do you mean?"

"I mean are you going to *work* at it?"

She looked at him and smiled. "You have to ask that of a pit bull bitch like me?"

He laughed again, and again she felt the pleasure of it.

"But, Louie," she said, "we need to talk about this. Even if it turned out—God knows how—that I could prove you got the car back on the sixth of July, painted blue, and junked it on the seventh, I don't know that it would make a damn bit of difference for you."

His face tightened. "Now you sound like that lawyer bitch. 'It's not about actual innocence, Louie,' she says, 'it's about mistakes in legal procedure, violations of your rights during the trial.'"

"Tanya knows the law," Molly said.

"Can't the governor give . . ." he struggled for the word, "you know."

"Reprieves? Pardons?" Molly sighed. "That's unlikely, Louie. She's committed to capital punishment."

"I know. But you could try."

"Let's see what happens here. But, Louie—"

"What?"

"Don't count on this. Make your peace. Get ready."

He exhaled hard through his nose. "That's what Sister Addie says, too."

"I'd listen to her," Molly said, standing up and looking at her watch. "It's almost five now. I'll fly to Fort Worth tomorrow and start looking."

She sat back down. "Louie, who else have you told this to?"

He shrugged. "Just Tanya and you. And Sister Addie. I tell her everything."

Molly stood and nodded to the guard.

As the guard took a step in his direction, Louie turned his head and watched his approach with the intensity of a batter watching a pitch cross the plate. The cords in his neck stood out like snakes and his eyes from the side looked as still as marbles. It occurred to Molly for the first time that she'd never once seen Louie blink.

chapter *16*

The kid was always black and blue
Scared to death and hungry too.
That's too bad, the teacher said.
Just be glad that you ain't dead.

So he learnt at home and school
The hunter's special Golden Rule:
In this world some blood will spill.
Make damn sure you're not the kill.

LOUIE BRONK
Death Row, Ellis I Unit,
Huntsville, Texas

▲　▼　▲

It was after nine o'clock and almost dark. The last fifty miles of the drive home Molly had felt like a horse galloping back to the stable; all she wanted was to get home, soak in the bathtub, and climb into bed with the stack of mail-order catalogues she'd been saving. The absolute last thing she wanted to do was what she'd promised herself she *would* do: sit down and work at her computer. Maybe it was age creeping up on her; she used to make this trip all the time and then work half the night.

She pulled up to her mailbox. Inside was a neat stack of mail bound with a rubber band. On top was a note written on a piece of lined paper torn from a spiral notebook. She drove into the garage and read the note by the overhead light.

"I've got some news. Call me if you feel like dinner or if you don't feel like dinner. Grady."

Molly paged through the mail and since nothing looked like a check or good news, she carried it into the house and dumped it on the table. She didn't feel like dinner or calling Grady. It could wait. She opened the refrigerator door and the icy blast felt so good she just stood there for a while, leaning over with her forehead resting

against the freezer door, surveying the meager contents—sliced turkey, bread, some beer, and a few shriveled tomatoes.

Finally she grabbed a Coors Light, popped it open, and took it
with her to her office.

She stopped in the doorway and looked into the dark room in
which she spent so much of her life sitting alone at the keyboard.
She sipped the beer and watched the red light on her answering
machine flickering in the darkness and the eerie bluish toasters flying across her computer screen. Since she always left the computer
switched on, she used a program that darkened the screen after five
minutes of no use. Tonight it was displaying her favorite screen-
saver—winged toasters flapping across the blackened background,
with an occasional piece of toast whizzing by. Talk about rabbit
holes, she thought. This, right here, might be the strangest rabbit
hole of all—a place where toasters flew and voices resided inside a
box, a place where she spent her days alone writing what was called
"true crime," but some of it was not true.

Maybe none of it was true.

Without turning on the light, she sat down at the keyboard. For
the first time, sitting at her desk, watching the toasters wing their
way across the screen, she admitted it to herself: it was possible, it
was just possible, that Louie didn't murder Tiny McFarland. Liar
though he was, he'd been pretty damned convincing. And Addie
Dodgin, who was nobody's fool, believed him.

It was possible.

And if Louie didn't do it, then *Sweating Blood* was largely fiction.
If Louie didn't do it, then David Serrano and Alison McFarland
must have been wrong or lying about seeing that car. If Louie didn't
do it, he was about to die for the one crime he did not commit. If
Louie didn't do it, then who the hell did?

The trip to Fort Worth tomorrow was unlikely to produce anything. But now the doubt was planted in her mind. She knew from
experience that, once planted, it was lodged there forever. Maybe it
would turn out just like the first crime she ever researched—Vernon
Cates's murder. She'd worked night and day, followed every lead,
however tenuous, and she'd gotten nowhere. That was the worst
outcome of all—not to know.

She straightened up in the chair and tapped the space bar to wake
up the computer. Time to get to work. If she wrote the Bronk story

well enough, Richard would not be able to resist it. But how was she going to write it? This morning it was all perfectly clear. Now she just didn't know what the story was.

She called up a new document with two key strokes. There on her full-page monitor was the computer version of the writer's dreaded blank page—all backlit and ready to go. She typed two question marks so the screen wouldn't look so empty, then stared at them and the blinking cursor.

She could go ahead doggedly and write the story she'd intended all along: after ten years on death row a notorious serial killer finally receives society's ultimate punishment. She'd describe his last words, the death chamber, the injection, the witnesses, the different reactions of everyone involved. Poignant interviews with the victim's family, with law enforcement officials, and with a woman who befriended him in prison. Everybody with a different slant on capital punishment. A good story, one she'd been thinking about for years —the appropriate end to the Louie Bronk saga. That story she could write half-asleep.

Or she could write the story of a writer who spent eleven years covering a serial killer and writing a book about him. Then, only days before the killer is to be executed, the writer discovers that the crime for which he has received a death sentence—the crime that was the focus of her book—was not committed by him. A story of delusion and failure. Yes, that could make a story, but she hoped to hell it wasn't true.

Or she could write the story of a family—a rich and powerful dysfunctional family—that was shattered by a random act of violence. The twist comes when years later it turns out that the family may have lied and is sheltering a killer. A real murder mystery, that story.

Or she could write the inspirational story of a woman who befriended a doomed killer, who accepted him as no one else had ever done, and converted him to humanity as well as to Christianity. Just in time for his date with death. The story of Addie Dodgin might make interesting reading.

Or—Lord, she was too tired to deal with all this uncertainty.

She needed a bath and some serious sleep. She sat back in her chair and stretched her arms out in front of her, curving her back, which ached from the drive. It was too hard. She couldn't do it right now. Richard Dutton was going to have to wait another day for the proposal, though this would be the first time in the eight years she'd worked for him that she hadn't delivered what she promised right on time.

As she stood, the phone rang. She looked down at it and thought about letting the answering machine take it. But she lost patience and picked up before the end of the third ring.

The voice over the line said: "Yup. She was one of mine, sure was. See, I can have any woman I want. Any woman. She was there at this big, fancy house, all dressed in white, not a spot on her anywhere, carrying a bunch of flowers she'd picked. Yup. Just as easy to do the rich ones as them you pick up by the side of the road. Ain't no difference when you get down to the basics."

Molly let out a long breath. "Grady. Don't do that. You're reading right from his confession, dammit."

"His very words, as quoted in your book. Just in case you find yourself softening toward him here in the final hours."

"I'm not softening. Far from it. But—"

"But what?" he asked.

"Tell me your news first. Then I'll tell you mine."

"Okay. This is news of the bad variety. If I had any good news to go along with it, I'd ask which you wanted to hear first, but since I don't, here it is: you got another note from your pen pal, and it's pretty ugly."

Molly braced herself by leaning her hip hard against the desk. "Read it to me."

"Okay. By the way, it was stuck to some more pages from your book, thirteen pages this time. Candice Hargrave." Molly pictured the autopsy photos of the willowy dark-haired teenager with her slender throat slit so deep her head was nearly severed.

Grady read in a monotone:

"Lady writer, here's my rhyme:
I can find you anytime.

You may think that you can stay
All detached, above the fray.

If you think life's like a book
Better take a second look.

You're a cinch—an easy mark,
your eyes wide open in the dark.

So as you witness Louie's death,
Think about your own last breath.

Tell me this, since you know it all—
when will the master poet call?

Molly's breath stuck in her throat. It was fear, the hot, raw, abject kind that made her want to cower in a corner. She hated it. She leaned over the desk to switch on the lamp, but stopped herself and straightened up. She was not going to give in. "Well, the verse may be improving a little," she said. "Eyes wide open in the dark—that's pretty good. I wonder how he knows."

"Molly, I've got a patrol car passing your house every half hour. If I weren't on tonight, I'd come stay with you."

"You're assuming I'd let you."

"Just for protective purposes, of course."

"Protective! You—the worst shot in the history of the Austin Police Department."

"I qualified once again this year," he said. "Now tell me what you started to say before, about Louie Bronk."

"Grady, it may just be that I'm tired, but—" She looked down at the computer screen, blank except for the two question marks. "I'm worried. There may have been a big mistake."

There was a silence over the line. Then he said in his take-charge, official voice, "I want to hear everything, absolutely everything."

"Hold on a minute." Molly carried the cordless phone with her to the small sofa. She leaned over and repositioned the pillows so one would be under her knees and another under her neck. Then she lay down and wedged the phone between the pillow and her ear. Sometimes it was better to talk about difficult subjects lying down; the change in posture sort of tilted the world so you could get a different angle on things.

"Okay," she said. "I just wanted to get comfortable."

Then she told him everything—beginning with Louie's claim of innocence and ending with her reluctant promise to him to apply her pit bull nature to the fullest in Fort Worth. As she talked, she pictured the man at the other end of the line—listening intensely the way he did, nodding his head and encouraging her to go on. Talking with Grady Traynor, she remembered, had always been easy: he really listened and was willing to play with the possibilities.

"So," she said, "here I am in my dark office trying to write my boss a proposal for the final Louie Bronk story. But I can't do it because I don't know what the story is."

"Molly," Grady said, "if you really think there's a chance this story of Bronk's could be true, it has repercussions for our two murders. It would take some doing, but I could justify calling Fort Worth right now and asking them to send some uniforms out to look for the car in the morning."

Molly thought about it. Then she could sleep late and stay at home all morning drinking coffee and writing the proposal. But no. She could do this better than some bored cop. And she'd promised Louie. Experience had shown her time and time again that it was better to do things herself.

"Thanks, Grady, but I better do it myself."

"I wish you wouldn't."

"Well, I need to. I promised."

"Molly, I don't think it's safe. Let me take care of it."

"No. And I wouldn't have told you if I thought you'd bully me."

"Well, how about this? I could send someone up there with you, or get you an escort in Fort Worth, a cop who knows that area, just to drive you around."

"No. Thanks."

"Still the loner," he said.

"I've never been worth a damn at delegating."

"Or at teamwork."

She sighed. "Or at teamwork."

"Will you call me from Fort Worth?"

"Okay."

"No matter what?"

"Yes."

"Molly, the more I get into it, the more I wonder about Charlie and that earlier murder. Did you know that Tiny McFarland was the one who had the money in the family and Charlie inherited millions from her? Up till then he'd been small potatoes. It was the bucks he inherited from her that allowed him to build a big business."

"Of course I knew that. It was all in my book."

"Oh, yeah," he said. "That's where I got it actually."

She thought for a minute and said, "Since I owe you some info, here's a gift that fits right into your theory. I bet you didn't know that Tiny slept around. Alison says her mother was chronically unfaithful. That was not in the book because I didn't know it until yesterday."

"No. I didn't know that. Thanks for telling me. But that was not the case with Georgia; everyone agrees it was a loving marriage, that they were devoted to one another. And faithful—that does happen occasionally, you know."

"Have you got anything back on David Serrano?" she asked, ignoring the barb.

"The ME thinks he preceded Georgia McFarland in death by about five or six hours, but it's just an estimate. He was killed with his own .38 caliber Smith & Wesson, registered to him. Not a print anywhere on it. Definitely not the same weapon that killed Georgia."

"What about your inquiries down in Brownsville?"

"Interesting. Makes me doubt my initial theory about Serrano. He's got no record. Matter of fact, he was a leading citizen. Very rich. But it came from legitimate business—funeral homes, just like he told you. He had a license for the gun. They'd had some bad business at one of his operations, so he took a security guard course and got a license."

"You working on a new theory?" she asked.

"Always." He yawned into the phone. "But let's talk about something else for a change. You said you're in your dark office. It sounds like you're lying down. Are you?"

"Uh-huh," she said, letting her head fall back onto the pillow.

"Are you dressed?" he asked, lowering his voice.

She smiled. "I should have realized by the way you started out that this was going to be an obscene phone call."

"What a good idea. From what I hear, the way it's done is for me to tell you in vivid detail what I'd like to do to you. Should I do that, Molly?"

She hesitated; there was no question where all this was going to end up if she didn't stop it now. It would be a big mistake to encourage him.

"All right," she said. "Tell me."

"I'd start by finishing the headache cure I began the other night.

You know how I hate to leave things unfinished. And a thorough headache cure neglects no part of the body. But I'd want you to get all comfortable first, out of your binding clothes and into a nice loose T-shirt like you used to wear to bed."

"I still do," she said.

"Mmmmm. White ones you can see through?"

"Sometimes."

"Good. Then we'd put on some nice slow dance music. Something from the old days—Johnny Mathis or Sinatra. Remember how slow we used to dance, Molly?" His voice had dropped even lower, to a growl. "I know you're tired, so while we dance you could lean against me, and I'd start pressing nice and firm with my thumbs all the way down your spine so that—"

Molly's fax machine rang once and then began its shrill electronic buzzing.

"What's that?" he asked.

"Just my fax."

"Well, we'd certainly turn that damn thing off first," he said. "Anyway, then I'd—" He stopped talking into the phone; Molly could hear several men's voices at his end. Then he spoke into the phone again. "I wish I could come show you now but I'm working and my chief is right here. Unfortunately, he's a man who doesn't understand spontaneity. How about tomorrow?"

"If I'm back from Fort Worth."

"Call me. I can see I need some more practice on this obscene calling business. And, Molly, please, please be careful."

After they hung up she lay in the dark for a while thinking about dancing with Grady Traynor and wondering how the years had slipped away without her noticing.

Then she got up and walked over to the fax machine. A single curled-up sheet on her agent's familiar letterhead had slid out. It said, "Sorry to be the bearer of bad news, but the Japanese are withdrawing the offer for translation rights to *Sweating Blood.* They say the *New York Times* article today made them nervous and they are going to pass it up. Best, Jonathan."

Twenty thousand down the drain. Damn.

She let the paper fall to the floor. She didn't have the heart or energy for a reply right now. It could wait until she got back from Fort Worth.

On her way to bed, she stopped at the foot of the stairs, turned, and did something she'd never done before. She checked the front door and then the back one, even though she was certain she'd already locked and bolted them.

The next morning Molly caught the eight o'clock Southwest flight to the Dallas-Fort Worth airport. A forty-minute flight, it just gave her enough time to drink two cups of coffee and speculate about how she might get the magazine to pick up the expense of her airfare and car rental. Just before they landed, she glanced over the *New York Times.* At least there was nothing more about Louie Bronk.

The Budget Rent A Car smelled like someone had thrown up in it not too long ago, but she didn't want to take the time to exchange it, so she rolled down the window and turned the air-conditioning on high.

She put on her sunglasses, glanced down at her map, and drove south out of the immense airport complex, resigned to a long haul. She remembered other trips to the Dallas area when she'd felt she'd been caught in one of Dante's circles of hell, condemned to driving for all eternity. The metropolitan area was huge, endless, even by Texas standards.

She drove west toward Fort Worth, then south on 820, delighted with the sparse traffic of a Saturday morning. She spotted her exit after only thirty minutes. That could be a good omen for the day.

The first order of business was to find the junkyard Louie had described, if it still existed—if it ever had existed—and then search for the car itself. Preferably before it got much hotter; it was already humid and eighty-four degrees at quarter to ten and climbing for the nineties. Then, whether she found anything or not, she'd try the auto painting places in the area Louie had described. She hoped to be finished in time for a late lunch someplace with excellent air-conditioning and a menu that had things like pasta and steamed vegetables. And wine. Yes, it was Saturday. Wine was a fine idea, a reward for going through the motions on this.

She turned off the highway at the Rosedale exit. With a sinking heart she surveyed the decaying, graffitied warehouses, the clusters of black teenagers hanging out in garbage-strewn alleys, the weedy parking lots, and cracked curbs. Well, if you had to pick the most appropriate place in the world for a serial killer to junk an old bloodstained car, it would be this very area of Fort Worth.

The stretch of Rosedale just west of the highway seemed to be devoted to the seriously disabled automobile—wrecking yards, auto body shops, service stations, used car lots. The shiny new cars sold and driven in the downtown area must get banished out here to the perimeter for their old age and death.

She drove for a few miles, then turned around and slowly headed back toward the highway, studying the possibilities on the right side of the road. They all started with "A"—ABC Auto Salvage, A-One Auto Parts, Aaron's Automotive Recycling Center. The one closest to the highway was All Okay Body Parts. That fit the name pattern Louie remembered and it was close to the highway. She'd start there.

She pulled up to a tin shack that seemed to be the office. A hand-lettered sign said "NO TITLE. NO PROBLEM. NO MINORS." Two cars and a truck in various stages of cannibalization rested on their axles near the door. The truck looked as if the entire front end had been amputated by a gigantic saw and one of the cars, a little red compact, was so crumpled it was barely recognizable as a car. Anyone inside would have been pulverized.

When she entered the office, two men in overalls looked up at her from where they were squatting on the floor unpacking some boxes behind the wooden counter. "H'ep you, ma'am?" the younger one said, standing and dusting his hands on the sides of his overalls.

Until this second Molly wasn't sure how she would play this. On an impulse she decided to start out as a customer, rather than a journalist.

"I hope so." She pushed her sunglasses up on top of her head. "I'm looking for a '72 Mustang hardtop."

"What parts?"

"Any parts you have. I particularly want a 351 Cleveland engine and doors and a notchback trunk. But I'd like to look at any Mustangs you have from before '75."

The man looked at her with his eyebrows raised. "Well, let me think. I know we got a old blue Mustang out there, way back in the old part of the lot, don't know the exact date. Jeff, we got any other Mustangs?"

"Check the computer," the older man said.

The man motioned her to the back where he opened the door to a small office that contained only one chair and a card table with a computer on it. Without sitting down, he typed in some commands and then typed some more, watching the screen flicker.

"Just the one Mustang," he said. "Blue one I mentioned. It don't have the model listed here."

"Could I see it?" Molly asked. She felt ripples of anticipation in her chest, that old thrill of the chase getting under way. She'd moaned about making this trip, but once she got into a search, there was nothing more engrossing in the world.

The man looked her over. "Sure. Come on."

He led the way to a back door. They stepped onto a grassy field that extended back for many acres and looked like a battlefield of burned-out car bodies, rusted metal parts, broken glass, and scraps of tires. It was the most unkempt place Molly had ever seen, and the ugliest. It was also unshaded and very hot.

"It's yonder," he said, pointing to a far corner of the field and striding off in that direction, "past where the driveway ends."

She followed, stepping carefully to avoid the debris that was scattered everywhere. The driveway he'd referred to was merely a beaten-down path in the overgrown grass and weeds. "How long has the car been on the lot?" she asked.

"Dunno. Long time. More than the six years I been here."

As they walked, Molly felt a sharp pricking on her ankle. She looked down and saw several huge mosquitoes there. Quickly she leaned down and slapped at them, leaving two blood smears on her skin.

In the daze of her early rising this morning she'd put on her khaki skirt because it had been lying out on the chair and looked clean. Big mistake. The flats with no socks were a mistake, too. Damn place must be a mosquito breeding ground; they were everywhere. She brushed her hand around her ear where one was buzzing.

"Real bad year for mosquitoes," the man said, looking back at her. "All the rain."

As she followed him, Molly eyed his thick overalls and long sleeves with envy. She felt a prick in the center of her back and tried to slap at the spot, but couldn't reach it. They were biting right through her damp T-shirt. She glanced around at the puddles of standing water and the tire segments and other junk that held water. It would be impossible to design a better breeding ground for mosquitoes.

"You got an old Mustang you're working on?" the man asked.

Afraid he'd test her knowledge if she said yes, she improvised. "Uh, no. My son. I'm scouting for him."

As they passed close to a tin lean-to where tires were stacked up to the high roof, Molly stopped in her tracks and let out a little gasp. There next to the path lay a big white dog, its head reduced to a bloody mess of bone and fur. Clusters of black flies stuck to the blood and swarmed around the body.

The man stopped and looked back. "Yes, ma'am," he said, shaking his head. "Ain't that a shame? Poor old Bomber. Best damn dog we ever had and look at that."

"What happened to him?" Molly asked, reaching down the back of her shirt to scratch a bite.

"Dunno. We come in this morning and he was laying out here dead. Someone nearly beat his fool head off. We ain't gotten around to burying him yet."

"Why? Was there a burglary?" she asked, looking around the yard.

"We couldn't find nothing missing, but as you can see, it ain't easy around here to know."

Molly forced her eyes away from the dog and continued walking, stepping gingerly around the broken glass and sharp metal shards that lay everywhere.

When they got to the back of the lot, the grass was longer, less beaten down, and it sliced at her bare calves. Sticker burrs caught on her skirt.

The man pointed to the area where the high barbed-wire fence formed a corner. There in the shade of a squatty live oak, with weeds grown up to the bottom of the windows and vines half covering it, was a pale blue car. Molly's heart sank when she saw how light the color was, but she plowed through the tall grass to get a closer look. The hood and the engine were gone. The windshield above the steering wheel had a small circular break with a network of cracks radiating out from it—the same exact configuration she'd seen on many of the cars they'd passed.

When the man saw where she was looking, he said, "Didn't buckle up."

He pushed his way through the weeds and managed to wrench the driver's side door open. He squatted down to look at the dirty old sticker on the edge of the door. "A '75," he said, squinting at it. "Engine's gone, but the doors look pretty good." He walked around to the back and pulled some vines away. "Back's a hatch, so that don't help you none."

Molly looked at a rusted patch on the roof and asked, "Is this the original paint job, do you think?"

He ran a thick index finger over a rusted spot and said, "Yes, ma'am."

"And no other Mustangs on the lot," she said.

"Computer says not," he said, turning around and starting to walk back to the office.

Molly walked beside him, feeling sweat trickling down her back. "How long has this lot been operating?" she asked.

"Twenty years, maybe," he said.

She was so hot now and the bites were itching with such an intensity that she decided to blow her cover and speed up the process. "Did there used to be a black man working here? A man with one hand?"

He turned and looked at her. "Oh, you must be thinking of old Calvin, nigger who runs A-One couple of blocks down Rosedale. Got in some trouble while back, armed robbery, I think. Served some time. But he's back in the business now. Wondered though if he'd got in trouble again what with all the cop cars there this morning."

"Cop cars?" Molly asked, feeling vibrations running down her arms and into her fingertips. Something around here was on the move in a big way.

As they walked back across the lot, Molly continued to slap at mosquitoes and scratch her bites. She had one particularly vexing one puffing up behind her left knee. As they passed the dead dog, she averted her head and held her breath, hoping they'd get around to burying him before long. It was getting hotter by the second.

Back at the office, she smiled and gave the man her card, asked him to call her if he heard of a 1972 Mustang.

As she drove the few blocks to A-One Auto Parts, Molly thought about how to approach this one. It would probably be best, and quickest, to identify herself as a journalist right away. But she would have to play it by ear.

She pulled into the gravel and dirt parking area next to the sign for A-One Auto Parts. There were no police cars here now. A big sign said "NO DUMPING. ORDER OF HEALTH DEPARTMENT. $1000 FINE," and another said "BRING YOUR OWN TOOLS." Louie did have a remarkable memory. Eleven years later and he still remembered that sign.

She walked through the opening in the Cyclone fence and climbed the cracked cement steps. At the top loomed a garagelike prefab structure. Behind it stretched acres and acres of junk-strewn fields filled with old cars, rusted radiators, hubcaps, crumpled license plates, black hoses, pipes, plastic bits, broken glass, and heaps of rotting tires. It looked like a place where nothing had been moved in decades. And the mosquitoes were everywhere. They'd already located her ankles and had worked up to her knees. She leaned down to slap and scratch. First chance she got she'd stop at a drugstore for some spray, if she survived that long.

When she looked around and didn't see anyone, she approached the garage, thinking the office must be inside. As she neared the door, she saw at the side of the building three large mounds on the ground. They were surrounded by swarms of buzzing flies. She backed up a few steps and covered her nose with her hand. The three dead dogs lay stretched out on their sides. Clouds of black flies almost obscured the bloody pulps where their heads had been. Judging from the bodies, two of the dogs had been tan and white pit bulls, and the third, a dark-bodied German shepherd. Someone did not like junkyard dogs.

When she looked up from the bodies, she saw a huge black man— tall and burly with gray hair and a toothpick hanging out of his mouth—standing in the door. In spite of the heat, he wore a black Windbreaker and heavy black pants. She looked to see if he was missing a hand, but both were stuck in his pockets.

"Howdy," the man said with a scowl. It sounded more like a curse than a greeting.

Molly's immediate impression was that this was a man who would never fall for a lie, so she decided to play it as straight as she could in the circumstances. "Howdy." She glanced over at the dead dogs. "Hear you had a little trouble."

"Lots of trouble, I ever find out who did that to my dogs." His voice was low and menacing. "Where'd you hear about it?"

"Man over at All Okay said he saw police cars here this morning."

"What's it to you?" he said, looking hard at her.

"I hate to see that happen to a good dog," she said, watching his face. "Are you Calvin?"

He paused, then said, "Yup."

"My name is Molly Cates. I'm a writer for *Lone Star Monthly* magazine and I'm looking for a car."

"What you mean?"

"I'm looking for a particular car—a 1972 Mustang hardtop, blue."

He took a step back and lowered his head but not before Molly caught the astonishment on his face. He couldn't have been more shocked if she'd asked for a Rolls-Royce in mint condition.

Finally he looked up and managed a smile around the toothpick. "You pulling my chain," he said.

"No. Why would I? Do you have any old Mustangs like that?"

His eyes narrowed. "You don't look like a cop. So you must of just talked with them."

"Cops? No. Why?"

"Because a car just like that got stole offa the lot last night."

She was half expecting it, but when it came she felt a jolt of surprise nonetheless: what had been a routine inquiry was now in earnest. She took a step closer to him. "Could you describe the car that was stolen last night?"

"Maybe you should talk to the cops, lady. I already told them."

"I'll probably want to do that, but first I'd like to hear it from you."

Calvin leaned against the doorjamb and looked off into the distance over her head. "Just what you said—Mustang, '72 model, blue. Someone drug it off in the middle of the night. Cut a section outta the fence, kilt my dogs, and made off with it."

"What else can you tell me about the car?" she asked.

"Engine was long gone, so I don't know about that, but it was notchback."

"What about the color?"

"Like I said, blue."

"What shade of blue?" she asked. "Light? Dark? Bright?"

He shook his head. "Bright, I guess."

"Was it the original paint job, do you know?"

"No. Course it weren't. Mustangs never come in that color. It been repainted."

"Do you know what the original color was underneath?"

He reached up with his right hand and took the toothpick out of his mouth. "Now how should I know that, lady? Car been on the lot years and years without anyone, including me, paying it no mind. Then it gets drug off in the middle of the night and next day you show up asking about it. I don't give a fuck about the car. My dogs got kilt." He jabbed the toothpick in their direction. "If I'd been here I woulda called 'em off and let the fuckers take it. Piece of junk. Weren't worth it."

Molly glanced down at the corpses. "I'm real sorry about the dogs." She paused to let that sink in before making her request. "What records have you got on the car?"

"Nothing. Anything that goes back more than two–three years we got no records on. I explained it to the cops. It ain't expected in this business."

"What about photographs or inventory records?" She glanced around the lot at the heaps of junk with a sinking heart. "Don't you take inventory from time to time?"

He shook his head.

"How do you know what you have here without any records?" she asked.

He took his index finger and tapped it against his temple for an answer.

"So there's not even a scrap of paper to prove that this car actually existed—an inventory or sales slip from when you sold parts of it off—anything that might mention it?"

"Nope."

"Did you work here eleven years ago, Mr.—?"

"Calvin. Yes. But if you're gonna ask me do I remember buying this car, no. I been in this business thirty years, off and on, and I bought a lot of cars."

Molly smelled a dead end coming unless she could make something happen here. She reached in her shoulder bag and pulled out a photo of Louie, the one she had taken in the hall of the Hays County courthouse. She held it out to him. "Does this face ring a bell with you?"

Calvin glanced at it, shook his head, and leaned back against the garage. His expression was bored.

Molly kept holding the photo out. "He's a small man, white, about thirty-five at the time. Skinny. Lots of tattoos on his arms. As you can see, dark hair, thin, combed back. Small eyes set close together. Long jaw. What you can't see in this picture is he's got lots of teeth, more than he should have. Moves kind of quick and jerky."

The man's face remained blank. "Sound like half the crackers come in here," he said.

Molly sighed. "Well, could I see where the car was, please?" she asked, unable to think of any other course of action, but not ready to give up on it yet.

Without a word he turned and disappeared inside the office. Then he returned in a few seconds. "Turned on the telephone machine. We got to make this quick."

He started walking along a gravel path leading away from the entrance. As he walked, he pulled his arms out of his pockets and Molly felt her pulse throb with excitement when she saw that the left hand was missing at the wrist. He turned his head quick to see if she was looking at it. "Viet-fucking-Nam," he said. "Souvenir."

Molly slapped at her itching ankles and asked, "What else was stolen last night?"

"Nothing I can figure, but we don't keep real good track here, not computerized like some of the newer places."

They walked in silence through row after row of mutilated cars. Many of them had the same characteristic circular hole in the windshield above the steering wheel. Molly resolved to be more consistent about wearing her seat belt.

Calvin stopped in a row of especially old and decrepit shells that had once been cars. Molly spotted the place where the car had been even before he pointed at it with his toothpick. The grass was dead and there were indents in the damp earth where the axles must have rested.

"Right here," he said, moving his lips to make the toothpick point at it. "Why you so interested in this?"

Molly walked around the outline on the ground, staring down. "A man who's in prison, on death row, says this car could prove he's innocent."

The man's nostrils flared. He threw his head back and laughed up at the sky. When he was finished he looked back at Molly, tears in his eyes. "And you believe that shit?"

"I don't know yet. I need to find the car first." She walked over to an old green Dodge that was right beside the empty space where the Mustang had been. It was that wonderful vintage of car that had the softly curved fenders. She rested her hand on the curve as she squatted down to look underneath it. The metal was so hot she jerked her hand away.

She walked around to where the back of the Mustang would have been and looked down at a pile of some rusty metal scraps. "How do you suppose they got the car out?" she asked. "It wasn't drivable, was it?"

Calvin shrugged his massive shoulders. "Probably drove a truck through where they cut the fence and towed it right out."

"Did it still have tires?" Molly asked, still studying the pile of metal scraps.

"Don't think so. They could of put some on."

She leaned over to look closer at a piece of rusted pipe in the pile. About a foot and a half long. She thought she saw some spots of color—bright blue color. Kneeling, she reached out for it. Yes, there were indeed some splatters of bright blue. Just as she was picking it up, Calvin cried out, "Watch it, lady! You got yourself in a mess of fire ants."

The second before he finished the warning, Molly felt the first fiery stings on the tops of her feet. She dropped the pipe, leapt to her feet with a shriek, and took some quick steps back to get away from the mound. Then she stamped her feet and bent over and frantically brushed at the small red ants on her legs and feet. Some of them transferred to her hands and stung her fingers. "Oh, shit," she said. "Ow. Damn." She grabbed the hem of her skirt and used it to swipe at them. "God, I hate them."

"Me too." Calvin's face was screwed up in distaste. He had backed up several feet to safety and his arms were crossed protectively over his chest.

She stood and held her skirt up and shook it in case there were some on the fabric. Then she ran her hands up and down the full length of her legs several times.

When she finally looked over at Calvin, he was watching with what she suspected might have been a suppressed smile, but she wasn't sure. "Mean fuckers," he said laconically. "Put me in mind of the Viet Cong."

Molly finally calmed herself down, though her feet kept making little involuntary steps and she scanned the ground constantly. Her feet and ankles felt badly burned; she knew from experience the bites would feel worse tonight.

"Let me see that thing you was picking up," Calvin said, using his toothpick to point at the pipe she'd dropped.

Molly darted in quickly, picked it up, and shook it. Then she examined it. On the coarse rusted surface were some brilliant blue paint splatters that looked as if they came from a spray painter. She ran her fingers over the roughness of the rusty metal, feeling how much smoother the droplets of paint were. Silently, she handed it to Calvin.

He studied it, turning it around, and said, "That's the color. Same as the car. This here's the tailpipe. Must of broken off when they moved it." He touched the jagged, rusty end with his thumb. "Or could of just rusted off before that."

"Didn't the police look around here?" she asked.

"Nah. They just took down what I told them and looked at the hole in the fence and give me the evil eye—you know, how they look at you when you got a record."

Molly looked around the ground, under the car on the other side of the empty space, and in the vicinity. But she saw nothing else with bright blue paint. This tailpipe seemed to be all that was left behind —precious little proof that such a car ever existed, but she was starting to believe it.

She reached out her hand for the pipe and he gave it back to her. "Calvin," she said, "you have any other old Mustangs on the lot?"

"No," he said. "Only a '87 ragtop, come in last week."

Molly took a last look at the space where the blue Mustang had been and sighed. "Is there anyone else working here who could confirm the existence of this car?"

He reached up and took the toothpick out of his mouth. "You don't believe me?"

"Yes, I do believe you, but I need someone else to say the same thing."

"No one else. Just me and that's why I got to get back to the office," Calvin said, his voice hostile again. "Got to take care of them dogs and cover the phone and customers and every other damn thing like some one-man band."

He started walking. Molly fell into step beside him. When they got back to the office, she thanked him and left him a card with her number on it—just in case something came up.

Back in her rental car, she wrapped the sharp end of the pipe in the *New York Times* business section, which she never read, and stuck it in her big bag diagonally so only a few inches stuck out.

Twenty minutes later Molly had found the intersection of Mansfield Highway and Loop 20. From there she could have located the place she was seeking by the stench. "Sam's Body Shop—Painting Our Specialty—Lowest Prices," the sign said, but the sign, which was several yards in front of the building, seemed to be the only thing that hadn't been damaged by fire. The blackened brick facade had crumbled around the gaping holes where the front window and door had once been. Pools of standing water around the base of the walls were black with ash and cinders. A smoky haze still hung in the air.

She pulled into the parking lot at the side and shut off the engine. Her stomach was churning over missed opportunities. That was how it had been after her father was killed: everywhere she went, every step she took, she had turned out to be a day late.

chapter 17

Four sister-bitches
Three were cruel snitches
One had to get stitches
One got death twitches
They all give me itches
Inside my britches.

LOUIE BRONK
Death Row, Ellis I Unit,
Huntsville, Texas

▲ ▼ ▲

Molly Cates rolled down the window, letting in a blast of hot air, and squinted against the noon sun. Sam's Body Shop appeared to be housed in two buildings. The front one, which must have served as the office, had been reduced to a blackened shell. A long butler building at the back of the property, probably the shop, looked untouched.

She studied what was left of the front building. The cinder-block sides and brick facade were still standing, but the windows and doors had been burned out. Enough light filtered in through the caved-in places in the roof to illuminate the blackness of total destruction inside.

Molly stretched her right leg, propped the foot up on the dashboard, and scratched at the itchy bite behind her knee. She'd have to get in touch with the fire marshal and the police to let them know this was arson, if they hadn't already figured it out. Some dead junkyard dogs, a stolen wreck of a Mustang, and now this. Someone was willing to go to a great deal of trouble over an old car. It was enough to get her juices flowing.

She opened the door and looked up and down the street. The neighborhood seemed quiet enough. Across the street stood a warehouse and on the corner an old auto parts store. Next door was a weedy vacant lot. No one was out on the street except for a small group of men standing on the corner a few blocks down.

She walked around to the front of the building and peered in through where the door had been. A flimsy strip of yellow police tape dangled loose from the door frame. Inside, the walls were blackened and wires and flaps of insulation hung in a tangled mess from the ceiling. The floor was littered with charred acoustical tiles that had fallen from the ceiling and solid chunks of unidentifiable objects that the fire didn't digest. Puddles of filthy black water stood everywhere.

She glanced around for file cabinets, even though she knew it was hopeless. Anyone taking extreme measures like this would have made sure that all the files were burned first; they were probably the tinder used to get the fire started.

She stood in the doorway and called, "Hello. Anyone there?"

When there was no answer, she stepped inside. The floor was slick with a muddy film of wet ashes. She wrinkled her nose against the stench and called again, "Anyone here?"

Still no answer.

A collapsing door frame led to another room at the back. Careful to avoid the puddles and keep her clothes from brushing against anything, she made her way through the room. She stood in the inner doorway and looked into a gloomy room smaller than the front one. There were no windows. The only light came from the door where she was standing and two holes where the roof had caved in. The air was hazy with the dirty smoke that seemed trapped inside; the sun rays streaming in through the roof holes silvered the little flecks of gray and white ash suspended in the still air.

"Hello." This time she spoke softly, apprehensive that any loud noise might bring the roof down.

In the far corner stood three metal filing cabinets, each with four drawers. They were blackened and covered with debris—ceiling tiles, burned plasterboard, and wire tangles. She walked around a heap of ashes in the center of the room to the file cabinets. The light in the corner was barely sufficient for her to see what she was doing.

The top drawer in the first cabinet was stuck, or locked, so she tried the next one down. It opened about an inch and then refused to budge. The fire and water seemed to have warped the metal. She worked at the drawer by jiggling first one side, then the other, gradually pulling it out a few more inches. She wished she had a flashlight to shine inside; she had just about every other damn thing in the world in her big shoulder bag, but not that.

Reluctantly, she reached a hand inside and felt around. The drawer was empty. She squatted down and worked the third drawer open. Empty, too. So was the bottom one.

She turned her head to look at the pile of ash and cinders in the center of the floor. Surely that was where the contents of these drawers had ended up.

She stood and tried the top drawer on the next cabinet. It made a rusty scraping noise as she forced it open. She stopped with her hands on the edge of the open drawer and listened, holding her breath. There it was again—a creaking noise she had not made.

She turned toward the sound.

Three men stood watching her. One was black, two white. The black man had already entered the room. The other two filled the doorway, blocking the light. Her breath caught in her throat. The way they stood. Their silence. Trouble. Bad trouble.

She looked around, desperate. She was trapped in a corner. In a room with one door. And the door was blocked. She was caught.

Her throat closed up tight.

A drop of sweat rolled from her temple down her cheek.

The man inside the room stood with his legs braced wide, his hands at his sides. Hanging from his right hand was a long rod—a tire iron, she thought. She remembered the junkyard dogs, heads smashed and bloody.

The man took a step to his right, the other two moved in. One stopped in front of the door, arms crossed over his chest. The other, a huge hulking shape, moved to the left. She was surrounded. It was happening. After all the years of covering crime. Her luck had run out. It was her turn.

She could have stayed home. She'd been warned. She could have had a cop escort. She had said no. Stupid. Stupid.

The man with the tire iron took a step closer. Muscle shirt cut off to show his flat belly. Camouflage gimme hat pulled low on his forehead. He took another step.

She opened her mouth. Had to try. Had to say something. No sound came out. Her throat was shut. She swallowed. "I—I have an appointment here," she croaked.

"With us." The man with the tire iron whispered it. "With us." He took another step toward her.

Molly stepped back. Her heel hit the wall. The edge of the world. Nowhere to go.

Now the other two were closing in. Slow. One step at a time.

She pressed her back against the wall and pulled her arms in tight against her sides. Her bag was there, under her left arm. Hanging from a shoulder strap. Open. Grady's tear gas! In there somewhere. She felt around with her fingers. God, such a mess. Keys must have sunk to the bottom.

The man with the tire iron was closer now. He slapped it into his palm.

She should scream. Someone might hear. But she couldn't. It would unleash her panic. Speed things up. It would be the end.

She had to talk. Her only advantage—words.

She held her right palm up. "Wait. I've got a police escort. Outside," she said. "Right outside."

"Po-lice escort?" the man with the tire iron said, wiggling his hips. "Lady here has a po-lice escort, Dooley." He turned his head to the big man.

The fingers of her left hand grazed the tailpipe wrapped in newspaper. She slipped her hand inside the newspaper and circled the pipe with her fingers.

The big man called Dooley took three steps and smiled, looking her up and down. He was only a few feet away.

She clenched her teeth. Goddamn. Going out as a victim was the pits. This was how Louie's victims felt—terror and shame at being too weak, too dumb to see it coming. If only she had a handgun, a machete, an Uzi, a grenade, an atomic bomb—she'd use them. With no remorse. If only she'd worked harder on her push-ups. If only she were Rambo, or Wonder Woman, or Charles Bronson—any-fucking-thing but the middle-aged, female sitting duck she was.

"You'd better check," she said in a high voice she barely recognized. "Out front. Go on. Take a look. What can it hurt?"

The man in the camouflage gimme hat said, "Fuck. That don't even work in the movies." He stopped two feet from her, his mouth hanging open.

Hot spurts of sweat popped out on her forehead and trickled along her eyebrows.

She gripped the tailpipe inside her purse. She had it by the smooth end. The other end was sharp and jagged. It could do damage. If she picked her time.

The man with the tire iron was right in her face. She could smell his sweat over the fire stench. Under the hat visor his open mouth gaped pitlike.

She was trembling. Every inch of skin vibrated.

Slowly he raised the tire iron.

Her head pulsated with hot terror. She held her right hand up. Her throat opened. "Listen," she screamed. "Listen. A siren!" She made a sound she didn't know was in her—a shriek, a wail.

From the side, the big man darted in. She saw his fist draw back. Then she saw a spinning light. It was like getting hit by a truck at eighty miles an hour. Her head was torn right off the neck. She crashed into the wall and slid to the floor. Blinded. Head jangling. Cheek blazing with pain.

When she opened her eyes, the big man was squatted over her. His fist was drawn back again.

Her left hand still grasped the tailpipe. She drew it out of her bag and passed it to her right hand. She scrambled to get her feet under her and rose to a crouch. She choked up on the pipe, lunged forward, and drove the jagged end at his face. Her intent was to kill. Or blind. She went for an eye. But it felt like bone as she drove it in. And twisted it. The roar of pain—she couldn't tell if he was roaring or she was. Or both. He fell back. The pipe went with him.

The man with the tire iron loomed over her, the iron poised over his head.

Crouched, Molly put her arms over her head and curled into a ball. The perfect victim. Just roll over and wait for the ax. Christ, there was nothing else to do. So she waited, her body shuddering. There was a moment of silence. She curled up tighter to keep the shuddering from shaking her apart. She thought she heard a car door slam. And then another.

A voice hissed. "Shhh. Fuck it, Marcus. Someone's here."

Voices drifted in from outside. From another world.

"Le's go. Come on, man," said an urgent voice. She held her breath and prayed. *Yes, go. Please go. Oh, please. God make them go.*

Then she heard the sound that made her heart stop—the snick of a switchblade opening. She pressed her face tighter against her knees and waited to feel it in her back.

"No," a voice hissed, "we ain't been paid to do no killing. Le's jus' go. Help Dooley."

The sound of feet scuffling. Moving away. Retreating.

Molly let out her breath and stayed curled up.

Then nothing.

She opened her eyes and lifted her head. She was alone.

Shouts came from outside. Then more shouts.

She struggled to her feet. The left side of her face felt destroyed.

As fast as she could, she stumbled through the debris and into the front office. Through the door she saw a red car with a light on the top. And a shield on the side that said "Fire Marshal." Lord, oh, Lord. Had she gotten lucky. She felt like falling to her knees. It was the kind of timing, she thought, that could happen only once in a lifetime. She felt like laughing. Or crying.

She straightened up and walked to the door. Two men in brown uniforms, one in a suit, and a woman with a huge black beehive hairdo stood around a tan car. One of the men in uniform was talking into a hand-held radio.

"Did they get away?" Molly asked.

They all looked toward her.

"Who the hell are you?" snapped the man in the suit.

"Molly Cates. Those three men attacked me in there." The words poured out. "Use that radio. Get a police pickup call out on them." She walked toward them. "Now. Do it now. One of them is hurt. The patrol cars can cover the area. They may be your arsonists, too." She had to stop and gasp for breath. She leaned against the red car.

The man in the suit nodded at the man holding the radio. "Do like the lady says," he said.

Three hours later Molly Cates sat on a bench at the Fort Worth Central Police Station holding an ice bag against her swollen cheek. She had made and signed her statement, had her face photographed for evidence, and she had identified with enthusiasm two of the men who had attacked her. The police had picked them up five minutes after the fire marshal had called it in—the leader in the camouflage hat, whose name turned out to be Marcus Gandy, and the big one,

Dooley Smithers. The third man seemed to have slipped away. So far, the two in custody had kept a sullen silence.

Dooley had gotten stitches at Fort Worth General for deep cuts in his cheek. A half inch up and he would have lost the eye.

A police paramedic had glanced at Molly's face, looked deep and long into her eyes, declared her not concussed, and had given her an ice pack for the cheek. A sergeant-investigator from FWPD Burglary and an arson investigator from the Fort Worth Fire Department had talked with Grady Traynor in Austin to check on Molly's story. Both the detective and Grady had talked with the patrol officers who had taken the call at A-One Auto Parts and they had all talked with Molly Cates—several times and in dull detail. Her throat felt raw from all the talking.

But no one really knew what the hell was going on.

Finally, at three o'clock Molly got a chance to talk with the one person she really wanted to talk with—Nelda Fay Ferguson, the sole owner of Sam's Body Shop since her husband Sam Ferguson had "passed over" three years earlier.

At an age Molly estimated near sixty, Nelda Fay had a hairdo larger than her skirt; she wore her dead black hair teased into a mound and her tight denim miniskirt showed off legs so thin that the shin bone resembled a razor. Once Nelda Fay started talking Molly couldn't remember why she'd been so eager to talk to her. The woman talked without ever taking a breath.

"This sucker don't look anywhere near's bad as some of them we get coming in," Nelda Fay was saying as she looked down at the photograph of Louie Bronk. "Don't get me wrong now—I wouldn't screw around with this one neither, but I seen much worse. No. I don't remember him. It's a real damn shame those records got burned, 'cause we keep the best damn records you ever did see. Got audited two years ago and that IRS auditor, she said she'd never seen such pretty documentation. Our bookkeeper, Willie Pettigrew, he does everything just perfect. A real fuss budget. Just like my late husband. Just the kind you want to do your bookkeeping. If you're on the up and up, of course. And we got nothing to hide. Not a thing at all. So we run a real honest, clean business just like when Sammy was alive and—"

Molly leapt in. "Mrs. Ferguson, were the records for 1982 in those metal file cabinets in the back room?"

"Sure were." She pursed her scarlet lips. The color had bled into the wrinkles surrounding her upper lip. "From 1969 when Sammy bought the business. All neatly filed alphabetically. All of them, every one. I did the filing myself." She waved the photo in the air. "If this sucker had a car painted, I coulda found his receipt right fast. Real shame, since it seems so important to you. Too bad you didn't come by yesterday. Can't believe it was worth burning the office down for."

Molly stopped listening; her head was throbbing and her fire ant bites were flaring up. She'd had enough for one day.

Finally the woman stopped talking and said, "Oh, dear, you don't look well."

"No. I'm sure I don't," said Molly, who had been reluctant to look in a mirror. She jotted Nelda Fay's phone and address down in her notebook and handed her a card.

When the police were finally done with Molly, one of them drove her back to the burned-out building to pick up her car and gave her an escort to the airport with his lights flashing. It was the best thing that had happened all day, Molly thought. It sure was the way to get through Metroplex traffic.

As she entered the terminal she caught sight of Grady Traynor slouching against a pillar with his tie unknotted and his jacket hanging open. In spite of her aching, swollen face and itching insect bites, in spite of her exhaustion, in spite of the fact she knew she looked, and smelled, like a bag woman, in spite of not having eaten all day, in spite of everything in the world that should work against lust, the sight of him sent ripples of heat radiating through her body. If she let herself, she would love him just as desperately as she had before. The best thing for her to do was turn around and get back on the plane, run for her life.

He caught sight of her, stood up straight, and waved to get her attention. It was too late for escape.

When she reached him, he put one arm around her waist and drew her out of the stream of passengers walking through the gate. He faced her without smiling and put the other arm around her, too, drawing her gently against him. He leaned down and very lightly touched the swelling on her cheek with his lips. Then he moved to her mouth and kissed her quickly, letting his mustache linger for a moment against her upper lip. He tightened his embrace, pressing his hips into hers, and kissed her again. This time the kiss was in earnest, long and active, involving movement of his entire body—his hips, tongue, and hands—definitely not the kind of kiss appropriate for a public place, but Grady had never been a man to worry about convention.

It was a kiss that took her back twenty-six years to the cab of a pickup parked at City Park. And just like then, it was a kiss that could elicit response from a snowman. She raised her hands to the back of his head and buried her fingers in his hair, feeling the change in texture that had come with the change in color.

She broke it first, tilting her head back and taking in a long breath. He moved his lips to her ear and whispered, "How bad was it, Molly?"

"Grady, I was so terrified I stopped being human."

"Oh," he whispered back, "I know that feeling too well. I'm so relieved you're safe."

He lifted his head but kept his arms wrapped firmly around her. "Guess what?"

She looked up at him.

"You're going to owe me a steak dinner," he said in a slightly hoarse voice, "and your apologies. It's just a matter of time before we nail Charlie McFarland for the murder of David Serrano."

"What happened?" she asked.

"We've traced back to McFarland some payments that went into David Serrano's account at the Bank of Brownsville. Eleven years' worth."

"Paying him off?" she said. "Blackmail?"

"I imagine. That's how Serrano was able to get his business started, with an initial thirty thousand from Charlie right after Bronk's trial." He brushed his lips and mustache against the sensitive skin just below her jawline. Into her neck he said, "After that, he paid three thousand a month."

"Wow," she said.

"You writers really have a gift for words." He lifted his head. "If you want to renege on the bet now, Molly, you can."

Molly ran an index finger lightly down the three raised scars across his nose. He closed his eyes and held his breath.

"What does Charlie say?" she asked.

"Mmm," he said, his eyes still closed. "Charlie says he always treats old employees generously, but he was unable to demonstrate any other case where he's paid a total of three hundred ninety thousand dollars to someone who's not working for him."

"That's not enough to charge him with murder."

"No, but we're working on some other angles, too. I can't talk about them right now." He pressed his cheek gently against her good one and said, "So how about Steak and Ale? You look like you could use a good meal." His breath tickled her ear. "What a day you've had, my poor girl."

"Steak and Ale is fine. I'll treat—for old times' sake. But the bet's still on and you haven't won yet."

He took a step back from her and quickly buttoned his jacket. Then he said with the flash of a smile, "Why don't we take you home first, Molly? You could change your clothes and we both could freshen up."

She felt an inexplicable rush of blood to her face. Lord, why not? It was futile to fight nature and—she looked up suddenly and listened because she thought she heard her name being called. Yes, there it was: "Paging Southwest passenger Molly Cates. Molly Cates, please come to the Southwest Airlines courtesy phone for a message."

Grady put his hands over her ears. "Don't take it, Molly. Whatever it is, let it wait until tomorrow."

"No. I need to see what it is." She broke away from him and walked toward the bank of telephones.

It was Charlie McFarland. His voice sounded dead tired. "Molly, I just talked to Richard Dutton. He said you were flying in from Dallas, so I've been paging you every few minutes."

"I just got in."

"Listen, I'm willing to talk to you for that article now. Not just willing. Anxious to have my say. Right now."

"Now?" she asked. She glanced up at Grady and saw him shaking his head vigorously.

"Yes. Can you come over here to the house on your way home?"

"I suppose so. But there are no strings attached, Charlie."

"No strings."

"All right. I'll come right now." She made a face at Grady.

As soon as she put the phone down, Grady stepped in and pulled her close again. "Okay. I won't fight the inevitable. But I'll go with you. Caleb dropped me off here, so I don't have a car anyway."

"What if I said no?"

"I'd have to call a cab, but it's much safer this way. You are clearly a woman in need of police protection." His face shifted to a sober look. "He's a dangerous man, Molly."

She paused and looked into the pale eyes that weren't laughing now.

"And then we'll go home together," he said. "Say yes."

She raised her hand and laid it on his cheek. "Yes."

"Hot dog," he said.

chapter 18

▲ . ▼ . ▲

On death row
Set to go.
You start to sweat.
Oh, man, you bet.
The time is right,
Clocks at midnight.
You feel it being born
Your gut is torn.
It's red and shrill
Like a fresh kill,
Like your worst dream,
Comes the red scream.

LOUIE BRONK
Death Row, Ellis I Unit,
Huntsville, Texas

Molly parked the truck just inside the entrance gate. Grady leaned across her and opened the door, nearly lying in her lap to do it. He brought his face up close to hers. "Just humor me here, Molly. Be sure he knows I'm out here waiting for you."

She slid out, but before she could shut the door, he added, "Bear in mind: this guy may be responsible for two murders in the last four days."

She slammed the door and turned toward the house. Every light was blazing. It looked like someone inside didn't want to take the chance of walking into a dark room.

She rang the doorbell and waited. Frank Purcell opened the door, the sleeves of his white shirt rolled up and the black automatic at his belt in full view for the first time since she had met him. "Evenin'," he said. "Charlie's in his study, waiting on you. His back's bothering him real bad."

"How's it going, Frank?"

He shrugged and shifted his eyes away.

"Me too," she said, giving him a pat on the shoulder as she walked past him. She continued on down the hall with the bluebonnet paintings.

Charlie McFarland sat in the same recliner he'd sat in five days before, wearing the same clothes, except that instead of boots he wore slippers now. He sat very still, his shoulders slumped forward, and he held a dark-looking drink in his hand.

Molly paused in the door. "Sorry to hear your back is acting up, Charlie."

He glanced up at her by just flicking his eyes, as if moving the whole head might hurt too much. "Molly, thanks for coming. Forgive me for not standing. Sit down. Sit down."

She sat in the same orange chair she had used before.

"Could Frank get you a drink?" he asked.

"No thanks. I can't stay long. I've got a friend waiting for me outside."

"Wouldn't your friend like to come in and wait in the living room?"

"No. He's used to waiting in cars." She watched his face as she added, "He's a cop."

Charlie raised his eyebrows and said in a flat voice. "I hope things haven't got to the point where you feel you need police protection coming here."

"Oh, no. He's my date. It's Saturday night, you know." She started to smile, but stopped halfway through because it made her cheek hurt with a fury. She put her hand to the swelling, but quickly pulled it away because it was tender to the touch.

For the first time since she'd walked in, he seemed to focus his eyes on her face and let them come to rest on her cheek. "What happened to you?"

"Pretty ugly, huh? When I was in Fort Worth, three men tried to beat me up in a burned-out building."

Charlie took a sip of his drink and looked at her over the rim. "What on earth were you doing in a burned-out building in Fort Worth?"

"Some research," she said, "on the Louie Bronk matter."

He set his drink down so hard it sloshed over the edge and Molly caught a whiff, deep and mellow, of good straight bourbon. He said,

"That's exactly what I want to talk about. I'm so fucking sick of hearing about that son of a bitch. God, it'll be a relief two days from now when he's history." He blew out through his lips as if literally letting off steam.

"Then maybe you'll all stop giving him publicity," he said. "I have some things I want to say about that. For the record."

"Good."

"You won't think it's so good when you hear what I have to say," he said, his lips barely opening as he spoke. "I'm goddamned mad, just fed up to here."

She found her recorder and pulled it out of her bag. "It helps if I can record what we say. Is that all right with you, Charlie?"

He gave a nod so slight it was really more of a twitch, a movement that left her in no doubt about his pain. She switched on the recorder, watched to see that the tape inside was turning, then placed it in her lap.

He sat forward slightly and gripped his knees with his hands, as if he were closing a circuit or grounding himself. "You aren't going to like this and you probably won't even print what I'm fixing to say, but I need to say it anyway. I think giving all this attention to these violent criminals encourages others to commit crimes." He spoke in a cold, firm voice, faster than usual, as if he had rehearsed it and wanted to say it as quickly as possible. "I believe Georgia was killed by someone imitating Louie Bronk and I think her killer learned how to do it from your book and from all the press Bronk's gotten. That anonymous letter you got clinches it for me."

Molly felt a clutch of dread in her chest. She didn't believe it. But still the dread was there. "Charlie, I really don't think—"

He raised a hand. "Hear me out. You asked for an interview and I'm giving it. I think this lunatic picked on my family because he was copying Bronk. I'm not saying it was just your book; there's all the other publicity Bronk has gotten—I blame everyone who keeps this animal in the public attention by writing about him, making him into some sort of celebrity. Now I suppose people have a right to know the facts, the bare facts of a crime, but when you write this long book that goes into his childhood and past and what the shrinks say and, Christ, even his poetry, it just makes me sick."

Molly took a deep breath. She was beginning to feel ragged; she shouldn't have come. "Charlie, serial killers, like Louie, don't read books; the only printed material they're likely to look at is pornography."

"How would you know that?"

"From my experience with them, and from the things I've read—research that experts in the field have done."

He took a long draw on his drink. "Hell, I've read some of that stuff, too. These serial killer fellows like Bronk often like to read about themselves in newspapers, right? And they all read pornography and detective magazines, right?"

"Yes," Molly admitted.

"So why not your book?" He looked at her hard, his eyes set back deep in the layers of flesh his face had acquired over the years. "Why not? How do you know that they don't get off on stuff like you write?"

"I have worried about that some in the past, but I really don't—"

"You don't think it's an accident this happened right after your book came out, do you? Hell, it triggered some crazy to try it himself." His face was darkening from its usual ruddy tan to a deep maroon.

"Charlie, I can see why you'd be angry, but—"

"Angry?" he boomed. "Angry does not even come close to how I feel. My wife was killed. My privacy is being invaded. My children are being tormented. The police are looking at my bank accounts, every aspect of my life. Here I am, a victim of crime, and the police come after me as if it's my fault." He turned his head away from her. "It's sickening."

He opened his mouth to speak again, but couldn't catch his breath. He gulped for air and then breathed in and out with wheezy gasps. For a minute Molly feared he was going to choke. She started to stand, but he gestured her down with a movement of his hand.

"The reason I haven't said anything public in the past is that I wanted to protect my family's privacy. But the dam has broken. Also I didn't want to do anything to give any more attention to this violent criminal. But what does it matter now? It's hard to imagine it could get any worse. I know you're not going to write this, but I just want my protest registered."

"Of course, I'll write it," she said, looking down to make sure the recorder was moving. "Anything else?"

"Yes. The solution is to give these criminals fair trials and execute them real fast, with a minimum of press coverage. It's a crime—no, a *sin*—it's a sin that Bronk is still alive eleven years after he slaughtered my wife and that he's getting all this attention now. He should have been executed right after the trial or right after his first appeal was denied." He lifted his hands from his knees and slowly leaned back in the chair, as if he'd totally exhausted himself.

Molly leaned back, too. She felt more beat-up and bruised than she had after the fight today. It had haunted her some, this idea that writing about crime in a dramatic way might encourage sick minds to try it, but she'd rejected it. Almost rejected it; there were still those 3 A.M. awakenings when she worried about everything, including this. There could be some truth in what he was saying and it horrified her to contemplate it. The irony here would be if someone had copied Louie in a murder Louie didn't even commit.

She looked down at the recorder in her lap. She wanted to get this over with, but she needed to ask one more thing. "What about David Serrano, Charlie?"

He shook his head. "He was always a nice boy, a good employee. I wanted to help him get started in life after what he'd been through. Now I'm getting blasted for it. I don't know what he might have got mixed up in over the past years. I'm not convinced his death is related to Georgia's."

"It would be one hell of a coincidence," Molly said. "Did you read about Louie recanting his confession?"

He lifted his head. "I can't believe a responsible newspaper would print that garbage."

Molly nodded. She was not about to give voice right now to her growing doubts about Louie Bronk; it might push this man into apoplexy. "Why have you decided to talk publicly now?" she asked.

He looked down at the backs of his hands. "I just needed to get it off my chest. Like I said, the dam has already broken and . . ." he hesitated. "And it's my last chance."

"Your last chance?"

"Yes." His eyes still cast downward, he said, "Six months from now, I'm not going to be around."

"Why not?"

He looked up. "If you use this in an article, please don't do it for another week. Until I've had a chance to tell my family. I found out last week that this pain in my back that I thought was a ruptured disk is really cancer. Had a scan and it showed tumors all over the spine, and in my lungs and liver. Everywhere. Doctor says I'll be lucky to make it to Easter."

"Oh, Charlie, I'm so sorry."

"Me too."

"Who knows this?"

"Georgia knew. Frank knows. Other than my doctor, only them. Before I go public I want to get a real good second opinion. I'm going to Anderson in Houston next week. I'll tell them then. At least the Bronk thing will be over by then. So you see, my kids will have enough to deal with—all this death—without you making it worse by digging up past pain."

His lips tightened. "People usually ask if there's anything they can do when you tell 'em your bad news. If you was to ask me that, Molly, I'd say what I been saying all along: 'Don't upset my kids with all this.' I think Alison is stretched to her breaking point. I'm trying to get her to come stay here. At least she'd be safe and away from that man she's living with. Stuart doesn't show the strain like she does, but he's suffering, too."

He picked up the glass. "Sorry. I think that's all I can take today." His head fell back against the chair again. "I get so tired. Can you find your way to the door? Frank will let you out."

Molly turned off the tape recorder. "Thanks for talking to me, Charlie. I assure you that I will write what you've said and I'll check with you before printing anything about your illness. All right?"

Without opening his eyes, he said, "Fine."

Frank was waiting for her at the door. She wondered if he'd been there all along or if Charlie had signaled him in some way. He deactivated the alarm by punching a series of numbers into a keypad on the wall, used a key to unlock the two dead bolts, then opened the door and stepped out. He stared at Grady Traynor sitting in the truck, then stood aside for Molly to pass.

As she approached the truck, Grady leaned across and opened the door. He looked at her face in the overhead light and said, "Shall I drive?"

She shook her head as she climbed in. "No. Driving always makes me feel better." She started the engine.

They drove in silence for the first minute. "So?" he said finally. "Are you going to tell me?"

"Huh? Oh, he's mad. He thinks people like me who write about crime glamorize the criminals and cause other people to commit crimes."

"Bullshit," Grady said.

"I hope so," she said fervently. "I hope you're right."

Then she said, "Grady, I've been wondering. It's possible that Louie set this all up—what happened in Fort Worth last night and today. I mean, when he told me about the car, he could have arranged for someone to steal a Mustang from that lot and burn down the auto body place, to make it seem like someone was trying to destroy the evidence that would exonerate him." She took her eyes off the road for a minute to glance at him. "Pretty farfetched, I know. But do you think it's possible?"

"Sure, it's possible. I've known guys in solitary confinement to plan bank robberies, kidnappings, even murders, and get other people to execute them. It's possible, but I don't think he did. Do you?"

She was silent, thinking about it. Four minutes later when they pulled up to her garage she said, "No. I don't think so either." She pushed the button on the door opener clipped to her visor and drove into the garage.

When she cut off the engine, Grady reached over and turned up the radio which had been playing low, tuning it to K-VET, the country music station. As if by some master plan of fate, the song playing was Patsy Cline's "Crazy," a song they had danced to at the Broken Spoke in 1968. "Mmm, that's just right for us, isn't it, Molly?"

He pushed the button on her visor, and as the garage door rumbled down, he walked around to her side. He held his arms up in their old slow-dance position, inviting her, waiting for her. She stepped into it as easily as if twenty-five years had not gone by. Together they began to sway to the mellow strains of the song. He bent his head down to press his cheek against hers.

"It's like riding a bicycle," Molly murmured.

"This is the sort of thing your body never forgets how to do. Oh, Molly."

It was as if one might really have a second chance at the things that mattered. She knew it wasn't true, but for this moment she chose to believe it anyway, because it felt so good.

The automatic timer switched off the overhead light, leaving them in total darkness.

Dancing with Grady Traynor had always been somewhere between dancing and making love in rhythm. And now, in the dark garage, to the smell of grease and old lawn mowers, they fell back into that familiar mating dance, the one that started so dreamy-slow you were caught up in it before you had a chance to escape, even if you wanted to. It started with the feel of another body, separate at first, and strange, different in its hollows and fullnesses. But gradually, with the music and the movement, the bodies softened, the outlines blurred, and one body began to flow right into the other as the dance went on.

She remembered the very first time she had danced with him, wanting to pull his shirt out and run her hands up his bare back right there on the dance floor. She hadn't done it then; she had waited until later. But she did it now, untucked his shirt and very slowly moved her hands up his back, feeling the smooth skin and the knobs of his spine underneath. When she moved her hands along his sides up under his arms, he sucked in his breath. She remembered back then being aroused by his arousal, and, amazingly, it was no different now.

Molly had always loved this stage of the dance, stretching it out, prolonging it until the tension forced the next stage. The song changed to Jennifer Warnes's "Right Time of the Night" and then Willie's "Always on My Mind." Grady wrapped both arms around her, resting his hands on the swell of her hips. She began unbuttoning his shirt, slowly. She rested her palms against his bare chest, moving them down the abdomen, pausing to feel an unfamiliar scar that ran under his belt.

"Appendix," he murmured, as she ran her fingers the smooth length of it, "at the damnedest time, right in the middle of the Westerman investigation."

Slowly, as they danced, they undressed one another, one button, one zipper, one hook at a time. Then, music and all pretense of dancing forgotten, it was no longer slow or languid. To Molly's surprise, it felt even more desperate to her now than when they were young. Maybe because now they both knew something that they hadn't known then: that they were mortal and that time was running down. In this world you never knew which dance was the last one.

"Want to go upstairs where it's comfortable?" she said, barely able to get her breath.

"Remember San Antonio?" he asked.

She laughed. She did remember. They had gone to a party in San Antonio, where they had danced, just like this. On the way home, unable to wait, they stopped in a cornfield and made love for the first time in the back of his old pickup under the light of a full moon. "Oh, yes," she said, "I remember."

"So do I." He picked up his shirt and jacket and spread them out in the back of her pickup. "This isn't called the truck bed for nothing," he said, lying down on his back and pulling her in on top of him.

Later, upstairs in bed, Molly could have drifted off to sleep, except that she was ravenously hungry. She lifted her leg, which had been resting on top of his, and rolled on to her back. He propped himself up on an elbow and looked down at her in the pale glow of the night-light she always kept burning.

"It's a little like going to a twenty-fifth high school reunion," Molly said. "You can't help but worry how you'll look to people who have a mental image of you at eighteen."

He laughed, picked up her hand, and pressed the palm against his stomach. "I know what you mean. The last time we did this, this area was concave."

She turned her head on the pillow to look down at him. "It looks good to me, Grady, and after all, it is fifty years old."

"Fifty?" he said, slowly pressing her hand downward. "Really? But who's counting?"

She withdrew her hand. "How about that dinner you promised me? All I've had to eat since breakfast was two bitty little bags of almonds on the plane."

"Oh, yes, ma'am, dinner." He looked down at her, his pale eyes predatory in the gloom, as he moved them along her body. Foolish to let all this happen again, she knew. But, after all, life was short, and she was certainly old enough to take care of herself.

He leaned down and kissed her, his tongue flicking along the insides of her lips as lightly as a feather.

He slid a hand under her back and raised her on to her side, brushing his chest against her breasts and slipping his leg between hers, trying to rekindle her interest. "Dinner now or later?" he asked.

But she couldn't answer because he'd pressed his mouth against hers.

He brought his leg up higher and rubbed. She found herself getting less interested in dinner.

A shrill electronic buzz made her pull away and sit up. It sounded as if it were coming from inside her head, but Grady sighed and pulled a tiny pager from under the pillow. "Damn," he said, looking at the digital readout that glowed in the dark. "I better check on this."

Molly collapsed on the bed and pointed to the phone on the night table.

Grady reached over to it and punched out the number. After a few seconds, he said, "What, Caleb?" He listened for several minutes and Molly could hear the low voice droning on through the receiver. "No shit," Grady said. Then again, louder, sitting up, "No shit." He listened some more and said, "Well done. Thanks for buzzing me. I'll get back to you." He hung up and sat there leaning against the headboard with his legs stretched out straight.

Molly looked up at him in the dim light. "Well, why do you have that look on your face?" she asked.

"What look?"

"Like a traffic cop seeing a Rolls-Royce zoom by at ninety miles an hour."

He glanced over at her. "That was Caleb. Fort Worth PD called to say that their check on Marcus Gandy, whom you will recall from your close encounter today, was as recently as one month ago employed by none other than the Fort Worth Division of McFarland Construction."

Molly was stunned. "Could it be a coincidence?"

He shifted his foot so it rested against her hip. "Molly, Molly," he scolded in a low voice, shaking his head.

"Well, could it?"

"Is it so hard to accept that Charlie McFarland finds you such a pain in the ass that he arranged to have you beaten up, maybe killed?"

"Yes," she said firmly.

"Well," he said, drawing his foot along the side of her thigh, "I think you might have a problem there." He lifted his foot and very lightly ran his toes from her knee up the inside of her thigh. "Now where were we?"

"Mmm, prehensile toes."

"I love it when you talk like that. Big words." He moved down so he was lying next to her.

She looked into his pale eyes, now only inches from hers. "Oh, I didn't tell you the rest of what Charlie told me tonight."

"Charlie who?" he murmured, kissing her throat.

"He's dying," she said. "Of cancer. That's what's wrong with his back—all these tumors. You better make your case quick. In six months he'll be dead."

He stopped what he was doing. "You believe that?"

"Yes."

"Who else knows?" he demanded.

"Georgia knew, and his doctor, and Frank Purcell. He hasn't told anyone else yet. He just found out a week ago. He wants to get another opinion."

"Who's his doctor?"

"I don't know."

"We'll find out and check on it," he said.

"Can you get that sort of information from a doctor?"

He pushed himself up to his knees and looked down at her. "I can do anything. Just watch," he said, leaning over her to begin a slow exploration with his mouth. Grady Traynor—a man who was never in a hurry; she had always liked that about him.

"This police protection isn't such a bad thing," she murmured, abandoning all thoughts of dinner.

It was ten o'clock before Molly's hunger pangs returned. "If we don't eat, I'll perish," she announced.

He sighed and swung his legs over the side of the bed. "We'd have eaten hours ago if you hadn't waylaid me. Can I use your shower before we go out?"

Molly leaned over the edge of the bed to gather up her clothes, which lay in heaps on the floor. "Sure. I'm going to get some ice water from the kitchen. Want some?"

"If you'll bring it to me in the shower."

In the glow of the night-light, she pulled her T-shirt on over her head and started down the dark stairs. Suddenly the front door swung open and the click of a light switch downstairs flooded the hall and stairs with light. Jo Beth gave a start when she saw Molly on the stairs.

"Mom, you're home! There were no lights on, so I thought—"

Jo Beth stopped in midsentence when Grady stepped out of the bathroom with a towel wrapped around his waist.

"Dad!" she said. Her face, looking up at them, was frozen in shock.

He stopped in his tracks and put a hand down to secure the towel. Molly had never seen him blush before, but his cheeks and neck had turned crimson under his tan. The man who was never at a loss was at a loss. "Oh, Jo Beth. Uh—"

"Sorry," Jo Beth said, putting a hand in front of her mouth. "I didn't know anyone was—uh, sorry. I'll come back later."

She stepped backward and let a giggle escape. "I'll ring the bell next time." As she closed the door, Molly thought she heard her daughter say "Wow."

chapter 19

I got me a few.
The dragon is blue
The dagger is too.
Jail-house tattoo—
Something to do.

Skeleton's grin,
The mark of sin,
Death and its twin—
Dreams from within
Inked on my skin.

LOUIE BRONK
Death Row, Ellis I Unit,
Huntsville, Texas

After a very late dinner and far too much wine, Molly had fallen into hard slumber. But she woke with a gasp, mouth dry as sand, skin prickling, heart hammering, eyes wide open. She knew what time it was even before she turned her head to look at the glowing green numerals of her digital clock: three o'clock. Always three o'clock—her witching hour, when the fears and anxieties she managed to keep in the closet during daylight hours broke out, reared up on their hind legs, and howled.

For twenty-six years she had suffered from these early morning terrors, ever since that humid summer night, when she was sixteen. She had awakened in a sweat. Her daddy hadn't come home and she was certain that he was in mortal danger. She had gotten out of bed and sat at the kitchen table, keeping vigil at the black window until sunrise, when she went out looking for him. For five days she searched. For five days she didn't go to school, didn't eat, or sleep, or cry. On the fifth day his body floated to the surface of Lake Travis, where it was found by three early morning fishermen.

After that night, the image she often woke from was a face barely glimpsed through dark rippled water, a face glowing green like the clock numerals, with streamers of decomposing flesh trailing behind like seaweed. She always tried to get closer, to see the face so she might comfort it. She'd reach out her hand, but as her fingers brushed the surface of the water, she woke, gasping for breath as if she had been the one under the water.

But this time it wasn't her daddy that woke her up.

No. This time it was Tiny McFarland.

Molly took several ragged breaths, closed her eyes, and on the backs of her lids, she conjured her up—not the pale, rigid body on the steel autopsy table, but the living woman. Though she had never seen the woman in life, she had her clearly in mind when she wrote that scene in *Sweating Blood*. The chic blond woman with the prepubescent body. Wearing a white linen dress and carrying an armload of red flowers from her garden. There she stood in the open door of the garage, looking at Molly.

Molly moved her lips, speaking to her with no sound: *There you are. Looking good in your white dress, a size four, if I'm remembering right. But why are you taking those flowers into the garage? You want to get cut flowers in water right away. Why don't you take them to the house? There's no water in the garage. And it's greasy in there. You, a woman meticulous about your appearance, you in an expensive white linen dress that you plan to wear to a luncheon, why the garage? To do some chore, maybe? But you have a man living right above the garage who does things like that for you.*

Mmmm. Yes. You have a man. Living above the garage. A handsome man. Young. And you have difficulty resisting men. I understand that. I have had that kind of trouble myself.

Are you taking him the flowers? Or did he call out to you? Now I know your secret as surely as if we two had sat down over a glass of wine and confided our sex lives. The two of you have been getting it on. You and David Serrano. Lady Chatterley and the gardener. A handsome couple, you so blond, he smooth and swarthy. Oh, yes. He was upstairs in his hot apartment, wearing only shorts, and he saw you out the window cutting flowers and he wanted you. You'd been away for three weeks and he was wild for you. He saw you in your white dress and he wanted you.

One of your children was home, true, but she was napping and you were eager for him, too, because you'd been away. Maybe he came running down the stairs and took you in his arms. Maybe you danced. Maybe you were both so eager you couldn't wait, just like Grady and I were tonight. Maybe it got out of hand, got too rough, or you fought. Maybe someone surprised you. Maybe your husband came home. What a shock to be making love in the dark and suddenly the light goes on and the garage door starts to lift, and there you are . . . or maybe someone else came. Molly's eyes flew open and the image vanished.

Molly lifted her head and looked down at Grady Traynor asleep next to her, cocooned up to his chin in her Aunt Harriet's old patchwork quilt. His face was relaxed and peaceful, his breathing deep and even. He slept as he always had, as if the years on the force and in homicide, as if all the horrors he had witnessed, had never touched him where it mattered—a man with no nightmares. She envied that.

She put her hand gently on his shoulder. The second she touched him, he became instantly and totally awake. God, she'd forgotten. You could wake him up anytime of the day or night, and he was immediately ready—to talk, or fight, or listen to the rain, or make love. In her experience, other men tended to be groggy or surly when awakened in the middle of the night, but not this one.

Grady glanced up at her face, then at the clock. He rolled over onto his back and said in a raspy voice, "Looks like the lurkies have got you by the throat, Molly. Three A.M. still a bad time for you?"

"Sometimes," she said reluctantly, hating to admit it was as bad a time as it had always been. "My fire ant bites are blistering." She pulled one leg out from under the covers to show him her ankle in the glow from the night-light. The top of her foot and her ankle were dotted with tiny pearly blisters.

He extricated a hand from the quilt cocoon he'd made for himself and wrapped his fingers around the ankle, completely encircling it. "Anything an old friend could help with?"

Molly leaned her head down close to him. "Louie Bronk didn't kill Tiny McFarland," she said, watching his face intently.

Grady stared straight up at the ceiling in silence for a minute, as if he were reviewing it in his head.

Molly discovered she was holding her breath in anticipation of his response.

Finally he said, "I have my doubts about it, too. What convinces you?"

Feeling too warm and too confined, Molly pulled her foot from his grip and used both feet to push the covers down to the end of the bed. "Oh, Grady. You know how you construct a story, you spin it from a few facts, it looks pretty good, and then somehow it's set in concrete?"

"Do I ever!" he said with a snort.

Aware suddenly of her nakedness, she reached down to the foot of the bed, pulled the sheet back up, and wrapped it around herself. "Well, that happened here, I think, with Tiny McFarland. Now that I look at it from this angle, there's so much wrong with my version. It's always been a messy case. First, it was so different from Louie's usual MO—away from the Interstate, choosing a blonde, killing her with so little blood, no postmortem rape, the nicks on her scalp. Then there were the stolen things that never turned up—the watch, the earrings, the stuff taken from the house; they were all distinctive. Something should have surfaced if they'd been pawned like he said. And the car, that goddamned Mustang. They dragged the lake twice and couldn't find the fucking thing."

The little blisters on her feet and ankles were itching like crazy. "And, Grady, when they questioned him about the case he was already in a frenzy of confessing. He confessed because they wanted him to, because he was in the mood, because it was a status crime, because it had his signature on it already." Though she'd been struggling to resist the urge, she scratched at the blisters; it just intensified the itch, but she kept on. "And they fed him information. Of course, I know that can happen inadvertently and Louie's quick to pick up on things. But I think this was deliberate. It probably was Frank Purcell who filled him in on those crucial bits about the scene and where the body was and what was stolen.

"But it's the car. That's the final thing for me. Lord help me, I believe him, Grady. I think he did have it painted before the Tiny McFarland murder. I think he *did* junk it in Fort Worth." She was trying to keep her voice low and in control, but it kept rising and she heard the edge of hysteria in it. "He said at the time of his confession that he'd dumped it in a lake near Fort Worth because he knew if they found it, they'd discover he'd had it painted days before Tiny was killed and it would invalidate his confession. He was never even there at the McFarland house. And he sure as hell didn't kill Tiny. It's all a lie. Which I helped propagate with my meticulously researched book."

Her whole body felt as if it were simmering over low heat now. She reached out and laid her hand on his chest, waiting until she felt the even thudding of his heart under her palm. "Grady, in"—she stopped to do the mental calculation—"in forty-five hours he's going to be executed for something he didn't do. I can't stand that."

He said quietly, "You're going to have to stand it."

"Can't you do something?"

"What? This isn't my case, Molly. But even if it had been, it's been tried and appealed. You know that. There's no recourse on this."

"There's the governor," she said. "Last year she gave Tommy Stark a thirty-day stay and Julius Boulton in April."

"Shit, Molly. With Stark the Bishop asked her to and with Boulton it was rock stars who asked. Even a she-wolf like our governor has one or two people who can get her attention. And Stark got executed anyway."

"Yeah. I know. But thirty days might help."

"How? How might it help?"

She shrugged. "I can work some more on the car issue. Convince someone. I don't know."

Grady sighed as if he knew he was in for a long evening now. "Molly, think this through. If you're right that Bronk was never even there, then Alison McFarland and David Serrano were both mistaken about seeing the car. Or they lied under oath."

"I think they lied. It had been in the paper, that police were looking for a car of that description in connection with the Greta Huff murder in San Marcos, that the Texas Scalper might be driving a car like that. I think they lied to make it look like the Scalper did it. To protect the real killer. And, goddammit to hell, it worked. It fooled the cops, and Stan Heffernan, and the jury, and it fooled me."

"Are you toying with the idea that David Serrano killed her and got the kid to support his lie about the car?"

"It's possible. I think Tiny and David were lovers. I'm sure of it. He was an exceptionally good-looking man and he was available, right over the garage. And she had a weakness. I think that's why she was in the garage in her white dress with her fresh-cut flowers."

"Well," he rumbled, "you would know about that, Molly. After all, you're the expert in—"

She put a hand over his mouth, hard, and shook her head to stop him from saying any more. "Don't," she said, and waited a few seconds before taking her hand away.

He took a long breath. "Okay. But consider this: what if her husband walked in on them?"

"Or someone else."

He lifted his head off the pillow, doubled it over, and rested his head back on it. "You want to know what I think?"

She nodded.

"I think when we find the person who did my two murders, we'll know who killed Tiny."

"You think the same person did all three," she said.

"Yes."

"So does Louie. He says if you get away with killing once, you'll do it again—eventually."

Grady smiled. "Louie. An expert on homicide if there ever was one."

Molly hugged her knees into her chest and rested her chin on them. "Are you still thinking that person's Charlie McFarland?"

"Everything points to it, Molly. I really don't know how you can pretend to be a reasonable woman and ignore the facts about Mc-Farland. May I review just a few of them for you?"

Molly rolled her eyes upward. "Okay," she said. "Shoot."

He held up the index finger of his right hand. "One. He tried to bribe you not to interview his children and to let the Bronk case drop. Right?"

She didn't respond, but he went on. "That's because he was worried you might dig up something new, that one of his kids might spill some beans."

He held up another finger. "Two. We suspect he used his financial clout with the publisher of *Lone Star Monthly* to get your boss to kill the Bronk story he'd already agreed to. Right?" He raised his head to see her expression.

"Yeah," she muttered. "I can't prove it, but I believe it."

"Okay," he said. "We come to three." He added a third finger and shook them in the air. It was a gesture Molly loathed; she saw it as an aggressive male gesture of intimidation. She reached out, took hold of the offending hand, and pressed it down to the bed.

"Three," he said, lowering his voice. "Yesterday he tried to have you killed."

Molly started to protest, but then she saw the three faces coming toward her in the dim light and Marcus Gandy's gaping mouth, the tire iron raised over her head. It had been a damned close call. Her cheek began to pulse and she put her hand to it.

"Well," Grady said, watching her face, "maybe their orders were just to discourage you forcefully. But he set them on you and you could easily have been killed. Now I would think, Molly, that any one of those would be enough to get you annoyed at McFarland."

Molly shrugged.

Grady snorted, a bitter, angry sound. "Of course, he doesn't know you like I do. He thought he'd be able to buy you off or scare you off, but he sure as hell made an error in judgment." For the first time, his voice had taken on that cold tone she remembered from the past.

"What do you mean?" she asked, even though she knew it would be better to let it drop.

"Well, hell, Molly, you don't ever let anything go. You're the only person I know who's still brooding over a twenty-six-year-old case."

"Brooding? What makes you think I'm still brooding over it?"

"What makes me think it?" He scooted up on the bed so he could lean back against the headboard and use his hands to punctuate his words. "It's what wakes you up sweating and shaking at 3 A.M.; it's what makes you a workaholic who doesn't know when to stop; it's what keeps you from having a stable relationship with a man; it's what drives you further than rational people are willing to go."

She turned her head away so she wouldn't have to look at him. "None of those things are true anymore, Grady. If they ever were true. Maybe when I was twenty. But you don't know me anymore."

"I can see it in your eyes, Molly. I hear it in your voice. That old obsession is still there. You finally ran out of possibilities on your father and had to stop, so you find it difficult to let go of anything that even remotely reminds you of him. It's crazy."

Now she really didn't like the direction the conversation was taking. "I don't want to get into ancient history with you, Grady. We were talking about Charlie McFarland and this has nothing to do with him."

"The hell it doesn't. The man even looks a little like your father. He walks and talks like him. He's the same age, same West Texas type. And now he says he's dying. This brings back all the old feelings about Vernon's murder—if it was a murder."

She was breathing hard. She squeezed a pillow against her chest. "Here I thought you were just a dumb cop who barely finished high school and it turns out you're a shrink who's qualified to label people crazy."

His silence told her she'd hit home.

Finally he said in the tight, hard voice she recognized as runaway anger in him, "Well, you tell me then, Molly. Is it crazy to stay up night after night in the dark staring out a window? Is it crazy for a married woman with a baby to go out and screw some paunchy old tobacco-chewing county sheriff while her husband's at work? Is it crazy for her to go into a fit of anger when he catches her—"

"Stop!" she yelled, putting her hands over her ears. "That's enough. For God's sake, isn't there a statute of limitations on these things?" She moved over to the edge of the bed and tried to get up, but one ankle was caught in the twisted sheet. "You stop right there," she said, trying to extricate herself from the sheet. "I knew you'd get around to this, Grady." She tugged at the sheet but he was lying on it. "You just couldn't let it rest, could you? I was very upset then. You knew it was a bad time for me, very bad. I was doing what I had to do for my father and you—"

"Christ. The dutiful daughter! You're still crazy."

She felt the old anger rising like hot bile pumping from her stomach, gagging her, spilling a sour, metallic taste into her mouth. "No. You never even tried to understand. He knew something. Olin Crocker had information about my daddy's murder, something he refused to tell me. I was prying it out of him—yes, *screwing* him. I would have done anything—anything!—to find out what he knew. Then you butted in. Into something that was none of your business. I was finally getting somewhere when you came home and threw your jealous husband tantrum. And the whole thing dead-ended right there."

She was shouting. "Did you know that? Crocker never spoke to me again after that. The whole case just dried up and blew away."

She finally extracted her ankle from the sheet with a violent jerk and stood up. "And you know something? If I had it to do over again and all it took was screwing that randy old bastard, I'd do it again and again and again." Grabbing her T-shirt from the floor, she pulled it on over her head. "I'd do much more than screw him."

"And you say you're not obsessed. Listen to yourself, Molly. You were a married woman with a child and you—"

Her next words came out in a banshee shriek. "Stop it! Stop it right there. I said I didn't want to talk about this, Grady. You promised you wouldn't bring it up. Now stop it or get out."

She heard the last shrill words echoing inside her head and she remembered the last time she'd screamed like that, twenty-two years ago. In a frenzy of anger and shame she'd screamed for him to get out and he had left, just walked out and left her.

He'd just walked out and left her.

The memory grabbed hold of her and shook her; it squeezed the breath from her and burned her eyes. Without warning it erupted through her eyes in a gush of burning tears. She tried to suck them back, but they were beyond control. She sat down on the edge of the bed with her back to Grady and let them come.

She had managed over the years to blot out huge chunks of the past, like her breakup with Grady Traynor and, before that, her wild, uncontrollable grief over her father. After he was killed, Molly had dropped out of high school, in spite of her Aunt Harriet's protests and everyone else's advice. None of them understood. She needed all her time and energy to concentrate on the problem of finding out who had killed her daddy. She had gone about it with a passionate intensity that recognized no limits.

A year after Vernon Cates was found in the waters of Lake Travis, she had walked into the Austin Police Department headquarters to try to extract some information on a new lead. There behind the desk stood Grady Traynor in his brandnew uniform. She was seventeen, he was twenty-four, and they couldn't stop looking at one another. They had begun a mating dance right there in the lobby, using only their eyes. His were the palest aquamarine under thick black brows. Six months later she was pregnant. They got married, and for a while, it seemed to work. She loved him, everything about him, and when Jo Beth was born, she felt as if her sanity had been restored and she might, after all, be able to live like other people.

For the first two years they were married, she'd thought all that craziness was behind her. She'd felt grown-up, like a mature wife and mother. But she'd been dead wrong. It had simply been a lull in the storm because she had exhausted all her leads. The minute a fresh lead appeared, she was caught up again by gale-force winds. Those two years had been just a sweet respite from the power of her quest, which reclaimed her with a vengeance.

She left Jo Beth with her Aunt Harriet most of the time and picked up the investigation of her father's death; when she ran out of leads again, she just brooded on it, sitting at the kitchen table night after night, staring at the dark window, waiting for something to happen.

Then, just when she thought she'd exhausted every possibility, Olin Crocker had come along. The Burnet County sheriff had interrogated a suspect in her father's murder. Crocker had some vital information, she was sure of it, but he wouldn't talk, even though she'd used everything at her disposal to persuade him.

It had ended in total defeat: Olin Crocker never told her what he knew and Grady Traynor had left her.

But she had weathered it, and after all, it was twenty-two years ago—a whole generation. No use weeping over it now. She drew in a few deep breaths and lowered her face to her shoulder to blot her wet cheek on her shirt. Grady was sitting up against the headboard with a puzzled expression, watching her. She turned away and wrapped her arms around herself to keep from crying again.

After a few minutes, she felt the bed move behind her. He was getting up to go. But then she felt his shoulder brush against her back. He rested his cheek against her shoulder. "Molly, Molly, I'm such a dumb shit. These old things have a way of sneaking up on me. I didn't intend to say any of that; it just escaped. It was like I was possessed and had to say it, but it's done now. I promise I won't do it again. It's over and done with, out of my system. Ancient history, as you say. I'm sorry."

He reached his arms around her and hugged, rocking her slightly. "Come on, lie down here next to me, even though I am a bully."

"Grady," she said, twisting to face him, gasping for breath, "I didn't mean to hurt you. I did what I felt I had to do. Maybe I was a little crazy."

His pale eyes opened in surprise; it was the first time she had ever come that close to an admission of regret.

"I know, I know," he soothed. He drew her back onto the bed. "There. It's all over." He tucked a pillow under her head and pulled Aunt Harriet's quilt up over them.

Beginning to feel the mellow aftermath of a good cry, Molly relaxed back against him. After a few minutes of silence she heard his steady breathing and rolled over to see if he was sleeping. His eyes were still open but barely. She wanted to keep him awake. "Grady, I suppose you've considered that Charlie's being so sick gives his kids a real motive to kill Georgia."

"If it's true he's got terminal cancer," he said groggily, "you're right; they might want to knock her off so they wouldn't have to share it when he dies. There are millions at stake. But I thought you said he hadn't told them yet."

"That's true. But maybe they know anyway." She yawned and looked over at him again. His lids were closing. "One last thing, Grady."

"Uh-huh," he said in a thick voice.

"How do you feel about the death penalty? You're the only person I know who's never said anything about it."

He was silent and she thought maybe he'd fallen asleep. But finally he said, "I've come to hate it. It means we can't make any mistakes and we make mistakes all the time."

When she looked over at him again, he was asleep. Even Grady Traynor had limits at this hour of the morning.

Molly got up in the dark, wrapped a blanket around her, and padded downstairs. She couldn't sleep, but at least she could keep watch at the window for a while.

When Grady Traynor came down at dawn, dressed and ready to work his Sunday morning shift, he came into the darkened living room so silently she didn't hear him until he spoke: "Still at your old post, Molly."

She gave a start, guilty, as if she'd been caught doing something forbidden and shameful. "Oh, I just got up," she lied. "My ant bites were itching."

He walked to where she was sitting curled up in the wing chair in

front of the window. He leaned down and pecked her on the cheek
—a cold dawn parting after such a warm night, it seemed to Molly.

He started to turn away, then seemed to have a second thought.
He squatted down next to her chair, looked hard at the dark window
that was just beginning to show a dirty graying near the horizon, and
said softly, "The same tragic and wonderful things will happen out
there, Molly, whether you're watching or not."

"But if I'm watching, at least they won't take me by surprise."

"I wouldn't bet on that," he told her.

As she heard the front door close, she felt suddenly exhausted.
Maybe she was getting too old for vigils.

▲   ▼   ▲

chapter 20

Here's the best deal—
Hands on the wheel
Go where you feel

Work for a day
Collect the pay
And drive away

Open highway
Going my way?
You made my day.

LOUIE BRONK
Death Row, Ellis I Unit,
Huntsville, Texas

It was a Sunday tradition.

Molly supposed she should have taken Jo Beth to church when she was little; everybody seemed to think it was a good idea to give children some religious training and Molly agreed in theory. But the few times she'd tried it, they had both hated it with such intensity that even now, many years later, a Sunday rarely passed when one of them didn't mention that the thing she was most grateful for on a sweet lazy Sunday morning was not being in church.

Instead, they had their own ritual: every Sunday morning, even in winter, they swam together in the clear, ice-cold waters of Barton Springs. Afterward, they went out for a leisurely lunch. They read the newspaper and each worked on her own copy of the *New York Times* crossword puzzle. It was Molly's favorite time of the week.

They had been doing this for twenty years, except for a four-year interruption when Jo Beth had been away at college.

As they walked from the parking lot to the pool, they were uncharacteristically silent, the only sound the slap of their sandals on the pavement. In the truck Molly had pointed out the patrol car following them and had given Jo Beth a blow-by-blow description of the events in Fort Worth the day before. Neither of them had said a word about Grady Traynor. Molly knew she had to say something but she couldn't seem to get started. She stole a sideways glance at her daughter's face and felt a stab of foreboding at the expression she saw there. Jo Beth's head was down and between her eyebrows a deep vertical furrow dented the usually smooth tight skin.

They each paid the entry fee and walked down the steps to the pool in silence. For Molly, Barton Springs had been a case of love at first sight. When she was fourteen and they had just moved to Austin, her daddy brought her here to swim. It had come to personify for her all the wild, slightly seedy, funky, laid-back beauty of Austin, especially Austin as it had been before the growth boom of the eighties.

The pool was mammoth, the length of three football fields laid end to end, and spring-fed. It was a hybrid, part of it constructed of cement like any pool and part of it enclosed by a natural limestone cliff—a municipal pool that felt more like a swimming hole or a spring-fed lake. Irregularly shaped and somehow soft-edged, it seemed to Molly like a long skinny rectangle drawn freehand by a two-year-old with a broken blue-green crayon.

At ten on a Sunday morning, the pool had just opened. The only swimmers already in the water were two sinewy, sun-dried women who were doing laps, skimming across the water like marine mammals. A few people sat on towels in the grassy areas surrounding the pool. One sleepy-looking lifeguard slouched on one of the eight high platforms spaced along the length of the pool.

Molly and Jo Beth took the long walk around the shallow end, where a few mothers and small children were inching into the water, and up onto the rock walk along the cliff that led to the grassy slope on the far side of the pool. There they dumped their big towels under a towering pecan tree—the same exact spot every Sunday.

They both wore thong-type sandals and long T-shirts over their swimming suits. In silence, they shook off their sandals, and in silence they both pulled their shirts over their heads. As Jo Beth folded hers and laid it carefully on top of her towel, she said, "Aren't you going to say anything about you and Dad? I didn't even know you two were on speaking terms and all of a sudden there he is walking naked out of your bathroom, for heaven's sake." She turned to look at Molly, who had stopped with her shirt in her hands. "That sort of thing can be a real trauma for a child, you know." Jo Beth managed a half smile.

Molly balled her shirt up and leaned over to tuck it under her towel. "It must have been a real shock for you."

"It was." Jo Beth's grin faded.

They stood facing the pool. The subject of Grady Traynor had been taboo between them for so long that Molly found herself mute now. If she got started, Jo Beth might again start asking about the real reasons for the divorce; in the past Molly had parried those questions with evasions, vague statements about her own immaturity back then and their mutual incompatibility. Molly's behavior at the end of her marriage to Grady Traynor was one secret she hoped to take with her to her grave. She had always felt grateful to Grady that he had kept her secret; according to Jo Beth he had never, in all the twenty-two years they'd been divorced, said a negative word about Molly.

"So what's the story?" Jo Beth asked.

Molly shrugged her shoulders. "Well, you know he's on the Mc-Farland murder, so I ran into him there and we had a drink afterward, and of course I had to make a statement about finding the body, and I've seen him a few times since then, you know, like the night they found David Serrano's body over at the Burnet Road storage place and we had things to talk about concerning the case and then he met my flight yesterday when I came back from Fort Worth and . . ." Molly saw Jo Beth's grimace of impatience; she'd been babbling. The two of them had never been secretive about sexual matters, but somehow this was different.

"Easy, Mom, easy." Jo Beth reached out and patted her on the arm.

Molly took a deep breath. "Honey, I'm finding this real hard."

"Yeah, I can see."

Molly walked down the grassy slope to the pool and sat down on the edge, letting her legs dangle. Her toes just skimmed the surface of the water. Jo Beth sat down next to her, still waiting.

Looking down toward the shallower water, Molly studied the familiar pattern the light made on the bottom of the pool, a bright pattern of big shimmering hexagons—one of the many things she had wondered about for years and intended to investigate, but had never gotten around to. How many things like that, she wondered, would be left unexplored when she died?

Without looking at her daughter, she said, "I guess I can't tell you much, because I don't know what's going on myself." She didn't know she was going to say the next thing until it came out of her mouth: "Really all I can tell you is that I've always loved him. Always." Molly glanced over at Jo Beth, who was staring straight down into the water, a glistening tear balanced on her cheekbone.

Molly reached her arm around Jo Beth's shoulders, which felt as smooth and sun-warmed as they had when she was a little girl. "Baby, what is it?"

Jo Beth's head sank toward her chest and more tears fell. "Oh, Mom. I'm in love with Ben and it's so utterly hopeless."

Molly leaned her head against her daughter's. Benson Williams, the senior partner in the firm and Jo Beth's boss, was married and had four children. He'd once been a U.S. congressman and everybody knew he wanted to be governor; a divorce was not likely.

Molly knew that Jo Beth had said all she was going to right now; asking questions wouldn't help. It would all come out later, when she felt like telling it. They sat like that for several minutes—two women, Molly thought, who conducted their love lives like something out of a country and western song.

Then Molly rose to her feet and said, "Come on. Let's do it before we lose our nerve."

Jo Beth stood up next to her and curled her toes over the edge of the cement, getting ready to dive. "One," she said, glancing over at Molly.

"Two," Molly said.

"Three!" they both shouted. They hit the water simultaneously.

It was always a shock, no matter how many times you'd done it. The first contact numbed Molly's skin and made her eyes throb deep inside her head. As she burst to the surface, she felt, as she always did after the first dive, charged with vigor and new awareness, more intensely alive. It was tempting to think in terms of purification, because that's exactly what it felt like.

She lay on her back in the water and kicked, stretching her arms out wide, feeling like a seal at play in an arctic pool. She tilted her head so the bruised left cheek was under water. Wouldn't it be wonderful if these waters that bubbled so clear and cold from underground could magically heal wounds? And wouldn't it be even more wonderful if they could wash away old transgressions and sleepless nights and regrets?

She let herself sink under the surface and, with her eyes closed against the cold, swam down to the bottom where she reached out her hands to feel the inrushing water surge up from a fissure in the rock. It was even icier and clearer down here at the source and she liked to think she was the first person in the world to make contact with this water. She stayed down as long as she could, then burst back up to the surface, gulping in the hot air.

Maybe it was because the Texas heat was so relentless, so scorching, so steamy, that Molly relished the iciness of this water. She had grown up in West Texas without air-conditioning, when the only relief from the summer heat had been water, and this water was the best she had ever known—better than the cattle tank in Lubbock, better than Lake Travis where she and her daddy had lived, better than the chlorinated pool at her condo. This was spring water fresh from the ground, sixty-eight degrees all year round; it bubbled up into the pool, uncorrupted by the Texas sun, had its first exposure to the air, and gushed out into the creek.

Molly saw that Jo Beth was beginning her laps, so she fell in beside her. Strong swimmers, they each did six lengths of the pool before stopping to rest. They sat on a rock ledge that jutted out from the limestone wall, positioning themselves so the water gushing from a cleft in the limestone swirled around their hips.

Jo Beth tossed her head to sling her long hair away from her face and turned her face up to the sun. The furrow between her eyebrows was gone; her skin glowed translucent and honey-colored. Like Molly, Jo Beth had been born in February under the sign of Pisces and considered water her element; for both, swimming was a dependable restorative, especially in difficult times.

"So, Mother," Jo Beth said, "before we got distracted by sex, you were telling me about Louie Bronk. You don't really believe he's innocent, do you?"

"I'm afraid I do." Molly squinted her eyes at the water and thought how much easier it was to confront all this now, in sunlight, than it had been last night in the darkness.

"But there's nothing to prove it," Jo Beth said. "I mean the trip to Fort Worth was a bust, wasn't it? Other than your coming out of it alive, of course. There's nothing at all to prove he ever had that car painted.''

"Not a bloody thing.''

"It must have been damned frustrating for you to be—what's the old saying? A day late and a dollar short?''

Molly ran her hands through her hair. "A day late. Yeah. It was damned frustrating. And Nelda Fay Ferguson, the woman who owns the body shop, kept saying it: if only I'd come twelve hours earlier she could have put her hand right on the receipt in seconds, so perfect were their records, so meticulous their filing. What a shame I hadn't come yesterday. I wanted to strangle her. I hate being too late. I hate missing things. The saddest words in the language are 'Oops, you just missed it.' ''

Jo Beth's long, dark lashes were spiked with water. "Hmmm. A business like that—auto painting and parts—my experience is that they rarely keep complete records. They usually have huge holes where the underground economy operates.''

Molly felt a little tingling buzz in her arms and hands—that old feeling when she got close to some truth that had previously eluded her. "When people barter or pay in cash, you mean.''

Jo Beth nodded. "And Louie Bronk strikes me as an underground economy sort of guy.''

"When he paid at all,'' Molly said thoughtfully.

"Yeah. But this is a service you can't steal. He'd have to pay to get his car back.''

Molly felt like she was just emerging from a fog. "Jo Beth, when businesses like that don't report a transaction, do you think they keep any records on it at all?''

"Well, they certainly wouldn't keep them with their legitimate records, where the IRS could stumble on them in an audit, but I've seen lots of businesses that keep private records. They might want to keep them for their own use, like sometimes when there's a guarantee involved, that sort of thing. Or they just want a record of the amount of business they really did, in case they want to sell the business sometime.''

Molly tried to recall the conversation with Nelda Fay Ferguson the previous day. She pictured the sharp, tense face with the scarlet lipstick. The mouth moving, talking and talking, and Molly barely listening, her head throbbing, her bites itching. Once she'd established that the records were all burned up and that the woman didn't remember Louie, she'd paid hardly any attention to her, to that endless chatter about perfect records and what a clean business her husband had run and the IRS.

She said, "I must be losing it. That woman did nothing but protest about what a clean business her husband ran; she was clearly worried about any inquiries into her records. I must have been comatose. . . ."

"Getting hit on the head can do that."

Molly scrambled to her feet. "Jo Beth, I need to give her a call. Right now. On the outside chance she's got something. I'll be right back."

Jo Beth smiled. "Glad to see that love hasn't turned you to total mush, Mom."

"You too, sweetheart," Molly said, patting her on the head.

Molly eased off the ledge and swam to the ladder nearest their clothes. She shoved her wet feet into her sandals, and as she hurried around the pool, she wrapped the towel around herself like a sarong. She stopped to get her hand stamped at the gate and pushed out the turnstile. The patrol car was still there, double-parked. She lifted a hand in greeting to the young cop who looked like he'd rather be anywhere else in the world. Baby-sitting the daughter and ex-wife of a homicide lieutenant was clearly not his idea of a good way to spend a Sunday morning.

When she got to the truck, she flipped through her notebook until she found the page where she'd jotted down notes about Nelda Fay Ferguson and Sam's Body Shop. Instead of using the little speaker clipped near the visor she picked up the receiver; that way there would be none of the echo effect you got from a speaker phone that tended to make people think a whole roomful of people was listening in to the call. This conversation would definitely require a delicate touch and a feeling of privacy. As she punched out the number, she felt thankful for her ingrained habit of always getting a phone number; there was always something she forgot to ask in an interview or some piece of information she discovered she needed later on when she was writing.

Leaving the truck door open, Molly perched on the side of the seat and punched out the number.

The phone rang eight times. She was about to hang up, consoling herself that it had been a long shot anyway. But on the ninth ring, a dispirited voice said, "Ferguson residence."

"Mrs. Ferguson, please."

"This is her."

"Mrs. Ferguson. I'm so glad I got you home. This is Molly Cates in Austin. I talked with you at police headquarters yesterday."

"Oh . . . yes." The voice came flat and reluctant, the auditory equivalent of a dead fish handshake.

"You remember we talked about the records from July 1982. I told you I was looking for a white Mustang that got painted blue?"

"Yeah."

"Mrs. Ferguson, lots of businesses do some cash transactions that don't get reported, you know, for tax purposes."

There was dead silence on the other end.

"Now no one's interested in that here. If your husband might have done some of those cash transactions back then, it's not anything anyone would get upset over. Not in the least."

"I wouldn't know nothing about that. See I—"

Molly cut her off in midwhine. A good way to get people to cooperate was to give them a sense of participating in a larger cause, something that had some heroism to it. "Please listen, Mrs. Ferguson. This is so important. Remember I told you yesterday about the man on death row who says this car business could prove he didn't do it? What I didn't think to tell you yesterday is that he was a drifter who never had a checking account in his life or a credit card. He would have paid in cash. If you could find any record of a cash transaction on a Mustang for that July third to eighth period, under any name, it could be very, very significant."

Silence.

Molly lowered her voice. "Please, Mrs. Ferguson, if there's any chance you might have some slip of paper or entry in a notebook, anything, it could help so much. And I can promise you there will be no trouble for you as a result." She held her breath.

"I'm feeling poorly today, Miz . . . uh . . . Cates," Nelda Fay whined. "And I surely don't know what you're talking about here. . . ."

"Just tell me if there's any chance some other records were kept," Molly persisted. "At home maybe."

Again there was a silence. *Slow down,* Molly thought. *You're pushing too hard; back off.*

Nelda Fay said, "No. All them records were at the office and got burned up. You was there, you saw what a mess it was. Now I'm not well at all. Sorry." The phone clicked.

Molly put the phone back in the cradle and counted slowly to sixty. Then she dialed the number again. The phone rang three times before it was picked up. The voice sounded even whinier this time.

"Mrs. Ferguson, Molly Cates here. I think we got cut off; it's this mobile phone of mine, damn machine doesn't work right half the time. You were talking about feeling poorly and I can sure identify with that. You know where my face got all bruised yesterday when I was attacked on your property? Well, it's sure giving me a bad time today and I'm wondering if there isn't some bone damage on the cheek or maybe even some damage to the eye. . . ."

"Miz Cates, I'm sorry to hear it, but my doorbell is ringing. I—"

"I may go to see a specialist tomorrow," Molly continued. "Now you shouldn't worry about that. Not for a second. It wasn't your fault it happened. Lord, I know how long it takes to get people to do things. Even something simple like boarding up a hazardous building like yours there on the Mansfield Highway. I mean you can't expect it to get done the day right after the fire. Although some folks might say—"

"Miz Cates." Nelda Fay's voice became anxious. "What is it you want me to do again?"

Bingo. She got her. "To look through the records your husband kept at home for anything that mentions a car being painted in July of 1982."

There was a lengthy silence. Molly actually had to hold her tongue between her teeth to keep from saying more. Silence was often the best persuader.

Finally the woman said, "I surely would like to help you."

"That's real kind of you, Mrs. Ferguson."

"Now that I had a chance to think about it, I remember that my husband did from time to time take pity on someone less fortunate who had trouble paying the usual prices. He might have given a discount for cash. Since there was almost no profit, he might not have put it on his tax return. Not often, mind you. But it happened sometimes, and I believe he did keep some of them records at home."

Molly felt like she was walking on a narrow bar and could tip either way. "Mrs. Ferguson," she said evenly, "could you look through those things now? I'd be happy to wait." Molly felt an absolute certainty that the woman, motivated by curiosity, had gone home yesterday and searched through the old off-the-record records. Now the box—a shoe box maybe, or one of those cheap metal lock boxes—was sitting on the kitchen counter and Nelda Fay was probably staring at it right now as she wavered. It was a hard decision: trouble with the IRS was specter enough to discourage anybody from being a Samaritan.

"I'll have to do some rummaging around. Couldn't I let you know in a few days?"

"Mrs. Ferguson, the man's going to be executed tomorrow just after midnight. There is no time. Please."

A long exhale went into the phone. "Just a minute."

Molly could picture Nelda Fay standing with her hand over the phone counting under her breath so a respectable amount of time would pass by.

Waiting had always been painful for Molly. Keeping the phone at her ear, she reached into the back seat and pulled a pen from her bag. She began to doodle on the notebook page headed "Sam's Body Shop." Without planning it, her fingers drew a rough sketch of a car, blocking in a door and making little crosshatches over it to indicate the door was a different color from the rest of the car.

She let her sandals fall to the ground next to the truck, and leaning back into the seat, she swung around so she could put her bare feet up on the dashboard.

After several minutes, Nelda Fay Ferguson came back on the line. "Miz Cates?"

"Yes." Molly made herself jump with the loud eagerness of her voice.

"There *is* something here."

"Yes?"

"It's looks like a carbon copy, kind of blurred and messy, but it's a receipt and it's in my husband's handwriting."

"Could you read it to me?"

"Just let me put on my other glasses here. So I can try and make this out. Darn these old carbons. Sam was always economizing. All right-y. It says, '150 dollars p-d,' you know short for paid, and the date is 7/6/82. Then it says, ' '72 Mustang, total body, grabber blue,' that's the color, you know."

Molly found herself short of breath. "Is there a name on it?"

"Well, let's see. It's kinda hard to read. These carbons always seem to get more worn out at the top when they been used too much. But it looks like the name is L. Bronson. Is that the one you wanted?"

Molly felt like someone had whacked her in the chest with a two by four. L. Bronson was the name Louie had told her he had used.

So it was true. There was no escape from it now. It was true.

"Miz Cates? Is that right?"

"Yes," Molly said, "it's what I was looking for."

"Are you sure this isn't gonna bring me no trouble, Miz Cates?"

"Absolutely. I promise it."

Molly stopped here; she hadn't planned for this. She really had no idea what to do next. "Mrs. Ferguson, are you going to be home for a while?"

"Well, I *was* planning on going out later."

"Well, I need to figure out a way to get this from you today."

"Get it from me? What are you going to do with it?" Her voice was shrill with alarm.

"Don't worry, Mrs. Ferguson. It's just to show his car was blue after July sixth. For evidence."

"Oh, golly, I—"

"Tell you what, I'll call you back in a few minutes, after I've arranged it. Okay?"

"Okay."

Molly put the phone down, leaned her head back into the seat, and closed her eyes tight. Why had she done this? She could have let it rest after making the trip yesterday. But now there was no going back.

That painstaking research she'd done—all lies. Her beautiful book —all lies. She felt a flush of hot thick blood flooding into her chest and arms. She'd been duped by Louie Bronk. So had everyone else, it was true. But hers was so public. Would she have to print a retraction? Recall the book?

Everyone would have to know. Or would they? She was the only one who knew about this, except for Nelda Fay Ferguson, who wasn't about to tell anyone. She could just let it go. It probably wasn't going to make any difference anyway; it was hardly the kind of evidence that would get the Bronk decision reversed. She could call Nelda Fay back and tell her it wasn't what she was looking for after all. And she could tell Louie it had just been too late. Too late. Too bad.

She opened her eyes and saw her face reflected in the dirty windshield—wet hair stuck flat to her head, the discolored cheek puffy, the rest of the face very pale. God. She certainly looked like the kind of person who could conceal evidence and present a lie to the world.

At the very least, she was the kind of person who could let her own petty concerns overshadow the fact that a man was about to die for a crime he did not commit.

She picked up the phone and called Grady Traynor's number. He wasn't in, but she got hold of Caleb Shawcross and got him to agree to call Fort Worth immediately and send a detective in plainclothes so as not to upset the lady to Nelda Fay Ferguson's address to pick up some evidence. Then she talked him into having the detective put it on a Southwest flight to Austin and sending a man over to pick it up at the airport that afternoon.

Molly called Nelda Fay back and told her to expect someone within the hour.

She got down from the truck, stuck her feet in her sandals, and walked back to the pool. Jo Beth was doing laps again. Molly walked fast along the edge so she was waiting for her at the deep end. Jo Beth stopped and grabbed on to the edge of the pool. She looked up, studied Molly's face, and said, "She found something."

Molly nodded. "A carbon of a receipt with the name he was using on it, the date, the type of car, and the color of paint used. It set him back 150 bucks. I shudder to think where he got the money."

"Now what?" said Jo Beth.

Molly dropped her towel and sandals where she was and tucked her keys under the towel. Then she dove back into the water. When she surfaced, she shook her head to get the water out of her ears and said, "Damned if I know."

chapter 21

▲　▼　▲

If I could be
Somehow set free
From being me
Here's what I'd be—
Wild Comanche
Painted with mud
And clotted blood,
Covered in skins,
No thought of sins.
Scalp takers
Skull breakers
Scream makers
Black hair lovers
Swift death givers.

LOUIE BRONK
Death Row, Ellis I Unit,
Huntsville, Texas

Molly sat at her desk looking at the telephone. Her shoulder muscles burned, as if she had just done a hundred push-ups, or as if sharp claws were digging in between her shoulder blades. She pictured an evil-looking gargoyle clinging to her, grinning down at her.

She jiggled her shoulders up and down to relax them. This was ridiculous; it wasn't her responsibility to act on this information. Tanya Klein was the one. After all, Klein was Louie's attorney, a specialist in habeas corpus law. The thing to do was just unload it all on her and let her carry it from here.

She picked up the phone and dialed the number of the motel where Tanya was staying in Paducah, Kentucky. She was there doing research on behalf of a client of hers, another death-row inmate. It had taken Molly a half hour to wheedle Tanya's unlisted home number out of one of her coworkers and then to beg her roommate to reveal the number in Kentucky.

"Slumber Rest Motor Lodge. How can I help you?"

"Tanya Klein's room please," Molly said.

The operator let it ring about fifteen times before coming back on the line. "Miss Klein doesn't answer."

Molly felt desperate; her shoulders were hunched up around her ears again. "Could you page her? She might be in your restaurant or the lobby or the pool maybe. It's an emergency."

"We don't have no pool, but I'll check the coffee shop."

After a few minutes, Tanya's world-weary voice came over the line: "This is Tanya Klein."

"Oh, Tanya, it's Molly Cates. I'm so glad I found you. I—"

"God. How did you track me down?"

"Tricks of my trade," Molly said. Then, unable to keep a breathlessness out of her voice, she poured out everything that had happened in Fort Worth. As if she were presenting some prize, she told Tanya about the receipt for painting the Mustang dated July sixth.

There was a long silence on the other end of the line. Tanya said, "Wait a minute here. Molly, you aren't saying you believe Louie Bronk is *innocent?*"

Molly took a deep breath and tried to lower her shoulders. "In the McFarland matter, yes. I am saying that."

"On the basis of a carbon receipt from an auto body shop? Something anyone could manufacture? Give me a break, Molly."

"I was thinking we might try to get DPS to date it."

"Oh, sure." Tanya let out a bark of a laugh. "It would be perfect for carbon 14 dating. You get it? *Carbon* 14?"

"Yeah. I get it. Tanya, how did someone so young get so cynical?"

"You know the answer to that, Molly. You've covered enough of these cases. It's dealing with a system where the Supreme Court of the land actually debates whether it is unconstitutional to execute someone who might be innocent. Where that same court agrees to hear the issues of a condemned man's case but refuses to grant him a stay so he'll be alive when his case gets heard."

"I know," Molly said. "It's ludicrous. But where are we now with the appeals?"

"I wrote up a Certificate of Probable Cause and sent it to the Fifth Circuit Court. We may hear back tonight."

"What can we do with this new evidence?"

Tanya sighed. "I guess I can go back to the state with a one-issue petition."

"Good," Molly said. "Let's do that."

"Of course there are a few little problems here. In Texas there's a thirty-day limit on filing claims of new evidence after a conviction, a limit recently affirmed by the Supreme Court. And—let's see—it's been more than three thousand six hundred and fifty days since Louie was convicted, so we're a little past the deadline. Now that doesn't mean we don't file these things. We do. All the time. You'd be amazed how often we find them: lost witnesses, newly uncovered alibis, confessions that were given by people now dead—you name it. Of course, the courts don't pay any attention to them."

"But those are bogus," Molly protested. "This is the real thing."

"Doesn't matter," Tanya said in a dead voice.

Molly took a deep breath and said, "So what are you supposed to do with new evidence that really does come up at the last minute?"

"Executive clemency is supposed to be the route for that."

"How does that work exactly?"

"Well, you know in some other states the governor can commute a sentence or give a pardon unilaterally, but not in Texas. The way it works here is the Board of Pardons and Paroles has to recommend clemency first. But it's never happened. Those pricks have never voted to commute a death sentence. Not once. And, anyway, all the paperwork has to be done in triplicate a minimum of five working days before the execution date and we've only got one day."

"Oh, shit. Where does that leave us?"

Tanya measured another long-suffering silence into the phone. "Well, the governor does have the power to grant a one-time, thirty-day reprieve. In order to give the Board more time to consider a case. Like she did recently in the Boulton case. But, Molly, even if by some wild stretch of circumstance she could be convinced to do that, it would just delay it a month. The Board is simply not going to recommend commutation in this case, no matter how many carbon copies you come up with. Louie really doesn't have any issues. Even if he did, it wouldn't matter—they are out for blood."

Molly dug her fingers into her right shoulder, trying to force the tension out. It was impossible. Surely she'd done as much as could be expected of her. She could stop here.

"Look. Molly," Tanya said, "thanks for calling. Really. Tonight

I'll fax a petition to CCA and the trial court simultaneously, and I'll include your new piece of evidence. Okay?"

"How long will it take them to respond?" Molly asked.

"At this point in the process, a few hours, usually. Just long enough for the judges to have a good laugh. They'll probably slap my hands and accuse me of abusing the writ, like they did last time."

Molly put down the phone. She felt stabbing pains in her shoulders; the gargoyle was settling in, hooking its claws in deeper. This whole thing was futile. The state was determined to execute a killer and there was nothing she could do about it. She should go see a movie and forget the whole mess. Yes, that's what she would do. But first she needed to talk to someone.

She called Stan Heffernan's home number. His wife said her husband was out sailing on Lake Buchanan and had failed to take his beeper with him. Molly left an urgent message for him to call her the minute he got home.

Then, not knowing what to do next, she started making calls, trying to find someone to talk to, anyone who might be available on this sunny Sunday afternoon.

First she tried APD. Grady Traynor was at a crime scene in East Austin, one of the other homicide detectives said—another drive-by shooting.

Richard Dutton didn't answer his phone and didn't believe in answering machines.

Barbara Gruber, who was usually available, had actually gone out on a date—with a man, her mother said.

Jo Beth had said she was going in to her office, but she didn't answer her phone there.

Molly even tried calling Jonathan Bellinger, her agent, to commiserate about the Japanese deal falling through. But Jonathan wasn't home either.

She pushed her rolling chair away from the desk, grabbed her big tote bag, and rummaged through it, scooping all the loose pieces of paper off the bottom and dumping them out on the rug. In the pile were two credit card receipts, a used Kleenex, several little triangular corners torn from her Day-Timer, and what she was seeking—the card Addie Dodgin had given her, which had gotten badly crumpled.

She smoothed the card out and winced when she saw under the name and address the slogan "We are forgiven." But it seemed less obnoxious now than it had the first time she saw it. Maybe she was warming to the idea.

Maybe she felt more in need of forgiveness now than she had two days ago.

Picking up the card and her cordless phone, she lay down on the little sofa and arranged the pillow under her knees. Again she looked at the card. Maybe all of us should print slogans on our cards, she thought—something pithy that would explain us to the world. We would be limited to three words. Three words. That would be a challenge. What would hers be? She rubbed her thumb over the slightly raised letters of Addie Dodgin's card and considered it. Maybe hers would be "Never give up" or "Honor the dead." That sounded so grim. When all this was over she'd have to make some changes. Work less. Live more. No more vigils. God, now she was thinking in slogans.

She dialed the phone number, certain somehow that Addie Dodgin would be in; she would be there. She *would*.

"Sister Addie Dodgin here." The voice was so cheery, so sugary sweet that Molly felt like slamming the phone down. This woman was not her sort; she would probably suggest they pray together or leave it in God's hands. Why had she made this call?

"Addie, this is Molly Cates."

"Why, Sister Molly, I was just thinking about you."

Molly let her head rest back on the sofa arm. "What were you thinking about me?" It sounded like a lover's question.

"I had a feeling you would call. Maybe I was just hoping it."

"I thought you might like to hear about the results of my trip to Fort Worth," Molly said.

"Oh, yes indeed. I surely would. Just a minute. Let me get settled here." There was a thump and some rustling, and then some clicks. "There. Now I'm settled with my knitting. I hope you don't mind. I listen better when I knit."

"What are you knitting?" Molly asked, surprising herself with the question.

"Oh, my. It's an afghan. For Louie." Addie sighed. "But I'm afraid it won't be finished in time. And no one else could stomach the colors. You know what colors he asked for?"

Molly remembered the horrible thing Addie had been working on in the warden's office. "Brown and pink," she said.

Addie laughed. "I forgot you're a writer; you notice these things."

"Oh, I wish that were true," Molly said. "So much gets by me. Sometimes I think I go through life swathed in cotton and preconceptions. I miss so much. About yesterday—" Molly cleared her throat and started in. She told her in detail about the stolen car and the fire that destroyed the records.

Addie listened actively with lots of oh, mys and dear, dears at the right times. Through it all Molly could hear the steady *click-click* of her needles.

When Molly got to the part about the three men attacking her, Addie said, "Goodness. You were blessed to escape that. Someone was riled over this."

"Yes. But there's more." Molly told her about the receipt Nelda Fay Ferguson had been persuaded to unearth. "It should be on its way to Austin now, for whatever it's worth."

Addie Dodgin sighed one of the biggest sighs Molly had ever heard. "I suppose you've told Tanya Klein about it?"

"Yes. I tracked her to Paducah, Kentucky, to tell her."

"And she said nothing would make any difference."

"Yes. But she's going to include it in a petition to the state anyway."

"But the courts are not likely to give relief," Addie said.

"That's what she says."

"So now you're stuck between a rock and a hard place, aren't you, dear?"

"Sister Addie, I can't remember ever in my adult life not knowing what to do next."

"That must feel strange."

"Oh, does it ever," Molly said.

"Tell me what you're thinking."

"Just so you know what I'm really like," Molly said, "my first thought was to do nothing. Just let it slide by. Then no one would know what a gullible fool I've been and my book wouldn't look like the worthless piece of shit it is."

Addie chuckled. "Isn't that just the kind of creature we are? Our first instinct is to hunker down and protect ourselves."

Molly felt her shoulders and neck relax into the sofa. "Yeah. And with me, it doesn't get much better. My next thought was: He's a killer. He may not have done this, but he's done others. What difference does it make which one he's executed for?"

Sister Addie whistled, a low quivering sound like wind vibrating the wires between Waco and Austin. "Now that's a real interesting question to ponder. What answer did you come up with?"

"Well, I'm still just nibbling around the edges of it, but it has to do with lying. Now I lie all the time. You wouldn't believe what a liar I am. I can't seem to get through a single day without telling lies right and left. You should hear me: 'Yes, that is an interesting idea for an article; thank you for sharing it with me. It's nice to see you again. No, you aren't bothering me. Why, I'd love to come to the Symphony Women's Fashion Show, but I'm going to be out of town.' "

Sister Addie laughed, a good belly laugh that made Molly smile. "Oh, those social lies," Addie said. "It sure is hard to live in the world without telling them."

"Yeah. I justify them as politenesses, but I get so inured to them, I don't even notice I'm lying, and before I know it, real lies creep in."

"What are the real lies?" Addie asked.

Molly let out a long breath and felt a small shudder deep in her chest. "Well, in my work—in writing—you start your lies small, with presenting some minor thing as fact when it isn't or fudging a quote slightly to make it better, or to make it fit better with the point you're making. But then it grows into something worse, like stopping your research at the point where you've got lots to support your point of view, but before you get to the really messy opposing stuff. And then the next thing you know, along comes a big bad wolf of a lie"—she felt short of breath—"like the long extended lie I tell about Louie Bronk in my book."

"That was a mistake on your part," Addie said, her voice firm, "not an intentional lie."

"No. It was a lie," Molly said. "Because I started with a preconceived idea—that Louie did kill Tiny McFarland—and then made all my research fit into that mold. I accepted other people's lies because they fit with what I wanted to believe. Louie says it best—he says when he confessed to Tiny's murder down in San Marcos he was just telling the law what they wanted to hear. And he did the same with me—he just told me what I wanted to hear. I had my mind made up what the story line was and he went along with it and gave me what

I needed to write my book. There were danger signals everywhere that he was lying, but I was in a hurry to get the book written before the advance money ran out. I didn't ask enough questions. I took the easy way."

"You sure are hard on yourself," Addie said.

"No, I don't think so. Because the inevitable result of that lie and all the smaller lies is something truly ugly—the absolute Godzilla of all lies."

Addie almost whispered it: "Letting a man die for a murder he didn't do."

"Yes. Remaining silent. And right before I called you I'd already decided that I'd done as much as I could to correct this, that it was an impossible situation. Not my fault. Not my responsibility. The only thing to do was just drop it and let the powers that be do what they will do."

"That doesn't sound like you, Sister Molly, dropping something because it's impossible. Anyway, it doesn't sound like Louie's assessment of you."

"Oh, I'm persistent all right, but only on the things that fit my preconceptions. Everything else I conveniently overlook. But, Addie, the lying has to stop somewhere. It's not saying much for me, but *this* is where I draw the line in the dirt. This kind of lie is enough to—" She couldn't find an adequate end to the sentence and anyway she had run out of breath.

"To darken the world," Addie Dodgin said. "I agree with you. It's intolerable. So what are we to do?"

"Tanya says executive clemency is the only thing left."

"That, or you and me trying to rescue him tomorrow night with guns blazing," Addie said.

"Yeah," Molly said, smiling at the image. "I think guns blazing has more chance of success."

Sister Addie laughed, and Molly thought how very pleasing the sound was. God, a few minutes ago she'd been about to hang up because she found the same voice too sugary.

"I tried to call the governor's office earlier," Molly said, "but I couldn't get through. I don't know if it's even worth trying."

"Why not?"

"Well, she's tough on law and order. She's got to be. And politically she has to support the death penalty. Stark and Boulton both had powerful advocates. And Stark got executed anyway."

"Even so, it's worth a try, I think," Addie said, "and I might could help you get an appointment to see her."

"How?"

Addie chuckled, and the click of the needles speeded up. "I've known Susan Wentworth, formerly Sue Ellen Haberman, since we were in the ninth grade."

Molly was stunned. "You have?" The two women were like different species. But now that she thought about it, they were both from Waco and about the same age.

"Yes," Addie said, "I know we seem like creatures from different solar systems, but we both grew up in Waco, went to different high schools, but we met when we competed against one another in a Future Homemakers of America bake-off. She did an apple streusel, her grandmother's recipe, and I did an angel food cake, my own concoction. I won. Funny. The Lord really does move in mysterious ways. That loss probably made her governor. She switched from Future Homemakers to debate club, went on to win state her senior year. I got married and continued to bake prize-winning angel food cakes. And eat them."

Molly found herself almost shouting into the phone. "Addie, why don't you go see her? Since you're old friends. Tell her what's happened. Ask her to give us thirty days."

"Oh, honey. I didn't say we were old friends. I know her well enough that I might be able to get an audience, but you're the one to do this. The request carries more weight coming from a cool customer like you, rather than a known holy roller like myself."

"Cool customer?" Molly said, unable to keep the hurt out of her voice. "Is that how you see me?"

"Well, I'm just talking about the temperature at the skin level," Addie said, "not way down at the heart and soul."

"I sure don't feel cool," Molly said. "Lately I've been having these hot spells where I feel sheer panic creeping over me. I don't know if it's my conscience or a preview of menopause."

Addie laughed. "Tell you what, Sister Molly. Give me a few hours to try and get hold of the governor. I'll call you back."

Molly put the phone down and tried to get up from the sofa. She needed to sit herself down at the keyboard and get cracking on this latest installment of the Louie Bronk saga. But she couldn't budge. Her body was pinned down, paralyzed. She let her head sink back to the sofa arm. It was too difficult. She was tired. And it was Sunday. The hell with it for today.

Molly spent the next hour lying on the sofa working on the *New York Times* Sunday crossword puzzle, which, for some reason she didn't understand, was an activity so riveting that it could hold her attention through a hijacking, or even Armageddon itself.

When the phone rang, she had finished the puzzle, all except for a few boxes in the lower left-hand corner. She sat up and grabbed the phone.

"Sister Addie here. The governor's going out of town tomorrow, but she'll see you at seven for coffee before she goes to the airport. She says you'll have ten minutes to make a case and that it better be damned good."

"How did you manage it?" Molly demanded.

"Don't ask," Addie said with a laugh. "She says to drive around to the back gate of the mansion on Lavaca Street and just holler your name into the intercom."

"What do you think I should say to her?" Molly asked.

There was a pause during which the only sound was the click of knitting needles. "Well," Addie said, "Sue Ellen Haberman was always a person who appreciated honesty and passion. Say what's in your heart."

"If I did that, Sister Addie, she'd run screaming."

"I doubt it, my dear. Sue Ellen's been through the fire herself once or twice. Will you call me afterward? Let me know what happened?"

"Yes."

After she hung up, Molly went upstairs and took a shower. Standing naked, washing her hair under the hot spray, she thought not about Louie Bronk or the governor or the execution, but about Grady Traynor in the dark garage. As she was drying off, the phone rang.

"I'm parked across the street," Grady said, "and I am craving barbecued ribs and a Shiner Bock. Always happens to me after a drive-by. Will you join me?"

"Oh, yes," Molly said. "Give me five minutes to dry my hair and get dressed."

"Sure. Let me in and I'll help you."

Molly pulled a big T-shirt over her head and ran downstairs to let him in, her heart thumping. In spite of everything, he was back for more.

When she opened the door and saw him across the street, leaning against the battered white Ford Tempo, her heart gave a sudden lurch. She stopped in the doorway and pressed a hand over her heart to quiet it, but underneath her fingers it gave a mighty kick. She was alarmed by the power of it until she remembered that many years ago that very thing used to happen frequently.

She grinned. That was the worst sign of middle age she'd experienced yet: to worry you're having a heart attack when you're merely falling in love.

chapter 22

You're the one
Who used the gun,
Had hisself some fun.
Tell us, they said,
You made them dead.
No use denying.
No more lying.
I might.
All right.
I'll bite.
I confessed
To all the rest.
I'm the best.

LOUIE BRONK
Death Row, Ellis I Unit,
Huntsville, Texas

▲ ▼ ▲

Molly arrived at the back entrance to the governor's mansion fifteen minutes early, so she pulled her truck to the curb on Lavaca and slumped down to wait. She didn't want to listen to the radio and she hadn't thought to bring the paper along. She let her head rest back on the seat and stared at the white-brick wall and the back of the Greek Revival mansion that had served as home to Texas governors since 1856.

It was six forty-five and the sky was lightening in the east. She lifted her eyes up, above the wall, above the flat roof of the mansion, and above the treetops to the rose-colored dome of the state capitol a block away. The repairs to the dome had finally been completed, along with the new underground addition. At the very top of the dome stood the recently restored Goddess of Liberty. In her right hand she held a sword and in the left, a gold star, which she raised aloft, 309 feet into the Texas sky. As Molly watched, the morning sun caught one of the star's points and made it wink, once, twice, and then the whole star was suddenly illuminated, sending out golden rays against the slatey sky. Molly felt a little quiver in her chest. If she were a person who thought in terms of signs and omens, this might mean something for her.

Molly Cates didn't have many heroes, but one of them was Susan Wentworth. Once an alcoholic housewife with four children and a philandering husband, in her forties Wentworth got sober, divorced her husband, and went to law school. In her fifties, she won a seat in the state legislature and then ran for governor.

During her first term Susan Wentworth became one of the most popular governors in the history of the state and was reelected four years later in a landslide. She achieved national recognition with her witty keynote address at the Democratic Convention and was often mentioned in the national press as a possible candidate for president. Molly's magazine had recently done a cover by superimposing the governor's head on a model dressed as Wonder Woman lassoing the state of Texas with one hand and the United States with the other.

At two minutes to seven Molly pulled her truck up to the closed gate in the brick wall, easing up to the intercom speaker. The instant she spoke her name, the gates swung open. She drove around the brick-paved circle drive and stopped under the porte cochere behind a white Caprice Classic with three antennas on the back. She glanced around for guards but saw no one. Then she noticed that she was surrounded by security cameras, hidden in azalea bushes and up in trees and next to pillars.

A man in a dark suit emerged from the white carriage house at the gate and approached the truck. "Follow me please, Mrs. Cates," he said. They entered the back door and he ushered her into the first room on the right. A large room with two full walls of windows, it was decorated all in yellows and beige. The first rays of morning sunlight seemed to bring it all to warm, glowing life. A huge octagonal table occupied the center of the room.

"Please sit down," the man said. "The governor will be right along."

Molly waited for less than a minute before Susan Wentworth entered, her three-inch spike heels tapping the hardwood floor at the doorway with an energy that made Molly stand and stare.

Though Molly had never actually met Susan Wentworth, she had seen her in person several times at press conferences and speeches. So she thought she was prepared for the vitality of the woman's physical presence. But when the governor entered the room—wiry and spring-loaded, frosted blond hair coifed within an inch of its life, wearing a vivid red suit and matching lipstick—Molly found herself staring in awe. She was—just for a moment, unexpectedly, amazingly—star-struck.

The governor carried a manila file folder which she set down on the table with a slap. "Morning, Miz Cates," she twanged. "You're right on time and that's good because I have to leave for the airport in just ten short minutes."

A man entered behind her with a tray bearing a silver coffeepot and two cups.

"You'll join me in some coffee, I hope," she said, pulling a chair out and sitting down at the table. "Sit down."

Molly sat. "Yes. Thank you."

The man put a china cup and saucer in front of the governor and one in front of Molly. He poured each a cup and walked out silently, pulling the door shut behind him.

The governor picked up her cup and took a sip, studying Molly over the brim. Her bright blue eyes were framed by scores of deep wrinkles radiating out from the corners. She set her cup down and said, "Miz Cates, I don't believe we've met before."

"No, ma'am," Molly said, her throat dry and scratchy.

"I have read some of your pieces in *Lone Star Monthly*. I particularly liked the one some years back about the archaeologist who investigated those old bones that got dug up during the construction downtown. Made me feel I missed a bet by not becoming an archaeologist."

"Me too," Molly said. "I felt that way every time I talked with Dr. Carrue. He died a few months ago. On a dig in Big Bend." Her voice cracked at the end of her statement. Molly took a sip of coffee to clear her throat.

The governor opened the file folder in front of her and rested her long, delicate fingers on either side. "Miz Cates, I have to tell you I'm real familiar with this case. I followed it closely back in '82. I was interested because I knew Tiny McFarland slightly—from the Planned Parenthood Board. And I have known Charlie for years; he's been a generous supporter of mine. I'm grieving for him now, what with losing another wife. You should know this has a personal dimension for me."

She lifted the sheaf of papers in the folder and ruffled the pages with her thumb. "After I talked with Addie Dodgin last night, to refresh my memory on the details, I got out Mr. Bronk's file—you know they send me these from Huntsville before every execution. And I have to tell you, I think he's exactly the sort we ought to be executing." She looked up and met Molly's eyes directly. "I'm curious. What on earth could you have to say in his behalf?"

"Nothing," Molly said. "I have absolutely nothing to say for him. He's far worse than you could know from reading that file, Governor. He's certainly killed more women than he ever got convicted of. He's a cold, brutal, manipulative, empty excuse for a man and he has no redeeming traits. . . . But I have come to be convinced that he didn't commit the murder he's scheduled to die for in seventeen hours."

The governor paused with her cup halfway to her lips. "Why?"

Molly had planned out what she was going to say, but she had forgotten it all. She'd just have to wing it. "Governor, I've covered this case for eleven years. I spent two years researching and writing a book on it."

Susan Wentworth flicked an impatient hand. "I know that."

Molly flushed. "Until last Thursday I would have sworn to you that the man was guilty of Tiny McFarland's murder. But something happened to change my opinion. When I read in the paper that Louie had recanted his confession, I went to see him. Not because I believed it, but I was curious to hear what he had to say. I was sure it was just the usual death-row scramble to avoid execution."

Molly's voice gathered strength as she got into the story. "Governor, the story he told scared me plenty. He told how he was able to make a convincing false confession, how the authorities fed him information and how he gleaned the rest. He confessed because he liked the attention; it felt good and this was a glamorous case that attracted more attention than the other murders.

"He said there was a way to prove his innocence. He said the car that was described by two witnesses at the McFarland house—you know all about it from the file so I won't waste your time—could never have been there on July ninth because he'd had the car painted on July sixth and junked it on the seventh. He described the place where he'd junked the car in Fort Worth and where he'd had it painted and asked me to go find it."

Molly pushed her coffee cup away so there would be nothing between them. "Now Louie is a liar—big time—so you have to watch him. He was convincing but I wasn't buying. Not then.

"Governor, by the time I got to the wrecking yard in Fort Worth the next morning, a car of that description had been stolen off the lot the night before. When I got to the auto painting place, it had been burned down and all the records with it; the ashes were still smoldering. All the records had been destroyed. While I was there three men tried to beat me up."

Molly leaned forward so far in her chair she was just perched on the edge. "Governor, someone didn't want me to find any evidence."

"Sounds like they were successful," Susan Wentworth said in a dry voice, "since it seems you came up empty-handed."

"Not totally," Molly said. "I persuaded the owner of the auto body shop to dig up a carbon receipt of a cash transaction—she was keeping the things not reported to the IRS at home—made on July sixth. It describes the car and the name—L. Bronson—is the one Louie told me he'd been using. So we do have that. We do have that piece of evidence."

Susan Wentworth set her cup down. "Doesn't sound like diddly squat to me, Miz Cates."

"I know it's thin. But, Governor, I've been covering crime for twenty-two years and I feel certain about this one. The murders of Georgia McFarland and another man—David Serrano—who used to work for the McFarlands—make me think we should hold off on the execution until we see what's going on. What harm can thirty days do?"

"What harm?" The governor sat up straighter and crossed one slim leg over the other. "My opponents in the legislature would say I was soft on mass murderers and every attorney with a death-row client would be beating on my door. Miz Cates, you've had eleven years to come up with something. It's too late and too little."

She lifted her cup and took another sip of her coffee. "Anyway, this is a matter for the courts and Pardons and Parole to deal with." She looked Molly directly in the eye. "Do you dislike the death penalty so much?"

"It's true I don't like it. But that's not the reason I'm here. Governor, Louie made a false confession to this crime. If we execute him, we're going along with his lie. We become a party to it. Our system has made an error here. We need to own up to it."

The governor sighed and looked toward the window. "You know that I favor the death penalty in cases like this. I have often said it."

"Yes, I know that's what you say publicly." Molly took a deep breath. "But I have noticed, Governor, that in the six years you've been in office you haven't yet attended an execution. It's customary for governors to do that from time to time."

Susan Wentworth turned back to face Molly, the corners of her scarlet, bow-shaped mouth twitching. "And you're reading into that that I'm secretly against it? Miz Cates, I've got a busy schedule and executions would not be a good use of my time." She let the smile break through and it was dazzling. "I *delegate* executions."

The governor stood up. "I'm denying your request, Miz Cates. I appreciate your being an advocate for Justice as you see it here, but I'm not convinced your new evidence is worth a hill of beans. You know, I don't make a habit of listening to eleventh-hour pleas, but it was Addie Dodgin who asked me to see you, and Addie is one of my heroes."

Molly was caught with a mouthful of coffee.

"Oh, yes," the governor said, "I don't have many heroes, but she is one of them."

"Why?" The word blurted out of Molly's mouth all on its own.

"Why? You don't know Addie's story?"

"Story? No. Actually I've only met her once, over in Huntsville."

"And she isn't given to talking about herself, is she?" The governor glanced at a tiny gold watch on her wrist. "Well, time is racing, but I'll give you an abbreviated version: about ten years ago Addie was at a convention of social workers in Houston. One night, she was attacked by two men in the hotel parking garage. She was raped and cut up so bad the docs needed a Simplicity pattern to figure how to stitch her up when she was carried into the emergency room. Well, they sewed her back together—she looks like a patchwork quilt—or, like she says, a Humpty-Dumpty success story, and somehow she recovered. Her husband left her while she was in the hospital and one of her children was killed in a traffic accident the next year."

Molly's eyelids stung.

"Enough to do anyone in, isn't it?" the governor said, watching Molly. "What Addie did with her grief was found her prison ministries and the first people she visited were the men who had assaulted her. She still visits them over in Huntsville—the sorry, miserable sumbitches." She tilted her head. "You didn't know all this?"

"No."

"I would think her story would be irresistible to a writer like you who seems drawn to the violent. She's far more interesting than Mr. Bronk." Susan Wentworth slapped the file shut and picked it up. "I'll tell you a secret if you'll promise to keep it."

Molly nodded mesmerized.

"I'm about to appoint Addie to the Board of Criminal Justice, to fill the new victim seat we created last year. I think she'll turn out to be one of my best appointments."

She walked toward the door, then stopped and turned to Molly. "I have a suggestion for you: how about writing more about crime from the victim's point of view? I reckon serial murderers sell books, but where are the stories about the Addie Dodgins of the world? People who survive the unimaginable and go on cheerfully— the stuff of real heroes."

Molly felt like an oversensitive second grader chastised by a beloved teacher. Her cheeks actually burned with the rebuke. "I'll think on it, Governor. Thanks for the advice."

As Susan Wentworth put her hand on the filigreed brass knob to open the door, Molly found herself panicky. This was her only chance. "Governor, wait!" She took a few steps forward and said, "Addie told me the best way to talk to you was just to say what's in my heart. It's this: you're the head of a mighty state, and you hold the power of life and death. Louie Bronk is a miserable worm of a man whose mother and four sisters beat and molested and humiliated him when he was a boy. He's guilty of the most horrible crimes, but he was falsely convicted of this one. Here's a chance to show mercy to someone who has never seen it before. Please, Governor. Give Louie Bronk a thirty-day reprieve. It could save us all from a grave miscarriage of justice."

She stopped. Molly found she had her arms outstretched in a beseeching gesture she wasn't aware of having made.

The governor pursed her red lips and let out a long stream of air.

"Well, Molly Cates. I like your passion." She put her hands on her hips and looked down at the carpet for several long seconds. "If anything would sway me on this issue," she said, looking up, "that would. But the answer is no. The request is denied." She smiled and said, "Go home." Then she turned the knob and walked through the door.

Molly felt like running behind her and tugging at her sleeve and she would have done it if there was the slightest chance it might do any good. But she recognized the finality of the answer.

There would be no executive clemency for Louie Bronk.

chapter *23*

On the Interstate
Feeling mighty great.
Nothing to do but drive,
Speed a steady fifty-five.
Cruising cops give me the eye.
Hell, I just pass 'em by.
This stretch of highway
I have things my way.

         ▲   ▼   ▲

LOUIE BRONK
Death Row, Ellis I Unit,
Huntsville, Texas

The worst of it, she thought as she drove up Lavaca, wasn't the disappointment or even the embarrassment over her ineffective arguing of the case. The worst of it was that she felt relieved.

Yes, here she was breathing easier than she had in days. She'd done everything that could be morally expected of her. She'd tried to bring out the truth, done her best. Yet nothing had changed: Louie was still officially guilty; her book hadn't been proved wrong to anyone but herself. It was out of her hands now. That meant she could go about her business—get back to work, sign books at the party the magazine was throwing for her on Friday. Maybe now the Japanese would reinstate their offer and she'd get a nice fat check.

Of course, there was still the problem of the article—what on earth was she going to write about Louie Bronk's execution? The story had changed so radically. It was no longer the story of a serial killer finally being executed. It was the story of a serial killer who had been unjustly convicted; it was the story of an unsolved mystery from the past—what had really happened to Tiny McFarland? Who was lying and why?—and it was the story of two new murders which must be somehow connected to the past. It was a story richer and more convoluted, messier and scarier than the story she'd thought she had.

So here she was, for God's sake, a crime writer with the story of a lifetime right under her nose. Why wasn't she home writing it? She stopped at the light at Lavaca and Martin Luther King, not sure where she was heading. The reason she wasn't writing the story was that she had gotten accustomed to stories that were finished, neat, standing still, not ones that were crashing around her. This was real life, messy and hard to pin down, and she hadn't a clue how to get her arms around it. Just thinking about it was enough to bring back yesterday's paralysis.

And then there was the execution tonight. Oh, God. She had committed herself to being there. But could she actually go and watch them execute a man for a crime he did not commit? Be a part of that big Godzilla lie? To go seemed dishonest and cold-blooded.

To stay away seemed dishonest and cowardly.

Right now the idea of just staying at home for the next twenty-four hours sure was an attractive idea. She could curl up with a bottle of wine and a good book, or a movie on the VCR. Maybe Grady would come over and offer some more police protection. It was supposed to get cool tonight. They'd put her goose-down comforter on the bed and get under it and not think about the meticulous, lethal procedure going on in Huntsville. By midnight she'd be asleep. By the time she awoke in the morning it would be all over.

There would be a small item in the City-State section of the *American-Patriot,* page three, telling about the execution; she had read and written enough of those to know exactly what it would say. It would give the time the execution started and the time the doctor declared him dead. It would give his last words, if any, and say he was the fifteenth person to be executed in Texas this year, the sixty-eighth since Texas resumed executions in 1982—the highest total by far of any state in the nation. It would list his convictions. And every good citizen who read it would say to his wife across the breakfast table, "Good. That's one animal who won't be back out on the streets. We ought to do more of that."

When the light changed, she turned left onto Martin Luther King and pulled into the parking lot of a garish pink Taco Cabana. Whatever she was going to do next, she couldn't do it without coffee. She ran inside and brought the cup back to the truck. Then she picked up the phone to make the call she hated to make. Sister Addie would be waiting.

Addie answered before the first ring ended.

"She said no," Molly said without identifying herself. "No executive clemency. Said we didn't have diddly squat and Louie was just the sort we should be executing."

Knitting needles clicked. Addie said, "Well, it's hard to argue against that." She clucked once. "And I just talked to Tanya Klein. The Fifth Circuit Court refused to grant relief and so did the state. Of course, she'll file the usual last-minute petition to the Supreme Court, but there's no chance, she says. It's all over. We need to let Louie know."

Molly hadn't even thought about that. Of course, he'd be waiting to hear.

"Would you like me to tell him?" Addie asked. "I was just waiting for your call before driving over there. To the old death row over at the Walls. You know, they transferred him there early this morning. I think it's better to tell him in person than ask them to give him the message, don't you?"

"Oh, yes. Much better. You tell him, Sister Addie. Please."

"All right. I don't believe it will come as that much of a surprise to him. You want to see him before tonight, dear? We could put you on the list."

The thought made Molly's stomach swoop. "No. I don't think so."

"Any messages?"

"Messages? Let me think. Yes. Tell him I tried. And I'm sorry," Molly said, feeling right down to her toenails the inadequacy of that message. "So sorry."

"Well, I'll see you tonight?" Addie said, her voice rising in a question.

"I don't know. I guess," Molly said. "It seems wrong to come and wrong not to."

"I know what you mean." Addie paused. "I don't want to play the busybody here, but—"

"But you're going to."

"Yes, I'm afraid I am. One advantage of my having attended too many of these melancholy occasions is that I have considered this question five ways to Sunday. Here's how I see it. Being there is not in any way a tacit approval or acceptance. You are simply witnessing the event, that's all."

Molly considered it in silence. Addie broke into her thought. "You haven't been to an execution before, have you, Sister Molly?"

"No."

"That place, the death chamber, is like no other place I've ever been. This is going to sound silly to you, but just wait—you'll feel it the second you walk in—the very air in there is corrupted. It reeks of misery. I think it's important that a few of us who disapprove should be present, so we can fill the air with our own vibrations of opposition."

It did sound silly. Molly said, "Prepare me for it. What should I expect?"

"It's, oh, my dear, it's, well, it's not—"

"You aren't going to tell me it's not really so bad as I imagine, are you?"

"Heavens, no. It's worse. Far worse than you imagine. They tell you lethal injection is humane, but sometimes it goes very badly. That's another reason for you to come. You should *know.*"

Molly sighed. "I'll be there," she said. "Have you finished the afghan?"

Addie laughed. "Not quite. That was the real reason I was hoping you might get a thirty-day reprieve. For me. So I could finish this dratted thing. Well, I need to get on the road, dear. Thanks for your good efforts on Louie's behalf. We tried."

Molly put down the phone and checked her watch. Seven-forty. She didn't want to go home and she didn't want to go out for breakfast. And she absolutely did not want to go to the office.

She put her coffee cup in the circular holder between the seats and headed the truck toward South Austin. What she really wanted to do, *had* to do, was talk to Alison McFarland about her testimony ten years ago. The discrepancy was driving Molly crazy.

She headed south on Guadalupe, crossed the bridge over Town Lake, and took Congress Avenue. When she pulled up in front of the house on Monroe it was not yet eight. Hell of a time to be making a surprise visit. But that was the least of it. What she was about to do was probably inexcusable, just what Charlie had asked her not to do —put more pressure on an unstable young woman on a day that was sure to be monstrously difficult for her anyway.

Molly walked up the cracked sidewalk to the front door. She frowned when she saw that the door was standing open. For a flash she wondered if they felt safe because they knew for a fact there was no murderer loose outside their house.

She knocked on the wood door frame and waited.

Mark Redinger came to the door in a pair of white shorts and nothing else. His tanned chest was finely muscled and covered with just the right amount of curly black hair. Molly wondered what he had looked like at seventeen. Pretty spectacular, she imagined. A handsome, wild boy—according to Stuart and Charlie both, a real bad influence. A boy who liked older women, who liked to spy on people. A boy who had reason to hate Charlie McFarland, then and now.

Through the screen she thought she saw Mark scowl when he recognized her. Well, who could blame him. "Good morning, Mark," she said. "I know it's ungodly early, but I wonder if I could have a word with Alison."

"Well, Mrs. Cates," he said in a cold voice. "She isn't dressed yet." He looked down at himself—his flat belly, narrow hips, and long muscled legs, and when he looked up he wore his flirtatious grin, as if he had just remembered to put it on. "Neither am I actually," he added.

"It's important," Molly said. "If she could spare me a minute I surely would be grateful. And I don't mind whether she's dressed or not."

"Just a sec," he said, and faded into the darkness inside.

When he reappeared, he'd thrown on a short-sleeved shirt but hadn't buttoned it, so a generous expanse of chest still showed. He opened the screen for her and said, "I'm going to put on some coffee. Will you have some?"

"I'd love some," Molly said as she entered. The hall was filled with cardboard boxes and large green garbage bags full of clothes and books. "Someone moving?" she asked.

"Alison's moving back home." Mark led the way back to the sunny kitchen.

In the kitchen, she watched as he went about the business of making coffee with graceful, efficient motions. Molly said, "I suppose Alison feels she can be more helpful to her father right now if she's home."

"I guess," Mark said, his eyes down, fixed on the coffee he was measuring into a filter.

In a minute Alison walked into the room. She carried a small calico cat in her arms. She was wearing dirty gray sweatpants, a huge blue T-shirt, and no shoes. She looked at Molly and said, "Today's the day."

"For Louie Bronk, you mean?" Molly asked.

Alison nodded.

"I think of it as today, too," Molly said, "although really it's tomorrow. The law reads that it has to be done between midnight and sunrise on the date the court has set, and the date's the twenty-ninth."

Alison shrugged. "Well, in any case, we're about to see the end of it."

"Maybe not," Molly said, watching her face.

Alison stopped still. "Oh? Has something happened?" The cat made a sudden twist as if it had been squeezed too hard. Alison leaned over and let it down on the floor.

"Yes," Molly said, "and I wanted to ask you about it."

Mark finished the preparations and switched on the coffee maker. He turned and leaned a hip against the counter, nonchalant, his shirt hanging open.

Molly paused. What she was going to ask would be best done in private. Maybe she should ask Mark to leave. On the other hand, it would be interesting to see his reaction to it.

"I'm not going to take the time to go into details," she said, "but in the past two days I've unearthed some new evidence. It's enough to convince me that Louie Bronk did not kill your mother, and that there was no white Mustang with a brown door at your house that morning. Louie did own such a car, but before the ninth of July, it had been painted bright blue and sold to a scrap yard in Fort Worth for junk. It could not have been in Austin."

Neither of the two young faces changed expression.

"So I wonder," Molly continued in a slow, neutral voice, "if you could have been mistaken about what you saw that day, Alison?"

Mark reached out and put his arm in front of Alison the way a driver reaches out to stop his passenger from flying forward when the brakes are applied suddenly. "Charlie was right," he said between tight lips. "You are a troublemaker. What are you trying to do here?"

"I'm just trying to find out what really happened that day," Molly said. "And I wish you'd both help me." The coffee maker emitted a loud grinding noise, very much like a Bronx cheer.

Mark kept his arm out in front of Alison. "Help you? Help you do what? Drive Alison crazy with this? Don't you think it's hard enough for her?"

Molly directed her words to Alison. "I think it's very, very hard. But I hope you'll answer the question, Alison. Could you possibly have been mistaken?"

The delicate lavender skin under the girl's eyes wrinkled; it was the only movement she made to show she was considering the question.

"This is enough, Mrs. Cates," Mark said, finally lowering his arm and standing up straight. "We don't need this today."

Molly held up a hand. "Wait. I'm talking with Alison. Give her a chance to answer please."

Mark turned toward Alison, but the girl didn't look at him. She continued to stare down at her toes. She said, "It's always possible to be mistaken. Maybe I was. But David, he was sure of what he saw."

"No," Molly said, "he wasn't. When we talked Tuesday night, David hinted that he was having doubts. I don't think he was sure at all. Alison, please tell me about the car."

Alison took a quick bite at the side of her thumbnail. "There's not much to tell. I was kind of sluggish and bleary-eyed, the way you are after a nap. And I was only a kid. When I looked out the door, I thought I saw a car. David made me promise to stay in the house, in the TV room, even though I was scared to be alone, and when he came back in, we talked about the car and I remembered it was white. He thought it had a brown door and I thought I remembered that, too. That's it. That's what I remember."

Molly felt a buzzing in her fingertips. "But David always said he stayed with you in the house after the two of you saw the car drive away."

"Did he? I think he was out of the house for a little while." Alison shook her head. "I'm just not sure."

Mark took a step forward. "Come on, Mrs. Cates, what are you trying to accomplish here? This guy was convicted five times. He's a killer. He confessed."

"That's all true, Mark. He's also a liar and has been known to confess to crimes he didn't commit. I think he lied when he confessed to Alison's mother's murder. Now, that means someone else killed her." She looked him in the eye. "Don't you think we need to know who it was?"

He didn't flinch from Molly's stare. "Wait a minute. If you really had some new evidence you'd have given it to the court and gotten Bronk a pardon, or whatever they call it. You don't have anything."

"Well, I don't have enough to interest the courts, that's true," Molly admitted. "But I have enough to convince me. Mark, that coffee smells done. After my rudeness, do I still get a cup?"

He smiled, though it looked like his lips had to make a real effort to do it. "Coming right up." He turned to open the cabinet behind him. "What do you take?"

"Oh. Nothing. Black, please."

He took out a glass jar containing little packets of Sweet'n Low, reminding Molly of what Georgia McFarland carried in the pocket of her terry-cloth robe. After he had poured coffee into three mugs he handed Molly one and then emptied a packet into each of the other two. He pushed one mug down the counter to where Alison was leaning. She didn't even glance at it.

Molly took a sip of her coffee. "Sorry to barge in like this so early, but I thought you'd want to know."

"Yes, I guess I do," Alison said. "Is there anything else you found out? Anything you haven't told us?"

Molly thought about Charlie—his cancer and the payments to David Serrano. Nothing she could tell. "No," Molly said. "That's it so far. I don't want to scare you, but I believe now that David was murdered because of something he was going to tell about your mother's death. When he and I talked Tuesday night, I think he was on the verge of telling me something important, something that had been eating at him. Do you have any idea what that might have been?"

Alison shook her head. "You know, when I woke up that day, I thought it was just another long, hot, boring summer day. I wasn't paying much attention to anything. If you only knew what moments in life were going to be important, you'd pay more attention to them."

"Amen," Molly said.

They drank coffee in silence until Mark said, "Sorry if I've been inhospitable here, but this is one hell of a hard day for Alison. I hate to see her made more unhappy. Anyway, who can blame a man for what he does before his first cup of the day? We're just going to have to agree to disagree here. I don't buy your theory for a second. Alison's always done just the right thing and this Bronk guy is as guilty as they come."

Molly took a sip of her coffee and watched the cat rubbing against Mark's ankle, meowing. Mark got a carton of milk out of the refrigerator and took it to the back door where he leaned over and poured it into a small bowl. The cat went for it right away. Then Mark put the carton back. Well damn, Molly thought, who knows? Maybe Alison has herself one hell of a man here. Maybe she ought to stay right here with him and not move back to her father's. Maybe it's safer here.

Molly took another sip of her coffee. "Mark, did you have any luck with the attorney general's office?"

"About attending the execution? No. They said I wasn't official enough. They do not allow the general public to attend executions and I guess that's what I am. I'm going over anyway, to drive Alison. I'll just wait outside for her."

"What about Stuart?" Molly asked.

"I think he's already left, early this morning, planning to do a little hunting on the way."

"What's in season?"

"That doesn't matter to Stu," Mark said.

Molly put her cup down on the counter and said, "Well, have a safe trip to Huntsville, you two. I'll see you there, Alison. Did they tell you where to go?"

Alison was chewing hard on her thumb. "Yeah," she muttered, "to the Information office across from the prison at eleven-thirty."

They both walked her to the front door.

Walking out to the truck, Molly felt she was only marginally wiser than when she'd arrived and she hadn't been very wise then.

▼

The rest of the day was the worst writing day Molly could remember in all her twenty-two years in the business, and she'd had some bad ones before. She'd sat down determined to stay at the keyboard until she had something she could fax to Richard—a start for the article, a teaser to interest him. But all she did was make false starts and erase them in disgust, stare at the wall, and eat microwave popcorn—two full bags of it. She might just as well have gone shopping or watched soaps all day for all she accomplished.

At five-thirty Grady called from across the street and gave her an excuse to quit. She opened the door and was surprised to see that he was carrying a bottle of champagne.

Once inside, he wrapped his arms around her and, holding the bottle in both hands, rolled it up and down the small of her back.

"Oh, feels good, nice and cold," she murmured. "Too bad I can't drink it with you."

"Why not?"

"Because I'm leaving for Huntsville in an hour."

"Don't go," he said.

"I have to, Grady. I promised."

He kissed her quickly. "Please don't go."

"I have to. What's the champagne for?"

"To celebrate the doggedness of cops the world over."

Molly held her breath. "You've got something new."

He leaned down and kissed her—a long involved kiss during which the champagne bottle eased slowly down her back and ended up rubbing the backs of her thighs. "Here's a question for you," he said into her neck, his breath hot, his lips moving against her skin. "Would you rather go upstairs and make wild love or stay here and talk about some dull police work?"

"Those activities aren't mutually exclusive, are they?" She unbuttoned two buttons and slid her hand inside his shirt. "What have you got?"

"I can only do one thing well at a time," he said, sliding his hands, champagne bottle and all, down the back of her baggy warm-up pants and pressing her hips hard against his.

"Champagne's losing its chill." She was suddenly short of breath. "Tell me what you've got."

"It can wait," he said, pulling her down to the rug.

▼

They never made it upstairs. It was nearly an hour before Molly got to the kitchen to put the champagne bottle in the refrigerator.

When she came back, Grady was dressed and sitting on the bottom step.

Molly sat down next to him. "Now tell me."

"Okay. Darden Smith, the detective from the Fort Worth Assault Unit, called. Marcus Gandy told all. He was hired by a local McFarland foreman named Carl Manning. When Detective Smith leaned on Mr. Manning some, he finally admitted the orders came from the home office in Austin, from the highest level."

"Oh, Grady, I am sorry to hear that."

"I thought you might be." He rested his hand on her knee. "We'll charge McFarland tomorrow. For criminal solicitation. We need you to come sign the affidavit."

Molly's thoughts were spinning. "But I wonder how he could have known. Louie said he told only three people about the car: me, Tanya Klein, and Sister Addie."

"Maybe Sister Addie's a spy," Grady said. "On the McFarland payroll."

"Maybe Tanya Klein is," Molly said mostly to herself. She looked down at her watch. It was almost seven o'clock. She stood up. "It's a three-hour drive. I'm going to take a shower and get dressed." She started up the stairs, but stopped halfway. "Grady, you must know about things like this. What do you wear to an execution?"

He leaned back on the stairs and looked up at her. "I'm fond of that red shirt you wore last night—the one with the missing button at the neck so it gapes open when you lean forward." He smiled. "Bronk might like that one, too."

Molly sighed and ran up the stairs.

When she was showered and dressed, not in the red blouse, but her usual khaki pants, white shirt, and orange blazer, she came down the stairs. Grady was sitting in the wing chair reading the newspaper. He looked up. "So when can you come in tomorrow to sign the complaint?"

"Oh, I don't know."

"Molly, they could have killed you."

"Even a dog gets one bite. Let's give him a break."

"Molly, don't be crazy. This is serious business. McFarland's a killer. This gives us cause to bring him in."

"I don't think so. Anyway, he's sick. Dying."

Grady put the newspaper down on the chair with a slap. "That, at least, appears to be true. I talked with Gerald Brumder, an oncologist Charlie's doctor sent him to. He confirms that he gave McFarland the diagnosis."

"Has Brumder told anyone else?"

"Just the son, Stuart McFarland, who's a colleague of his. Charlie asked him not to tell anyone, but he told Stuart as a professional courtesy, Brumder says."

"I see," Molly said. "That's interesting." She sat down. "I wonder if Stuart told his sister and his cousin the news. If he did, that gives both children, and Mark, a real powerful financial motive for killing Georgia before Charlie dies."

"I'd call ten million a real powerful motive, yeah."

"Better than any motive you've been able to come up with for Charlie."

"That's for sure," Grady said, "since I haven't come up with any motive at all. He had multiple motives for killing the first wife, but none that I can find for Georgia." He came up behind her chair and leaned down, resting his cheek against her head. "Molly, I wish that just this once you'd take my advice: stay home tonight."

"Come with me. When it's over we can find a nice place to spend the night."

"I can't. I have to go back on this drive-by. We've got a suspect to interrogate. I could send a uniform to drive you."

"No. If you're not coming I don't want anyone. I'm going to work in the car, talk into the tape recorder, and figure out some things."

"Well," Grady said, "they're predicting a norther. Bundle up, at least."

chapter 24

A rolling stone,
A restless bone
Ain't got no boss,
Don't grow no moss.
I make do with what I find.
I don't leave nothing behind.

LOUIE BRONK
Death Row, Ellis I Unit,
Huntsville, Texas

▲　▼　▲

She gave herself the first hour, from Austin to Caldwell, for listening to Willie Nelson and letting her mind float. Some loose easy time for thinking about Grady and how sweet it would be to get home tonight and find him there, in her bed, and press up against his back and sleep for ten delicious hours while the norther rattled the windows.

Her hour was up when she hit Caldwell. She switched off the tape player and tried to focus on the problem of how she was going to write this story. One thing was sure: it couldn't be just the usual execution story. She'd read plenty of accounts of death-row procedures. She knew exactly what had happened to Louie on this, his last day. Early this morning they had transferred him and his possessions. They had driven him, shackled and cuffed, the fourteen miles from the Ellis Unit to the Walls Unit inside the city limits of Huntsville, where the law mandated executions should take place. There his guards had passed the buck and turned him over to new guards, who had locked him in a holding cell on the old death row a few yards from the execution chamber.

That cell was barred and reinforced with fine mesh so visitors couldn't pass him any contraband—no tranquilizers, no drugs, no poisons to cheat the state of its duty. Two guards had been posted near the cell all day and the chaplain, in this case Sister Addie, had sat with him, outside the cell. He could have visitors, as many as he wanted, but no contact visits were allowed. In Louie's case it didn't matter. There was no one who wanted contact—no family, no friends. His three remaining sisters wanted nothing to do with him.

He had been asked what he wanted for his last meal—it could be anything, so long as they had it on hand in the kitchen.

Sometime during the day the warden had come to see him to talk about arrangements—the disposition of his worldly goods and the disposal of his body. The thought made Molly's stomach contract.

And this, for a murder she was absolutely convinced he didn't commit. The only true elements in the account she'd written of Tiny McFarland's death were that it happened on the morning of July 9, 1982, and that Tiny was shot dead. But not by Louie Bronk. By someone else—someone Tiny knew, someone she loved, someone in her family.

She was rich. She was married. She was a mother. She liked to take chances. She was promiscuous. All those things may have contributed. Plus that one other ingredient that all murder victims shared: she got unlucky.

Molly had started the story in her dreams two nights ago. Now she struggled to flesh it out.

Tiny McFarland, dressed in a white linen sheath and high heels, had cut an armful of red gladioli from her garden. On the way back to the house, she'd run into a lover. A lover in the garage. David Serrano—young, attractive, hot-blooded, available. She had dropped the flowers so her hands were free for a lover's purposes. The big garage door must have been closed; lovers require some privacy. Little Alison was asleep and no one else was home, so it wasn't such a big chance to take.

At this point the story got difficult.

First Molly thought it through with David killing Tiny in a jealous rage over someone else, a new lover maybe, or Tiny's desire to end the affair.

Then she envisioned Charlie coming home, using the automatic door opener and finding them there. Nightmare time.

She could see Stuart coming home early and finding them there and killing his mother in some sort of Oedipal rage.

Or even Alison, a nervous girl with great possessiveness toward the men in her life, coming on them and panicking, thinking someone was being hurt. No. She was only a little girl—eleven years old.

Or Mark. Maybe he was infatuated with Tiny. Maybe he'd spied on some of her trysts; he had a history of that. Maybe he was getting revenge on Charlie.

One thing was clear: whoever did it had a clever idea that worked better than he could possibly have foreseen. He'd been reading the paper about the Scalper and decided to make the murder look like just another Scalper killing. What a thrill it must have been when Bronk actually confessed to it. Of course, Frank Purcell had fed him some information, she felt sure, but that must have been after Louie had already confessed.

As for the recent murders, surely David had been killed over what he knew about Tiny's death. He had gotten too nervous and was about to tell it all. Georgia—well, that just got too complicated for her at this late hour. Time was running out.

When Molly pulled into Huntsville, the whole town was dark and buttoned up—just after 11 P.M. on a Monday night in a small East Texas town. She was thirty minutes early and so tense that she found herself craving a greasy cheeseburger even though she'd given them up a year before. A beer might help, too. She drove around a little and didn't see anything open, so she abandoned the idea. Anyway, executions, like surgery and some crime scenes, were probably done best on an empty stomach.

What she really needed was a walk, to get the kinks out of her legs after three hours of driving.

She parked the truck across from the big modern Walker County courthouse on the town square. It was well lighted and there were several sheriff's deputy cars parked on the street—a good place to walk. She slipped on her tennis shoes, laced them tight, and did four circuits of the square, increasing her speed each time, until she was nearly running. When she finished, she felt even tenser and more keyed up than she had when she began. She felt as if the volume of blood in her body were building up, pressing from the inside. God, that sounded like one of Louie's poems.

She got her notebook and pen out of the truck and changed from tennis shoes to a pair of black suede loafers, under the notion that it was inappropriate to wear tennis shoes to an execution; her Aunt Harriet would certainly approve of that notion. Then she headed toward the prison, an easy five-block walk.

She passed the bus station and walked through the incongruously pleasant residential area that surrounded the old prison. It was a lovely neighborhood with handsome Victorian houses and a scattering of more modest but well-kept frame bungalows, green lawns, and flowerbeds.

She'd never been here at night before and as she neared the prison she was awestruck. Against the dark sky, the massive forty-foot-high brick walls, washed in white security lights, loomed over everything. The inmates, and everybody else in Texas, called this place "the Walls." The oldest structure in the Texas prison system, it reminded Molly of a medieval walled town. Inside, on 140 acres, was a nearly self-sufficient world: a textile mill, a machine shop, cell blocks, a chapel, school rooms, an exercise yard, kitchens, garden plots, even an arena for the annual prison rodeo. And, of course, there was also that small separate structure in the northwest corner —the death house, the one place in the prison she had not yet seen.

As she approached, Molly remembered back about a year ago, when she was doing a piece on sex offenders. She had been sitting on the low wall across the street from the prison, waiting to interview Timothy Coffee who was being released after serving thirteen years for several aggravated rapes. That day they had been doing a mass release, because the number of inmates had gone over the court-set limit. One hundred twenty-five men were being released early, before their terms were up. As she waited, they emerged in groups from a small side door. All were dressed identically in the pastel long-sleeved shirts and work pants they were issued on release. Each group did the same thing: the men walked until they were a few yards past the prison wall, and then suddenly they started running. At first, they jogged slowly. Then they picked up speed. They ran as if the devil were chasing them, down the street, down to the bus station.

Molly stopped. The memory made her want to turn and run. There was nothing to stop her, nothing making her go through with this. She could run back to her truck, lock the doors, put the cruise control on sixty-five, and hightail it back home, as if the devil were in pursuit.

She stood rooted to the sidewalk.

Ahead of her, a tiny cluster of demonstrators was gathered near the front door of the prison. A pretty pathetic demonstration—five people dressed in black, holding candles and chanting in low voices words Molly could not make out.

She looked at her watch. It was already past eleven-thirty. Almost time. She started walking again, reluctantly, one foot in front of the other, feeling herself pulled forward by whatever force it was that kept her in motion, doing what she did. It was habit maybe. Habit and curiosity. The curiosity spurred her on to look for the most grotesque things she could find, and habit made her keep on doing it. Appetite for violence and death. Just like the buzzards she'd watched from Charlie McFarland's house.

She passed the demonstrators without a word to them and headed toward the flat-topped, two-story administrative building across the street from the prison. The rosebushes that lined the walk were perfectly pruned and mulched. There was no better maintenance anywhere in Texas than in and around the prison buildings, she thought. And tonight the execution would be exactly like that—a neat and well-maintained death.

Her chest tightened as she walked up the stairs—just the usual pre-Louie jitters, she told herself. *Relax. You don't even have to talk to him tonight; your only job is to watch him die.* It was something just to be gotten over. In four hours she'd be home in bed.

All the lights on the first floor of the administration building blazed. No doubt executions required administrative overtime; it was probably even in the budget. Molly headed down the hall to Darryl Jones's office, where the witnesses had been told to gather. When family or friends of the condemned were attending, they gathered separately, in the basement. But there was no family or friends for Louie Bronk. As she approached the door, she heard the murmur of voices, low, but with an undertone of excitement. The vultures were gathering for the kill, and she had chosen to join them. She was one of them.

The director of public information for the Texas Department of Criminal Justice, Darryl Jones, was in charge of dealing with the press, so Molly had met him often before. He hurried to the door of his office to greet her, like the host of a party, a very subdued party. A tall, slender black man with the profile of a movie star, Darryl gave her the full impact of his splendid smile. "Molly Cates," he exclaimed, "have you come to expose us?"

She smiled up at him. "Darryl, anytime you want to expose yourself I'll be front and center. But I don't really think it would be appropriate right now, do you?" Oh-oh, she thought, crime scene humor slipping out. She was going to have to watch herself.

Darryl gave a perfunctory laugh. "Well, you know everybody?" He gestured into the room. Fifteen people, more than she'd expected, stood talking in groups. Clustered around Stan Heffernan stood six reporters, leaning forward trying to hear what he was saying. Molly recognized Judith Simpson from the *American-Patriot* and a man whose name she couldn't recall from the Associated Press. Stuart McFarland, dressed in a dark suit and tie, stood in the corner drinking coffee out of a foam cup and talking to Tanya Klein.

"Who are the men over there in front of the window?" Molly asked, indicating a group of five men.

"The tall man in the three-piece suit is Tom Robeson, chief of the enforcement division of the attorney general's office. The fat guy with the cowboy hat is Rider Kelinsky, the state prison director, my big boss. The others are just TDCJ brass, no one special."

"Why are they all here?"

"Some of them, like Tom and Rider, have to be. The others, well, they just like coming." Darryl grinned at her. "We could solve our cash flow problems by selling tickets to these damn things if they'd let us. Hey, I've got to make a call, Molly. Why don't you help yourself to a cup of coffee over there." He pointed to a credenza against the wall where a Thermos, some cups, and a plate of cookies sat on a tray. "It'll be another few minutes." He walked off.

Molly looked around the room again. Alison McFarland was not there, which gave her a tiny pinch of misgiving. But there was still time.

She should get out her notebook like a good writer and go interview the various officials, but she couldn't face it tonight—the low droning male voices, the righteous indignation about recidivism and federal court interference, the outrages of Ruiz vs. Collins—she'd heard it all before. She wanted something she hadn't heard. She wished Addie Dodgin were here to talk to.

When she saw Tanya Klein turn to talk to one of the reporters, Molly walked up to Stuart. "Have a good day off?" she asked him.

He reached up to adjust the perfect knot in his tie. "Actually, yes. It makes me realize that the rest of the world doesn't have to work every minute. Yes. A fine day. How about you?"

"Oh, I tried to write and couldn't. I should have taken the day off, too. Have you seen Alison?"

He scowled. "No." He looked at his watch. "She'll be here, though. Mark was going to drive her so she'll make it on time. I talked to her at noon to check." He paused. "She told me about what you said this morning."

"Oh?"

"I wish you hadn't done that, today of all days. She was pretty upset. I hope you won't harp on this tonight and make it worse."

"You mean I shouldn't harp on the fact that a man is being executed for something he didn't do? I shouldn't harp on it because it might upset your sister? Stuart, I don't want to upset you or Alison. I know this is a hard time for you both, but the person who really killed your mother may be the one who killed your stepmother and David Serrano. Doesn't that worry you?"

His face darkened. "This is all crackpot theory, Mrs. Cates—your theory. You're the only one who thinks this. Alison told me what you said about Louie Bronk and that damn car. If there were any truth to it, the people investigating at the time would have found it. Or his lawyer. You're not helping matters by interfering here. You're not qualified. Leave this to the law enforcement people."

Molly felt her combativeness rising but she swallowed it down. This man did not need any additional problems right now. "I can certainly see your point," she said.

He nodded, held up his coffee cup, and said, "Excuse me."

Molly watched him walk to the credenza and pour himself another cup of coffee. Then he leaned against the wall and began eating Oreo cookies off the tray. He popped one after another in his mouth, staring off into space while he chewed.

Molly looked around and saw Tanya Klein standing alone. When Molly approached her, Tanya took a step back and frowned. She doesn't trust me any more than I trust her, Molly thought, and I don't trust her at all. "What's happening?" she asked.

"The Supreme Court denied our last petition for a Writ of Certiorari a few hours ago. Louie Bronk is history."

"Have you seen him?" Molly asked.

"Yes. Right after we got word, I went to tell him."

"How'd he take it?"

"Like a trooper. I hear you went to see the governor this morning."

Molly nodded.

Tanya arched a dark eyebrow. "Oh, well. We never had a chance with this one. There are some others coming up, though, that are real cases."

Molly tried to fight down the irritation she felt. It was so unjustified. This was a woman who worked hard in an impossible job that rarely allowed any victories. They were on the same side, opposed to the death penalty. They should be natural allies. But Molly's suspicions had been brewing and now they were bubbling over. "Tanya," Molly said abruptly, "do you know the McFarlands?"

"Well, you just saw me talking to Stuart," Tanya said with a shrug.

"Yes. But do you know Charlie, the patriarch? Ever talk to him about the Bronk case?"

Tanya looked at Molly through narrowing eyes.

"Have you?" Molly asked, her voice more aggressive than she'd intended. "Ever give him any information about what Louie was telling you?"

Tanya's face tightened in anger.

"Maybe about the car he junked in Fort Worth?" Molly was on a roll now and couldn't stop if she'd wanted to. "Ever get any contributions from him for the Center?"

Tanya's nostrils constricted and she shook her head, clearly not in answer to Molly's question but in dismissal, as if Molly were a fly buzzing around her head. She turned and walked out of the room.

Wow, Molly thought, I am really on the warpath tonight. But she had hit a nerve there. Suddenly she felt better. Some of the tension had dissipated. A few more fights and she'd feel almost human. She poured herself a cup of coffee even though she had a rule about never drinking it after noon. What the hell.

A few minutes later, Alison McFarland entered the room. She had dressed up. She wore a long brown skirt and clean white blouse, dangly earrings, and she'd washed her hair. When she saw Stuart, still leaning against the wall gobbling cookies, she made a beeline for him and put her arm through his as if she needed to hold herself up.

He stiffened and pulled back slightly. Molly was close enough to hear Stuart say, "You clean up good. You ought to do it more often."

"Yeah, I know. What happens now?" his sister asked.

"Damned if I know," he said. "I wish they'd get on with it."

"I'm so nervous, I'm afraid I'll have to pee right in the middle of it."

"Why don't you take care of that now, Al?" Stuart said, his mouth grim.

Alison left the room. Molly watched her leave and decided she should go to the bathroom, too. Why pass up a chance?

In the ladies' room, Alison was leaning over the sink staring into the mirror. She didn't turn when Molly entered, but gave a tiny smile into the mirror. "Hi, Mrs. Cates."

"Hi, Alison. I don't know about you, but I'm as nervous as a cat. Makes my bladder kind of chancy."

Alison straightened and turned to face Molly. "You know what I hope?"

"What?"

"That in his last words he'll do the right thing and own up to it, settle all your doubts."

"I can't imagine that," Molly said, "but there's no telling with Louie."

When they got back to the office, Darryl Jones was standing in the door saying, "All right, folks. If you're ready, let's walk across the street."

They all filed out, two by two. Alison grabbed her brother's arm and walked pressed up against his side. Stan fell in silently next to Molly. "I hear you went to see the governor this morning," he said as they crossed the street.

"Word does get around," she said.

At the front door of the prison, the demonstrators came to life. They picked up placards and raised their voices. "Execute Justice," they chanted, "not people!" No one, including Molly, acknowledged their presence.

The brass hand railing up the steps to the prison door gleamed, as if it had just been polished for a big party. And the whole thing did have a party feel—the undercurrent of excitement and anticipation. It was concealed under a somber facade, but it was there.

Inside the door several of the men wearing Stetsons stopped to check their sidearms at a caged-in desk.

They filed into the visitors' lounge. There an assistant warden and a few other officials from TDCJ waited. The only one Molly recognized was Steve Demaris from the Ellis Unit.

There are so many of us here, Molly thought—wardens and assistants and reporters and witnesses and elected officials—because this way no one is responsible. Safety in numbers. This is all an exercise in passing the buck.

"Ladies," Darryl Jones said, after they'd all gotten inside, "please leave your handbags in here. They'll be safe. Officer Steck will be staying here with them. Members of the press, you are allowed to take into the chamber only a pen and notebook. We are required now to search you for recording devices. Bear with us, please, so we can get this done right quick."

Three young corrections officers began to search them.

Quickly, routinely, they moved from person to person. When it was Molly's turn she lifted her hands so the guard could feel her pockets. " 'Scuse me, ma'am," he said as he patted Molly's jacket pockets and the back of her pants.

They stood around for several minutes. Molly looked at her watch, staring at the face until it was exactly twelve. Just like New Year's Eve, standing around waiting for midnight. Waiting, but not to be kissed.

When she looked up, Molly was surprised to see that, somewhere along the way, Frank Purcell had joined the group. He was wearing a Stetson and boots instead of the business clothes she'd seen him in before. When he saw her staring, he nodded.

Alison still clung to Stuart's arm. He looked as if he'd like to be anywhere but where he was.

The phone rang.

Darryl Jones picked it up and listened. He nodded, then said, "It's time."

He led the way through the visitors' room, out a door, down a long corridor, then outside into the night air. The temperature had fallen. Molly wrapped her arms around herself for the brief walk down a cement path to a small freestanding brick building.

The second Molly stepped inside and got hit with the dank odor of ancient dungeons, she felt herself falling backward to another century. She kept her arms wrapped across her chest. The chill. She'd never felt this before. It was as if this place, this killing place, had absorbed into its walls and floor and bars all the terror and death that had passed through. It seemed to be present now, all hundred fifty years of it swirling around her head. This is what Addie meant when she talked about this place. She had called it "corrupted air."

This could not be happening. This was 1993, the year of Our Lord 1993, September. An enlightened age, an age of computers and faxes. It was not an age where people were put to death in cold damp prisons. But this was real. They were here, a group of people gathered behind brick walls at midnight to enact an ancient ritual. To try to cure the tidal wave of violent crime by making one blood sacrifice.

They passed by the eight tiny, empty gray cells of what had been the old death row, before the state of Texas had outgrown it. In the cell nearest the door, the one reinforced with tight mesh, stood three cardboard boxes. Probably Louie's stuff, all packed up. Her chest ached.

Darryl Jones waited at the door until they all gathered. Then he shepherded them into the chamber. It was a small brick room, very brightly lighted and painted an intense cobalt-blue, the kind of garish color you saw on walls in Mexico. The room was empty, no chairs, no distractions, nothing. Molly found herself blinking and wishing the fluorescent lights were not so intense.

Bars painted the same color of blue separated this room from the execution chamber a few feet away. A white curtain was drawn back so they could see through the bars a tableau so strange that the only thing she could think of was a Halloween haunted house where she'd once taken Jo Beth. A gurney was bolted to the floor. On it Louie lay strapped down, his thin arms extended. He was dressed in an immaculate white prison uniform and shiny black shoes. His hair had been trimmed since she had seen him four days ago and he was freshly shaved. The state of Texas had spiffed Louie up for the party.

His scrawny bare arms were stretched out and strapped down at the wrists. IV tubes ran from both arms and disappeared into a tiny square hole in the wall, next to a one-way mirror. The slack pale skin with its network of crinkled blue tattoos looked like some grotesque illustration from an anatomy text. Like skin and limbs and veins long dead. Yes, Molly was suddenly certain that his arms were already dead. So now it was too late to go back. The only humane thing was to go ahead and kill the rest of his body. She tried to swallow but her mouth was utterly dry. God, she was losing her mind. What if she wrote all this? Richard would be convinced she had gone mad. So would everyone else. She forced her eyes away from the dead arms.

At Louie's head stood the warden of the Walls Unit, dressed in a dark business suit and paisley tie instead of his usual tan Western outfit. He, too, had dressed up for company. In a sudden lapse of memory, Molly couldn't quite dredge up his name. She wasn't doing very well. Here she was, the star crime reporter for *Lone Star Monthly,* and she'd forgotten her notebook. Furthermore, she had no idea where the real story was, where it started or where it would end, what she would write, or whether she would write anything at all. Her legs felt rubbery and her stomach so hot and churning she was grateful she hadn't put anything in it.

Sister Addie stood at Louie's side, holding his right hand. She wore the same pastel house dress she'd worn when Molly had first met her, and draped over her shoulders was the ugly pink and brown afghan she'd been knitting for Louie. Her head was bent down to his and they were talking in low voices, but when the group filed in, Louie looked away from her and turned his head toward the witnesses on the other side of the bars. His eyes darted and stopped on Molly. He gave her a slight nod. She nodded back and tried to smile. Instead her mouth fell open, as if she'd just got a shot of Novocain and lost control, or as if she were about to let out a scream.

The door on Louie's side of the bars opened. John Desmond, the state prison director, entered. "Warden," he said in a deep voice, "you may proceed."

The warden turned to Louie. "Do you have a last statement to make?"

Louie glanced quickly up at Sister Addie. Then he turned his head toward the witnesses but kept his eyes fixed on a spot above their heads. In a quavery, whiny voice, he said, "I want to say I'm sorry for the things I done. I want to thank my sister Carmen-Marie who's not here but she's been real nice to me in the past and I wish I'd been a better brother." He paused and ran his tongue over his thin lips. Molly thought she saw him blink once, as if to force back a tear.

"And Molly Cates," he continued, "who tried to help. I left you something." His chest rose and sank several times. "Thanks. Mostly, I want to thank Sister Adeline Dodgin for sticking by me and trying to show me the way to salvation. The only good thing I leave behind in this world is my poems."

He'd spoken the last words rapid-fire and now he had to take a breath. "Oh," he said, as if he'd just remembered something important, "I forgive everyone who's involved with this. Jesus forgives us all. We are forgiven."

He rolled his head on the gurney so that he was looking up at Addie. She smiled down at him, looking directly into his eyes. The room was absolutely silent. Then as if she had received a signal, though Molly couldn't discern any movement on Louie's part, Addie looked at the warden and nodded. The warden stepped back and nodded to the one-way mirror in the wall where the tubes from Louie's arm led. "We are ready," he said.

Death seemed instantaneous.

Louie took a deep breath, his eyes opened wide in surprise, he coughed twice and was still. If she had blinked she'd have missed it.

The only sound was the scratching of pens as the journalists wrote on their pads.

The door in the execution chamber opened. A man in a white coat entered, carrying a stethoscope. He leaned over Louie and put the stethoscope to his chest. Then he stood up and looked at his watch. "Twelve-fourteen," he said, and walked out.

Louie lay still, his eyes wide open.

Molly looked around, feeling confused. That was it? As easy as that? Life hadn't even resisted. There was no fight, no scream, nothing to mark it. The line between being alive and being dead was so narrow it was almost imperceptible.

That's something Louie must have known, she realized—known better than anyone. A bullet or a knife in the right place and it was done. Quicker than a blink. No big deal. Happens all the time.

chapter 25

▲ ▼ ▲

Here's Louie Bronk's rules
For crime-fearing fools:
There's lots out there to fear.
Don't believe all you hear.
Keep your distance from strangers
And all them deadly dangers.
Keep your car in good repair.
Don't let it get stuck out there.
But here's the truth, what the fuck,
The whole damned thing's a
matter of luck.

LOUIE BRONK
Death Row, Ellis I Unit,
Huntsville, Texas

Back in the visitors' lounge, Molly sat on one of the sagging brown sofas and listened to her own breathing. Stan Heffernan walked over to her and rested a hand on her shoulder. It felt so heavy, so hot, so authoritarian that she longed to shake the damn thing off.

In his whispery voice he asked, "What did he leave you?"

"Huh?"

"In his statement he said he left you something. I wondered what it was."

"I don't know," Molly said.

He lifted his hand. "So, Molly, what do you think?"

"What do I think?" Dazed, she looked around at the people coming into the lounge talking quietly. "I think—" She looked up at his face for the first time. "I think that in all my years of reporting on crime I have never seen a more premeditated homicide."

His big head nodded slowly.

"What do *you* think?" she demanded.

"I think, considering the weasel he was, he went down well. I was half expecting him to give in to the red scream."

"The red scream?" Molly said, feeling a vibration inside her chest. "Oh, yes. If he'd done that, it sure would have been a different show, wouldn't it? Not near so neat and tidy. If I were worth a damn, I would give it *for* him. Right now."

She looked around the room at the prison officials, the journalists, the politicians, the curiosity seekers, all looking relaxed and relieved that it was over and had gone so well. What would happen if she stood up, opened her mouth wide, and let out the red scream that had been building up inside her all night?

She didn't, of course.

Instead, she sat on the sofa with one hand over her heart and the other in her lap until the scream retreated and she felt confident enough to stand and talk with people.

Molly was getting ready to leave, gearing herself up for the long drive back, when she saw Addie Dodgin standing in the door of the visitors' lounge. Addie waved and walked over to her, pulling out of her bag a folded paper. She held it out to Molly and said in a very quiet voice, "Louie asked me to give you this."

"Is this what he meant when he said he left me something?"

Addie nodded.

Molly unfolded the paper. It was a page of wide-ruled school paper, the kind that Louie had always used for his poems; she saw at a glance that this was another one, a little longer than usual. She looked up at Addie. "Have you read this?" she asked.

"No. He said it was for Molly Cates's eyes only. And that's a direct quote."

Molly looked down and read silently:

For Molly Cates
Special rates
From a friend who waits
At heavens gates.
I'm all through
Don't you be blue
Heres the news that intrests you—
That thing I did or did not do.
Tiny yes and Tiny no

Eeny meeny miny moe.
I've said no and I've said yes
I've said all right I confess—
What a bloody mixt up mess
Now for the hot line—
Was she one of mine?
Yes
Yes
Yes
PS
About the car—
It took me far.
Make no misteak
Its in the lake.
Dont that take the cake?
Im sorry, I guess
Goodby and god bless
Your friend at the end
Louie Bronk

For one second she was tempted to believe it, to ignore Fort Worth, and go with a dying man's last words. But only for a second.

"The son of a bitch!" she said. "The sick, sorry son of a bitch."

The whole room fell suddenly silent. Molly looked around her. Every head was turned her way—Stan Heffernan, Darryl Jones, Frank Purcell, Steve Demaris, Alison McFarland, Stuart McFarland, the assistant wardens, the journalists, the guards—all looking as if she'd blasphemed in church. Their shocked expressions made her so mad she said it again. "He was a sick sorry son of a bitch who never *could* tell the truth."

She looked at Addie. "Why didn't you give me this before?"

"Because he asked me not to deliver it until he was gone. What does he say?"

"He says he *did* kill Tiny and that the car is in the lake. Says he guesses he's sorry."

Addie sighed. "Pure Louie to the end." She pointed to the paper in Molly's hand. "Do you believe it?"

"No." Molly rubbed the paper between her fingers, feeling the cheap quality of it. "No. I don't believe it. Do you?"

"No," Addie said. "I'm trying to figure out why he wrote it. To make you feel better about your book maybe?"

"That's a charitable thought, Addie, but I don't think Louie's capable of that." She looked around to see if everyone was still looking. They weren't, but she lowered her voice to make sure no one else could hear. "Addie, do you know when he wrote this?"

"This evening, about nine, just before he ate."

"Did he have any visitors right before?"

"Yes. Tanya Klein. As soon as she left, he sat down and wrote it. Took him about an hour. Then he folded it up and gave it to me. Made me promise I'd wait until he was dead."

"Did you hear their conversation?" Molly asked.

"No. I took a break so they could talk privately."

Molly looked around the room for Tanya. "Did she leave already?"

"Tanya? No. I think she's picking up some of Louie's effects at the side door."

"Effects? What effects?"

"He marked her name on one of his boxes. Some papers, I suppose. The rest of his stuff he donated to my church group that works with the homeless."

Molly was thinking so hard she could hear a rushing in her ears. "Oh, damn. Addie, I may be totally deranged, but I think I know what's in that box. Tell me—what was really important to Louie in this world?"

"His poems," Addie said immediately.

"Uh-huh. Those wretched poems. You know, two years ago he had me sending them around, trying to get them published, but it was a lost cause. I used some of them in my book, but there are zillions of them, enough to fill a cardboard box."

Darryl Jones knocked on the door frame to get attention and said, "Folks, thanks for coming. They want to close up here, so let's get out of their way. Any members of the press who want to talk are welcome to come back to my office for a spell."

People headed slowly for the door, very slowly, as though they didn't want to leave or couldn't face being alone. Molly certainly felt that way.

Seeing Stuart and Alison McFarland, she caught up with them and said good-bye. They both looked subdued and burdened, she thought as she watched them walk out together. If they had hoped that witnessing the execution would make them free from the past, it hadn't worked.

"Louie didn't like Tanya much," Molly said, leaning down to talk to Addie as they walked, "so he certainly wouldn't leave her his poems. But, to get them published, I think he would have agreed to almost anything, don't you?"

Addie thought for a minute and said, "Yes."

"I think someone used that as an incentive to get him to assure me that he killed Tiny so I'd stop being such a pain in the ass and let it go. That's why he wrote me this last lie." She waved the paper and stuck it in her bag. "Do you think that's incredibly farfetched?"

"Yes, but it's probably true," Addie said. "You think Tanya made him the offer?"

They waited at the front door until it was buzzed open. They stepped outside into a cold wind that took hold of Molly's thin cotton pants and fluttered them around her legs.

"She's a lawyer," Molly said. "They're usually acting for someone else. I think she's just the agent for someone who agreed to put up the money to publish, probably at one of the vanity presses where you can get anything published if you pay for it yourself. God, just think of it—*The Complete Poems of Louie Bronk.*" They stood at the top of the steps for a minute looking into the darkness. "It's enough to send you screaming into the night, isn't it?"

Addie shivered in the wind. "Yes, I believe it is." She reached into her bag, pulled out a thin pink sweater, and threw it over her shoulders.

As they walked down the steps, one of the assistant wardens approached them and said to Addie, "Sister, if you'd like, I'll drive around the side with you and load everything up for you."

"Oh, thank you, Jim Bob. That surely would be a help." She was struggling to put her arms into the sweater sleeves.

As he reached around to hold it for her, the assistant warden asked, "Sister Addie, don't the idea of it, you know, driving back like that, don't it give you a creepy feeling?"

Addie laughed. "No. I wasn't afraid of him while he was alive and I'm certainly not afraid of him now." She turned to Molly. "Maybe we can finish our talk tomorrow over the phone. I am just plumb beat right now."

"Yes, of course. You've been here all day," Molly said, feeling the hair on the back of her neck prickle. "Addie, what's happening with Louie's body?"

Addie was looking down, trying to button the little pearl buttons on the sweater. "Well, his sisters didn't want anything to do with him, dead or alive. And there's no one else. So we're going to bury him at our church. Nice little cemetery overlooking Lake Waco."

"That's what they're going to load up?"

"That, and some boxes. I have a station wagon. Fortunately." She chuckled. "I don't know what I'd do if I still had my little Volkswagen bug."

Molly was stunned. Almost too stunned to register the story possibilities. "Do they . . . put him in a box, or what?"

"No box. There's no budget for it. They wrapped him in a sheet I brought and my afghan. It turned out to be finished enough."

"What will you do when you get back to Waco?" Molly asked.

"Drop him off at the funeral home there. It was too costly for them to come here to pick him up and since I'm making the drive and have room, well, it's the sensible thing." She laughed again. "Gives me some company on the way home."

"Well," Molly said, "drive safe." She was hit suddenly with the image of Addie being stopped by a highway patrolman who would peer into the back of the car and see Louie wrapped in the pink and brown afghan. It struck her so funny that she began to laugh.

But once she had started laughing, she couldn't stop. She stood on the sidewalk and laughed, helpless, until tears ran down her cheeks. She tried to stop, tried to take a deep breath and control it. But she just could not stop. She was caught in the ridiculousness of it all. As she raised a sleeve to blot her cheeks, she caught a glimpse of the warden looking alarmed and Sister Addie looking worried. Still she could not stop.

Sister Addie reached out and put her arms around her. She hugged her in close and they stood together like that on the sidewalk, while Molly laughed and the tears ran down her cheeks. Finally, worn out, Molly came to a gasping stop. She stepped back out of Addie's embrace, embarrassed by her loss of control, and used her sleeve to blot her wet face.

"Sorry," Molly said, pushing her hair back. "I don't know what happened. All of a sudden it all just seemed so ridiculous."

Addie smiled up at her. "Well, it is that. Were you thinking of me being stopped on the highway with Louie in the back?"

Molly let out a hiccup. "Yes. Exactly."

"It is a funny image, me trying to explain it to the highway patrol. Are you going to be all right driving home or would you like to come along with me and Louie? We could put you on a bus to Austin in the morning."

"No. Thanks." Molly rummaged in her bag for some Kleenex. She hiccuped again. "I'm fine. I need to get back."

"Yes. Maybe you'd like to come to the service for Louie on Thursday."

"No. I don't think so. Thanks, but I . . . ." She didn't know how to finish it.

"It's not your brand of worship," Addie said.

Molly nodded.

They said their good-byes and Addie walked off across the street with the assistant warden. Molly headed along the sidewalk toward the town square.

After she had walked half a block, she heard steps behind her and turned to look. Frank Purcell was barreling down on her, his Stetson low on his forehead, his boots hitting the sidewalk hard. "Mrs. Cates," he called, "where are you parked?"

She looked back to the prison where Stan Heffernan and a few reporters were crossing the street and she called out in her loudest, most carrying voice, "Good night, Stan!" She turned and waved. Stan, looking a little puzzled at her enthusiasm, waved back at her.

At least, she thought, they have seen this man with me and he knows it. If he has any plans for me, that should nip them in the bud. "I'm parked on the square, across from the courthouse," she told Purcell.

He fell into step with her. "That's a good idea," he said. "Nice and safe with all the sheriff's men around there."

"That's what I thought, too. I had a bad experience in Fort Worth on Saturday." She patted her cheek. "You remember when I came by the house. It made me a little cautious."

"I'd say, Mrs. Cates, you are one of the least cautious people I've run across."

She looked sideways at him. "I am?"

He smiled and it was a pleasant smile although she couldn't see if it reached his eyes because they were hidden in the shadow of his hat brim. "You are. That scene back there in the visitors' lounge." He *tisk*ed. "Now everyone knows you don't believe Louie was guilty and it's well known that you are not one to give up a bone you're chewing on. That combination plate might make you a target."

Molly opened her eyes wide, pretending she was young and innocent. "You think so?"

He smiled again. "That's why I want to get you safely inside your truck and headed home. My boss's orders actually."

"Well, I'm obliged. To you and to Charlie."

They passed the bus station and Molly could see the top of the courthouse. She felt the impulse to ask him about feeding information to Louie Bronk eleven years ago. It would be in keeping with her indiscretions of the evening and she really wanted to see his reaction. But she fought down the impulse. Another time.

"How's Charlie doing?" she asked instead.

"Poorly. Very poorly."

"Sorry to hear that." She really meant it. Charlie had his hand in lots of the subterfuge going on here. But he was no killer, she was certain.

When they reached her truck, she had her keys out and ready. "Thanks for the company," she said. She unlocked the door and climbed in. Just as she was about to close it, Frank moved in and took hold of the door handle. Alarmed, she started the engine, put her hand on the gearshift, and looked down into his face.

He quickly lifted his hands, showing her his palms. "Don't shoot," he said with a smile. "I just wanted to ask you something." The smile faded. "Do you have enough fuel to make it all the way home without stopping?"

She nodded.

"Then do it, please. Lock your door and don't stop."

"Now why should I do that?" she asked.

He sighed. "I could say it's just that Mr. Bronk there, the late Mr. Bronk, reminds me of the dangers a lady faces out on the highway."

"You could say that, but I wish you'd tell me the real reason."

He looked down at the toes of his boots, then back up at Molly. "You and me both know there's a killer, a living one, out there." He gestured with his head toward the road in front of her. "Ain't that enough?"

"Your boss knows who that killer is," Molly said. "You probably do, too."

He tilted his head down so his face was hidden by his hat brim. "Do like I said and have a safe trip," he said.

"Well, put your mind to rest, Mr. Purcell. That's exactly what I intend to do." She took hold of the door handle, slammed it shut, and locked it.

Molly waited until he stepped up on the sidewalk before she drove off.

She let out a long breath. It was done. Now she could go home and sleep, which was the only thing in the world she wanted. She turned on the heater, first time that year, and headed north toward Route 30. If she could do seventy part of the way, she might get home by three-thirty. There wouldn't be any radar traps to worry about this time of night.

As she was leaving the city limits just before the turnoff for the highway she saw some movement ahead at the side of the road. She looked again. Yes, at the outer range of her headlights something was moving. She slowed down and checked to see if her doors were locked. Damn. Frank Purcell certainly had gotten to her.

As she got closer her headlights caught a blur of white on the shoulder of the road. A figure rose and moved onto the road. It was a woman, wearing a skirt, a long brown skirt and a white shirt. She raised her hands and stumbled into the middle where Molly's lights exposed her.

Molly caught her breath. It was Alison McFarland. Her hair was a wild mess and she had a smear of blood under her nose. She was cradling one arm up against her body with the other. Molly looked in the rearview mirror to see if anyone was behind her. The road was clear. She slowed. Other than the girl, the road was deserted. On one side, nothing but a barbed-wire fence and open fields; on the other, the same thing. No place for anyone to be hiding; the girl was alone. And in trouble.

Molly reached for her phone to call for help. She picked it up and saw in the display window the red letters "No Svc." Damn. She was out of the service range of her system. She slammed it down.

In the road, Alison started to limp toward the truck, tripped, and fell to her knees.

Molly braked. Alison tried to rise from her knees. Molly could hear her crying now. She opened the door and looked both ways before getting out.

"Oh, Mrs. Cates." Alison was weeping so she could barely get the words out. "It's you. Thank God. Mark threw me out of the car. My car," she wailed. "I think my elbow might be broken. I landed on it. Can you drive me to a hospital?"

Molly put an arm around the girl's narrow waist. Alison looked ghastly. Her skirt was torn. Her blouse had mud stains and a few bright red blood drips. Tears were mixing with the blood which was seeping from her nose. Molly supported her to the passenger side of the truck, but found the door locked when she tried to open it.

"Hold on to the handle. Here," Molly said. "I'll go around and open it."

"Hurry," Alison gasped. "I'm afraid he might come back. Please hurry."

Molly ran around, hit the automatic lock, and hurried back around to help the girl in. Alison let out a little squeal of pain when she brushed her arm against the door getting in. "Okay," Molly said. "I'm sure there's a hospital right in Huntsville. We'll find it. Hold on." She closed the door, ran around, and got in. The first thing she did was hit the door locker. The engine was still running, so Molly shifted and turned the wheel sharply and drove forward onto the shoulder. As she was shifting into reverse and looking behind her, she felt it—cold metal digging into her neck, right under the jawbone.

It was a surprise so total she felt the blood in her veins stop flowing.

chapter 26

▲ ▼ ▲

A monster, a beast,
A devil at least.
No human being,
They're all agreeing.
He has taken life
Shed blood with his knife.
We'll show him his error.
Make him taste the terror.
Suck out his last breath.
We'll put him to death.

LOUIE BRONK
Death Row, Ellis I Unit,
Huntsville, Texas

In the coolest voice Molly had ever heard, as if she were giving a stranger directions to the nearest service station, Alison McFarland said, "We're going to continue on the way you were going, for one mile. Then you take 19 west. If you take a hand off that wheel for anything, I will shoot—like this." She pressed the gun under Molly's jawbone and jabbed upward to illustrate. "Up here, into your head. It's already cocked. The smallest twitch of my finger will fire it." All this was spoken in a drone. No emotion.

Too shocked for real fear, Molly drove the mile in silence.

"Here's the turn," Alison said, "19 west. Take it."

Molly made the right turn onto the dark two-lane road. Her hands clenched the wheel. She struggled to regulate her breathing. Get calm. Think straight.

For two miles they drove in silence, without passing another car. Beyond the strip of road illuminated in her headlights lay total blackness. If she was going to die out here in the dark, at least she wanted some answers first. "Where are we heading, Alison?"

"Lake Livingston, a place called Point Blank," Alison said. "In six more miles we come to the turnoff. Don't worry, I'll tell you."

"What would I have to worry about?"

"That's right. Just drive."

Molly kept her hands on the wheel and held the truck steady. She tried her daddy's old calming trick—listening to her own breathing. Breathe out, breathe in. She heard it deep inside—in, out, in, out. But some other noise intruded itself—a tiny almost imperceptible noise, like . . . like a mouse gnawing. Molly's eyes flicked sideways. It was Alison. Chewing. She was turned toward Molly, pressing the gun against Molly's neck with her right hand and chewing furiously on her left thumb.

As though a shot of painkiller had suddenly worn off, Molly felt the muzzle bruising her skin and, worse, the pressure of hot panic simmering in her chest. Her nerves couldn't take any more silence, or gnawing. "Bad habit," she said.

"What would you know about anything?" Alison snapped.

"Good point," Molly said. "But I sure would like to know." She waited to see if Alison would reply, but there was only silence. "Mark didn't kick you out of the car."

"Of course not. He wouldn't have the balls. I forced a big fight. It wasn't hard since he's so mad about me moving back home to be with Daddy. I said I was going to take the bus back. And I will take the bus back." She pressed harder with the gun. "There's one leaving Huntsville in two hours."

"Two hours," Molly said. Whatever Alison was planning to do, she thought she could do it and get back to Huntsville in two hours. Molly began to let up on the accelerator, very gradually. Slower was better here. Alison didn't seem to notice.

Only the hum of the engine and the whir of the heater broke the silence inside the cab.

"Sure is one dark, lonely stretch of road." Molly tried to glance sideways without moving her head.

There was no response.

"How did you feel tonight, Alison, when you saw Louie die? Any misgivings?"

A long exhale of disgust was the only response.

"You might as well tell me the story," Molly said. "It will keep me calm."

There was only silence.

"Well," Molly said, trying to keep her voice low, "I'll start it off. I think that first one was an accident. Your mother must have been a difficult woman to have as a mother, neglectful and self-absorbed. But what happened was really more an accident than anything else, wasn't it?"

The only response was a resumption of the gnawing sound. Molly felt her palms getting slick on the steering wheel. She wanted to wipe them off, but remembered Alison's warning and believed it. She gripped the wheel tighter.

"Let me see how close I can get." Molly kept her eyes straight ahead, on the dark ribbon of road. "You wanted to go with the boys that morning. Poaching rabbits. But they wouldn't let you. So you went out to shoot targets. When you got back to the house you wondered where your mother was. You looked for her. Felt a little panicky at being alone. She wasn't in the house or the garden, so you decided to see if her car was in the garage. The door was closed, so you poked your head in the side door. It was dark inside and you must have been scared when you saw them there together, confused. I can imagine how upsetting that would be."

Molly tried to see her out of the corner of her eye but in the dark she could make out only the shape of the bent head. Alison was chewing on her finger again, as if she were intent on consuming herself. Like those animals that gnaw their legs off when they get caught in a trap.

"You had your gun with you, one of those little .22 rifles kids often learn to shoot with. And in a moment of panic you shot. It hit her in the back and killed her. An impulse. An accident. Am I close, Alison?"

There was no response. This time Molly kept silent, too.

Finally Alison spoke. "She knew I hated being left alone but she did it all the time. That's why Daddy got David to come live with us, because she was always going off somewhere. Then Stuart called. From Mark's house. He was upset, crying so hard he could barely talk. He said he wanted to talk to her. I called and called and looked out in the garden, but I couldn't find her. Stu told me what had happened. Mark had just told him that Mom was doing all these dirty things with David. Mark said he'd watched them. He told Stu all these disgusting details and Stuart told them to me over the phone. I didn't believe people I knew would do things like that. Stu said he was coming home to ask her about it."

Alison kept the gun muzzle pressed hard against Molly's neck. "After he hung up, I thought about looking in the garage to see if her car was there. They didn't even notice me. They were half undressed and making all these weird noises. I didn't know if he was hurting her or she was hurting him, or what. It was dark. I don't know how, but the shot got her in the back. Just that one shot. When David backed away, and she dropped to the floor, it was a moment so . . . well there was never anything like it. One second, and she was dead. All it took was a tiny movement of my finger. I hadn't even willed it. Not really.

"It was so easy. That was the thing. I think about it all the time, how easy it was. Like tonight. People consider it this huge dramatic thing, but really it's easier than switching a light off."

"Yes," Molly said softly, "I got that feeling tonight, too. But what happened next must have been hard."

"Oh, no. That was easy, too. I'd been reading about the Scalper in the paper and watching it on television. I knew all about it—the shaved heads and the car they thought he might be driving. I told David what to do and he did it. I should have done it all myself. If I'd done the shaving, there wouldn't have been any of those cuts."

"Because David was scared and you weren't," Molly said.

"David was more than scared. He was a sniveling wreck. The thing he feared most, though, was my father finding out what he and Mom were doing. So he did what I told him to do."

"Where did you put all the stuff—her watch and earrings and the things from the house?"

"Oh, we buried everything, way out past the house, in this cedar thicket where no one ever goes. Her hair, too."

"And the gun?"

"That, too. I hated to. I wish I still had it."

"You must have been scared while you were doing that."

"No. Really. A little hurried because Stu was on his way home. That's all. It was like a wonderful adventure. I never had such a good time. Like while the boys were out doing this silly stuff, shooting at rabbits, I was doing something real, far more important and exciting. Something I would never ever tell them about."

Molly kept her eyes fixed on the yellow stripe unwinding in her headlights. Alison was not so different from Louie Bronk, she thought. Both lived down the same sort of rabbit hole, where killing people was the best sport.

"Stuart didn't know, did he?"

"No. By the time he got home, we were all finished and David had called the police."

"Does he know now?"

"I don't think so. But he doesn't want to know."

"Mark?"

"God, no. You'd never tell Mark something like that. He's such a blabbermouth. Such a baby."

Molly moved her eyes sideways, straining to see Alison's face in the dark. "When did your father find out?"

Alison sucked in her breath. The gnawing sound filled the cab again and Molly clenched her teeth against it. Her own fingers could feel the flesh being ripped away from the nail.

"That was the bad part," Alison said. "I hated that, and it was so unnecessary. He never had to know. For the first few days, he didn't. But then David broke down and told him. By that time, he was more scared of the police than he was of my father."

"And then Louie confessed. That must have been a surprise."

Alison made a small popping noise that sounded like an exclamation of delight. "It was the most wonderful moment of my life. It was magical. Like I'd made it happen. Like there was this invisible connection between me and him. Like it was all meant to turn out that way. He came along at the right time and he'd done so many murders it didn't matter if he took on one more. He was just perfect." The girl's voice was more animated than Molly had ever heard it.

"Especially after your father got Frank Purcell to supply Louie with the essential information about the murder so his confession would stick."

"I guess. I didn't have anything to do with that. Daddy did that, for himself, I think. To avoid scandal. Maybe a little for me. He believed it was an accident."

"It was an accident," Molly said.

"Mmm. It's hard to remember exactly," Alison said in a dreamy voice.

Molly started to nod, but the gun jabbing into her jawbone

stopped her. "How about David? I guess the execution was just too much for him."

"Oh, he was a gutless old woman. He was thinking about telling. After all this time." Alison's voice dripped with contempt. "Conscience. Religion—those aren't real things. And who cares whether some scummy lowlife like Bronk gets executed?"

"I do."

"You and that fat church woman."

"And David, of course. He cared. So you shot him."

"I had to. I did it Tuesday night, with his own gun. And put him where he wouldn't get discovered for a while."

"I can certainly understand why you had to kill David to keep him from telling. But Georgia—that's another matter. To kill for money, Alison!"

"No." The gun ground into Molly's neck. "Not for money. If you think that, you don't understand anything." Her voice was earnest, fervent.

"Tell me," Molly said, "so I will."

There was such a long pause that Molly thought Alison had finished talking. But finally the girl said, "My father and I were happy together. Close. Georgia ruined that. She made him act like some silly adolescent. I didn't want to leave home. I wasn't ready. I wanted to stay there with him, but she drove me out. She spent all this money making our house ugly and they were like these stupid moony honeymooners. I couldn't stand it." The gun muzzle prodded Molly's jaw. "There. Turn right on 980. Right here."

Very carefully, Molly made the turn onto the narrow road. They were getting close to the end of this trip. She had to grip the wheel hard to keep her hands from shaking. She glanced down at her bunch of keys dangling from the ignition. In the light from the dash the little tear gas canister Grady had given her gleamed among the jumble of keys, just inches from her right hand.

"So money didn't enter in?" Molly asked.

"Well, it wouldn't have been right for her to get any of my mother's money. You can see that. But mainly it was to get her out of the house so I could go back and take care of Daddy. He's sick."

Molly kept the questions coming while she tried desperately to come up with some plan of action. They were coming to the end of the line. "The master poet stuff—I suppose that was to make it look like there was another crazed killer at work. To direct suspicion away from your family."

"I got the idea from you. From the poems you included in your book. So I wrote you some verse, put you under a curse. Now I'm going to do worse, send you home in a hearse."

Molly couldn't see her face but she suspected the girl was smiling.

"Why me?" Molly asked. "Why threaten me?"

"At first it was just to get your attention and make it look like a homicidal maniac was out there. I thought you might write about it, make it public, so everyone would think that. I didn't really intend to kill you. Not then. Not until I saw that you would never give this up. See, you're like me—you stay with things forever."

A sign on the left said Point Blank. Their destination. Too fast, too soon. She wasn't ready. Maybe she could rattle this girl, get her to lose concentration. "Well, it turned out there really was a homicidal maniac out there, didn't it, Alison? And your plan didn't work since they're getting ready to arrest your father."

From the gasp, Molly could tell she'd made a direct hit.

"No, they're not," Alison said.

"Yes," Molly said. "They are. I heard it from Lieutenant Traynor just before I left Austin tonight."

"I don't believe it. Okay. There's the sign. Turn left right here, on this unpaved road."

Molly slowed down and started the turn. "It is true. They're going to arrest him and they don't give a damn that he's dying. He'll take the blame for you."

The gun jammed into her jawbone, savagely. Molly gritted her teeth.

"How do you know he's dying?" For the first time Alison's voice rose in anger. "How do you know that?"

Molly completed the turn. Gravel pinged against the bottom of the truck. "He told me."

"He told *you?*"

"Yes. And I bet you heard it from Stuart, who learned it from his doctor."

Alison's voice turned icy again. "Turn left here onto the grass and drive on past those trees."

In her headlight beams, Molly saw a circle of tall pines and beyond that a narrow grassy point that seemed to slope down into the darkness. She couldn't see it, but the lake had to be in that darkness, somewhere below.

Carefully, she turned off the gravel. The truck bumped onto the grass. God, the gun was cocked. One of these bumps could set it off. She slowed down and headed toward the trees. When she reached them, she applied the brakes gingerly, coming to a gentle stop.

"Keep going," Alison said.

Molly gave the gas pedal the tiniest pressure. The truck inched forward, bumping out onto the narrow promontory. The grass sloped downward. About twenty feet from where the land fell off into black space, she stopped.

Alison shoved the gun against her neck. "Not yet." Her voice was back to the dead drone as if now she was just dealing with dull logistics. "Go on. Right to the edge."

"This will never work, Alison."

"Everything else has."

Slowly the truck moved out to the edge. About five feet from the edge, Molly braked again.

"A few more feet," Alison said.

Molly inched the truck forward and stopped. In the headlights, aided by a thin drizzle of light from the cold sliver of a moon, she saw the gleam of black water below.

She raised her left foot to press the emergency brake.

"No!" Alison ordered. "Just put it in neutral. And leave the engine running."

Molly gripped the wheel. So that was the plan. The truck was going into Lake Livingston. With Molly inside. Probably already dead with a bullet in the brain. Or was it going to be an accident? Molly would drown, like her daddy. That face in her dreams, glowing green through the dark water, flesh trailing like seaweed—it would be her own face, her own fate.

She hesitated with her hand above the shift. Inside the dark cab, cold tremors rippled along her spine. The gun still pressed into her neck, her jugular, her spinal cord—her lifeline. In just seconds it would be blown apart. She had to do something.

She could just take her foot off the brake, push the pedal to the floor, and send them both hurtling off into space. Take whatever came. But the shock would make the gun fire, right into Molly's neck. She put her hand on the shift and eased it into neutral. With her foot above the brake, she waited to see if they would roll. The truck moved forward an inch, another inch, then stopped. The slope was decidedly downward, but the long grass seemed to be holding them.

"Put your hands back on the wheel."

Slowly, reluctantly, Molly did it.

"Now stay right there." Alison moved the gun away from Molly's neck for the first time. Molly glanced sideways. Alison had shifted the gun into her left hand. She opened the passenger door and backed out carefully, keeping the gun pointed steadily at Molly's head.

Molly glanced down at the tear gas canister dangling among the keys. Now or never. But first she'd have to turn off the ignition and pull the keys out.

Leaning into the cab, Alison said, "Move your hands up to the top of the wheel where I can see them." Molly winced. Now. She was going to do it now. Her temple throbbed where the bullet would hit. She started to slide her hands up. Then she did two things at once. She turned the key in the ignition and ducked down. She jerked the keys out and threw herself flat onto the passenger seat. The gunshot boomed inside the truck. The cab shook. Glass shattered.

Molly fumbled for the canister, got a grip on it. With a shaking hand she aimed up and pressed. A spray hissed out. It hit the dashboard and sent a cloud of mist back at Molly. God damn. Her eyes were on fire. She glanced up through the tears. Alison stood in the open door, holding the gun level with both hands, aiming down at her. But Alison's eyes were streaming, too, and her face was contorted. Molly sprang forward and whipped the heavy key chain up into the hand holding the gun. It hit home with a bone-cracking thwack. The girl screeched and jerked her hand back.

Molly's lunge flung her against the dashboard. The truck started to roll forward. She scrambled for the open door. Before she reached it, the door slammed shut, knocking her to the floor, under the dash. With the weight shift, the truck picked up speed.

The fall was a swooping descent, down into a black hole. Then the impact—a head-on crash into concrete. Her body slammed against the seat. Then nothing. No breath, no heartbeat, no light. A moment of suspended nothing. A hesitation in time and space. Then a liquid gurgle from the darkness. Black icy water trickled around her, then cascaded. A tilting of the globe, a lurch, and the truck sank like a boulder.

Molly reached up and grabbed the seat, struggled up from the floor. But in the dark she wasn't sure it was up, or down, or sideways.

Water gushed and swirled everywhere. Then it crashed down on her, a roaring tidal wave. Where was it coming from? An open window. Yes, the gunshot had broken a window. She could climb out. But where was it in all this darkness? She felt the force of the gush and moved toward it, but it drove her back and pressed her against something hard. The door. She reached behind her and groped along the hard surface—metal or glass. The water had risen to her waist. She had to find the door handle. It was happening so fast. Her groping fingers found something. She scrabbled at it, got her hand around it. The door handle. She jerked on it and pushed with her shoulder. But nothing gave. It felt welded shut. She tried again, ramming her body into it again and again. The pressure on the other side was like a menacing beast of supernatural strength. She could hear it gurgling and slavering, forcing its way in.

She'd read something once, after the Kennedy incident. How to get out. What was it? Something about pressure equalizing. Something about waiting. But there was no time. The inky water was swirling under her arms, sloshing up into her face.

She turned her head and saw a faint haze of greenish light in the blackness. The headlights. Good Lord. She hadn't turned them off and they were still working down here. A sputtering sound came from her lips. A damn good battery. That's what her daddy would say. Those Chevy trucks, they last and last. Get yourself a Chevy truck, darlin'. You won't regret it. Oh, you were right, Daddy. But what about me? What should I do? Tell me. Tell me *now*.

Water splashed into her open mouth, gagging her. Panicky, she gulped for air and sucked in more water. The level was up to her neck, eddying around her head, pushing up her nose, into her mouth. She was drowning. It was the end. Give in now, she thought. Abandon the struggle. Get it over with.

The swirling water lapped into her ears. It growled and rumbled. Darlin', it said. Darlin'. You are made of water. It's your element. You are Pisces. A fish baby. Keep your head up. Up is where the air is. Down is the water. Keep your head up. And wait. You can wait.

You're in your element. A fish. A mermaid. Never afraid of the water. Not you. Remember? Even the ocean that first time. Just wait. There's plenty of air. In my pocket. Breathe the air in my pocket. Breathe in and out. Listen to your breath. Slow and easy. Stretch your head up. Wait for the right time. Soon now.

Molly stretched her face up into the darkness. She sucked in the little air that remained. She was floating up off the seat. Her nose butted against something. Only one breath of air left.

The water roared in her ears. Now. Find the door handle now. It will open now.

She took a deep, long, shuddering breath and submerged. Her hands groped for a door. They swept over smooth metal. Glass maybe. She pictured the recessed handle, but she couldn't find it. Then a finger caught on something narrow and smooth. She grabbed with both hands and pulled. She pressed her shoulder against it. Nothing happened. She fluttered her feet until she found something to brace them against. Then she pushed again, throwing every ounce of strength against the door. It softened, then gave slightly. Again she pushed, forcing it—harder—until it opened a few inches, then a few more, then just wide enough for her to squeeze out. She slipped through, flowed through, undulated through, made of water. Pisces.

She swam free into the black water. But her air was used up, her lungs scorched. She didn't know which way was up. In both directions stretched black nothingness. She stopped swimming. A tickle of something rippled up her leg. Bubbles. Air bubbles, heading for the surface. In the faint cloudy green light from the headlights she caught a glimpse of them—a line of silvery bubbles shooting up, seeking their own element. It was the last breath of air escaping from the truck. She followed it. Up and up. With a desperate final surge, she burst to the surface. Air. She drew in racking great gulps of cold night air and looked up at the slender crescent of moonlight.

She rested back in the water, letting it support her as she greedily inhaled and exhaled. The water made soothing sounds in her ears. It felt purifying, and after what she'd heard and seen tonight, some purification was sure in order. Beside her, a chain of bubbles burbled to the surface, then stopped abruptly. She looked down into the water and thought she saw a distant greenish glow—the headlights still burning. Oh, he'd enjoy that. A reliable battery. How much he'd enjoy that.

She heard a gunshot, but it sounded miles away. Nothing to do with her.

After a time, she submerged and swam out to the middle of the lake, as far as one breath would take her. The cold water numbed her eyes. When she surfaced she heard another gunshot. But she just smiled and leaned back to let the water float her. Nothing to worry about.

Like Br'er Rabbit in the brier patch, she'd been thrown right into her element.

The beat of the music was relentless.

"Five," Michelle called from the front of the room. "Six. Keep those abs sucked in."

The push-ups were hurting more than ever, Molly thought. That's what happens after five measly days off. Five months to build the muscle, and five days to lose it.

"But, Mother," Jo Beth said, pushing up and down with ease, "this Prison Ministries is a Christian group—it doesn't sound like your sort of cause at all."

Molly pushed herself up and groaned. "They do good work. Anyway, only half of it goes there. The other half—and we're making a big assumption here that there will be any royalties at all—goes to the Assistance Center."

"Seems pretty extreme," Jo Beth said, "but if it makes you feel better, I will draw it up tomorrow. You really want to include the Japanese money, too?"

Molly grunted. "Yeah. The whole ugly wretched thing. I can't bear to look at any of it. Just do it, honey. Get it over with."

"Okay. It's your money."

"Ten," Michelle called. "Keep breathing."

"Dad says Alison McFarland is setting up for an insanity plea," Jo Beth said.

"Yeah. So I hear." Molly was panting. "I have no problem with that. She is insane. So was Louie, of course. But she's rich insane and he was poor insane. Big difference." Sweat was rolling into her eyes.

"Thirteen . . . fourteen," came the call.

"What about her father?" Jo Beth asked.

"They're thinking about indicting him for criminal solicitation and conspiracy to obstruct justice. He's in the hospital now, so I don't know." She stopped talking for a few seconds to catch her breath.

"Now I want to hear about the important stuff," Jo Beth said. "How about you and Dad?"

"Oh, Jo Beth, I wish I knew. When he came to pick me up at that campground on Lake Livingston, I've never been happier to see anyone in my life. And it's like that every time I see him. When he appears at my door, I feel like I'm having a heart attack." Molly looked up at Jo Beth. Her daughter had tears in her eyes.

"How about you, honey?" Molly asked.

She shook her head. "Oh, Mom. Don't ask."

"Seventeen . . . eighteen . . . nineteen."

Molly's arms were quivering and her back burned. "Goddammit," she muttered. "I watched an execution . . . I escaped a dangerous killer . . . and a watery grave . . . I swam across Lake Livingston in the dark . . . surely I can do twenty-five miserable—" Her breath ran out.

"Twenty-one . . . twenty-two . . . twenty-three."

Molly was gasping, straining. Her arms shook wildly and her shoulders felt like they were wrenching out of the sockets. She looked up to see Jo Beth watching with wide, excited eyes.

"Twenty-four . . . twenty-five."

Molly did the last one, then collapsed with a yip of triumph.

"Mom," Jo Beth whispered, "you did it. Now how about your Louie Bronk story? Have you gotten going on it yet?"

"Tonight," Molly said. "Richard's promised me as much space as I need. Powers-that-be be damned, he said. I'm going to start it tonight."

From the front of the room Michelle bellowed out, "Very good. That was so good we're going to do twenty-five more. Ready? Abs in. Let's go!"

Without showering or changing out of her exercise clothes, Molly sat down at the computer. She banished the flying toasters with one tap on the space bar and started to type. Her hands skimmed across the keyboard fluidly, as though the ideas in her head were pouring out through her fingertips. The words seemed to appear on the lighted screen of their own volition.

At midnight on September 29, seventeen of us, upstanding citizens all, gathered behind high brick walls in Huntsville to commit a homicide—as cold-blooded and premeditated a homicide as it is possible to imagine. We stood by silently, we witnesses—journalists, prison officials, politicians, and ordinary citizens—as Louie Bronk was strapped to a gurney and a large dose of sodium thiopental was injected into his vein.

He went pretty gentle into that East Texas good night, considering that he was a man given to deadly violence and considering that he was inno- cent of the murder for which he was being executed.

No one tried to stop it. Not one of us. I knew he was innocent, but I did nothing. I didn't object or cry bloody murder, or give in to the red scream— that shriek of terror and rage death-row inmates talk about. I just stood and watched—a passive witness.

But no more.

Here is my red scream.

To understand how such a monstrous miscarriage of justice could hap- pen, you have to go back eleven years to that hot July day when . . .

She wrote long into the night with no awareness of time passing. The screen just kept on filling up with words.